# BOMBAY DU

# BOMBAY DUCK IS A FISH

Kanika Dhillon

**westland ltd**
Venkat Towers, 165, P.H. Road, Maduravoyal, Chennai 600 095
No.38/10 (New No.5), Raghava Nagar, New Timber Yard Layout, Bangalore 560 026
Survey No. A-9, II Floor, Moula Ali Industrial Area, Moula Ali, Hyderabad 500 040
23/181, Anand Nagar, Nehru Road, Santa Cruz East, Mumbai 400 055
47, Brij Mohan Road, Daryaganj, New Delhi 110 002

First published by westland ltd 2011

Copyright © Kanika Dhillon 2011
All rights reserved

10 9 8 7 6 5 4 3 2 1

ISBN: 978-93-80283-87-6

Typeset in Adobe Caslon Pro by SŪRYA, New Delhi
Printed at Manipal Press Ltd., Manipal

This book is sold subject to the condition that it shall not by way of trade or otherwise, be lent, resold, hired out, circulated, and no reproduction in any form, in whole or in part (except for brief quotations in critical articles or reviews) may be made without written permission of the publishers.

*To*
Mr Shah Rukh Khan—for the phenomenon that he is,
for the person that he is and for the legend that he is.
The legend that makes everyone believe in
the Bollywood dream.

*To*
Every person who dreams a dream—big or small.

*To*
*Bobs*
Who will always be a part of my journey.

## SUICIDE, SIDDHARTHA AND ONION BHAJJIYA

It was two in the morning in Mumbai.

I was sitting on the ledge of a five-storey building. Contemplating jumping off it, after walking this earth for exactly twenty-six years, seven months and eight days.

Thank god for small mercies: my nails were painted a soft shade of pink. My long, black hair was recently washed and smelling of honey and apricot. I would definitely make a pretty picture, lying dead in the street below. I wish I knew the right angle to jump so I could land with my face up and without my body getting distorted too much. If I stood on the parapet and jumped backwards, looking up at the sky, maybe I'd fall in that position.

Well, I guess you have to leave some things to chance.

Before I planned the details, though, I wanted to enjoy the breathtaking view. My original plan had been to jump off the ledge just before dawn. (So my body would not lie around for a long time, unattended. I have a phobia about dogs and I'm convinced it will follow me to my next life as well. I'd decided, after a lot of deliberation, to jump between three and four in the morning; early morning joggers around the area would definitely spot me before a bunch of dogs gathered around and scared my dead body away.) But I wanted to look at the view just a little bit more, before taking the final plunge ... That phrase 'just a little bit more' ... that must easily be the root cause of all the problems in the world. Especially mine right now.

Coming back to the view ... I was thinking about the much talked-about jewel in the Mumbai skyline—the Worli Sea Link, which has been in the making for about ten years and is going to be inaugurated soon. Unfortunately I won't live to see it come alive. The first I heard of it was almost a year ago, when I had hesitantly stepped out of the Chhatrapati Shivaji Terminal. I remember, when my plane was starting its final descent, looking down through its tiny windows at the twinkling city full of dreams, promises and stars—Mumbai.

I had conjured up the images of all the gods and goddesses I could think of. I just had one thing to say to them before my plane touched down: 'Please make my dreams come true.'

And then, finally, the Jet Airways flight that had brought me from Amritsar reached its destination. I had left my home town far behind; and with it, I had also left an angry, sceptical father, who thought his daughter was throwing away common sense and a first class in a management degree to become some assistant to some director in the jungle called Bollywood. I'd also left behind an anxious and excited mother, in whose eyes I could already see stars. In fact, I could see my whole life unfold in her mind, before I had a chance to live it.

Before I left, she'd whispered excitedly in my ear, 'Try and do a movie with Shah Rukh Khan.'

I'd rolled my eyes. My mother was a die-hard fan, and of course she did not know—as I did—that I might never get to see the man, let alone *work* with him.

I was absolutely wrong. Thank god for that.

Anyway, I knew there was more to come; my mother was just warming up. She whispered again, 'In fact, see the way he made it big in Bollywood. He started from nothing, nowhere, knew no one! And now look at him!'

I'm sure Shah Rukh Khan has no idea that he is this beacon light beckoning an entire galaxy of people to come and struggle in Bollywood. There are superstars and legends, and then there is Shah Rukh Khan. No godfather, no uncle, no magical surname to open the golden gates, no legacy to help him. He'd made it on his own. And that's what set him apart from everyone else.

He was one of us who crossed over and managed not just to survive, but rule.

There was another guy, though, who had something to do with my journey. I was standing in the airport thanks to him. Siddhartha. He had a huge role to play in my decision to try my luck in Bollywood. He was my father's best friend.

See, my dad and I never seemed able to have an actual conversation, so I had never told him, all this while, that I wanted to be a film-maker. When I tried, for the millionth time, to tell my mother, we were sitting in our veranda. Our gardener was planting tulsi under my mother's keen eyes while she chatted with our neighbour about the dinner menu and announced 'my' future plans of taking up a job in New Delhi, with an MNC.

For any middle-class household, working in an MNC is a version of the American dream. Our neighbours and friends would look at us with a tinge of envy; my parents would preen and I would take another sip of the hot coffee, wondering if there would ever be a pause in this conversation so I could tell them that it was not a cushy managerial chair that beckons me, but cinema and the screen and stories.

I had spent many a Sunday afternoon waiting for that pause. It was a simple line I had rehearsed: 'I want to make films. I want to tell stories.' At night, standing in front of my bathroom mirror, it all made sense to me. In the morning, seeing my dad immersed in Siddhartha's life, it seemed flimsy.

As time went by, and the tulsi plant grew several inches, I was still clueless about how to present my case to my parents. I was running out of time now: I was to start my job in a month!

And then it hit me. Siddhartha!

I picked up the book my father loved: *Siddhartha*, by Hermann Hesse. He read it at least once every two months—finding solace in it, companionship, and of course looking for his answers.

My dad and I could never see eye to eye. Maybe there was a key to breaking through to him somewhere in this book. My father was known to be a spiritual man and many people came to him for advice. Often, he would just quote from this book. Perhaps if I discovered spirituality, if I read this book, I would connect to him in some way.

And maybe then I could find a way to tell him that I wanted to go to Mumbai to make movies.

I finished reading the book in one night.

And then read it again, over and over, till it was imprinted in my heart. Word by word.

Nothing.

My suitcase was being packed. Fifteen days to go. I had read the book fifteen times over, and then it hit me. If I waited for the perfect pause, I would have to wait forever. I had to go in and make it myself. Announce it.

I walked into my father's study, but found my mother there

instead. I had to say something. And finally it all came pouring out to her. It started with how I wanted to go to Mumbai and ended with Siddhartha's story. How Siddhartha had convinced his father to let him go and explore life. How he had stood on one leg for hours together to prove to his father how committed he was to his decision. Well, I was as determined. Okay, I was not even thinking of standing on one leg for more than a minute, let alone days, but I *was* committed to what I wanted to do.

My dad walked in then. 'What's happening here?' he asked.

My mother simply looked at me and said, 'She has found Siddhartha . . . she wants to go away.'

'With Siddhartha? Who is he? When did you meet him? How old is he? Is he an MBA at least?'

This was definitely not going as planned. 'No, no. Your *book*, your Siddhartha . . . I have read it many, many times, I have tried to understand it to make you understand that I want to do something different with my life.'

And then began my repeat performance. I remember it was raining that night and Shivshankarji was serving us onion bhajiyas with tomato sauce. Shivshankarji had been with our family since the time I was in diapers. He was the most free-spirited person I knew. He could walk into the middle of a bitter fight between Mom and Dad and nonchalantly continue to pick up the glasses left around the room, or clean the mirrors, or polish the wood. He was completely unaffected by any emotional turmoil around him. That's what made him wise—or weird, depending on which way you wanted to look at it. Shivshankarji always had a chore to be done, and nothing could stop him from doing it.

Talking about my dreams and Shivshankarji's chores—that

day his chore was to serve us bhajjiyas, and even if I were slicing my wrists with a sharp knife, Shivshankarji would have first finished serving the snacks and then gently taken the knife away from me. As an afterthought, if I may add.

So, in between my passionate speech about my dreams and desires, Shivshankarji was handing out steaming hot, crisp bhajiyas and asking my mom if she would like some more sauce with it.

Well, she did.

I waited for Shivshankarji to finish serving the tomato sauce so I could resume my well-rehearsed monologue on hopes and plans, and my dad waited patiently for me to finish my long speech before he said, 'You don't understand a word of that book Neki, or life or spirituality. You are young. You think you know, but you don't. So stop this foolishness and start packing. You are going to Delhi.'

My mom offered me the plate of fried onion saying, 'Eat something. Onions inside are tender and the coating is crisp and crunchy. Shivshankar has added a tinge of garlic this time in the batter. It tastes lovely with the ketchup.'

If my mother ever visited a therapist, she would end up making the doctor a good cook: she would only talk about food, recipes and nutrition in her sessions. Every week she discovered a new food item that a scientist had declared could prevent cancer or some other ailment listed in the medical encyclopaedia. So if there was raw tomato served as salad on our dining table for a week, rest assured a scientist somewhere was involved.

Shivshankarji hated all scientists. They always meddled with his recipes and dinner menus.

'Do you need me to pack your suitcase for Delhi?' my mother asked. Probably hoping that the uncomfortable issue would be quickly resolved and the family could go back to its glorious and uneventful existence.

But not this time: I had to show my dad that I did learn something about life from *Siddhartha*. If you want something to happen for you badly, you need to want it very badly. And you need to show how much it means to you to the right people.

I decided to stay in my bedroom, and refused to eat or interact with anyone, including Shivshankarji. I heard him tell my mother quietly it was all because of those horrible TV channels. My mother became hyper about my state within a few hours, and by the end of the day, when she thought I'd not eaten a morsel of food (I did have an old chocolate bar in my drawer, which I nibbled on, but obviously no one knew about it) she was positively frantic. The morning of the second day, I was summoned to dad's study. It was show time! All I had to do was say nothing.

A round of talks and lectures followed. The pattern was, my dad would talk endlessly and I would look at the clock ticking in his study. He would get tired and stop. Then I would say as a parting shot, 'I still want to go to Mumbai and be a film-maker.'

The second day passed with my mother almost on the verge of collapsing, my father weighing his options and Shivshankarji cooking enough food to feed an army in case I was ready to eat.

On the third day my father relented.

I had learnt well from Siddhartha. Well done.

And now we were at the airport.

Instead of New Delhi, I was booked for Mumbai.

And here was my mother, mumbling things about Shah Rukh Khan and stardom in my ear. 'I promise if I ever go beyond saying a hello to Shah Rukh Khan, I will get you an autograph,' I said.

I could see that my mother was already imagining the autographed paper hanging on our drawing room wall. In a frame made of pure gold and engraved with an intricate design. 'Make sure that he writes my nickname okay? Ruby, not Geeta, okay?' she said.

I could see the nerve on my dad's left temple twitching. I knew he was ready to explode any minute, haul me right back to our car, with my mother in tow, and take us back home. I turned towards the boarding gate before my dad changed his mind.

Just then I heard him call out my name.

'Neki! I have given you six months. If you get somewhere by then, fine, otherwise I am coming to get you!' he said, staring at me sternly. It was not a warning but a threat. He had every intention of carrying it out. 'And you do not understand anything yet.' He glanced at my brand new paperback edition of *Siddhartha* peeping out from my bag. 'Just because you have read it ten times over does not mean you are ready to understand the complexity of life. You need to live it and only then you understand. It's a passing fancy for you. Don't be stupid and throw away your life in a mindless pursuit. I hope good sense prevails.'

On that note my longest conversation with my dad ended.

My mother's shrill voice butted in, 'And I hope you have lots of palak and sarson ka saag and curd with milk. It will keep your bones healthy. Scientists say palak helps fight skin aging. It keeps the skin clear too.'

My father was still looking at me as I turned to leave. The look in his eyes reminded me of a man who was helplessly watching his precious jewel roll down a hill, directly towards a garbage can. I was supposed to be the victim here, but somehow, at that airport, my dad was the one with the air of having been victimised.

The irony is, as I sit here planning my suicide, I realise, I *do* understand.

I could not find the key to my father in that book, but I found much more.

Living in Mumbai, I forgot my father's scepticism, and I forgot the anxiety of leaving my small town, Amritsar. Of leaving behind the strains of morning and evening prayers from the Golden Temple, permeating narrow, crowded streets. I forgot the school friends I'd left behind (all married and in various stages of hating their husbands); I forgot the laziness in the days and the slowness of time.

All I remembered were the stars in my mother's eyes.

The glamorous world she could see for me even before I started living it. I could see the stories she wanted to tell all her friends and relatives before I had the time to even make them up.

This is what this whole journey was about.

My mother's dreams for me.

And my father's quest for a spiritual life.

I for one was not going to shatter the dream.

Having said that, here I was, sitting on a parapet with an empty bottle of wine. Enjoying the view—and planning my death.

My parapet—I was convinced—had the best view in Mumbai. It was the wall of a dilapidated terrace of an old building which looked unlikely to survive another monsoon. But who cared. As long as I could open the rusty iron door to the terrace and make my way through the junk dumped there by the landlords—an old iron cupboard, bedraggled sofas, discarded tables—and reach this little clearing. Get to this parapet. And look at the breathtaking view. Mumbai was all mine. Who cared about the junk behind me, as long as my back was turned to it all.

My legs were dangling from the ledge; there was a soft breeze. I was flying. The sky was just a leap away, and my diary, as old as my time in Mumbai, sat faithfully next to me.

The most important question in my life, sitting here, drunk and alone was, should I buy a new diary to record the next year of my life in Bollywood?

Or should I burn the old one before I jumped off the ledge?

## NANO AND I

The brown leather cover of my diary was well worn. It was inviting. I wanted to read it one last time before destroying it. It was exactly 2:08 a.m. on my watch. I had ample time.

They say when you're at that point in your life, which may be your last, all the beautiful moments of the life you've lived flash by. Nothing was flashing though, in my drunken head. My shameless subconscious was letting me down and refusing to show me any beautiful images ... maybe there wasn't anything wonderful to show me? Just to be sure, I took out a few photographs tucked between the last pages of my diary. The first picture I pulled out was of five girls. My high school friends and I—all dressed-up for our first illicit party—were holding our name cards and smiling at the camera with sweet abandon. I looked at my friends—all so stunningly pretty. I'd always felt too tall and too scrawny next to them. My mother and my cousin Nidhi saw it differently though. According to them, I had almond-shaped eyes to kill for, long lustrous hair, full lips, and a figure which could easily take me to any ramp show. There, I'd got a flash! Obviously my subconscious mind had only been waiting for flattery.

Nidhi had lived with us for a while, as her parents were always travelling. Also, I barely spoke to my mother or father, and they thought it was a good idea to have someone my age around—they felt it would make me more social and outgoing. The therapy did not work out as planned: I followed Nidhi like her little lamb wherever she went, and when she was not around, I was back to being a loner

And then I got another flash—back to when I was about ten.

It was of Nidhi and me crying and laughing at the same time. I remember my harassed mother had locked us out of the house that day. We were standing on the street. Nidhi was laughing, thrilled with the prank we had just played on my mother, and crying because there were street dogs around. Yes, she had a phobia about dogs too. I was laughing and crying with her as well—simply because I was brainless. I would follow my cousin blindly in her every action and reaction. Of course, the flea-infested dog wagging his tail down the road did not help.

I'd read up on phobias once and consulted Freud on the matter. Instead of finding an answer, I found out that Freud blamed our collective dog phobia on the id. I think he was wrong in our case. For us, the phobia is a family thing. My mother had it, all her sisters too, and it had carefully been handed down to our generation as well.

I jerked back to reality. Great. The one thing I was able to remember before I ended my life was that I used to be a spineless lamb, petrified even of street dogs! Clearly I needed to skip memories from my childhood and teenage years. I rifled through the photographs, looking for a more recent one. And then I saw something that made me tremble. I was one of the ten people around the famous choreographer and number one director in the country today, Fiza Kareem. The whole of Bollywood danced to her tune. Literally. The photo had been taken on my tenth day on the set of her second film. As the 'runner AD' (short for assistant to the director), I'd been dashing to get a printout when I saw the entire production team and the direction team standing around Fiza Kareem and posing for the camera. I remember thinking it was a good opportunity for me to stick my neck in the frame. No one in the group would notice and my mother could hang it up in the drawing room. After all, I was only five heads away from Fiza Kareem's face. This was my moment of glory. The first moment of glory since I had come to Mumbai!

Well, now, *this* was a memory I appreciated. I needed to revisit the important chapters of my life, so I could feel like some parts of it were worth living before I ended it. But my brain was playing traitor and refusing to supply anything, clearly working in collaboration with the wine. I had to rely on Nano, my diary. (Yes, believe it or not, that's what I had named it. But Nano was a fitting name. My life was here, in these pages. Everything worthwhile captured in this little diary.)

I opened my Nano and stopped on the first page itself, at the sentence that I had written in capital letters *and* underlined: 'MY FIRST DAY IN MUMBAI'

~

MY FIRST DAY IN MUMBAI
28 June 2008. 9:08 p.m.
Dear Nano,
Luck has been with me since my plan to move to Mumbai materialised. Nidhi left Mumbai for London for a new job, so her place in the PG fell vacant. It is an all-girls' accommodation obviously. Her friends needed to find a replacement and I stepped in. Perfect.

I took a taxi from the airport to the flat. In my mind, Mumbai is beautiful; in reality, it stinks. Thankfully memories don't smell, so when I read this a few years from now I will be able to forget the musty smell and re-live this moment stench-free! My grandfather used to say, 'Memory is a tricky thing. When you revisit a moment, it becomes sweeter, the colours brighter, the pain stronger.' That's why I am writing this down, so my memory does not trick me.

The taxi guy got me to the flat without any problem. My mother was a little worried about my reaching safely, but I was not. I am an independent girl after all.

I was finally outside a tiny little building called 'Rose Mahal', right in the heart of Pali Hill market in Bandra. While driving through Pali Hill, I'd felt like I was passing through a mini fair. Stalls selling clothes, shoes, bags, caps, books, crockery, lingerie, jewellery, food—everything was displayed there in little shacks and stands, even on the street and the pavements. The taxi driver pressed down on his horn the whole time, cussing at regular intervals. My mother had warned me not to get into a taxi if the driver had incense sticks burning in the car. Apparently, it's not incense that the taxi drivers are burning, but something that would render a passenger unconscious so they can then rob them. I had dutifully peeked into the taxi before getting in, and then, to my horror, the driver had lit an incense stick about ten minutes later, at a traffic light. I didn't know how to get out. But then I rolled down both the windows and stuck my nose out all the way so the effect of any substance released in the taxi would not get to me. On second thoughts, I would have preferred to be unconscious because I was already gagging with the fumes and pollution I was breathing in.

As the taxi pulled up in front of Rose Mahal, I took a look at the building. The paint was peeling, and it looked drab—till you spotted the green and blue stained glass windows glinting in the setting sun. That's the exact point when Rose

Mahal would look beautiful. I saw it as a sign—I was going to love Rose Mahal.

As I was admiring it, a droplet fell on my cheek. I realised it had come with the scent of the salt-laden sea. Suddenly the droplets gave way to pelting rain. Mumbai monsoons. I hurriedly dashed towards the safety of the staircase.

My flat number was 442, and I had to climb four storeys with my luggage. There was no lift. I had four bags, and I insisted on taking all four with me, going up a few steps at a time hauling two bags, and then going down for the others.

Like I said, I'm an independent girl, and part of being independent is not to trust a stranger, especially with your luggage.

So floor after floor, my bags and I climbed the stairs. Finally, fifteen minutes of sweat and toil later, I rang the bell to my new home. A girl—as beautiful as a Bollywood actress—opened the door.

I smiled at her; she did not smile back. From my cousin's description, I knew she was Roshni Seth. Everyone called her Rosh.

'Hi, I'm Neki,' I said. 'I'm Nidhi's cousin . . .'

'Rosh' looked me up and down, exactly like a butcher would a lamb, wondering if he should cut it before his lunch break or after. She had made up her mind, and suddenly her nasal voice hit me. 'I know. The room in the far end is yours. Zoya is your roommate. The kitchen is right there, this is the living room cum TV room cum whatever you want to do here. Your bathroom is next to the balcony; it's not attached, that's why you get to pay less rent than Shikha and I. We have an en suite. That's Zoya, and that's Shikha.'

She stepped back and I looked in. The entire house was as big as my room back in Amritsar. Then I saw Zoya, cigarette in hand, sitting on the windowsill. She was wearing only a T-shirt. Her hair was cut very short, and she had one tattoo on her arm, and another on one of her long naked legs, near the ankle. Just about recovering from Zoya, I spotted Shikha. She was buttoning up her blouse and stuck to her, with his arm looped around her waist, was a very handsome man. He had a familiar face. The underwear ad! He was on the hoarding of an underwear ad, next to my lane back home! I was strangely relieved—at least one familiar face around here. So what if I was used to seeing him only with his briefs on!

Rosh skirted around me and walked out of the flat. Followed by Shikha, followed by my only hope, the underwear model. My bags were still outside the door. I could hear the rain pelting down on the roof. I stood there nervously. Zoya smoked as she looked at me. I had a feeling she was enjoying my discomfort. I was her cigarette entertainment.

Finally I dragged my bags into my room and sat down to write to my mother.

*Dear Mom,*

*I love this place. It's in a beautiful building called 'Rose Mahal' and it has coloured windows. It even has a small balcony. The building is right next to the market. I have three wonderful girls living with me. We are already like a little family. Zoya works in a company, Roshni works in a bank and Shikha works in Roshni's rival bank.'*

~

Remembering my lack of imagination on my first day in Mumbai, I felt ashamed. Surely, I could have come up with some better jobs for them! Zoya could have been an astronaut, Roshni a scientist (mom would love her and Shivshankarji would hate her), and perhaps Shikha could have been a lawyer.

## BREAKING THE BOXES

10 August 2008. 9:00 p.m.
Dear Nano,
The monsoons continue to drown Mumbai, filling up the lakes and the streets and the potholes. I continued to stay away from my flatmates while looking for a suitable break in Bollywood. How stuck-up my flatmates seemed for a long time. I had put each one in a box. Zoya in the 'wild—stay away' category; Rosh in the 'dubious starlet—stay away' category; and Shikha in the 'confirmed slut with contacts—stay away' category. The funny thing is, I realised the boxes I'd built for them made me a very lonely girl in this house for a long time. The day I broke those boxes, I realised that I do have friends around.

I shook my head again, at the memory of how severely I had misjudged my flatmates. I needed to read something from a better day. I flipped through the pages again. Just then, I noticed that my phone, which was lying on the parapet next to me, was blinking. I ignored it and went back to my diary.

## POV

1 September 2008. 7:00 a.m.
Dear Nano,
I have not slept all night! Today I'm going to meet the very famous Fiza Kareem. She knows all the superstars in Bollywood. She is as big as they get. I had never imagined I would ever get to be in the same room as her, let alone so early in my career! But I think Lady Luck is with me. My mother told me that the family astrologer she consulted back home predicted I was going to be very famous, very soon. Dubeyji is usually accurate in his predictions, and in my mother's head, that's why I've got this huge opportunity.

But in reality, this is how it happened: Shikha's friend is an AD on Fiza Kareem's next film, *Hare Rama Hare Krishna*, and he told Shikha that she was looking for another AD. Shikha immediately told me about it, and I thought I would apply. I've already met the first AD, the second AD, the third AD, the fourth AD and the fifth AD. Actually, I did it in reverse. The fifth AD met me first. Today I'm finally meeting Fiza Kareem. If all goes well, I'll get to work with her.

I've been very careful about how I've dressed today. I was given detailed pointers by my flatmates on 'How to dress for my first meeting with a famous director'. Rosh (who is a struggling actress) is my chief advisor. Zoya (who is an animator) is my chief critic and Shikha (who is in event management) is my 'chief contact'—I get to see all the models from all the hoardings walking in and out of the house with her. The event management company she works for is big and manages the portfolios of models and actors along with events.

I'd first worn a long kurta with jeans and kolhapuri sandals. It was immediately and brutally rejected. Rosh thought Fiza Kareem would run away thinking I was a nosy journo. And she called it 'verni'. Zoya, blowing circular loops of smoke towards me, simply said, 'Cheap.'

Rosh took matters in her hands and I tried the second outfit for the day. Jeans with a tight, fitting top that almost restricted free access of air to my lungs.

Rosh said, 'Sexy.' Zoya said, 'Tarty.'

You see, today, parading in front of the full-length mirror in my room, I understood one very important thing. It was called 'Point of View', in short, POV.

'What do you mean POV?' Rosh asked when I told them what I was thinking.

I struggled for the best way to explain it to her and then chose a simple example. 'Have you seen that beautiful spread of salads five star hotels have in their buffets? Well, for some people, they might look great, beautifully displayed, but for a lot of people, it's just a crime to let something like this exist. It's like the salads are mocking them and saying, while you die from hunger, I exist just to be beautiful. I can save you from starvation, but it's more important for me to just stand here and look beautiful.'

I looked at their very silent faces, and then Rosh muttered, 'But why would the salad say anything to anyone?'

Zoya and Shikha burst out laughing. 'Let's move back from

the salad to what you're going to wear Neki. You're freaking me out with all this salad-talking conversation!' Zoya said.

The reminder of the issue at hand had me in a nervous state again.

Clearly the POV about the outfit in which I was to meet Fiza was divided. Jeans. White shirt. That was my decision, I announced. Evidently I knew something about good dressing, because Zoya nodded her head and said, 'You should have used your brains all along.'

But then Rosh sulked, threatened, and then pleaded with me to at least wear my yellow pumps. They are beauties—my mother's farewell gift, which she had quietly wrapped in delicate pink butter paper and put in my suitcase. I discovered her note with the shoes as I was unpacking. The note had read, '*Dubeyji says yellow will bring you luck . . . you will reach for the stars in these and everyone will want to be in your shoes.*' My mother's awful pun didn't put me off the shoes fortunately: they were shiny, narrow in the front with a fragile flower perched on one side. They had a three-inch heel. They projected strength and confidence sitting there on my shoe rack. That's what I needed most today.

And anyway, what damage can yellow pumps cause after all, I suppose.

~

I laughed when I read that line. 'A *shitload* of damage,' I said aloud. A sleepy crow from somewhere behind in the dumping area of the terrace protested at being disturbed. It started cawing as if irritated and telling me to get lost. Even the crow did not want me there. I quietly went back to my diary.

~

Nano, my fingers were shaking while spraying myself with perfume. I'm wearing Rosh's fake Gucci watch. She insists branding is important when you are trying to be somebody, and apparently, in this industry, the perception that you are somebody is everything.

This is a make or break day for me, Nano. For the past two months I have met people, friends, friends of friends, hoping to start work on a film project soon. I was ready to start off as a runner, the last AD. But what a beautiful way to start my journey—with Fiza Kareem. I will have something to tell my dad about, not to mention my mom.

I have no choice but to impress Fiza Kareem.

I'll leave in about five minutes. I'm supposed to be on the set of the film in Film City Studios, Floor no. 10 at 10 a.m. It's about 7:15 now, but I don't want to be late. Zoya says I'll be cleaning the floors if I go so early. It will take me about an hour so I should really leave only at 9. But I'd rather be there early than even a second late. It is Fiza Kareem after all.

. . . Till later. Wish me luck, Nano.

## MY YELLOW SHOES

1 September 2008. 11:07 p.m.
Dear Nano,
I'm back.
Zoya and Rosh are sleeping. Shikha is in her room, but she's with somebody. The underwear model I think. So Rosh is in my bed. I'm in the living room.

I met Fiza Kareem. She told me to get lost from the set. Well, not in so many words, but I think she hates me.

Let me start from the beginning.

When the auto driver took me to Film City, I had goose bumps. Not because it was a definitive point in the life of an aspiring director wanting to make her film in Bollywood kind of moment, but scared-silly goose bumps.

Film City is a deceptive name; there is nothing city-like about it. It was like going through a jungle, and I could just imagine a leopard leaping out any minute from the wild thick forests around. Attacking my rickety auto on the lonely stretch of road. I'd anyway been a bit scared already; it had taken so long to reach this godforsaken place from Bandra, I was convinced the auto driver was abducting me. I had Zoya on speed dial.

Film City, the place where beautiful celluloid dreams are

created, is *ugly*. It's a leopard-infested jungle with pot-holed roads, wide barren expanses, a smelly canteen, and rusty brown metal doors at least ten feet high which have numbers placed crookedly on them. There are sixteen gates in all. Perhaps it's behind these brown metal gates that the magic happens, I thought. Because standing outside in that deserted area, I for sure could not see any dreamy or magical sights.

As I paid the auto guy and started walking towards gate number ten, a security guard screamed at me, 'Where are you going, Madam?'

I told him I was there to meet Fiza Kareem who was shooting for her film. He told me the crew was not there yet, and Fiza Kareem was only expected at around noon.

I found a plastic chair and after ten minutes or an hour, I can't say how long, Sameer Suri, the fourth AD and Shikha's friend, spotted me. He has a medium build, a sweet face and an impish grin. He smiled. 'All set?' he asked. Then he noticed my shoes and his face changed. 'Will you be able to walk in those? I mean, ADs have a lot of running around to do,' he said hesitantly. I looked at Sameer's shoes, they were a flamboyant pair of black Nike shoes with a bright orange motif.

I wanted to strangle Rosh. Before I could say anything, the other four ADs walked in. I saw Karan first—he is the chief AD, who speaks very little and is curt with everyone. He has a beard, which makes him look older than his age, and a medium build, although he towers over everyone with his heavy voice and scorching gaze. He was dressed in jeans and a kurta. I hurriedly glanced at his shoes; he was wearing a sturdy pair of white sport shoes, which screamed—serious, wearable and durable. Shivani, the second AD, who is in charge of costumes and who I can sense does not like me very much trooped in behind Karan. She is almost thirty, plump with a mass of curly hair and—I'd heard—knows everyone in the industry from the spot boy to Fiza Kareem. She was wearing flat pink slip-on canvas shoes—comfortable and in control. Then came the set and prop in-charge, Pratap Jeet. I've heard him say the weirdest things at the weirdest time. Tall, well built and very attractive, he wears his hair in a ponytail and has a tattoo on his forearm and a piercing on his brow. He was in jeans, a shirt and chunky Caterpillar boots. Rugged, dependable, and expensive.

Sameer, or Sam as everyone calls him, is next in the food chain. He assists all the other ADs and is in charge of crowd control. The fifth AD is Kriti Kapoor, the daughter of a famous producer. She is going to make her debut as a heroine in some film next year. A very pretty girl, wearing DKNY from head to toe. Even she was wearing glistening golden sports shoes. As I was struggling to figure out the message her shiny footwear was sending I realised she was staring at my shoes.

I wanted to kill Dubeyji this time. My yellow pumps amongst the other confident footwear mumbled dainty and helpless.

After exchanging a polite hello with the team, I went back to my little plastic chair to wait for Fiza Kareem. There was a beautiful make-up van nearby, painted white with black polka dots. It reminded me of one of my mother's silk saris. She kept it wrapped in a muslin cloth in a wooden trunk in our storeroom. Twice a year she would take out the trunk and show me her treasured sari collection. It smelled of mothballs and old times. I looked at the van and had an overwhelming urge to call my mom.

Suddenly, everyone around me seemed to start moving at

the same time. The spot boys and the ADs rushed in one direction. Fiza Kareem had just walked onto the set.

I stood up, not knowing what to do. I had been told by Sameer to wait, so I just stood there, without moving or blinking, ready to sprint when called, going over all the lines I had rehearsed over the last twenty-four hours. At the point where I was suffering from panic-triggered amnesia, Sameer walked over to me. 'I'm getting her dude,' I heard him say into his walkie.

I could hear PJ, as everyone calls Pratap Jeet, yelling into the walkie from the other end, 'Fiza is losing it—costumes for Kashish Kapoor are way off the brief, and Sam, I have a question for you, do you think aliens are going to attack us soon, because if they are, there is no point in me running around and doing this job if we are going to die anyway. Who cares if Kashish Kapoor's ass is too fat to fit into the mini dress? Anyway she is hardly there in the film. Two songs tops!'

I realised the Kashish PJ was talking about was the very famous actress and one of my favourite stars. I was about to confirm this with Sam when another voice barked into the walkie. It was Shivani. 'Shut the fuck up PJ, and get to the costume room now!'

Sam rolled his eyes. Both of us helpless bystanders in the 'walkie-war'. Just then the walkie started screaming again. It was Karan this time. 'Sam, I need you on the floor now!! There is a cleavage issue. Minty's dress is totally off. Get more cleavage on that, now!'

I was not sure I had actually heard what I'd just heard.

Sam looked at me. I could see his brain working, trying to figure out where he could deposit me for the time being. He looked over at the polka-dotted van.

'Neki, wait inside the van, please? I will come and get you soon. That's the van for the ADs,' he said and ran off.

I climbed into the van. It was like an icebox. On one side there was a sofa with flowery upholstery and, above it, a huge mirror. The van was a relief from the scorching sun outside, but within ten minutes my teeth were chattering. I did not have the courage to get out of the van and tell someone to do something about the temperature of the AC, though. Maybe people in Bollywood like the cold, I thought; that's why they always shoot in Switzerland!

I had to distract my shivering body so I lifted the curtains and peered out. I saw some people in white costumes gathering outside the shooting floor. I couldn't hear anything they were saying. Suddenly a thin boy with a bandana came up and gestured to the people—all of them wearing white tights and silver belts, silver headgear, silver shoes, silver bangles and silver eye shadow. He made them stand in a row and started walking down the line, checking them out. Just like you have an inspection in school. Some were stretching their legs and hands to impossible angles, doing intricate moves. Glistening bodies, perfect shapes. I assumed they were the graceful dancers we see behind the main actors.

Then, after talking into a walkie, the man in the bandana ushered them inside the floor. I saw Sam come out and hurry them in. One of the girls lagged behind and Sam held her hand. She pinched him and giggled.

A little distance from the floor, I saw a few men carrying water, tea, biscuits and talking into their walkies. They were the spot boys.

And then, in the middle of the crowd, I saw a little man walking with a file, a sad expression on his face. He picked up a plastic chair and sat right outside the AD van. He was a dwarf and he had a very familiar face. Suddenly I remembered who he was—I had seen him in a sitcom, my mother's favourite, called *Dekh Uncle and Aunty*. It had aired on Doordarshan some fifteen years ago, and my mother had loved it so much, she'd taped it on video and watched it over and over again. I remember that he was called Goku in the serial.

I saw Sam running up to the van. Goku tried to say something to him, but Sam hurried past him and barged in. 'Quick. Today is a bad day, but you have to meet Fiza somehow. We have to lock the AD team today,' he said.

I hurriedly followed him; half-frozen and numb. I noticed that Goku tried again to say something to us, but we both rushed past him to the floor.

I stepped in through the rusty brown gate. It was chilly inside, but not as bad as the van. It took me a couple of seconds to orient myself, and then the lights, the sound, the smell, the people, the sights began to seep in.

I realised the huge hall was crammed with almost two hundred people—workers and technicians, mostly men—standing next to the generators, fans, lights, sound systems. Some of them were screaming from the roof. Actually it was not a roof. They were standing on wooden boards hanging from the huge roof, which I got to know later were called 'taraphas'. The floor was practically carpeted with wires. I could hear various languages being spoken at the same time. Everyone was talking, screaming, cussing. And then I saw it. It was in the middle of the floor. The crux of this whole make-believe world. The set. The stage. Lit by a hundred or more sparkling bright lights. A huge cut-out of a milky-white moon sat in the centre of a raised white platform. On one side was a huge kidney-shaped pond with aquamarine water and pink flowers gently floating in it. On the other side was a beautiful fountain, with water gushing out. It was magical. And the magic was not just in the beauty, but in how suddenly it came upon you. In one minute I had left behind the heat, dust, fear, worries, leopards, everything I'd thought about the whole day. The moment I'd stepped on this floor, I was transported to a perfect place. It was a dream. As I was taking everything in, I heard Sam say, 'Fiza, this is Neki Brar.'

I whipped around to see Karan standing next to Fiza Kareem and murmuring something to her. I was caught completely off-guard. There, in front of me, was the familiar, famous face. I had watched her interviews, read her success story, read what people thought about her. I knew her favourite colour, her favourite dish, her best friends. I knew everything about her that the media could lay its hands on.

I did not hear what she asked me, and because Sam was nudging me furiously, I began rattling off information, that I was from Amritsar and had a Master's degree in Business Administration, and that I had no film experience. I think she'd asked me something else and I'd just given her a completely irrelevant answer.

And then she saw my yellow shoes.

It seemed like she stared at them for at least a minute before she turned around and told Karan: 'Why the hell are you guys wasting my time? Take her away.'

In effect, this had been my first big opportunity. And I'd been told to get lost.

I had blown it.

Karan smirked while Sameer looked at me sympathetically. Fiza turned away from me and I bolted for the door. I heard someone calling my name but I ignored it. I could hear Fiza's voice on the mike and I sensed Shivani and Kriti smirking at each other. I could feel my insides churning. I was going to throw up. I ran out of the door, into the heat, and towards the van to collect my handbag.

Just as I reached for the van door, Goku came running up to me.

'Please Madam. Please listen to me. One minute. Please give me one chance.'

I looked at him. I could not understand what he was saying. I could feel the tears welling up in my eyes, and I did not want him to see that. I opened the van door and he followed. He seemed desperate. He did not even notice my tears, because his own eyes were welling up.

He thrust an album in front of me. 'Please Madam, please see them once,' he said, his shiny shirt clinging to his body, wet with sweat.

I had no choice. I did. Pictures of Goku dressed as a strict policeman, a serious lawyer, a kind doctor, a comic Sardar, a meek gurkha. It was a strange thing to see this man living so many roles, but when I looked into his eyes, right in front of me, all I saw was a fading resemblance to a man who was once famous and had made the whole country laugh. Goku.

He was telling me his story without stopping even for a second, lest I tell him to leave the van. As he spoke, my tears were for some reason drying up. 'Madam, you are an AD, please give me a chance. Any character I am ready to do. You see I have played the famous role, maybe you don't remember, Goku, many years ago. You see we dwarves don't get good roles in Bollywood. Earlier we used to do comedy slots but now the actors do comedy themselves. You know that film, *Koi Mil Gaya*, na? I was shortlisted for Magic's role, but I lost the role to another guy just because he had done a

Hollywood film. Now that is not fair. He was one of the hobbits in that film, *Manor of the Rings*.'

He took out a neatly-pressed white handkerchief to wipe the sweat on his face. Even the AC is not helping, I thought, and then realised his perspiration had nothing to do with the heat.

'You know, in Hollywood they have main roles for dwarves as well, but here things are different. I want to make a film myself one day. I have even written the story. If you don't have a role for me at least hear the story. It will move you to tears. I narrate it to my children now and then. They all cry every single time I tell them the story. But it has comedy as well, along with a love track and situation for four songs. Including a disco number. I have made sure it is full commercial. Madam please. Think about it, I have to feed my family. Please see if you can do something?'

I didn't know what to say. That he'd just spent ten minutes with someone who wasn't even an AD on the film? 'I'll try,' I mumbled.

He folded his hands, thanked me a hundred times, and gave me one of his pictures with his vitals and phone number written behind. He was smiling when he left. I seemed to have made his day.

I wanted to call him back and take his autograph for my mother, but could not for some reason. I watched him walk away and promised myself that I was not going to quit. I might or might not get this film, but I was going to come back the next day and try again. Just like this man had been trying, so long and so hard.

Just then the door of the van opened. It was Sam. 'Wait here,' he said, and dashed off again.

I sat down on the couch again. Thinking about Goku.

At around 9:30 p.m., they packed up. Sam came into the van, looking exhausted. He looked at me and screamed. 'Oh fuck! You're still here? I forgot to tell you, sorry! She loved you. Start from tomorrow. Reporting time is 7 a.m. for you, since you are the junior-most in the team. The rest of us will come at 8 a.m.'

'But I thought she hated me! She said—'

Sam cut in, 'You don't know her. In fact, she said it's your first day and you looked very nervous; calm yourself down and come back tomorrow. So you're on. Karan will tell you about your duties after talking to the production house. Got to go now, bye . . .'

I nodded, completely stunned. I looked around as everyone left the set. Kriti sat in her Mercedes with Shivani. Karan and PJ in a Honda City and Sam in his Maruti Zen. I got into an auto which had a poster 'Stop TB. Do not Spit' pasted on the back. The other ADs zipped past; I was left far, far behind. Well, the comforting thing was, at least my vehicle carried a social message!

Film City was even more scary at night; the sounds of frogs and crickets adding to the creepiness. It was cold. I hugged myself and looked down. I could see my yellow shoes, glinting in the streetlight now and then, almost guilty, wondering if they had played their role correctly; had they proved lucky for me today?

As I reached my room and remembered all the faces staring at my yellow pumps, I knew what their fate would be. I took them off, wrapped them in the pink butter paper, the way my mother had, shut my suitcase and pushed it under the bed. They were never coming back on my shoe rack again.

And then, as promised, I emailed my mom about my day. This is what I said:

*Dear Mom,*

*Today I met Fiza Kareem. The big director. I have landed myself a dream job as her AD. She loved me. The film even has Shah Rukh Khan in a guest appearance. I saw Film City for the first time; it's beautiful. Most of the films are shot here. If you look closely you will see lush green trees, long, winding roads, and even a beautiful blue lake in the middle of it all.*

*Today I sat in an AC van the whole day. I was wearing a Gucci watch. I also met 'Goku' from your favourite serial. He was trying to sell me his story. Things move fast here, so much so that from watching Goku on TV, I was assuring him that I will hear his story one day and maybe help him make it here. You see, Mom, in one day I've covered a lot of ground in my yellow shoes.*

*Looking forward to tomorrow. Till later.*

*Love, Neki*

*P.S: I wore the yellow shoes today. They are beautiful. Everyone including Fiza Kareem looked at them for one whole minute. So I have wrapped them safely and will wear them on the next big occasion. They will bring me luck.*

## A 'TORCH'EROUS COMBAT

I held the wine bottle over my mouth, hoping there would be a few drops left. It was empty though; annoyed, I put it down next to me. It tottered for a second and then fell all the way down. The light from the street lamps bounced off the aquamarine bottle, paying homage to its beautiful slender shape.

My grandfather used to say, there is beauty in destruction. When a thing is about to be destroyed, in that moment it is the most beautiful ever. Because we know, after this second, it will cease to exist. 'What does not exist is always more beautiful than what does—for the former has the insignia of imagination added to it.'

Anyway, I was certain that the most beautiful wine bottle that ever was had crashed into a million pieces on the ugly concrete road. I heard a yelp—a man's voice, I thought. Or it could have been a dog. I peered down; any further and I knew I would join the smashed bottle on the road. I saw a figure dart by; or imagined it. Somewhere a light was switched on and off.

It sparked off something important in my memory: the torch signal. How could I have forgotten that? We'd prepared so much to shoot a scene for which I was in charge of bringing a torch. I leafed through the pages of my diary till I reached the right entry.

~

27 September 2008. 12:07 a.m.
Dear Nano,

Two amazing things happened today: I have discovered that the man of my dreams does exist in a physical form. Ranvir Khanna is the second lead in the film. He is tall, dark, handsome and intelligent. The other thing I have discovered is that my brain has a hibernation mode. It simply stops working when Ranvir Khanna is in the vicinity.

Ranvir Khanna's first film was a box office disaster; so was his second. But with his good looks and wit, he's very popular with the women. Rumour has it that he is seeing a prominent politician's wife, which is how he got his first break in the film industry. Apparently 'Mrs Politician' arm-twisted the director and producer into casting him.

The thing about rumours is, they stick. If you don't deny a rumour, there is always a possibility that there's some truth in it. And if you *do* deny it, consider it confirmed.

Anyway, Ranvir is so good to look at, it's easy to forget the rumours.

BUT, that is not what this day was all about—it was about me preparing for combat.

Today I was given the responsibility to handle an important prop for a scene. It's the first respectable job I've been given, considering the mindless chores they've dumped on me for almost a month. I've been used as a runner to fetch the make-up assistant when Minty's fake eyelashes stuck out at an awkward angle as the glue was not strong enough to hold it together, making her look like a fearsome witch rather than a doe-eyed picture of perfection. I've also been used as a fan holder, standing for what seems like hours to make Minty's dupatta billow so she would look like an angelic vision; or to get the curtains to flap in the background; or so that leaves could fly around like there was a storm brewing. I can definitely be called the weather girl for the month so far. I've also been used to collect a wig from the wig-maker who always accuses me of paying him less and asking for a wig made with real hair. I obviously had no clue why he was ranting at me; all I wanted to do was snatch the wig and hand it over to Karan or Shivani. I've also been doing Kriti's dirty work—like knocking on the vans of the artistes and politely asking their assistants, 'How long will Ma'am take? The shot is ready.' Or 'We'll be ready for Sir in ten minutes.' I'm the human version of a countdown that Kriti has invented for her personal entertainment. This has been the story on the set so far, but during the non-shooting days, I have been evolving as an intelligent film-maker—by ordering tea, coffee, snacks and dinner for the entire AD team, sitting and working till late in the production office.

On set, the only guy who hasn't palmed his work off on me and used me as his personal assistant is PJ. And Sam, who probably just hasn't had a chance to hand over his workload to me as I'm so busy running up and down and all over the floor. But the good thing is, all the spot boys and make-up dadas and costume dadas, the ones at the bottom of the food chain like me, they are my friends now. Something from 'Sid' just popped up in my brain: 'In the pursuit of a goal to woo a fair maiden in the village, you befriend the local barber's assistant.' Well, thankfully something made sense to me now in that book; I had instinctively befriended the barber's assistant.

~

I had to pause and laugh at how naive I'd been. I may have befriended the barber's assistants, but I forgot to befriend the barber himself.

So of course I'd landed on this rooftop, planning my suicide. . . .

~

But today, finally, I was actually given something important to do.

We were filming a robbery scene. For us ADs, it was a mini war. We had to get everything right in a short span of time. We had very specific requirements for the scene. Five actors were required to play the thieves, and the director wanted all of them to have real beards. They had to be unattractive, speak in a certain Bhojpuri dialect and act well. We had been hunting for these actors for over a week. We were all stressed because the main hero of the film—Ahmed Khan—would be in the scene along with Ranvir Khanna.

Ahmed Khan is a HUGE star. The first day he walked in, I hid behind a massive light and some skimmers, and stared at him. For a full two minutes. Just to make sure he was the same person I had seen on the silver screen. Just then, a mosquito bit him and he began scratching his arm. Then I saw the same mosquito descending on his spot boy, who was standing behind him, holding a glass of water, cigarette, towel, perfume, and anything else the star might ask for. I could have happily run after that mosquito and squashed it for making my Greek god uncomfortable. He was as good-looking and as perfect as he appeared on screen—till, two minutes later, I saw him pulling at his crotch. Surely I was hallucinating. No, he was grabbing his crotch again and scratching this time. That was it. No amount of silver jubilee hits, romantic dialogue or heartrending scenes could redeem this hero in my eyes. Ahmed muttered something and left, his entourage—which included a hair and make-up assistant, his personal assistant, his personal trainer, a few pumped-up friends, and his spot boy—trailing behind him.

It had taken a scratch at the wrong place and the wrong time to put things in the right perspective for me. He was all flesh and blood in the end. I laughed at my little joke and turned around to see the entire AD team staring at me.

My face was burning hot; they must have seen me gaping at Ahmed Khan like a star-struck idiot. 'I was not staring at him,' I muttered. 'I was thinking about how a mosquito doesn't differentiate between a star and a spot boy . . .'

They all looked at me as if I was a lunatic—I definitely sounded like one. Karan lost a bit of colour on his face as well. 'If she is dumbstruck looking at Ahmed Khan, then I want her off the sets when Shah Rukh Khan is shooting with us. I don't want her fainting or going loony,' he announced.

They all turned around to leave and Kriti—clad in various shades of blue from head to toe—gave me a wink and muttered, 'So fresh.'

'Thanks, I use Liril, it has lime. Mom says lime and citrus have vitamin C which keeps you fresh, keeps the stench away, you should try it . . .' I blabbered.

'Are you for real? So verni . . . by fresh I meant vernacular; verni; it was not a compliment, babe.'

'I didn't think it was one . . . I was just recommending that you use lime, for freshness.'

'What the hell do you mean?! I stink?'

'Yes . . . I mean . . . in a nice, designer way, of DKNY . . .' It sounded all wrong, and as Kriti stormed off, I hastily added, 'In a good way!'

Reeling from my series of colossal stupidities, I heard someone say a friendly hello. I turned. Ranvir Khanna was standing there smiling at me. I promptly dropped the scene printout that I was carrying. He gallantly bent down to pick it up for me and gave me a good view of his lovely, muscled back. I admired again his rugged good looks, the tall, lean frame, the curly locks, the chiselled profile. And then I saw his lips moving; he was saying something to me and handing me my papers. As I took it from him, his hand accidently touched mine. It was the fraction of a second in real life; in my head it lasted the whole day. I couldn't stop thinking about the texture of his hand—not too soft, not manicured, not supple. Hard, cowboy hands. Dammit. The fact was, Ranvir Khanna had said hello to me every day for the last five days, as well as bye, *and* asked a few questions about the script. This was easy for me to answer, as I've memorised the script and can recite the entire thing aloud with dialogues verbatim and punctuated.

Before I could thank him, he was called away by Fiza Kareem on the mike. My walkie came alive just then. It was Sam. 'Neki! In the costume room, now! 007!' That was Sam's code for 'Problem!' In two minutes I was in the costume room, the five actors we'd selected for the shoot standing in front of me, lined up.

I could hear Karan over Sam's walkie. 'Sam, are the robbers here?' he asked.

Sam immediately replied, 'Yes!'

'Do they all have beards?'

'Uh . . . mostly.'

'What do you mean *mostly*?' Karan shrieked.

'Well, one of them is clean-shaven.'

There was a pause. And then Karan's voice hissed with controlled rage from the walkie speaker.

'Who is responsible for this? I want everyone in the costume room, *now*!'

I hugged my torch—the big, blue torch that Ahmed Khan had to give Ranvir Khanna in the scene—which was the only thing I was responsible for today. I felt so glad I'd had nothing to do with this disaster whatsoever.

Meanwhile, the clean-shaven actor who was causing so much stress was looking at us sulkily. He had a nice face, I noted.

He saw me looking at him and promptly started talking. 'See, I want to be an actor, and with the beard no one will recognise me. Also, I've been trying for a role for four years! Maybe this will be my only chance to be in the same frame as Ahmed Khan. If I'm with a beard, people in my town won't recognise me!' he said.

'Dude,' PJ said to Sam, 'your robber is going to get us screwed. My job was to shortlist, I shortlisted. He looked good with the beard in the audition. This better not land on me.'

Just then Kriti, Karan and Shivani walked in. All set for battle. The make-up man accompanying Karan was carrying glue and a fake beard.

'Fix him,' Karan ordered angrily.

The actor stood his ground. 'I'm not doing this role with a beard.'

'But we told you that you need to have a beard for the role!' Karan said.

The actor did not budge. 'Sir, you said a beard is required for auditions. I told my agent I don't want to do it with a beard, he said go on the sets and they will adjust!'

Karan was frothing at the mouth now. 'ADJUST?! Adjust what?! Who made the confirmation calls to the agents?'

Sam quickly said, 'PJ did the short-listing, Shivani was looking into casting and finalising details.'

I was learning another basic rule of survival: to play the blame game and play it well. Pre-empt and extricate yourself before the problem snowballs.

Shivani's face went red, 'I did perfect casting! Then Kriti was supposed to call the coordinator and confirm the requirements.'

Without hesitating, Kriti said, 'I had my yoga class, so I told Neki to make the final calls. I explained to her in detail what needs to be done.'

Suddenly all eyes were trained on me accusingly. I didn't know what to say. Kriti had said nothing to me about confirming that the actors' had beards; I was only told to confirm the time for the shoot.

Another lesson of combat: lie and lie well. Kriti had evidently mastered it and was looking at me squarely in the eye. I was embarrassed that she was lying so blatantly, but she was so convincing, even I almost believed her! I knew we had a huge star in the making. She was going to be an actress to reckon with.

There was another home truth there; if you believe in your lie enough, at some point it does become your truth.

Karan looked at me menacingly and said, 'I need an actor who looks filthy, can act well, and has a real beard in the next ten minutes—ready in his costume.'

I stared at him. I felt like I was in a horror movie. Karan stormed off, as did the two girls. Sam looked at me sympathetically and PJ said, 'Do you think anyone would care if *I* was in a yoga class or getting a kidney transplant done? If I had messed up, I would be thrown out of the film! Which idiot said "what's in a name"?'

I looked at him, incredulous. PJ noticed and said, 'Don't you dare answer that question Neki.'

Sam gave PJ a look, and then all three of us ran out to find an actor with a beard.

I have never scrutinised men so closely. The tea boys, the sweepers, the cleaners, the hair and make-up assistants, the drivers, the light boys—I was checking out each and every amused face for someone who might work for the robber's role. After fifteen minutes, just when I was losing hope, I remembered that the costume assistant's dress dada—the tailor who does the last-minute clothes alterations on the set—has a beard. I ran all the way to the costume room and opened the side door. It led to a small adjoining make-shift room made of cardboard. It seemed deserted. Two sets of sewing machines were placed facing each other. Just then I heard some noise. I peeked through the discarded costumes hanging on the stands to see Sam and Kriti lip-locked, practically eating each other alive. Kriti's jacket had been discarded on the floor, as well as their walkies. Kriti was moaning softly. I was hugely embarrassed. They were making out, and for some reason *I* was having a panic attack.

What was the usual protocol when you see your co-workers making out at your workplace? Do you clear your throat and announce your arrival, or do you make a discreet exit. When I saw Sam's hand popping Kriti's Guess buttons, I decided discreet disappearance was my style. Just as I was backing away from the scene, I heard Karan asking for Kriti on the walkie, reminding her that she was supposed to get Ranvir Khanna on the set. At the same time, I saw Shivani opening the costume room door, presumably to look for Kriti. I had to shift to plan B.

I stepped out of my hiding position and patted Sam on his shoulder. He squealed and let go of Kriti, who glared at me accusingly. Accusing me of what, I don't know. I cleared my throat and muttered, 'Karan is calling for you on the walkie and Shivani is here.'

Kriti hastily straightened her shirt just as Shivani reached us, huffing and puffing. The angry gleam in her eyes changed into a suspicious one. There was some tension in the air and Shivani was smart enough to catch on to it. She immediately became the judge of the situation and we three were standing in a witness stand.

In a serious tone she asked, 'What's happening here?'

Before I had time to blush, get embarrassed, cover up for my friends and play the Good Samaritan, Kriti spoke, 'I'm sorry, it's my fault!'

I was shocked, impressed with the girl's honesty. Beneath the silky hair, creamy skin and fetching figure, there was a heart. I warmed towards her instantly and then turned ice cold when I heard the rest of what she was saying. 'I had to break them up—they were at it! In the middle of the shoot! I was looking for actors.'

Shivani's eyes danced with excited anger—she knew she was going to have fun eating us alive. 'What the fuck, are you serious? You guys . . . this is not happening!'

'Keep it down, Shivani,' Sam stopped her. 'I've zipped up on you and that stunt man, Hassan. He lands up in all our action shoots . . . Anyway, the point is, you owe me.'

Shivani glared at him and then said, 'There is nothing happening with Hassan. And you better stop this; next time it happens she's out!'

I realised that the 'she' here was me.

Shivani stormed out, saying something on her walkie to Karan.

Kriti looked at me and said, 'Listen, my dad's a well-known producer and I'm a public figure. This could be in the papers tomorrow. *You* have nothing to lose. So stick to the story?'

I gaped at her, dumbstruck; then she suddenly smiled at me—for the very first time. 'Thanks!' she said. 'I'm going to find you someone to play the robber. Don't worry, okay?'

She turned, leaving me standing there, aghast. In exchange for a robber, I was giving her my reputation. I turned to Sam angrily. 'How could you not say anything? My reputation on set will be ruined!'

'But babes, who will care about that? Now it's important for Kriti—she's going to be launched as a heroine! And why do you need a reputation? You are an AD . . . the last runner at that. You practically don't exist! Relax, this is the best time of your life! Enjoy it!'

I was furious. 'But my mother will kill me and my father will kill me again after my mother has finished killing me!'

Sam was clearly taken aback by my reaction. 'Who will tell them? How will they find out? Nobody is interested in talking about your flings, least of all to your parents. Don't you see how lucky you are? Poor Kriti lives under a microscope. Not to mention that her boyfriend will kill her. And her parents. Her public image will be ruined too.'

'What public image? Nobody knows who she is!'

'But they will, and they know her father!'

'You're all delusional! What world are you living in?'

'The same one you're trying to fit into now,' Sam said. 'Listen, relax. It's not a big deal. It was just necking. And you and I didn't do anything; we just have to let people assume we did, and they will forget in a day or two.'

'Neki!! Robber—I need him now!!' Karan yelled over the walkie. My modesty could wait. I had to find our robber first! I ran out—straight into Ranvir Khanna, who was walking to the set with his personal trainer, who everyone strangely referred to as Bunny. One could barely see his face, his long hair covering it the way it did. I almost tripped but Ranvir Khanna caught me.

Unfortunately, the moment wasn't accompanied by background music, bells and a soft, gentle breeze. It was hot, I looked like a baked potato and was almost on the verge of hysteria. On top of it, I was completely tongue-tied, so when Ranvir smiled, winked and said in his deep, raspy voice, 'What happened, darling, you okay?' I could only stare back at him. Thankfully, Sam came up just then and began telling Ranvir about our hunt for a robber. And how my neck was on the line if we didn't find someone, and soon.

Ranvir looked at me directly. I was upset, but with him looking at me, I felt a little hope. Someone was on my side. Not to mention that I would gladly run into his arms for a comforting hug. I smiled a little.

Ranvir smiled back sympathetically. His trainer Bunny gave him a little nudge, and said, 'It's hot, let's go in the vanity bro.'

Whoever chose the name 'vanity van' for the actors' vans was a genius. He knew what he was talking about. The van witnessed such unadulterated displays of vanity; the emperor was allowed to be without clothes in the van and he could indulge in hours of looking at an imperfection or admiring it and because he's only surrounded by his fawning entourage, there's no one to shout *'The emperor is wearing no clothes!'*

Ranvir's twinkling eyes jerked me back to the robber dilemma. He looked at me with a glint in his eyes and said to Sam, 'Will he do?' He pointed to Bunny. That was the exact moment I think I fell for Ranvir Khanna. Without looking at the appalled Bunny, I simply said, 'Yes!'

Sam looked at me with a little admiration for hijacking the cool trainer for the robber's role. When Ranvir walked away, Sam whispered in my ear, 'I wish I were a pretty girl with doe eyes; I would not move an inch on the set.'

Karan walked up then, ready to shout at us. I quickly said, 'Found the robber,' and pointed to the beefed up Bunny, who was looking distinctly grumpy now.

Sam added, 'Ranvir gift-wrapped him and gave him to Neki just because she is cute. I want to be cute.'

'At least someone is getting some work done,' Karan said and went back onto the set.

I had redeemed myself! I hugged the torch—today was going to be a wonderful day, I thought. As always I was wrong.

## HERE COMES MANDAKINI

The robber situation resolved, we were all summoned on the set. It was dark inside, and the set had been done up to look like a street. Fiza announced on the mike, 'One rehearsal!'

I saw the actors taking their positions. I had eyes only for Ranvir. He was memorising his lines and, for some reason, jogging on the spot. Bunny, the 'robber', was glaring at me from under a black blanket. I ignored him and focused on Ranvir again. Just then Karan said, 'Neki, the torch!' That was my cue. I ran up to the actors. I could feel all two hundred eyes on the set on me, and I prayed I wouldn't trip. I managed to reach them without incident and parted with the torch I had bought from the market the previous day.

I quickly went back and stood next to the monitor so I could watch the shot. Fiza Kareem had her own monitor, but the rest of the set wrestled with each other to look at the fourteen-inch screen to make sure their work in the shot was okay. The hair department checked whether an actor's hair fell at the right angle while he was talking, laughing, crying or dancing; the art department checked for the bulbs in the background, or the floor or the curtains, depending on the scene; the costume department checked whether a dupatta was draped right, or the crease of a pant was perfectly straight. The family and friends of the stars just sat in front of the monitor and occupied chairs, getting in everyone's way.

My granddad was right when he said that, in life, god was in the details. In film-making too, I realised, god was in the details. After all, we were all trying to imitate life.

The rehearsal went off well. At the end, Fiza Kareem said, 'Ranvir, switch the torch on twice in the scene, like a signal, and then hand it to Ahmed.' Ranvir nodded.

The camera started rolling. All two hundred people concentrated on the scene about to unfold in the next one minute, willing that their part in this make-believe magic should go correctly. For their sake, I hoped everything would go well.

Just then PJ came and whispered in my ear, 'What if there was an earthquake and all our robbers ran away or were buried under the set—then we'd have to dig the robbers out and do the scene! After all, shooting this one scene costs us four lakh rupees. You know how much the robbers get paid? One thousand rupees a day.'

'Shut the fuck up, PJ!' Shivani said on the walkie.

The camera rolled. The robbers did their bit, running helter-skelter to their marked positions. Ranvir raised the torch to his mark and clicked. Nothing happened. The camera kept whirring, the robbers kept running, Ahmed Khan kept looking at Ranvir, waiting for him to hand over the torch, and Ranvir kept clicking ... I knew all eyes were slowly going to come my way. The floor was spinning. I wanted to die.

Fiza Kareem screamed, 'Cut! What is happening? What the hell is this? Can we manage to get a torch that actually works?! What is the AD team doing?'

Karan ran up to Ranvir, looked at the torch and realised a battery cell was missing. He gave me a pointed look.

Fiza Kareem continued to scream on the mike. I could not comprehend half the words. 'The batteries will be here in a minute,' Karan said apologetically to her.

Kriti came up to me. 'You mean you did not check the torch before giving it up there?'

I didn't respond. By this time I thought everyone in the room could hear my heartbeat—it was so loud and so fast. A little man wearing a red jacket, oversized shoes, faded jeans and a warm smile came up. His name was Punjabi. He was one of the spot boys, and he had probably realised that my throat was parched. He offered me water in a plastic glass. As I was drinking it, I saw Shivani standing with Ahmed Khan, Ranvir and Fiza. Shivani was apologising as she handed over the torch—batteries now loaded.

'Sorry about this, it was the new girl,' she said, duly pointing to where I was standing drinking water. The three of them looked at me. I didn't know what the protocol was, after a screw-up. Was I supposed to crawl from the set floor or just stand there as if nothing was wrong? My walkie gave me the answer—it was Karan calling me outside.

I scurried out as Punjabi said, 'Don't worry, do you want a chocolate biscuit? I will get a new packet for you.'

I wanted some poison, but obviously did not tell him that. I smiled my thanks and rushed out. But not before I saw another pair of eyes watching me. Ranvir. He gave me an encouraging thumbs-up sign from where he was standing.

Karan was standing outside with Sam and PJ, obviously waiting to spell out my sentence. I walked over to them like a prisoner.

Karan simply said, 'When you are in charge of a prop, check it. Make sure it works.'

'I swear I did! It was working last night,' I said.

'Well, then keep checking it till the last minute. Double check, double check everything! Keep extra cells. You never know what can happen!' he said, and walked off.

PJ looked at me broodingly and added, 'What he is trying to say is, a good opportunity is like a slippery fish: you have to keep checking if it's still in the net. You never know what could happen, and unfortunately in your case Neki, the fish didn't just escape the net, it had a heart attack!'

'Let her be, PJ,' Sam said, and then turned to me. 'Actually I was supposed to go with the production guy, but Karan feels you are not ready to be on the floor yet, so I'll stay here, you go with Aslam. You got that, babes? Will you manage out there on your own?'

He pointed to a dark, portly, balding man wearing a white shirt, white trousers, white patent leather shoes and a gold chain. He waved to me with the hand holding a Nokia communicator.

'What am I supposed to be doing again?' was the question I wanted to ask.

Sam moved away as PJ gave me a once-over. 'You know, with your sweet face, you are not bad to look at, so be careful when you're with Aslam. He might sell you off and buy a new communicator.' He laughed wickedly and began walking away. Of course he was joking. But I still had to find out what it was I was supposed to do, and even more so now after hearing PJ's advice.

I ran up to him. 'Can you tell me where I'm going and what I'm supposed to do, PJ?'

PJ pulled me closer. He was a foot taller than me; I realised he was quite good-looking. He had a lean, muscular body and used the same cologne as Ranvir did. Only the amount varied.

'Never commit to a job without knowing what it is. You have no clue what you're doing, and you're not going to survive this one. Please stop wasting your time and screwing with ours. You know, my friend was supposed to be an AD on Fiza's film, instead of you. He was more committed, more deserving—but you're Sam's friend and now we know the details, after the costume room episode that Shivani just told me about. Karan opted for you, I guess for some eye candy on the sets. But I promise you, you're going to be out by the end of this week.'

I was stunned to hear the usually easy-going PJ ranting like this. I wanted to explain the whole costume-room episode, but suddenly I was only angry at how he was treating me. Without flinching, I looked him squarely in the eye and said, 'But I'm here and your friend isn't—so get used to it.'

PJ eased his hold on my arm, his hand staying on just a little bit longer than necessary. I moved away to the delighted Aslam.

We got into a smelly Sumo. Aslam started the car and an old dilapidated tape recorder began playing a Kishore Kumar song. In a way, I was glad to be escaping the war zone, but realised that I'd better figure out where it was that I was headed. When I asked Aslam, he laughed and said, 'You don't worry, Nekiji. Just sit in a corner and have lemon juice—I will finalise the poster man.'

I would have liked to spill some lemon juice down his crotch, but I only smiled and asked, 'Poster man?'

Aslam nodded. 'The director wants a hand-painted feel for the film posters that will come out eventually, so we're checking out and short-listing artists who can be considered.'

'But somebody who knows the creative brief should be with us, no?'

Aslam looked at me and smiled. 'I am the creative and I have the brief!' he said, laughing like a pig.

I ignored his crude joke. 'So what are the criteria you will shortlist the poster painters on?'

'I've already done the ground work. I know two guys who are in our budget and have a body of work to show, so I'm just going to check them out before finalising on one.'

I sat back, taking the information in. I might as well sit in one corner and drink lemon juice, I thought.

After weaving through traffic, vendors, people and animals on the road, the bulky Sumo finally stopped. The street was lined with shops displaying hand-painted posters. A skanky guy with flashy jeans came up to Aslam. I thought he would go down on the floor and lick Aslam's shoes any minute. Aslam was no longer the seedy side-kick with white shoes, here he was GOD. I could sense the change. This was his circus, and he was the ringmaster. My granddad popped in my head. 'Life is about role play my girl; play your part the way you are supposed to, and you'll be fine. The moment you try to be you, it's all over!'

Right now, my grandfather's advice made some sense—I should just let Aslam play God.

As if on cue, he waved his hand like a king and ten men moved at the same time.

'Give Madam a comfortable chair and some fresh juice, in a clean glass.' He turned to me. 'I'll be back,' he said.

Aslam and his little worshippers moved away towards a small shop at the far end of the lane. I sat on a little stool as someone handed over a glass of juice. It was some kind of yellow and orange concoction. 'What is this?' I asked, just to be sure.

'Ganga-Jamuna,' the boy said impatiently and ran away.

I sipped it tentatively and then relaxed. For now all was good. My feet were resting, the sun was warming my tired back, and my thirst was being quenched. I started looking around me, and slowly, as I stopped wallowing in self-pity, I realised I was sitting in a beautiful place—a place that had escaped the rush of time. The small shops, cobbled street, wooden frames and old hand-painted posters—one could imagine that Rajesh Khanna was still ruling the roost.

A particular poster caught my eye and without thinking I picked up my Ganga-Jamuna and walked over. It was a half-clad Mandakini, beautiful and very different from the real Mandakini, but I knew the film instantly from the clothes or lack of it—*Ram Teri Ganga Maili*. As I admired the sweep of the bold strokes, the mixture of colours, I wondered why a digital picture could not captivate me for so long. The answer was simple. When I looked at the painting, I could see the two days' work the artist must have put in it. Perhaps he was thinking of his wife's beautiful smile, pondering over his child's latest tricks, laughing at a joke with a warm, salty breeze ruffling his hair . . . In short, those two days of his life and more had been captured bit by bit in every stroke of this painting.

Just then a gnarled old hand came in my line of vision and waved a finger. 'Madam, please take the glass out. One drop can destroy the whole painting. Also I don't take chances with my Mandakini—she is my favourite.'

Just as he said it, I realised how foolish it had been of me to barge in. I quickly went out and placed the half-empty glass on the stool outside.

I went back inside to the old man. He was wearing a loose Pathani suit and had a long grey beard. His age showed on his face, but what caught me were the eyes. Twinkling and bright. He was surrounded by his creations and he was proud of them.

I sat down in his little shop, I knew he didn't mind. Slowly he turned to me and pointed to an illustration of Amitabh Bachchan in angry hues of red and orange. '*Zanjeer*!' he said and then looked at the picture for a few seconds. I knew he was not just admiring his work but reliving an era.

'I was the only one who could paint red and green around angry, young, gun-toting Bachchan. I could do it with my eyes closed. You know, in our time, the people would guess what a movie was all about based on our posters. It was all in the colours. A hero should have hero colours, and a villain should have villain colours.'

I realised then why my yellow pumps had been such a disaster—stereotypes work. The old man had given me a tip and I was going to hang on to it. My new wardrobe was in order: the set was a warzone, I was in a battle and the gear I needed was COMBAT (read Adidas and Nike for women). If I was to be perceived as a serious contender at work, I had to look like one.

If I were to make a poster of my life now, I would be so far away from what I wanted. In my head it would have to be a big poster with bold colours, with me in the centre, holding a rifle; but all I could see currently on the poster of my life were discarded yellow pumps, a useless torch, a helpless girl. Disaster.

I snapped back to the wise old man.

'You know those great artists—M.F. Husain and Bala Krishnan—they were poster designers to begin with. One of us! Now Bala Krishnan travels abroad with his work in big-big planes . . . But it's all time's play, you can't stop change, you can't stop ideas. But I wish we were not left so far behind!'

He looked at me and at that point I felt the burden of our

entire generation which had raced ahead. I wanted to comfort him, to give him a chance. Actually I could. He could paint the posters for our film. He fit the bill: experience and budget. I knew any money offered would be welcomed

Just then Aslam walked in. He was still playing god, his happy cronies following him. 'We can go,' he said to me. 'These two will come to set tomorrow with the work.' The two middle-aged cronies grinned happily. As he walked away, I noticed that Aslam was carrying a poster exactly like the one I could see in the back of the old man's shop.

'That's very similar to yours,' I said softly to the old man.

He laughed. 'Because it *is* mine. That other painter knows people. I am old, I don't know anyone. At least he can get some work and give me a little money.'

Full of promises I had not made to the old man, I got into the car next to Aslam. The shoot had packed up when we reached. Aslam went up to Karan and began selling his men to him. I was sure the sum he was quoting was more than what would really reach the cronies. Fiza Kareem was on her phone, standing about ten feet away from us.

My head was screaming—talk or shut up forever. I decided to talk.

'I can get the same work at half the cost,' I interrupted Aslam. 'Because I know the source your guy will anyway get his poster from. We should directly tell him what we want— it will be cheaper. Also, it's the right thing to do.'

Aslam's face changed all kinds of colours. Clearly offended, he asked in a condescending tone, 'Do you know anything about poster-making?'

I looked him in the eye. It was now or never. I folded my arms and shot back at him, 'Did you know one single film poster required six months of work from conception to mass production in those days—the finished panels were carted and assembled on streets into advertisements sometimes up to 120 by 60 feet? And that famous poster designers like Bala Krishnan can charge 2,000 rupees per square foot?'

There was a moment of silence. I'd shocked everyone around me. I loved it. I sent up a silent thanks for my good memory. My mother had a photogenic one too.

'So, you see, I have done my research,' I said curtly. I knew whatever information I'd just rambled had nothing to do with proving my point—but fortunately Aslam couldn't see that. He was just stunned into silence by the names and figures.

Suddenly, from behind me, I heard Fiza's voice saying, 'Karan, try her guy out too.' She'd witnessed the whole stand-off!

My smile was as big as my jaw would allow. PJ looked at me and winked. 'Nice move,' he said. I was not sure whether PJ was an enemy or a friend, but he definitely made the battle interesting. Shivani and Kriti looked at me with differing degrees of hostility. I was too happy to care though. I felt as if I was invincible. And the thought of the old man's face when asked to do the job made me happy. Maybe, in a way, I could tell him, 'We didn't leave you behind.'

When I reached home, all I wanted to do was sleep, but there was a little party going on at the house. There were a few people I knew, including the underwear model, who is now referring to me as 'Babes', and some I had never seen before. Every one of them was drunk though. I went into my room and closed the door, but a very wasted Zoya barged in. 'Hey kiddo! I took a battery from your torch for the TV remote and forgot to put it back! Here . . .' She threw the battery to me.

I looked at the tiny cell and the big role it had played in my life today. I could throw it in the bin, burn it or save it as a lesson learnt. Of course I saved it.

Sleep eluded me.

I stepped out of my bed. Crossed the little kitchen. Opened the back door of the kitchen, and stepped out. Leaving the thumping music, blinding smoke and broken glasses behind me. We have a small balcony, big enough for only two people to stand. A winding old staircase connects the balcony to the little unkempt overgrown yard behind. A drain runs through the entire yard. But that's only in the day; at night, with a beautiful moon and brilliant stars, it's a little stream. Standing there, I calmed down and then thought of Ranvir Khanna. I was eager to start another day.

I sat down on the top step of the curving staircase, opened my little laptop and wrote to my mother.

*Dear Mom,*

*Today I shot with the superstar Ahmed Khan. In fact the whole crew, including Ahmed Khan, had to wait for me to shoot the scene, as I was in charge of the most important prop. I even ordered Ranvir Khanna's friend to play a role in the scene, and he had to! I was in charge of finding someone to make posters for the film. I found a very talented old man. Fiza Kareem liked my work and smiled at me. I came back home and there was a party going on—girls only as boys are not allowed. It was a lovely day today because I know I am not scared of growing old anymore. I know now that when I'm old, I will have these moments I spent in the pursuit of my dreams to narrate to a young life. In short, I can't wait to grow old—but don't worry, I will get married on the way!*

*Love, Neki*

*P.S: When I saw the old man, I realised that—even to a stranger—it's evident from looking at your face if you have lived a life you've 'wanted' or you have lived a 'wanting' life. The old man has definitely lived the life he wanted. Thank Dad for letting me live mine too.*

## NAME DROPPING

I thought I could hear that song, *Hare hare Ram*; it was probably coming from a tea stall somewhere. It stopped as abruptly as it had started—like the listener had suddenly realised the lateness of the hour. Thankfully the lane I was going to fall in to was behind the house. It was even quieter than our front lane, except for the buying and selling of pot, coke and smack that went on occasionally. Sam had given us a lecture on the beauty of this lane and the system. The girls and I were thrilled because it brought down the rent in the neighbourhood as families did not want to stay here. There was no rendezvous scheduled for tonight, I could see. The cosmos was giving me a clear signal to 'Jump away!'

I thought about the lyrics of the song I'd just heard. For me, it was not just a hit song from a film slated to be *the* blockbuster of the year, it had sentimental value as well. It was the first song for which I'd been part of the shoot. Every time I heard the song, I could not help but sing along. I knew every beat, every word and every note of that song. I began singing along now as well—horribly out of tune, unfortunately.

I turned the pages of my diary . . .

10 October 2008. 2:34 a.m.
Dear Nano,
Today, I feel like I've stepped over a threshold. I think I've now lost the ability to morally judge people. I don't know if it's a good thing, or a bad one, but it *is* liberating!

It all started early in the morning, before my seven o'clock alarm went off. I woke up to our doorbell ringing repeatedly. Zoya and I looked at each other groggily and darted to the living room. Zoya gingerly walked towards the door and peeked through the eyehole. She turned around mouthing a filthy abuse and opened the door. It was our bai, Smita. She looked terrified; she was out of breath and her hair was all over the place. The beginnings of what promised to be awful bruises showed on her face and arms.

'What happened?' Zoya asked.

Breathing heavily, Smita said, 'The police are after me!'

'What?! Why?'

Smita looked at us and, wiping away a tear, she said calmly, 'Because I beat up another woman. She's sleeping with my husband. I caught them red-handed last night in my kholi. She is not even nice to look at: I'm much more fair!'

I didn't know what to take out of that statement. The vanity of a woman, the desperation of a wife, the disillusionment of a relationship. The insanity of the human mind. It was all thrown at us in one go. Zoya started laughing. 'I need a cigarette!' she said.

Rosh joined us sleepily and sat down on the couch with a sigh. Zoya settled on the windowsill. I was rooted to the spot. Smita looked at my pained expression and knew who her victim was.

'You need to put something on that . . .' I told her. I gave her some ice which she rolled up in her pallu and began pressing on her bruises.

'I broke her nose!' she suddenly exclaimed, not without some pride.

'Obviously the police is after you, then,' Zoya said dryly. 'Who attacked whom first?'

I saw some blood near Smita's mouth. She had clearly lost a tooth for the other woman's nose. 'I work the whole day for my husband who just sits around and lazes. I have no problem with that. I can feed him. He is my man. The father of my two children. But I am not sharing him with an old hag. And that also in my kholi! I walked in and she was on top of him, sucking his cock!'

Zoya chuckled.

'What will the world say? I am so bad and can't satisfy my husband? That he has to get it from this hag who is his mother's age. What will the society say about me?!'

Rosh got up and returned with a tub of lotion. She sat back in the couch and began massaging her legs, continuing to watch the drama like it was a soap opera on TV.

'So you pulled her and broke her nose?' Zoya asked.

Smita looked at us incredulously. 'Of course not! I screamed and threw her half-naked outside. Banged my head on the wall, threw a pan at my husband. The old hag ran away to her kholi across the road. Why should I beat her up when it is the man who was enjoying it as well? She is a prostitute. My man should have known better. I had to talk to him first.'

I was impressed with her assessment of the situation.

'So then what happened?' Zoya asked.

'The poor guy cried. Said the old hag came and raped him repeatedly while I was away in my village for my delivery. She came one night and said her man was not giving it to her. She opened her blouse buttons in front of my husband's face. He swore on the gods that he did not move. Then the witch told him that if he did not do it with her she would tear her clothes and run out and scream that she was being raped! To protect us he *had* to take her. Then she would come night after night and my man had to suffer her!'

Zoya had stopped smoking.

Rosh had stopped applying her lotion.

And I had stopped thinking.

Zoya and Rosh burst out laughing at the same time. Smita started crying and said, 'I am telling you, my man is innocent. He did it to protect his family. So I went into her kholi and beat her up. Now she's got two constables looking for me to beat me up. They also come to her kholi very regularly. You have to help me. My husband is going mad with worry! Please call someone, do something. You all are big people. I don't know where to go for help!'

Zoya snapped, 'Shut up! You are at fault! You should have broken your husband's face first!'

Just then an alarm rang. It was Rosh's. She was leaving for Delhi for an ad shoot. She was going to be one of the girls in a hair-oil ad who would shake their fake, glossed-up hair in front of a camera. She looked at us in alarm. 'I hate to do this but I have to leave for the airport in twenty. Keep me informed, okay?'

She went into her room to get ready.

Smita turned her scared eyes to me and Zoya. I didn't know what Zoya was thinking but I sure had no thoughts in my head. Just then my phone alarm went off. Reality hit. I knew I had to help Smita, but right now I had to reach the set on time, or else all the hard work of the past five weeks would go down the drain.

I turned to Zoya. 'I have a song shoot today. Fifty dancers and fifty junior artistes. It's a huge song. I have to leave!'

Zoya looked at me, panicking. 'I have to give a presentation to the boss at eight! I don't know what to do!'

I saw Smita's eyes welling up again. 'I'm sorry to trouble you. I should not have bothered you. You are busy people. If the police leave me, I will come tomorrow to make dinner, otherwise you will have to eat from a hotel,' she said and began walking towards the door. I ran to my room, pulled out a few hundred rupees notes from my wallet and rushed out to give it to her.

'Here keep this. It will help.' Smita thanked me. She had forgiven us. Zoya took out something from her purse and handed it to Smita as well. Smita smiled a bloody, broken-toothed smile.

~

I got a flash of Smita's eyes welling up. So I'd done something worthwhile there, no? And then came the aftertaste of that moment. I guess the money had been able to get rid of the guilt, but not good enough to get rid of the aftertaste! Assuaging a guilty conscience with money was just like scratching an itch—only a temporary reprieve.

~

My cell phone rang—it was Sam. I would need to reach the set by 7.30, he said. It was already 7. I told him I had fever and I was running a bit late, and before he could say anything further, I hung up.

Just then there was a commotion. Two hawaldars were bounding up the stairs with a fat woman who looked like she'd been quite badly beaten. Before any of us could react, the lady hurled herself at Smita. The hawaldars were eyeing Zoya's bare legs and were too distracted to separate the women. Zoya finally pulled the heavy woman away and I got Smita to one side.

Zoya screamed at the policemen, 'You cannot come barging into girls' accommodation like this. I will report you to your seniors. You will be in your own jail, rotting for harassment!'

The hawaldars were as cool as cucumbers in their dirty, crumpled uniforms. 'We all know how chaste you girls are. Half-naked you're roaming around, living alone Madam—with boys! Anyway, let's settle this. Tell your bai to give this one money for medicine and if she ever lays a hand on her again we will break every bone in her body!'

Smita screamed at them, 'But she raped my husband!'

The hawaldars laughed derisively.

'Fine, she will stay away from this woman. Please leave her alone now,' I said.

Zoya cut in, 'You guys should arrest her husband and this witch and put them behind bars together!'

Smita screamed, 'No, don't touch my husband. Just tell this old hag to stay away!'

'Tell your husband to keep his cock in check!' the old hag screamed back.

'You keep your clothes on!'

I was horrified. This was just like a dramatic film scene out of the '80s. Only it was not as pretty. It was real, and without a matching soundtrack. The stench of the sweating hawaldars was in the air that we were breathing in. The drops of blood from Smita's mouth were on the floor that we were standing on, and the cops were blatantly ogling Zoya and me.

My phone was ringing nonstop. Shivani, Sam, Karan and PJ were calling me, one after the other.

The hawaldars finally threatened Smita. 'If you don't say

you'll stay away from her, you're coming with us.' They grabbed Smita's hand and hauled her out.

There was simply no time to think. We hurriedly put on our shoes and jeans and ran out behind them. They were practically dragging Smita along the street. The shops were all still shut and streets deserted. People were sleeping on the pavements.

'If you don't stop we will scream!' Zoya shouted.

Someone from the pavement threw a can towards us. 'Shut up you whores!'

We were clearly disturbing a lot of people.

I saw the hawaldar whacking Smita hard. Without thinking I ran up to him and thrust my phone in his face—rage radiating from my body. 'I work for Fiza Kareem. This is her number. If you don't get lost right now I am calling her and getting you arrested.'

'She does work with her—this one's man told me!' the old hag said.

Thank god for the pillow talk! The hawaldar stared at me, waiting to see if I would back down. For those few seconds I made myself believe that I had the power to destroy this man. I think the hawaldar saw it too. He believed in my make-believe confidence that I could decide his destiny.

The hawaldar duo left with a feeble warning, taking the old hag with them.

Smita was laughing and crying at the same time. 'You see, now I will teach them a lesson. If they trouble me we will all go to Fiza Kareem!!'

We were all giggling out of relief. Smita hugged both of us and left. Zoya and I ran to our house and back down the stairs after getting ready in record time. 'Say thanks to Fiza Kareem—she saved our bai!' Zoya called out as I sat in my auto and bid her goodbye to start another day on the set.

## THE EQUATION

As I reached the set I could hear a loud song thumping in the background. I entered the set. It was a huge waterfall this time. Ten of the dancers, 'white, foreign' girls, were wearing bikinis. The remaining twenty—Indians, ten women and ten men—were dressed in swimming suits embellished with feathers. Ranvir was standing bare-chested in the water. Lights were blinking underwater—on the beat—and the whole set was reverberating with the lyrics 'Hare, hare Ram' as a choreographer rehearsed a step.

The moment I stepped in, I forgot Smita, the guilt, the hawaldar. All there was, was the spectacle and the urgency of the moment as everyone dashed around to get some work done. The set was very crowded, and I knew why that was. The American dancers were charging 12,000 rupees per shift and the production people wanted to wrap up their part as soon as possible. And obviously bikini-clad babes were a big attraction.

I spotted Shivani and Kriti standing with Fiza Kareem behind the monitor. Sam, wearing an electric-blue raincoat, was in the water with the dancers to show them their exact positions in the camera frame. Karan was shouting at the costume assistants who, heads bowed, were cutting fabric from the costumes that the Indian dancers would be wearing—so more skin would be shown, I guessed. PJ was holding some towels and looking straight at me. He handed the towels to a spot boy and began walking my way.

He was wearing half pants and a Hawaiian shirt. I saw that he'd got his hair cut—it had been cropped short, and he looked quite handsome. Without thinking, I blurted, 'You're looking nice with the new haircut!'

PJ grunted. 'You're late,' he said. 'Don't think just because Fiza Kareem talks to you now and asks you to do stuff for her directly that you can start coming late.'

'My flatmate met with an accident. I had to take her to the hospital,' I mumbled.

'All my flatmates have met with various accidents, so don't give me that,' he said dryly. 'But just in case, give her some flowers from me.'

I walked up to Karan who was now talking to Shivani and Kriti. 'I want you to take the dancers and junior artistes to the make-up rooms for costume change and touch-up. I'll call for them in a bit. Make sure they are all touched up!' he instructed them. Just then he noticed me and snarled, 'You cannot NOT answer my call. We need to talk. We cannot let this happen ever again. Just because Fiza called you yesterday to give Ranvir his lines does not mean you have arrived!'

'My flatmate met with an accident!'

Karan looked at me. He came up close and said very clearly and very slowly, 'I hope you know that you have one flatmate and she can meet with an accident only once. I don't care if she is accident-prone, but all our flatmates can meet with an accident only once. I hope I'm clear!'

Just then Fiza walked over. I stopped breathing. Sam was with her, dripping wet in his raincoat. Karan, Shivani and

Kriti stood stiffly, waiting to run at the first word of instruction. I braced myself as well. PJ was the only one who looked vaguely amused.

Fiza looked at Karan and said, 'I need the Indian dancers changed into their mermaid costumes and placed behind the foreign dancers, and the junior artistes need to be in transparent white wraps.' She was about to leave, then stopped and said, 'And I hope the boys don't waste their time ogling at the dancers, or else I will personally make you strip and stand in the water.'

Silence.

I laughed, then. And everyone followed. Score one for Neki. I had caught Fiza Kareem's joke and laughed before the rest of them.

Fiza looked at me and said, 'Not bad, you had them ready at nine sharp. We've got two shots done already.'

I smiled shyly and thanked her. She moved away. And then I could feel the daggers. I turned around and realised that I had scored another point. Fiza had given me credit for work I had not done, and I, like a scumbag, had accepted it. Well, as they say, all is fair in love and war. This was war. *My* hard work had been credited to these people so many times.

Before I could say anything, Kriti spoke up. 'I slaved my ass off getting them ready on time, you were not even here, and you said thank you! What kind of a person does that?' The others turned and left; PJ smirking, Karan disinterested, Sam confused, Shivani with respect, as if saying, 'You wanna play? Let's play.'

Before Kriti could go though, I said softly, 'The kind who tries very hard and has no choice.'

Kriti just looked at me weirdly and said, 'You know, you were a sweet, dumb girl when you came. What happened to you?'

Because she'd hit home—after all, I had not liked what I'd done—I retorted sharply, defensively, 'I'm just learning the tricks of the trade from my seniors!'

Kriti made a face and walked away to the costume room. I followed with heavy steps, feeling guilty for what I'd done. I had to make up to Kriti somehow. Just then I noticed Ranvir flexing his arm and wiping water from his torso. My stomach churned. Either I was hungry or had a serious crush on the guy. I caught Ranvir's eye and quickly looked away. I was met with PJ's icy look. I took a deep breath and walked out.

As I walked into the costume room, I could see the demarcation clearly. The foreign dancers had the best rooms. The Indian dancers were in a stuffy hall, and the fifty-odd junior artistes—JAs as they were sometimes called—were in the long, stifling corridor. Karan was delegating responsibilities to the ADs.

'Shivani, you take the foreigners ready with the new look and standby in twenty. PJ, the Indians are with you and Sam. Kriti, you take the JAs and divide in ABC and tell them the rows.'

Kriti was clearly sulking. And then suddenly she started breathing heavily. 'I can't breathe, I'm going to faint. I need to sit down,' she gasped.

Shivani muttered, 'It's all Neki's fault. Kriti is devastated. She worked so hard so that Fiza would tell her parents how well she's doing. She has ADHD and Neki triggered it off!'

Karan barked, 'Let Kriti rest. You guys get cracking; Neki, you take the JAs and divide them in ABCs for one, two, three rows. Sam—help her. I'm going on the floor.'

Karan walked away. I glanced at PJ and Shivani hovering around Kriti, telling her to take deep breaths, and then turned to Sam and, in a flat voice, said, 'I have three questions.'

Sam looked at me and replied in the same flat voice, 'Shoot, but only three, I don't have time for a fourth.'

'What the hell is ADHD?'

Sam replied with a straight face, 'This is Kriti's version of Attention Deficiency Hyper Disorder.'

'Do they have an official medical term for that?' I asked, wondering if Freud would place this condition as the handiwork of the conscious mind or unconscious mind. Sam interrupted my thoughts effectively.

'Is that the second question?' he asked.

I shook my head and asked sheepishly, 'What does dividing JAs into ABC mean?'

Sam rolled his eyes. 'It means A grade people, B grade people and C grade people.'

I was confused. 'How would we know, we hardly know them . . . I mean . . .'

'You're not grading them on their personality and IQ levels—you're grading them on looks. Key criteria being shape and colour. The ones who are fair and fit are A grade, those who are wheatish and medium fit are B grade, and those who are dark and unfit are C grade. But if there is a choice between colour and shape, then go for the fitter ones. Colour can be adjusted with make-up.'

I was shocked. 'That's horrible! And . . . and racist or something! How can you treat human beings like that?!'

Sam laughed. 'Are you crazy? Stop kidding and get to work. This is film-making and I'm sorry if your rosy dreams are shattering in this costume room. I'm wet and hungry and was told this morning that I've been thrown out of my apartment for playing my music too loud. By the way, I'm staying at your place tonight. I called Shikha and she said I could.'

I could not think of anything to say. It was like branding sheep. I looked at the mass of fifty people—thirty men and twenty women—who were mostly middle-aged. And mostly unfit. I ran after Sam.

'What is one, two, three? And why are you staying at our place? There are four of us already—well three since Shikha is out of town.' Shikha had been away for a few weeks, visiting her family in Dehradun.

With his eyes as wide as saucers, Sam said, 'You mean you've not figured that out? Grade A will stand in row one, B in two, and C in three. Anyway you can't go wrong as the foreigners will be in the front rows, then the young dancers and then these people. Nobody will bother about them. Let's just get them ready in time. And yes, I'm staying at your place; I have nowhere else to go right now.'

Saying that Sam walked away.

I was left standing there, staring at the sea of people I had to segregate, brand and ridicule. For some reason I could not move and then I heard Shivani hollering, 'Neki Brar, move your ass or get out of the way!'

My choice was obvious.

I was still thinking about the equation I had just heard: JA + ABC + 123 + ADHD = life on the set, when PJ came up and said, 'Reality check? Don't have it in you to segregate? Can't do it? Morality issues? Just say it and sit on the bench with Kriti and let us do the dirty work.'

Why was he always goading me, I wondered. 'I'm fine PJ. Thanks for the concern,' I said, and with a determined stride walked up to the JAs.

I ran my eyes over the people in front of me and told them I would be separating them into three groups. They all had a knowing grin on their faces—they had gone through the drill before. With a deadpan face I completed the task and sat down for Sam to come over and inspect my 'segregation'. I glanced at the person next me, a forty-plus man, dressed in a flowing white kurta and pyjamas. A somewhat familiar face, I thought. I had seen him in some serial, no, a movie . . . no, yes, he was a face on a wall; a photograph in my favourite film *Love-Shove*. He was the deceased father of the hero, and his photograph was framed and hung up on a wall. I remembered thinking how lucky he was to be a part of this whole world. At least he was in a photo frame.

And here I was, sitting next to him. I smiled at him. He nodded back.

'We will be leaving for the set in ten minutes,' I volunteered some information to fill the silence.

He nodded. 'It's okay, we are here the whole day. You have put me in the third row. It's good, I can just doze off and no one will notice.'

I smiled politely and then asked, 'So how long have you been a junior artiste?'

'Around thirty years now. I came to Mumbai from Haridwar to become a hero. Like most of us here.' A few men around nodded and chuckled. They were all C graders.

One of the women in the group said, 'I was the front row dancer in Juhi Chawla's *Bol Radha Bol*.'

The man next to her said, 'This Charu-di, her entire life she has lived on that movie!'

They all laughed. The other woman sitting next to Charu-di added bitchily, 'But she was messing around with one of the dance master's assistants! That's how she got the front row!'

They laughed again. I looked at Charu-di—she was laughing too. She had no regrets. 'At least I got to do that and show

I had something,' she said, pointing to her breasts, 'but you did not end up anywhere!'

The other woman shook her head and whispered something to the man next to her.

I thought about how this conversation, and the casualness with which they approached the subject of sexual favours, would outrage people back home. They made the whole thing such a non-issue.

So all the sordid stories I'd heard about big bad Bollywood were true. But if you were in the middle of it all, it was much more than just right or wrong. It was only a matter of choice.

I was about to walk away, when the photo guy continued. 'If Charu-di's best is that song, my best is that film, with my photo on a wall! The hero, Rajendra Sheikh, was always talking to my picture and taking advice. I played his deceased father.'

'I know. I recognised you from that film!' The words were out before I could stop them.

He looked visibly moved. His lips trembled. The men around him thumped his back jovially. 'See, you are also famous, everyone knows you Kamalji!'

'You know, my entire family has seen that film ten times,' Kamalji said, clearly overwhelmed.

One of the younger men groaned. 'A photo makes you so happy. You all are happy with one cheap dance and one cheap photo! Now, for pocket money, these college kids have started doing the work of extras. They call them "models". They treat them well, pay them well, keep them in the first row. Great! They are more expensive but the producers feel they are worth it. Why can't you give us nice clothes and nice make-up and make us worth it?'

Kamalji laughed. 'Voltage—stop it. The camera is not on.'

Everyone burst out laughing. But Voltage continued. 'These people want slim and fit and nice-looking people in the malls, theatres and streets—that is not India, Madam! *We* are the face of India! People like us go to the mall, the cinema hall and the disco! In reality, India is fat and dark!'

For some reason, Voltage was directing his anger towards me.

Just then Shivani barged in. 'What the hell Neki, what's taking so long?!'

Then she noticed Charu-di, Kamalji, and the seething Voltage. She greeted them, addressing them by their names, then turned to scold me again and went away. I was taken aback. She knew their names, she remembered them, and she'd given them respect. If what they said was true, that a person's true character shows when she is dealing with someone under her, then Shivani the monster was Shivani the angel! How could that be?

Just then a sexy little thing passed by in a mermaid dress and went up to Sam. 'Dude,' she said, 'this outfit is really uncomfortable. There are wires and stuff inside. How are we supposed to sit in the water with this?'

Sam cleared his throat and walked away with the girl. I was stunned to see that each of the dancers could give any leading actress a run for her money. And I could also see the queen bees, the most beautiful of the lot, commanded respect and got it instantly.

Charu-di noticed me gaping at the girl. 'This Tara is another thing all together,' she said. I realised that this must have been the girl Sam had been talking to the other day, outside the polka-dotted van. 'That big south Indian director is crazy after her. She has made a fortune sleeping with all the biggies. God has blessed her with a good body and face. I hope she makes enough to settle down well and does not squander it away on luxuries!'

I moved away to take a good look at Tara's lovely face again. For the first time I was face to face with the grim side of glamour—the morally debauched one. But somehow debauchery in this space was bearable. I was confused. I was losing the luxury of being able to instantly term things right or wrong, good or bad, black or white. The grey areas were taking over. It's a sign of growing up, I thought. When the colour grey takes over your hair, your beard and your brains.

The call came from Karan. The shot was ready. Everyone left in batches: the 'foreign babes' first, then the beautiful Indian dancers, then the second row, and then the rest. I wondered about the people pushed into the C-section of the third row—were they feeling bad? Just then I heard Kamalji say something and the entire third row, C-section howled with laughter. Including Voltage.

Well that answered my question.

## LIP SYNC AND LIP LOCK

It was time for final placements on the set. All the dancers were taking their positions, followed by the JAs, when there was suddenly a slight flutter on the set. All heads turned to look at the superstar Ahmed Khan as he walked in. He took his position in front of the camera and with ease performed the steps he had rehearsed the day before with the choreographer. The extras standing behind him followed.

Since the choreographer and dance-masters were in charge at the moment, the ADs were taking a breather, except for Sam who was standing in the water again.

I spotted Kriti in a corner and started walking towards her, to apologise. I knew this was the time to make amends. She was still breathing heavily. Just then I overheard a conversation I would rather not have. Two foreign dancers were on the verge of tears. A huge crowd had gathered around them, but I realised that not one person was listening to them as they were too busy staring at the women, dressed in bikinis and with towels wrapped around their waists. 'What if we get electrocuted?' one of girls was asking Karan.

Karan made soothing noises and then turned to Aslam and said to him in Hindi, 'I don't have time for this. Call the coordinator, calm them down, and get them in the water!'

'It's their first shoot. They are Russians. Let me explain it to them,' Aslam said.

One of the girls was evidently getting more angry than teary. 'There is open wire, electricity, water—what if we get electrocuted?' she asked.

'No one will get electrocuted; we have Mata Rani looking after us!' Aslam said.

The girls looked around. 'Where is she? I want to talk to her, to give us a guarantee. We are not even insured!'

Karan turned to PJ, who was just walking up, and said through gritted teeth, 'Fiza is asking for me, PJ. Get them in the water before I get back!'

'What's the problem?' PJ asked.

Aslam replied sheepishly, 'She wants a personal guarantee from Mata Rani. That they won't get electrocuted and die.'

PJ looked at the angry foreigner, at a loss for words. I rolled my eyes at how ridiculous the conversation was. What was Aslam going to do? Get one of our many goddesses to sell insurance to a Russian dancer? But Aslam was obviously good at thinking on his feet. That's what made him a perfect line producer.

'Well, I can't bring her to you, but Mata Rani insures the whole of India, she is a big entity. Ask anyone. They all know her!'

The dancers looked at him suspiciously, but not having much choice, they went back into the water.

Sam came running over. 'What happened?' he asked.

Aslam just laughed. 'See how smart these phoren people are. They know they can die any minute. Electrocuted. The plugs points are covered with plastic sheet only. The minute water goes in, wham, they're gone!'

Sam stared at him.

'Sam!' Karan yelled out, coming up to us. 'I've been calling you! What the hell are you doing standing here?'

'Aslam just told me I could have died standing there in the water!'

Karan turned on Aslam, furious. 'No, no,' Aslam muttered. 'Of course not! I told him we have made all the preparations. The plug points are all covered with plastic sheets. Did I or did I not?' he looked at me directly. I nodded. Because, in fact, he *had* said that. Aslam scurried off.

PJ looked at me. 'Scared?' he whispered.

I looked at him, knowing he was trying to needle me. 'No. As you can see, I'm not in the water.'

'Well, just remember, film-making can get dangerous. Those candyfloss dreams can have a price. You know a film called *The Conqueror*? It was released in 1956. Out of the two hundred and twenty people that worked on it, ninety-one contracted cancer. Forty-six died.'

'What rubbish! How is that possible?'

'It is, when you have radioactive fallout from atomic bomb tests in nearby areas. They were shooting near Nevada. But that's not what makes the story tragic for me.'

I looked at him. He was in a cynical mood.

'What makes it a tragedy for me is that, after all that suffering, the producer thought the movie was really bad. He bought every copy and refused to distribute the film. He was the only person who ever saw the film. The tragedy was not that all those people died of cancer. The tragedy was they died in vain.'

'And the irony is, instead of the people, you mourn the loss of the piece of work they created. Their supposed "Art".'

PJ shrugged. 'Art can be cruel. It's a jealous mistress, and can make someone a bad husband and a bad father. My dad's first film as a producer was *Jang*. All his life he has waited to make another sequel. But the point is, if we all get electrocuted today, who cares about the sequel to *Jang* right?' PJ said the last bit derisively.

'PJ you are dark and crazy and confused. Stay away from me!'

PJ laughed. 'You don't have to be scared of me; it's the water that should worry you!'

I laughed. 'Relax, we're far, far away from the water!'

Just then Shivani came up to us, talking on the walkie. 'Ranvir is calling you in the water,' she said, with a 'something's cooking' look in her eye.

'Why?' I asked, thinking I'd been a bit hasty in feeling fortunate that I didn't have to get into the water.

She looked at me sharply. I had given her a weapon and she was going to use it. 'To apply some sunscreen lotion I guess!' she said and sauntered off.

Mentally reciting the names of all the gods I could remember, I waded into the water. I tried not to look at the plastic covering, instead catching the eye of the Russian girl who thought Mata Rani was handling our insurance. She was smirking at my petrified expression. I could clearly understand the words she was not saying: 'Welcome aboard!'

I moved closer to Ranvir and suddenly lost my footing. He immediately held on to my arm and I become very aware that he was stripped naked to the waist. His stunning eyes and handsome face were just inches away. I was sure I was not breathing. He looked like a Greek god. I realised the Greek god was talking to me. 'I have a difficult scene tomorrow, would you mind going over the lines with me?'

Automatically I pulled out a script from my pocket. I usually carried the scenes for the entire week in my little sling bag in case Fiza Kareem asked for them. I started reading out from the paper in front of me. 'Ext. Street. Night . . . We see a huge moon in the background as you and Minty sit on the car bonnet—'

He cut in with a cute smile, 'Maybe the van would be a better place to do this? I'm shivering out here! Anyway, the camera is going to take some time to set up.'

I was shivering too, but definitely not because of the cold. I nodded, and we began to walk towards his van. I could feel all eyes on the set on me. Including Fiza Kareem's. Ranvir gestured to Fiza that we were going to rehearse lines. Fiza smiled and nodded.

And wading past all the curious smirking looks, we walked out of the set.

As we reached Ranvir's van, I saw Kriti lounging around outside.

'I see you're rehearsing lines with *her* today.'

Clearly she was over her ADHD attack. I'd never heard her talk to Ranvir in that tone. Maybe it had something to do with Fiza not being around. She continued petulantly, 'Dad may call you for dinner today. Come over no, maybe we can rehearse some lines there.'

Ranvir just smiled. I stood there awkwardly, ready to bolt. I couldn't help being excited though. Ranvir had chosen *me* to go over lines with. Despite Kriti's designer clothes and clout.

Ranvir stepped inside the van saying, 'Neki, I'll just get dressed.'

I nodded and turned to look at Kriti, who was still standing there, staring at me. Suddenly she smiled and said, 'You just can't handle it; a little bit of attention and you lot go crazy! Oh, and remember to call Kashish Kapoor's designer and remind him that we will be doing a water scene in the next schedule and Kashish needs to be padded up from front and behind.' She gave me a once over. 'Actually, you could use some of that too.'

I smiled back politely and said, 'I'll keep that in mind.' I stepped inside the van and banged the door shut in Kriti's face.

Ranvir was drying himself. His staff and help left and Ranvir walked into the tiny little bathroom to change. I sat down on the sofa and looked at myself in the huge mirror hanging on the opposite wall, with bulbs around it. Some of my hair had escaped from the low knot I'd tied it in and was framing my face. I began to adjust my hair to look more presentable when the bathroom door opened and Ranvir emerged in a white tee and jeans ... comfortable and sexy. He came and sat inches away from where I was sitting. I stared at the paper in my hands.

'You've got lovely, long fingers. Do you play the piano?' he asked.

I think I must have been shivering again, because the paper I was staring at was shaking. If only those lovely long fingers could hold the paper firmly so I could read a line or two, I would be grateful, I thought.

He leaned closer and took the script from my hands. 'I'll send Kriti in to read the scene,' I blurted out.

He took my hands in his and started rubbing them. 'You're freezing!' he said, smiling.

I desperately tried to think of something witty and sophisticated to say. All I could manage was, 'Yes, I'm usually cold and freezing. I like cold and freezing!' And that too in a croaky voice.

I knew I had to leave. I snatched my hands away and was

about to get up when Ranvir grabbed my hands again and said, 'Just relax, Maybe this will warm you.' And before I knew what was happening, I was in his arms and Ranvir Khanna was kissing me senseless. He tasted of mint and smoke. I had limited experience, but on the basis of a woman's instinct, I was sure he was the best kisser there was, ever. By the time the kiss ended, in my head I was married to him, we were living in a little bungalow, with two kids, a boy and a girl, with curly hair. Just when I was deciding the colour of the walls in our bedroom, I realised two things. One that Ranvir was heavily turned on, and second that the van door was open.

And Kriti and PJ were standing outside, staring at us.

I froze, and as soon as Ranvir realised why, I was thrust away. Feeling a bit dazed, I simply got up and walked out of the van. I wanted to fly and die at the same time.

I had a funny smile on my face the entire day. I was thinking about the kiss the whole time. At one point, I was holding the towels for the dancers to use after each shot, when Shivani walked up to me and snatched all the towels from my hands. 'You're not supposed to just sit with the towels,' she hissed. 'You have to give it to the dancers so they can dry themselves and not die of pneumonia! Don't forget what you are here for. For Ranvir, this is normal; girls throw themselves at him all the time. Don't be one of those hundreds.'

I looked at her angrily. So she'd already heard what had happened. Of course, I should have known Kriti would tell everyone on the set. But who cared. It was my personal life.

As soon as Shivani left, Sam came up to me. He stood in front of me in his ridiculous raincoat and stared at me for one full minute. And then he finally said, 'What the F.C.U.K?'

I smiled. 'It's not what you think . . . it's different.'

Sam had turned around to walk away. Hearing my reply, he turned back and said again, 'What the F.C.U.K?'

He walked away. Just then I saw Ranvir coming on the set with Kriti. I tried to catch his eye, but he didn't look my way. I saw Shivani sitting next to Fiza behind the monitor and I could imagine them talking about me. I looked over at PJ, but he was expressionless as he had been since the event. Karan, of course, was too caught up in getting things organised on set.

Ranvir walked into the water and Fiza called out, 'Neki, give Ranvir the lines for lip sync, and check it!'

'Lip sync' was when an actor would pretend to sing a song, and 'checking' meant that I was supposed to stare at his lips to make sure each word was sung as per the song. Any other day it would have been a regular part of the job, but with our 'lip lock' now public, checking 'lip sync' was embarrassing to say the least. I straightened my back and toughened myself against the imaginary snickers and stared at Ranvir's perfect lips.

I caught his eye shyly as the first shot got over. 'Neki, lip sync okay?' Fiza asked.

I knew Ranvir had missed the first word; he was a second late in catching the song. 'I think the first word was off,' I said softly.

Before anyone could react, Ranvir turned around and snapped, 'What is off is your timing. It was perfect, but let's go for one more shot . . .'

A moment of silence and many murmurs later, Fiza's voice shouted, 'Roll camera! Action!' After that, the only words I registered were 'Pack up!'

So I'd fallen for a guy *and* been rejected, all in a matter of half a day. Welcome to film-making. But my instinct said he was attracted to me and had feelings for me. Why else would he kiss me? They say a woman's instinct is always right—maybe because she never admits it was wrong to begin with. In this case my instinct was screaming that there was something special about Ranvir and me, and that was how it was going to stay in my head.

As I dragged my feet heavily towards the exit, I saw PJ and Sam walking towards me. Sam reminded me he was staying over at our place. He said bye to PJ; I turned around to wave at him but PJ had simply walked away. I could feel his anger. It bogged me down even more and I took it out on Sam. 'Why do I have to go home with you? Why are you coming to our place at all?'

'That's rude. I have no place to stay tonight because my landlord is upset with me. Stop behaving like an idiot.'

I looked at Sam. The good thing was I could be rude to Sam, and he was so slick, that the insults and rudeness would simply slide off him. He was untouchable.

'You're a pain in the ass, Sam!'

'And this pain in the ass is driving you home!'

I sat in Sam's Zen and we zipped back home. Sam looked at me. I knew he was going to say something about Ranvir.

'Neki . . .' Sam said.

'Shut up,' I replied.

~

Zoya was in the house when we walked in. She and Sam greeted each other like old friends and were soon standing by the windowsill, sharing a cigarette. I excused myself and went into my room.

*Dear Mom,*

*Today my bai was in big trouble with the cops but I scared them away. They almost fell at our feet when they realised I work with Fiza Kareem! At work we shot for a beautiful song. It was a dream sequence and Ranvir Khanna insisted I rehearse the scene lines with him. We have become great friends and I am sure he would love to meet you one day. We were shooting in water and it was exactly like Pooja aunty's US holiday pictures. In fact, better. Fiza is very happy with my work and even said so in front of the entire team. I am taking on more responsibility by the day—to the extent that now I am in a position to 'reject' or 'accept' people based on their looks, to decide if they are good enough to be in front of the camera. I decide their destiny with a simple nod! It is an awesome feeling—but I hope I can continue to enjoy it for a long time, because I know, with every nod and every shake of my head, I make or break a beautiful dream.*

*Till later.*
*Love,*
*Neki*

## THE APPLE FEELING

The vegetable market scene—I knew there was a reason why it was coming to mind right now.

Background action in a film is what goes on around the main actors while they're enacting a scene. A hospital setting would have serious nurses and doctors hurrying down a corridor. A man pushing a stretcher on which someone lies covered by a blood-smeared sheet. A nurse pushing a wheelchair on which sits a sad-looking man . . .

Unfortunately, right now, I could sense that there was something amiss in my real-life setting. A scene where a girl is about to jump from a building—logical background action would be a guard doing his rounds or perhaps a dog barking somewhere down the road, or a drunken man staggering down the street. *Some* sign of life. But it was so quiet that I could hear the crickets and the creepy insects crawling about and doing their business. I could sense a shadow huddled in a corner in the street below, adding to that uneasy feeling. It was like someone was waiting with bated breath for something to happen. Yes, something was wrong with the background action. I could say this with so much confidence because I was the champion of 'background action'. In fact, I have proof, right here in my Nano.

1 November 2008. 2:20 a.m.

Dear Nano,

Things have been so crazy since I last wrote, I don't know where to start ... so let me start from the beginning. The whole of the last month has gone by with me torturing myself with excruciating mind games: is Ranvir into me or is he not? Does Fiza like my work or does she not? Is Karan a robot with a timer or is he not? Is Shivani a devil or is she not? Is Kriti really as stupid as she seems or is she not? Is Sam sex-crazed or is he not? And lastly, does PJ have a crush on me, or does he not? Well, today is a historical day in my personal calendar because I have answers to all these questions! Well, almost.

Today we were shooting an outdoor scene in Kamalistan studio. The scene, set in a vegetable market, included Ranvir Khanna and the side actress Minty, the one who always has a cleavage issue. She has a love angle in the film with Ranvir. According to the scene, Minty comes to the vegetable market (in her Mercedes, wearing her high heels) to look for her old school friend. The local women around are fighting with a vendor, haggling over the price of vegetables. Eve-teasers start to harass Minty, and obviously Ranvir emerges to rescue her.

This was Ranvir's introduction in the film, and also, because Ahmed Khan is getting most of the dramatic hero moments in the film, Ranvir wanted this scene to be perfect in every sense. Of course I was very excited and I wanted everything to go well for him in the scene.

Ranvir had told me how important this scene was to him last night, in his vanity van. Since our kiss, he had been vacillating between over-friendly, relatively friendly and downright curt. But yesterday he'd suddenly called me to his van, and we'd had our first proper chat post that kiss (though he still didn't mention the kiss). He hoped everything would go off well, he said, and I was personally going to make sure it did, for him.

As I entered the set, I saw that the whole area was covered with fresh vegetables. I knew that these had been picked up from the market at dawn; Karan had said he wanted all the vegetables in the front row to be absolutely fresh, and they were. The other ADs and I ran around getting the forty-odd JAs ready. They were to be dressed in casual downmarket clothes. The middle-aged, pot-bellied ones were to be the shopkeepers; the others would be the crowd.

I wanted to personally make sure the four vegetable sellers in the frame with Ranvir were perfect and ready for the role. I short-listed Kamalji, Charu-di, Voltage and a few others to play the important, dialogue-speaking parts. It was obvious even to me that I chose them instantly because they were familiar faces. In real life, if familiarity breeds contempt, then in Bollywood, familiarity breeds work and opportunity.

I started rehearsing the background dialogues with them with full gusto.

'Get brinjal for half the price.'

'Fresh papaya here.'

'What Madam, you are haggling on this as well.'

I looked at Kamalji and said, 'Change that to, "Why don't you grow your own veggies in your own kitchen! They'll be free then!"'

My little team rehearsed their lines loudly and with full enthusiasm as I stood there, egging them on. Suddenly, they all fell silent. I saw that they were looking at something behind me. I turned around to see their object of interest and instead of one, I found three. Namely Fiza Kareem, Shivani and Karan.

The three of them were looking at our little hysterical practice with various degrees of amusement or anger.

'What are you doing, Neki?' Karan asked, a little nervously.

Sheepishly I answered, 'I was going through the lines with the main shopkeepers.'

Shivani rolled her eyes. 'The dialogue-speaking shopkeepers who are in the frame with Ranvir have already been selected. They have rehearsed their lines and are in the make-up room right now. Can you just get the rest of them ready and on the set, sweety?'

From being the leader of my little team, I'd been reduced to a brainless twit. The last ten minutes of passionate speeches and rehearsals with these ten people weighed heavily on me, not to mention the half-smile on Shivani's face.

Thankfully Fiza Kareem had not commented on the little scene. I looked at her surreptitiously and saw that she was busy telling Karan she wanted more yellow lanterns over the shacks behind, showing the hint of a shanty town, for the evening shot. They all moved away.

Just then Aslam joined our little party and got into a hectic conversation with the bunch of JAs. I realised Aslam was focused on a different scene all together: he was cutting deals with Kamalji and the other JAs about who could take the vegetables and fruits home with them after pack-up. He told his assistants to check with his wife if she needed anything. The orders were coming in fast and I was sure by the end of the day there was going to be no need to clear the mass of vegetables—they would be exchanged for favours.

Aslam suddenly spotted me in the crowd and realised that I'd caught on to what he was doing. So of course he attacked me. After all, the best defence is offence. 'What Madam! You gave me requirement for fifty junior artistes and now you are utilising only forty-two! Who will pay for the rest eight? My producer catches my neck and you youngsters make your own decision! What am I supposed to do? My job is on the line!'

I heard myself saying, 'I am so sorry! I thought Fiza ma'am said fifty yesterday but today they have changed the brief . . .'

'It's okay Madam,' he shrugged. Then he winked and said, 'Oh, by the way, Ranvir sir is on the set.'

I walked away without replying. Aslam was *the* man on this set, and if I was to survive here, he had to be my friend. Because Aslam was a politician. He had the talent to find trouble, disguise it with ignorance and then unveil it with aplomb. At the right time. When it would do maximum damage.

As I moved towards Ranvir's van, I looked around just to be sure Aslam was not watching. Of course he was. And with a half smile on his face, he even waved at me. With a defiant look I reached for the van door. It was locked. His spot boy Inder was on alert and told me he would come and call me as Sir was 'busy'. Just then the door opened and a blushing Minty, wearing a mini dress, emerged, escorted by Ranvir. Whose arm was around her waist.

He registered me looking at the arm pointedly. He waved bye to Minty and went back into the van. In a minute Inder came up to tell me with an apologetic face that 'Sir' was asking me to come in.

I was worried about the look on Minty's face and didn't know how to bring it up with Ranvir. Before I could say anything, Ranvir ran a finger down my cheek. Slowly. And then he stopped. 'How is it going?' he asked in a husky voice. 'On the set.'

I did not reply immediately. My mind was wandering. I wanted to bring up what had happened between us, but I didn't know what to say. What was appropriate in a situation like this? 'Hey, by the way, we kissed, remember?' Or maybe, I should giggle and say, 'You know, it's funny ... I think I dreamt that you kissed me.' Through the options racing through my brain I registered Ranvir's quizzical look. I pulled myself together and gave him an update. Then he asked some questions. What did I think about the script? What did I think of Fiza's perception of the role? Was he going to get enough mileage? Who did I think would take the final call on the film edit, Ahmed Khan or Fiza Kareem? I knew he really valued my opinion and all doubts about our relationship disappeared.

I remember reading somewhere that the only foolproof method to test if you are truly in love is to ask yourself, 'Would you happily be destroyed by this person?' If the answer is yes, it's true love. At that point I realised my answer was a 'yes'.

But there has to be a reason why Ranvir has not said anything about the kiss. I'm sure I'll find some explanation in Freud's theories; in fact, even without reading Freud I'm sure he would have said the reason Ranvir is not talking about the kiss is that it affected him at a deeper level, or the deepest level. On the other hand, it could also mean that the kiss didn't matter to him at all and he's completely forgotten about it. But I'm sure Freud was a nice human being and he would never have such a pessimistic analysis of a delicate situation.

Just then Shivani walked into the van with the scene to rehearse with Ranvir. She glared at me and hierarchy dictated I leave the van and Shivani continue the scene reading with the actor. I stood up. So did Ranvir. He stood between Shivani and me and politely told her that he wanted Neki to stay and do the lines with him since we'd started rehearsing the scene already.

My name had never sounded so musical before.

A warm feeling went all the way down to my toes.

The feeling was equivalent to what a tired, parched traveller trudging down a long, dusty, hot road feels when, rounding the bend, he sees a lush tree laden with apples. Well it was the 'apple feeling'. Looking at Ranvir standing up for me was my 'apple feeling'.

Shivani just smirked, said, 'Of course', and walked away with a not very happy expression on her face.

We went back to discussing the scene. On the face of it, I was telling Ranvir how important his introduction scene was to the script and how, if done well, it would really stand out in the film. But in fact my mind was totally focused on Ranvir's perfectly sculpted arms two inches away from me, on his hands, which accidentally brushed my shoulders at regular intervals while talking, on the fact that for a couple of minutes, he casually held my hand and caressed it with his thumb.

Well by now the tired traveller was standing under the apple tree and it had started raining. The heat was gone; the dust had settled down, the green was glistening. There was fresh dewy water all around. The tired traveller could not ask for more.

But I did.

I knew that my sitting next to him, wanting a little bit more, was not making sense at all. While Ranvir spoke, I noticed that the inside of his left wrist had a mole. That he had a tiny scar near his left brow. It was so small, so minute that I would have missed it on any other day. But today was different. I was so into him that I could see every curve, every dent, every mark on his body, in all its beauty, in all its ugliness. I understood in my own way what Sid meant when he said, *'If you listen closely, all else fades'*. We have superhuman vision, if we choose to use it. We have all this ability inside us, if we choose to listen closely.

The difference lies in what each of us chooses to hear, and what we choose to fade out.

As soon as Fiza Kareem came into the van to have a word with Ranvir, I left and walked back into the vegetable market. Just as I was busy getting everything ready for the first shot, I spotted Zoya on the set.

Zoya! My Zoya!

The first thought that hit me was that something was wrong. I ran all the way to where she was standing and saw her hugging Sam. It struck me that Zoya was not there to see me at all.

I'd been so busy with my own life and matching up to the others in the AD team, that I'd missed the meaning of the frequent visits Sam had been gracing us with. They were having a scene right under our noses! What hurt me was that Zoya had not told me about it. Why the secrecy? As I walked up, I noticed that Zoya looked a bit agitated. I realised her eyes were pink, like she'd been crying. I looked at Sam accusingly. 'What's up? What did you say to her? What's happening here guys?'

Sam just ran his hands through his hair and muttered, 'Shikha is back in town tonight.'

'Ya, I know that, and we were thinking of celebrating—she is coming back after almost a month! But what does that have to do with all this. You guys have been—'

Before I could finish my sentence, Sam gulped, 'I know that ... but ...'

'Neki,' I heard Zoya's husky voice. I turned towards her still not understanding the situation here. Zoya looked at me and with guilt-ridden eyes. 'Sam and Shikha have been dating for the last two years.'

I was shocked. What was wrong with Sam? He was having a scene with Tara the dancer, and with Zoya, and with Kriti, and now Shikha! 'How did I not know about it? What about the underwear model? What's happening?' I asked, thoroughly confused.

'Shikha and I have been on a break for the last five months—to give each other space. But Shikha called yesterday and told me she wants to get back.' He looked at the expression on my face and continued, 'I'm just trying to find the right person for me. I thought it was Shikha. But with all this . . . I don't think it is. Since Zoya, it has been no one else.'

I looked at Zoya. This was not looking good and this would not end well at all. I did not need to spell it out for Zoya. Some things we can rectify but some things we have to live with, and this one Zoya would have to live with for a long time. Without saying anything to Zoya I turned to Sam, all my anger directed towards him. His cute, chocolate-boy face reminded me of a miserable pug. I felt like he had some kind of wanderlust, an itch to conquer new people. I don't think he could help himself. It was a package deal with him: charming and unfaithful.

Karan hollered over his walkie that he wanted Minty on the set.

Sam held my hand and said, 'You can't say anything about this . . .'

I glared at him and said, 'Neither can you Sam, you can say nothing to justify this.' I jerked my hand away and walked off to get Minty for the shot.

## SYLVESTER TO THE RESCUE

The door of Minty's van was open. I walked in and saw her sitting with a cigarette in her hand. Busy writing in a little pink book, she did not notice me come in. She picked up her phone, dialled a number and then said, 'One for hospitality service. Will stay over two nights only in the nine-star hotel. Food and laundry paid for along with any shopping items. One party entertainment only, given the money. And no kinky business!'

Just then she looked up and saw me. She froze. The pancake on her face could not hide the blush. I could see she was considering hanging up. She seemed to weigh the importance of my having overheard her, and then dismissed me like a piece of furniture. The good thing about people perceiving you as a nobody is—that they reveal their true natures to you. Minty saw me as a mere flunky, so she did not feel the need to be guarded. She continued, 'Three of them for photo opportunity only. I will send the pictures. You approve. First class air tickets, hotel stay and payment by cash only.... Will be done.'

I remember Aslam telling us that Minty had started her own casting business on the side. Apparently she had a huge database of actors and models and she got them roles. While she dealt with another prospective client on the phone, I realised she was not a bimbo with a cleavage issue. She was obviously good at this number-crunching business, yet on the set she knew how to play dumb. She was seriously smart.

When she was done with her call I duly conveyed that she was required on the set right away. She nodded and took one final look in the mirror. A little bit of sprucing up and she was ready to be 'Minty the side actress, trying to make it big'.

As Minty took her position next to Ranvir, his eyes and mine met. He smiled. I felt a bit light-headed and then someone tapped me on my shoulder. It was PJ; like everyone else on the set he had come to terms with the kiss and rumours floating around about Ranvir and me. But I could tell from his ever-changing demeanour that it was the most difficult for him. Strangely the thought made my heart warm towards him.

But lately it was getting worse. Sometimes angry, sometimes friendly, sometimes protective, sometimes ignoring me. He would definitely confuse even a brain-mapping machine if it were to gauge his emotional quotient. Freud would have happily adopted him. I heard him clearing his throat and looked at his very amused face. 'Tell me Neki, what if the entire slum community attacked us today? I mean, we've bought tons of vegetables for the shot, and have displayed them—and in the very next lane people are dying of hunger. What if they come over and attack us all, starting with Ranvir the hero! Then what would have been the point of teaching the JAs how to sell veggies? What do you think?'

'I think you have some serious emotional issues,' I retorted. PJ threw his head back and laughed. 'Oh by the way, Fiza has invited everyone to have dinner with her today. So post pack-up.'

I was stunned. 'Me too?'

'She did say the AD team. So unless you have switched job profiles and become PA to Mr Ranvir Khanna, ya, you too.'

I wanted to respond with a sarcastic remark, but my case wasn't being helped by Ranvir's spot boy Inder coming up to offer me some juice. Through the course of the day, Inder offered me cold water, a wet muslin cloth to fight the heat and, just while Karan and the whole AD team were discussing the background action, he came up with a chair for me to sit down. That was the point I had to threaten him not to come within twenty feet of me on the set. But I couldn't help feeling warm and fuzzy: Ranvir had obviously told him to take care of me. I could live on that feeling for the next one month. He was wooing me through his spot boy. And in the life of a humble AD, it meant the world.

But I couldn't think about it for too long, because the rehearsal wasn't going well, and there was tension on the set. Fiza was losing it in the heat. Ranvir was sitting under an umbrella nervously biting his lips. The vegetables were wilting. The make-up on the artistes was melting. The simple background action of the vegetable vendors reacting to the goons was just not falling in place. And in between all this, Sam—who was in charge of instructing the JAs—found the time to come to me and say guiltily, 'I don't know what to do about Shikha. I love Zoya: it's true love!' I wanted to sledgehammer his brains out.

I always thought there was something wrong with the phrase 'falling in place'. Things never 'fall in place'. You try and throw them in a manner that makes sense to you and hope for the best. But then it all goes wrong anyway. Why did you make the effort to begin with? Because you need to be able to tell yourself you tried everything you could to make it work.

I was going to do just that. Throw things around in a way that made sense to me. I felt the background action was not working because the JAs were not reacting naturally to the goons eve-teasing Minty. They were turning when they were supposed to, they were screaming when they were supposed to, they were shouting when they were supposed to. But something jarred about the whole scene. Maybe the instructions Sam had given the JAs were incorrect, I thought. When the goon is talking rudely to the girl, all the people in the background were stopping and yelling at him instantly. Wrong. All they had to do was shake their heads and walk away.

Reality was subtle. Exaggeration was drama.

I looked at Ranvir's hassled face after the fifth retake. It was time to act.

I jumped in and explained my point to PJ, Sam and Karan in the middle of the field. Karan's mike was on. 'We are trying too hard,' I blabbered. 'The action is abrupt. People should not start protecting the girl, they should shrug and walk away till it gets messy. Then they should stand around and *then* the hero should come. People on the streets don't have the time to be virtuous here—they're busy struggling with their daily routines and bills and heat and traffic and delayed public transport. They don't have the luxury of moral righteousness. The hero is supposed to be the idiot who is not affected by all these daily problems and only thinks of the higher good!'

Silence. I realised that had not come out well at all: somehow the hero had an idiot attached to it. I was expecting a rude 'Shut up' over the mike, but a few things worked in my favour.

First, because Sam was feeling guilty about his little love

triangle, he instantly agreed with me. He was hoping his support would make me more sympathetic towards him.

PJ agreed too, and it was probably because he had a crush on me. I could tell by now. His eyes constantly followed me on the set. He grabbed every chance he could to have a fight with me. And, most importantly, he tried too hard to ignore me.

Kamalji, of the photo fame, who was playing a shopkeeper, also agreed with me because I had spoken to him nicely the other day and he thought I would give him a better placement in the crowd, maybe even next to the hero.

With so many people instantly agreeing with me, and the silence from Fiza's mike indicating that she agreed as well, Karan shrugged and said, 'Set it up, Neki.'

In retrospect, I can see that I got that chance to prove myself not because I was talented, but because it had just worked out that way. I guess I now know why PJ was always being cynical and saying, 'Your talent never makes things work here.... If things around you work, only then you work!'

I looked at the JAs and picked up Kamalji, Charu-di, and Voltage. The way they responded to my instructions, it was clear they were ready to die for me out of gratitude.

We began rehearsing. I said 'Action' for the first time—a special moment for a struggling film-maker! Everything went smoothly: the stand-in for Minty got into an argument with the goon, my C row actors performed brilliantly, and the scene fell into place. On the mike Fiza's voice said, 'Good. Let's take!' I was thrilled. I'd just crossed a huge landmark in my film-making career. And then it got better. Fiza called for me on the mike and said, 'Neki—just give the shopkeepers their marks for the scene.'

And with that sentence, I had arrived on the set—officially.

Ranvir got up, gave me a broad smile and winked at me. I preened with pride and turned to see Shivani glaring at me. Maybe it would ease the tension if I asked her to help, I thought. Plus, I really needed her assistance. It was imperative for me that this shot went off well. Fiza had trusted me with a task. This was my one and only chance—make or break. It had to be perfect. It had to 'fall in place'. I walked up to her.

'Shivani, would it be possible for you to make sure the children cross the camera in the background with the mother as soon as Fiza says "roll camera"? Because I'm giving the cues to the shopkeepers here.'

Shivani looked at me, smiled and said, 'Of course, it would.'

I was relieved, 'Thanks so much . . .'

Shivani smiled a bit more. 'If I were doing the background action I could make the kids climb the trees, if required. But I'm not, you are, so all the best!'

'What are you saying?'

'I think what I am trying to say is—no.'

And she walked away, pretending to be busy with something else. She was a master at pretending to be busy. I'd realised over the last month that half the battle was won for an AD if they knew how to look busy! Shivani was an old player. I did not stand a chance against her.

Just then Sam came up from behind and said, 'Don't worry Neki, I will handle the children!'

I looked at him scathingly. 'Don't think I'll think you're less of a scumbag if you do. I can manage.'

Sam just shrugged and walked off. Panicking a bit now, I looked around for PJ. I called his name on the walkie and he responded in a heavy voice, 'Neki—it's 004!'

'What does that code mean?'

I could hear the static on the walkie. And then PJ's voice burst through. 'I'm taking a dump! Stomach upset!'

I spotted Kriti giggling with the art assistant and ran up to her. 'Hey! I need help with background action!'

'Who doesn't?' Kriti smiled and continued spraying water on the sparkling green vegetables.

'Please, it's important! Fiza wants the kids to run in the background. Somebody needs to send them when Fiza calls for action. I am going to be on the other side, with the shopkeepers. PJ is taking a dump, Sam is doing something else and Shivani is not doing this.'

'I would *love* to help you. But I'm spraying the vegetables. Maybe you can ask Ranvir to help out?' Kriti smiled innocently.

'Ready Neki?' Fiza called out on the mike. 'Going for take!'

My heart stopped beating. They were heartless. What was I to do? I realised I was going to cry. I sent out a quick prayer and walked over to the two children, who were barely three and five years old, respectively. Their coordinator was happily standing under the shade of a tree fifty yards away, enjoying a cup of tea with Aslam. Darn it! I went up to the kids and the very disinterested woman playing their mother. I spoke very slowly, as if talking to a slow child.

'Listen carefully okay? When the director says "Action", you have to walk there.' The lady just stared back at me with a blank look.

I explained to her in detail about the pressure of the situation, how if she did not get it right we would need to go for a retake, which would cost a lot of money and be a waste of time. As I finished my speech, I realised she simply didn't care about any of those things. In that scorching heat, with the overpowering smell of vegetables, mint and lemons in the air, I saw pure unadulterated freedom. For this lady was free of fears, worries or consequences. She had nothing to lose, because she chose not to. I had no idea whether she would actually do as I'd asked.

I turned around to run back to my position. Just then I saw Punjabi, the spot boy, holding a cup of tea in his hand and grinning at me. 'Ma'am some tea?' he asked.

'No. Some poison,' my head screamed. I shook my head hurriedly and started running to the other side. Punjabi began jogging by my side in his oversized sneakers. He was wearing faded jeans and a T-shirt with the word 'SYLVESTER!' scrawled on it.

Suddenly, I thought of something. I stopped abruptly. 'Punjabi, can you do me a huge favour? Can you tell the little children and the mother to walk in front of the camera when Fiza Ma'am says "Action"?'

Punjabi froze. 'You mean like an AD? Of course I would love to! I have been a spot boy in twenty films now. I know everything. Of course I can do it!' He stopped one of the other spot boys taking a bottle of water to someone. 'Hey you! Hold this. I need to do some AD work!'

The other spot boy looked at Punjabi, newfound respect in his eyes. Reverently he took the cup of tea from Punjabi.

I reached my little corner and saw Punjabi leaning next to the children and the mother. A couple of spot boys were looking at him from a distance.

Over the mike came Fiza's call: 'Roll camera!'

My fingers crossed, I repeated a million times in my head, 'God please let this shot be okay! Please let this shot be one-take okay. Please let Fiza say okay to this shot!'

'ACTION!'

I saw the kids move into the frame and then, to my horror, along with them came Punjabi!

Fiza said, 'Cut!' My heart stopped. And then she said, 'Okay!'

∼

I stopped reading the diary and laughed. Little did I know that this 'Okay' would nearly cost me my job!

I went back to Nano.

## SPOT THE SPOT

The shot was okay—but Punjabi had run into the frame! So two things were proved beyond doubt: one, that God is always listening; he'd answered my prayers for this shot to be one-take okay. And two, he has a sense of humour.

Around me, everyone heaved a sigh of relief, but I felt like I was going to pass out. Air was not reaching my lungs for some reason. My mouth was parched. I ran up to Karan to tell him about the faux pas.

He turned around and for the first time said to me, 'Well done Neki!' Before I could say anything, everyone ran to the monitor to double-check the shot, happy to have it done with, because this shot had been okayed after many retakes.

I knew any minute the mistake would be discovered and I would be thrown out.

The shot started playing on the monitor. Just when Fiza was looking at the shot, Ranvir started discussing his role with her. She turned away from the monitor, trusting Karan and the AD team to double check the shot and continued her discussion with Ranvir. I held my breath, waiting for someone to spot Punjabi in the frame. I could see him so clearly—that T-shirt with Sylvester written across it was impossible to miss. I turned around to tell someone, but fear took over and I was quiet.

To my horror, Karan did not spot the 'spot'.

They moved on to the next shot.

I went up to PJ who had also been watching the shot. 'Listen, there is a problem. You saw the guy wearing that Sylvester T-shirt? The one with the kids ... that's ...'

'Sylvester's story is the best rags to riches story of all times, did you know that?' PJ asked.

I shook my head, wondering what he was talking about. All I could think about was that they had okayed a shot that would be played on the big screen and everyone would see Punjabi bobbing around with the kids. What would they do to me then?

I tried to interrupt PJ's rambling, but he ignored me. 'You know, when Sylvester Stallone first went to New York to try out acting, he couldn't seem to get a break so he decided to try writing while waiting for a role. He wrote *Rocky* while waiting for an offer! Eventually someone did like the story but didn't want Sylvester to play Rocky. They offered him insane money for the script. Sylvester kept refusing them. He even had to sell his dog! Finally they came around. Offered him the part, with the script. Paid peanuts. What was the first thing Sylvester did? Buy his dog back! If you want to see greatness, it's right here, all around you!'

I stared at him for a second, and then grabbed his arm and dragged him to the monitor. I took the remote and replayed the shot. I paused at the exact point Punjabi had walked in. 'Great! Yes, I'm sure Sylvester is great. I'm so inspired, but that guy wearing the name of greatness on his T-shirt in the background is the spot boy Punjabi!'

PJ stared open-mouthed. I felt ill: this really was serious. I was going to get killed for this one. PJ snapped out of his shock and called Karan on the walkie. 'We need to talk,' he said abruptly.

All the ADs—standing in various corners of the set—were alerted to the tone. It had 'disaster' written all over it. The ADs began walking towards where we were. I pleaded with PJ, 'Is there any way we can hide him?'

'You mean remove him from the film? No!'

'What *is* the solution then?' I asked him, dreading the answer.

PJ looked at me, sympathy all over his face. 'Re-shoot the scene. The light is different now, so we'll probably have to re-shoot tomorrow.'

Karan walked up and PJ told him what the problem was. Karan went very still. As did Sam, Kriti, and Shivani when they heard.

They were not even gloating, I thought. I was in serious trouble.

Karan looked at me. 'Why did you tell Punjabi to walk into the frame?'

'I only told him to help me with background action,' I replied in a small voice.

'If you need help, you have to say it on the walkie!' he shouted. 'Get an AD to help you! You don't tell the spot boy to do background action for you! You could have asked Shivani!'

Shivani jumped in, 'I was busy with the other lot; if I knew she was sending the spot boy in the frame, I would have left everything and helped her, better still done it myself. God, there is a height to stupidity!'

Kriti instantly added, 'I was already helping the art assistants. Fiza wanted the veggies fresh in the shot!'

I could tell Sam was genuinely feeling sorry for me. 'Can we tell Fiza that Punjabi came in the frame on his own?' he asked Karan.

Karan shook his head, 'He'll be kicked out!'

'If we don't, *she'll* be kicked out,' Sam said.

'Rightfully—she screwed up. She should go.' Karan turned around and walked towards Fiza. The other ADs looked at me and I knew for the first time that I had won their sympathy. Silent good-byes. My Bollywood dreams were over with Punjabi and his Sylvester T-shirt.

Just then Punjabi came back with a cup of tea as an excuse. 'Ma'am, I was okay? If you need anything else, please tell me. And some tea?'

As usual, I wanted poison.

I looked over at the monitor where everyone was now huddled. PJ called me over. I went. Fiza was staring at the monitor. 'Why didn't anyone point this out earlier?' she asked. 'Before we changed the set-up? We could have quickly taken another take.'

'We didn't realise till it was pointed out. By then the cameras were removed,' Karan muttered.

Fiza turned to Karan, 'Who pointed this out?'

Kriti, in a hurry to earn some brownie points, said, 'Neki came and told everyone. But if she'd told us earlier we could have rectified it!'

I was creamed. Fiza turned to look at me. The question was, was she going to hurl the chair at me or the mike? And then I heard Fiza say, 'At least she realised the mistake! And she is the one who is new out here! Neki, next time come and tell me directly!'

Flabbergasted, I watched Fiza walk away. In their hurry to report the mistake, they had missed out the crucial part—that *I* had sent Punjabi into the frame to begin with. I was the hero again! My mother must be praying very, very hard back home in Amritsar. I smiled with relief. I was going to stay in

Bollywood. Flukes and narrow escapes were definitely my style!

Kriti seemed to realise as well that they had not told Fiza why the error had occurred. She started walking towards her when PJ caught her arm and said, 'Forget it!'

Kriti looked at Shivani for support. Shivani looked at PJ's stern expression. She looked at Karan and shrugged. Shivani the bitch was an angel again! She was horrid at being a normal person. I could not figure out if she was the 'good guy' or the 'bad guy' in my story. She was so difficult to deal with.

PJ and Sam smiled at me. I almost hugged them in relief. Karan simply walked off. Keeping in mind my loyalty to Zoya and Shikha, I should have continued to ignore Sam, but on the set, loyalty, friendship, grief and loss—everything was momentary. Maybe that was the magic of making magic!

Fiza Kareem called me to discuss something then. That walk was the longest and most exhilarating one for me. I went and stood by Ranvir and Fiza. The guy in charge of taking stills of the film was there with his camera, trying to take 'working stills'. I desperately wanted him to capture my moment of fame so I could cherish it for eons to come. 'Director Fiza Kareem in creative discussion with assistant director Neki Brar'. This was it. I was a serious contender in the team now. The great thing about Fiza Kareem was that she did not believe in hierarchy. Her only criterion was good work.

The 'creative discussion' Fiza had called me over for was to ask me to tell the shopkeeper in the main frame to look more agitated.

Oh well. At least I'd been given the task by Fiza herself.

The rest of the shoot went well. The first good day I'd had in the entire shooting schedule so far. Well, almost. And the best was yet to come. Ranvir came up and patted me on my back. The part where his hand had touched me tingled.

'Okay,' Fiza called out on the mike, 'tomorrow we start with the shot we have to re-take, thanks to my ADs! Pack up!' All the ADs glared at me, and in an AD's life, that was supposed to be a good sign—a sign that meant you were climbing the ladder. Only in my case I was climbing it the wrong way. But atleast I still had my foot on the ladder.

## THE PESTICIDE PRINCESS

After pack-up, I ran to and fro on the set, getting things done to make it up to the other ADs.

'Make sure you tell the boys to do the spray on the veggies,' Karan told me sternly. He was still sore with me for the Sylvester episode.

I ran to the set assistants and production boys and in my haste to rectify my mistake, I told five assistants to 'do the spray'. I was curious to find out what 'do the spray' meant. Within minutes all the vegetables had been sprayed over with pesticide. Satisfied, I turned around and walked into Aslam's huffing and puffing face. He was red with anger. I realised that it wasn't just him: half the JAs were glaring at me.

'You sprayed all the carts? It is my department! Please tell me in future what you need and let me handle it!' Aslam said.

'Everything that happens on this set is my department!' I replied haughtily. After all, I had earned Fiza Kareem's approval today! I walked off feeling important.

Just then Voltage came up to me. 'Madam, you are doing your work, but a little charity is good if it does not harm anyone . . .'

'I don't know what you're getting at!' I stared at Voltage.

'Aslamji had promised us some vegetables.'

'Yes, but we need it for the shoot tomorrow,' I said.

'But half of it will rot anyway, and you will replace them with new ones. We could have taken that half home.'

I felt bad, but didn't know what could be done now. 'Well ... let Aslam figure it out,' I mumbled.

Aslam pounced at me, dabbing his face with a white handkerchief. 'What can Aslam do now, when you have got the entire vegetable market sprayed with a concoction of pesticides? Even the mosquitoes and cockroaches won't touch them!'

Aslam carried on muttering something to the crowd of people. As they were dispersing with disappointment, my euphoria was dying down. Just then, Punjabi came up to me. His eyes were brimming with excitement. 'Madam how did I do in the shot? You think I can be your assistant in the next film?'

All I could say was a horrified, 'What?!'

'Thank you Madam,' he said happily, as if I had assigned him the role of being my assistant already. He scurried off, to tell his peers I was sure, about a promise I'd never made. Illusion. He survived on it. Half the people on this set did. These illusions made them happy, and these illusions made them sad. In the industry, we played the game in our heads.

They say your source of happiness is within you. Well, in my case, my source of happiness was sitting inside a buttercream AC van, ten feet away from me. I ran up to the van. Ranvir's spot boy Inder looked at me with a knowing smile. That was an indication that I was in the actor's inner circle.

Inder opened the door for me, and as I stepped inside the van, I saw out of the corner of my eye Ranvir's trainer, Bunny, running towards us with a horrified expression on his face. I walked in and realised Bunny had been trying to stop me. Ranvir was standing there, inches away from a woman. I could not see her properly—her back was turned towards me. It seemed to me as if Ranvir was going to hug her. He saw me just then, and a strange expression flitted across his face. I hurriedly made an excuse, mumbling that I would come back later, and dashed out.

Bunny was outside, glaring at me. I glared back. Inder was sulking. His slim frame seemed even smaller. He'd clearly got a dressing-down from Bunny. I walked a couple of feet away and waited. I wanted to have a word with Ranvir.

I remembered all the rumours I'd heard about him being popular with the women . . . in the rosy haze that the kiss had brought about in me, I'd completely forgotten about them. And really, did I even have the right to ask Ranvir about the rumours, about the woman he was with in the van? Who could I turn to for a theory here? Siddhartha? Freud? My flatmates? Or the man himself, Ranvir? Feeling cold inside, I thought about the situation I'd put myself in. I knew I was in deep already. And I knew with deepness comes darkness. I could walk away. I could stay in the bright, warm sun. I had a choice. Ultimately we all do.

Just then PJ joined me and broke my train of thought. 'Good work! You must be so happy with yourself. You screwed up and you are the hero and the most hated person on the set today! The pesticide princess!'

I glared at him. 'I did not know what the spray was for.'

'The spray is to keep the insects away and discourage people from taking the vegetables. Otherwise they would disappear within minutes.'

'It's cruel you know, what if someone ate something without knowing about the spray?'

PJ smirked, 'Everyone knows about the spray. Forget it. By the way, I like what you're wearing. Looks nice.'

'Why are you wasting my time with this polite conversation?' I asked nastily.

PJ looked at me and laughed, 'Oh I guess you're busy waiting for your hero to finish his rendezvous with his girlfriend slash godmother!'

'Excuse me?' I glared at PJ.

'You know who is in there? Prateeksha Devi Ansari. The RDM party leader's wife who's supposed to be promoting Ranvir because she has *vested* interests in him and pun totally intended!'

'God, you're sick, and mean . . . and . . . sick!'

'You already said "sick". Come on, everyone knows Ranvir got a break in the industry because of her. She is producing a film for him. He is having a scene with her and many more like you on the side, not to forget almost all his actresses plus side actresses!'

'You sound jealous,' I said, refusing to accept what he was saying.

PJ laughed, 'And you sound like a fool. A big one.'

My anger was rising by the second. 'You're the biggest pessimist I know, PJ!'

PJ bowed, 'I take that as a compliment because I have read somewhere that ninety per cent of the time pessimists are right and the remaining ten per cent they are pleasantly surprised!'

I glared at PJ. Just then Aslam walked past us with two women, garishly dressed, photos in hand. Aslam winked at PJ, who smirked. Instinctively, I knew. 'What the hell! Aslam is into this casting couch thing as well? Who has called for them?'

'Someone who needs to be kept happy on the set. That's the thing: everyone knows about it but no one will tell. You see that production van up there? Many girls like those two get in that van looking for work. They don't want roles, just a steady clientele! It's all a part of the side business. The smaller shark provides for the bigger one!'

'Listen, you are disgusting and cheap!' I snapped.

'What do you think your almighty Ranvir is up to today—he is doing the same thing those girls are doing!' PJ replied scathingly.

'Of course not! He would never do something so cheap!'

PJ looked at me and smiled. 'Just because he is an actor and Aslam is a lowly line producer? Listen, this dirt on the road, when you look at it, you call it dust. And when you look at the same thing inside a beautiful globe, sparkling and pretty, you call it gold dust! But the point is, whatever you choose to call it, if it gets into your eye, it will hurt you. So you can call someone cheap, call someone else classy, but the act is the same! You are sleeping around, doing favours to get work. It can be as respectable and as cheap as you want it to be. But that's the bottom line!'

PJ was horrible and annoying and so right. He reminded me of Sid. He reminded me of a song which said, we all burn under the same sun. I didn't want to hear it though. So I said, 'Shut up PJ! Can you off-load somewhere else?'

'Fine, anyway, just came to remind you that we are leaving for dinner. We're going to Mystic China; Fiza loves the food there. You can come with us if you want or go with Ranvir, if he will allow you. But we won't wait for too long, we leave in ten minutes. We'll be waiting outside gate two.'

PJ stubbed his cigarette and walked away.

At the same time, the beautiful Prateeksha Devi stepped out with Ranvir behind her. They spoke for a couple of minutes at the door—Ranvir did not look at me even once—

and then she left. The moment her car had left, he walked over to me. 'So sorry Neki, you know who that was, she is family.'

I could sense there was something Ranvir was not telling me and there was something he was apologising for, that I did not know.

I heard myself say, 'What's happening, Ranvir? I'm hearing crazy things about you and that woman ...'

Ranvir smiled and said casually, 'Ya, me too.'

'It's not funny Ranvir ... I don't know what's happening. Where are *we* in this whole equation? Is there even an equation?'

'You tell me Neki ... is there?' he was looking at me intently as he stepped closer. He was just inches away from me now. 'Is there an equation here?' I looked at him, filled with longing. I couldn't bring myself to say a word.

'Listen, all you guys are going for dinner I heard? The place is right next to my house. Why don't you come over after dinner? Of course the rest won't know about it—but we can talk then.'

He waited for an answer.

This was my chance to say no and walk away. Choose the bright sun over the darkness.

I nodded my head in agreement.

He gave me quick hug, got into his car, and left.

So the next big step in the relationship had happened—I'd been asked out on a date. Prateeksha Devi and the rumours were forgotten momentarily as euphoria set in.

I walked to gate two and saw Sam's car leave. I panicked. I was just a few minutes late. But then I heard a horn blare and turned to see PJ in his car. He was waiting for me. When I got in, PJ said, 'We knew the pretty boy wouldn't be seen dead with you.' I looked at him and made a face.

'I'm just saying, I'm pleasantly surprised,' he laughed.

'Can you drive a little faster?' I snapped and settled back in the seat, hiding my smirk. What would PJ say if he knew about our plan for a secret rendezvous? I was ecstatic.

~

I chuckled when I read that. I wish I'd known then, that although ecstasy comes with a robe of grandness, it has another friend, hidden in the deep folds of the beautiful red velvet cloak of grandeur, taking account of each moment spent in happiness. For every moment spent in ecstasy, we have to pay with a moment of anguish.

## WHAT'S IN A DUCK?
## AND WHAT'S IN A FISH?

I didn't know about the rest of the team sitting on that table in Mystic China, with its gleaming cutlery and stark-white, stiff napkins, but I felt very self-conscious in the restaurant. Not because the place was so upmarket, which it was, but because I was suddenly in such a different setting with people from work. I was not used to eating with them. There were about fifteen of us, including some of the cast, and Fiza was interacting with everyone. Despite my discomfort, I was very aware of how lucky I was. There I was, the famous director Fiza Kareem two seats away from me, actually bothering to talk to me. I was doing well at work, *and* I was falling in love. So many good things had happened in such a short span of time.

About twenty minutes after we got there, to my surprise, Ranvir joined us. We shared a look but he didn't say anything. Somehow I knew he was here for me. There, sitting in the Chinese restaurant with the smell of vinegar and soya playing with my senses, I had my 'apple feeling' again. Ranvir was here for me. The episode with Prateeksha was becoming hazy and distant. I was two seats away from Fiza on my left and two seats away from Ranvir on my right. The rest of the table did not matter to me. I heard Ranvir order the Zhangcha Duck, and rave about how crispy the skin was on the outside and how soft, how tender it was on the inside. Heavenly, he said.

I remembered my mother telling me, 'It's important that boys should feel you are a homely girl. You should make an effort to like what he likes.' It was one of the many lectures my mother had given me over the years, on how to be 'ideal marriage material'—IMM, I called it. She'd been trying to train me to be IMM since I was in pigtails. I'd laughed at her then but I was not laughing now. I wanted to impress Ranvir and so decided to order the duck as well. If Ranvir liked duck, I was happy to love it too.

Even though we never ate duck at home, I remembered my mother telling Shivshankarji about an article on its medicinal properties. The waiter came to take my order and I announced my choice loud enough for Ranvir to hear, so he would know the effort being made here.

And then, for additional effect, I said (mentally thanking my mother for her incessant rambling at the same time), 'You know, duck fat has Omega six and Omega three essential oils, it has anti-cancer effects, and can help with psychotic disorders and depression? On the other hand, too much of Omega six can increase the likelihood of breast cancer in post-menopausal women . . .' I tapered off, thinking that this was not coming out the way it had sounded in my head. Someone at the table cleared their throat, I think it was Shivani. After a short pause, everyone resumed their conversations. I mentally shrugged: at least I was well informed, unlike the rest of the people at the table.

The food finally arrived. The waiter served Fiza and Ranvir and then turned to serve me. The mark of a good headwaiter is that he always remembers who ordered what at the table. If only I had remembered that, I could have saved myself.

The waiter placed my dish in front of me and announced with a flourish, 'Enjoy your fish, Ma'am.'

I reacted immediately. 'I didn't order fish,' I said loud and clear. 'I ordered Bombay duck!'

When you've had a good day, you're a little slow to catch on to the fact that it can turn bad any second. High on my achievements and heady from the attention Ranvir had given me through the day, I did not catch on to the very amused reaction of everyone at the table.

I repeated, more firmly this time, 'Sorry, you've made a mistake. I ordered Bombay duck, not fish. I hate fish.'

The sympathetic waiter cleared his throat and tried to be as quiet as he could for the sake of my ego. 'Bombay duck *is* a fish, Ma'am.'

And that's all I heard in my head, playing over and over, till I realised the dinner was over. I ignored the following people through the evening: the entire AD team, Ranvir and Fiza. The only person I interacted with was the patronising headwaiter. He had the nerve to ask me if the 'fish' was nice. I wanted to shove my fork down his throat. I was a complete social embarrassment.

∼

I looked up at the inky dark sky and laughed. It was the *sine qua non* for surviving Mumbai. You never took things for granted, and things were never what they seemed. In Mumbai, if you want a duck you need to ask for a fish! If you think you are seeing a fish, it could very well turn out to be a duck. So neither can a duck be taken for granted here, nor a fish. If you learnt that fast enough, you were here to stay. If not, the train back home was the only option!

I whispered it over and over, sitting on the parapet. Knowing that no one was listening except the broken furniture behind me and the chirping crickets. 'Bombay duck is a fish! I still don't get it. But I *know* Bombay duck is a fish!'

The chirping of the crickets suddenly seemed to get louder. I remember PJ telling me that in Brazil, Barbados and Zambia, the loud chirping of crickets was a sign of a windfall in financial gains and luck. Unfortunately, for me, crickets in Mumbai only meant fungi and organic decay.

Since I could not go to Brazil or Barbados, I decided to go back to my Nano.

~

Having gulped down more wine than I was used to, to hide my embarrassment, I was quite buzzed by the time we were all ready to leave. PJ offered me a ride home, but I declined. I needed to see Ranvir. He'd already taken off in his car, so I walked up to his place awkwardly and rang the bell.

He opened the door, and I looked up at him, teary eyed. He gently led me in and said, 'No biggie—smile! It should say on the menu it's a fish right?'

I was ecstatic. He knew why I was upset. He understood me. And then we kissed. It made me forget everything—Mumbai, duck, fish, life and me, in that order.

I woke up in his bed at two in the morning. I had made love with Ranvir Khanna.

Twice.

I turned to watch him breathing steadily, his back gently rising and falling. My high from the wine had worn off and my head was hurting. Reality began to sink in. This was unexpected. This was sudden. This was either a disaster or a dream; I needed to figure out which. I had to get away.

I hurriedly tiptoed out of his house and hailed a cab. I no longer distrusted cab drivers. In fact, a cab driver was the only man I could trust to drop me home safely at this hour. I wondered if the cab guy was thinking about what I'd been up to. Why I needed to hail a cab at two in the morning. But the cabbie was not judging me at all. His unperturbed, steady gaze at the road in front of him made me realise why I'd fallen in love with this city—Mumbai.

I reached home, purposely not allowing myself to think about anything. I sat on my bed, opened my laptop and wrote to my mother:
*Dear Mom,*
*I think you should know this. Bombay duck is a fish.*
*Love,*
*Neki*

## 'FUNNY' IS A FUNNY WORD

As I was going through the pages of my diary, I spotted the heading, 'A funny day'. I had to read it. Perhaps it would lift my spirits. Or encourage me to jump without reading my Nano any further.

'Funny' is such an accommodating word. It could mean anything from humorous to weird, from hurtful to pathetic. . . . When you don't know how to react to a situation, think of it as 'funny'. You want to run away on the day of your wedding, you say you have a 'funny' feeling in your stomach. And this day as I see it, was a really 'funny' one.

~

5 December 2008. 3:02 a.m.
Dear Nano,
I have realised my life is not just funny, it's hilarious.

For the past one month, I'd been counting the days to my first outdoor shoot. We were scheduled to go to Manori island for one day to shoot the 'holiday in Goa' scene.

Manori is a stretch of beach barely a ten-minute ride on the ferry from Marve beach on the outskirts of Mumbai. I had imagined Manori to be one of those magical, stunning beaches I'd seen in the James Bond movies.

When I saw it, I realised that Bond movies were shot in Greece.

Let me start from the beginning of the day.

I was sulking all the way to Manori because PJ had decided to woo me. And his idea of wooing me was to take me to Madh island under false pretensions. He had messaged me that we were supposed to go to Madh island for a location recce in the morning before going to Manori for the shoot in the afternoon. I was puzzled at the last-minute change of plan, and that the cinematographer and the direction department weren't coming along as they usually do for a recce, but being a junior in the AD hierarchy doesn't really allow you to question anyone. In any case, I was quite excited about going to Madh island. PJ had said it was where most Mumbai crews shot, and that it was gorgeous. Plus, I was looking forward to the ferry ride.

As we walked to the place from where we were supposed to catch the ferry, and PJ continued his commentary on the beauty of this Madh island, I realised we were walking through narrow lanes that were definitely not quaint or atmospheric. People were literally living on those lanes and there was barely any place to walk. The air was warm, thick and humid. It smelt of fish. Naked, sun-burnt kids streaked with mud were running around, neatly side-stepping the chickens that were pecking at dirt on the road. People were walking with piles of fish and dried shrimps. Some women had spread out a cloth and left a pile of tiny, shrivelled fish-looking objects to dry out, and a few cats hung around, waiting to nick anything they could lay their paws on.

'Isn't this beautiful, Neki? So raw, so primitive,' PJ said.

As I tried to come up with a fitting reply, I saw a man

squatting by the side of the lane, taking a bath with his underwear on. He slipped the soap in his underpants, lathered himself, and then poured a mug of dirty water. A little boy hovered around, playing with the pure white soapsuds, strangely made from the dirty water. He was making soap bubbles. They were floating around lightly, bobbing in the smelly air, some glistening white and some with rainbow colours and then disappearing or bursting brutally before they could float up to the rickety old kiosk right there, selling bread and eggs and cigarettes.

PJ looked at my face, 'Do you see the beauty in this, Neki?

The only beauty I could see was the pure white soap bubbles in the dark dirty water. Even the dirty water was capable of something pure and beautiful. The child had seen that.

PJ stopped. He rolled his jeans up all the way to his knees and looked at me. I was in a flowing white skirt and flip-flops. He checked my outfit out and laughed. 'Hike the skirt up!'

'Are you kidding me?'

'It rained last night Neki, pull up your skirt!'

'PJ, can we just get to this beautiful Madh island now?'

'The ferry is a minute away,' he assured me.

We turned a corner, and PJ pointed towards an expanse of—mud and garbage. In the middle of this garbage, a stream of people was lined up to get on to a rickety slab of wood, one end of which precariously rested in the mud and the other on a huge ferry. People were climbing on to the plank with scooters, cycles and huge piles of fish in baskets. PJ started jogging. 'Hurry Neki, we have to catch this ferry.'

I started running after him, my flip-flops almost giving way in the mud. As I navigated the wooden plank, I felt it sway dangerously. PJ climbed into the ferry and then held out his hand for me. I grabbed it and climbed in as well. There was barely any place to stand and for the entire ride I stood, barely able to breathe, between a woman carrying a huge basket with some mixture of crabs and shrimps on my left and a man holding on to his cycle on my right.

'How is it? I told you it will be a ride to remember!' PJ whispered in my ear.

The man holding the cycle looked at us and smiled. PJ turned to him, 'She is going to Madh island for the first time,' he said.

'Holiday?' the man asked.

I muttered, 'Work. We may be shooting there soon.'

'Actually, we are not shooting there, I just wanted you to see the island, so yes it's a mini-holiday,' PJ smiled cheekily.

I gaped at him. 'So why are we going to Madh island? I mean, what are we doing? Why am I on this fish-infested ferry if we are not even doing a location recce?'

I was almost screaming. People around were looking at me with strangely calm expressions. They were probably glad they had something to entertain them during the ten-minute ferry ride.

PJ smiled. 'Just enjoy the ride, Neki,' he said.

Just then the woman with the crabs standing next to me decided to sneeze. All over me.

PJ continued, 'What if there was an earthquake and the whole of Mumbai were destroyed? You know what you will regret the most? That you did not see a beautiful place that was right under your nose—Madh island.'

The fish woman next to me sneezed again.

A couple of crab legs were now sticking out dangerously from the basket. Almost scaring me enough to shut me up.

Thankfully I remembered my mother telling Shivshankarji, her main pupil, how crabs have their teeth in their stomach. That gave me some comfort.

We reached the shore of Madh island. The wooden plank was brought out again and all the passengers filed past me to get off the ferry. Livid, I refused to move. I was not going to get off the ferry. I stood right there and waited for the ferry to fill up with people, and to take us back to the other side.

'Since we have come this far, are you sure you don't want to check it out?' PJ asked hopefully.

I saw a glimpse of some trees huddled together beyond a small concrete structure. I could see a road curving and going up somewhere. The ferry turned and the road became less visible, and more inviting.

'We have time . . . we have to report at Manori only after lunch. That's why I organised this trip.'

I continued to look at the receding shore silently. What was I going to miss out on? A beautiful experience or a mosquito-infested walk to nowhere? Who knew? It was human to look back and wonder. And it was super-human for me to resist shoving PJ off the ferry. He was looking at me and it seemed like he knew exactly how I felt.

I didn't say a word to PJ the entire ride back, though he tried to cajole me out of my silence. Finally he gave up, accepting the animosity I was radiating. We were on the rickety plank again when PJ told me, 'You know what I see when I come here? Not the fish or the smell or the dirty water . . . I see another way of life.'

I looked at the women, children and men, going about their daily chores. You could see into the one-room houses they lived in. PJ continued, 'Working in films takes you away from reality, so I come here sometimes to reconnect. I wanted you to experience this. As an aspiring film-maker, you need to have seen and experienced different things!'

I snorted. 'Thanks! It was a fantastic lesson in film-making!' I said scathingly.

PJ looked at me and said gravely, 'You are welcome Neki, and you will need new clothes.'

I looked down to see my white skirt was soaked in mud.

I refused to talk to PJ again.

We joined the rest of the crew on Marve beach, where they were waiting for a ferry. A half hour later, I was finally at the promised paradise, Manori island, looking like a walking cake of dried mud. Walking alongside another cake of dried mud, PJ.

But I was happy to see Manori island after all and I ran to our allotted cottages to change. I was determined to forget the morning's drama and enjoy the rest of the day. I felt like I really needed this break. For one, I was tired of feeling guilty about lying to Shikha. I had not told her what I knew about Zoya and Sam. So there I was, stuck in the middle of a merry-go-round, with Shikha confiding in me about her love for Sam, Zoya confiding in me about *her* love for Sam and Sam begging me to stay silent till he mustered up the courage to tell Shikha the truth. A love triangle was ruining my piece of mind despite the fact that I wasn't even one of the angles. I desperately wanted to jump off the merry-go-round.

That was currently the first joke in my life.

The second was that nobody in my life knew I had a boyfriend. In fact, even I didn't know for sure if I had a boyfriend. Ranvir had been blowing hot and cold. Since the night at his house, we had met alone exactly twice. Briefly. Kissed exactly three times. Very briefly. And spoke on the phone twice. Ranvir hates text-messaging, and he hates talking on the phone. But I was increasingly getting agitated. The stolen glances were not enough anymore. I wanted to spend some real time with him.

Meanwhile, Aslam, for some reason, had become my spy. Without my asking, he was informing me of everything Ranvir did. And the funny thing was, I didn't stop him. So even if I was busy on the set, I knew that the beautiful Prateeksha Devi, Ranvir's 'godmother', came often to visit him. Apparently they were discussing a film project that she was producing for Ranvir. And I knew that Minty and Ranvir ate lunch together every day.

So for me, being near the beach, even if I was working, was definitely a break. Having settled in, and getting into work mode, I realised most of our JAs were firangs. Aslam had caught them all at Colaba, hanging around Leopold Café. They were mostly backpackers and tourists who were trying to make a quick buck; some Bollywood experience would be a souvenir to take back from their Indian holiday.

The scene we were going to shoot would introduce another key character, being played by an actor from the UK, David Brown. He is one of the main villains in the film. I had seen David's pictures in the casting file. He is in his early thirties and is a handsome guy with sharp features.

Shivani introduced David to the team; they had worked together before. They seemed to be on friendly terms. He smiled when he was introduced to the girls, and started flirting with us instantly. Without wasting any time. He kissed Kriti's hand and she smiled. Then he took my hand and kissed it too. I replicated Kriti's action and smiled. Now, if it were any other normal side actor kissing our hands, Kriti would have killed him and I would have slapped him. What made David different? Was it his charm or his complexion? It's funny that after six decades of freedom, the colour white may not be making our public policies, but it is definitely still making us a little weak-kneed.

I was in charge of getting the goras—as the foreigners were called on the set—ready for the shot. I went into the make-up room and sat next to David, who was getting his face done up. My mind, though, was on Ranvir. He hadn't arrived on set yet and I was wondering when he would come. PJ entered the room and greeted David like they were long-lost friends. PJ looked at me and smiled. I ignored him. 'You need to lighten up, Neki,' PJ said. 'You take everything too seriously.'

'And around this guy, you cannot take *anything* seriously!' David laughed and winked at PJ.

Their camaraderie was annoying me. I turned by back on PJ and asked David, 'Obviously you weren't one of the backpackers hijacked outside Leopold Café. So, how did you get in? I mean are you a professional actor?'

PJ was called over the walkie. There was a crowd gathering—the locals were coming to watch the shoot, and they needed to be controlled. PJ excused himself. David turned to me and replied to my question, 'Yes, I'm professionally trained. I came here five years ago on a holiday to recover from a break-up—and never left!'

'How did you break into Bollywood?'

'Well after roaming the Himalayas and in the south, I came to Mumbai for a few days. I bumped into this agent who offered me what he called a holiday-cum-shooting package in Udaipur. All I had to do was pretend to shoot a villager with a rifle! It was a paid trip and sounded like fun, so I took it!'

I laughed. Just then Shivani and Sam barged in. 'Can we

take the gossip outside and set up? The actors will be ready in thirty minutes,' Shivani snapped.

I got up, startled. 'Ranvir is here? But I didn't know!'

Shivani dripped sarcasm, 'Sorry, I didn't know we were supposed to inform you!'

I stood there, red in the face. I did not know what to say, so I simply walked out.

While walking towards the room allocated to Ranvir, I tried to calm myself down. When a day begins on a bad note, I told myself, the law of averages says it should end on a good one. Little did I realise that the 'bad part' of the day was yet to come!

And that was the funniest joke of the day.

## SHOT BREAKDOWN OR SHOT-BROKEN AND DOWN

I was almost at Ranvir's door when Inder came racing up to me and said, 'Ranvir sir is not in the room, he is sitting with Ahmed Khan sir.'

I knew Ahmed Khan's room was out of bounds for me. Disappointed, I turned away and saw Aslam heading towards us. 'Has anyone seen Mintyji? She came in an hour ago and we can't find her.' He stopped abruptly, and there was an awkward look between him and Inder.

Inder was glaring at Aslam, and I knew Aslam was up to something. He had not walked all the way here just to enquire about Minty's whereabouts.

The walkie crackled as everyone was called on the set. Fiza Kareem was sitting under a huge umbrella where the monitors were set up for her. The cameraman, Dharmesh sir, was setting the frame as Kriti hovered around him. 'You better light me up as nicely in my debut film, as you are doing Minty,' she giggled. 'With your light, if Minty looks nice I will look stunning!'

Dharmesh sir nodded. Kriti was the only AD he spoke or responded to. I had heard someone say he hated the lot of us. Thankfully, Dharmesh sir did not show his hatred so openly.

I passed them and walked over to Sam. I pointed towards Kriti and the cameraman. 'What's happening there?'

'Chill, it's outdoor,' Sam said.

'What do you mean?'

'Babe, haven't you heard—anything goes in outdoor shoots? You'll see a lot of people go "whoosh"! But it's all okay, it's outdoor!'

'What do you mean, "whoosh"?' I asked.

Sam chuckled. 'This is the time to flirt and chat up people you've been wanting to, and bond with the crew.'

I suddenly remembered I was supposed to be upset with Sam so I gave him a 'whatever' look and was about to walk away when a visibly annoyed Karan came up to us. 'Guys we are on an outdoor, not on a holiday! Can someone get Minty and Ranvir out of the room they have been locked in for over an hour?'

I felt my face going red. Shivani was looking at me. She'd known all along!

'Neki, do you need me to write a letter to you, for you to go and get them?' Karan asked impatiently.

I could not seem to move. I registered that Fiza was talking to Kriti and PJ. I could see Sam leading the goras to their positions. I could see everything but I could not move. Before Karan had a heart attack at my lack of response, Shivani stepped in saying, 'I will get them.'

I turned and walked towards the monitor. Suddenly I needed to do something, have a task given to me. I wanted to set something right. Something that was within my control. If not my life, at least setting the frame in the camera right would be some compensation.

I joined PJ in placing the foreigners in the frame. I was beginning to get angry. All I wanted to do was kill Ranvir along with Minty, using Minty's hideous pink nail file. Instead, I charged towards all the JAs and told them where to stand. I went up to a fat gora in neon pink shorts and told him go further back in the water. If I could not scream at Ranvir for cheating on me, at least I could shove this guy further into the sea.

The guy snapped at me though. 'You want me to drown or something lady? I told you already I can't swim, and you have told me three times to move deeper into the water!'

Shocked, I looked at him. 'I have? You can't swim?' And then, in the same tone, I said again, 'Why don't you take a step back in the water and stand there?'

Just then PJ came and led me away. 'No time to go loony, Neki,' he said softly. 'Keep the brains in place till pack-up—then you are allowed to be devastated by the cheating boyfriend, not before that. And here he comes.'

I looked up to see Ranvir walking on set. He was dressed all in white. Minty was also in a white dress; a dress so transparent, she did not even need to undress, I thought bitchily.

'Neki, go over the scene with David!' I heard Fiza over the mike. That was it. Nothing else mattered.

Ranvir looked at me as I walked past and gave me a warm smile. He opened his mouth to greet me, but I looked through him. My eyes were glued on David Brown. Like a soldier on a mission, I marched up to the actor.

I knew he had read the scene already in the make-up room. Still, I explained it to him. 'Basically you have to walk in and shoot at the unsuspecting tourists. Ranvir and Minty will rush towards you and try to catch you. You are supposed to push them away and run.'

'Got it! Thanks, you make a horrid action scene sound lovely!' he said flirtatiously.

I smiled back at him. I could sense Ranvir's eyes on David and me. Great!

Just then Aslam jumped in. 'Now tell me where all you need to block the beach off? My army will take over!'

PJ joined us, answering Aslam's query. He pointed to his left and right. 'Make sure the people watching the shoot don't come closer than twenty feet of the set at any given point of time.'

Aslam walked away as did David. I looked at PJ; he was staring at me. He pulled out a small pistol from his pocket. Black, gleaming and menacing. 'You know, there is no point stressing about cheating boyfriends in life, because you never know when an accident is waiting to happen out here,' he whispered. 'Especially with a gun and all!'

I scoffed, 'Oh you and your morbid disaster stories—just because it's my first film does not mean I'm an idiot! I know the gun is not loaded!'

PJ smirked. 'Correct! All I am saying is, accidents happen. I can prove it to you. You heard of the film *The Crow*? Bruce Lee's son Brandon Lee was killed by a prop gun—a .44 Magnum to be precise. They fired a full charge of gunpowder at Brandon, but unfortunately a bullet was already lodged in the barrel and hit him in the abdomen.'

I was shocked. 'What rubbish! No one checked it? The crew, the firearm technician?'

PJ laughed. 'What did you say? You are using big words huh? We are the crew and I am not about to fire a shot and check it.'

Just then I heard Karan call me on the walkie. 'Ranvir needs the scene. Can you come here Neki?'

I looked up, panic on my face. PJ tried to calm me down. 'Can you stop thinking about Ranvir and Minty? I am talking about guns, shots, and accidents here, Neki. Give yourself a break!'

'What I need is a break from people who lie to me and take me on a boat stuck in a mud pool!'

I could sense that PJ was getting angry, as was I.

'Ya, I know, because you only want to hang out with people who make a fool of you. Like Ranvir. You should be happy I took you to Madh island because no one here would have taken you there, not even your wonderful Ranvir, in fact never him, because he wouldn't be able to stand the smell of raw fish. He can only handle the one served steaming on a white plate with a slice of lemon on it!'

Karan was standing behind us, looking at us with a jaundiced eye. He spoke sternly. 'Let me remind everyone here of the rule. No dating in the team.'

'Don't worry, there is no one worth dating on the team,' PJ said pointedly.

I glared at PJ.

Karan continued in the same menacing tone, 'Well, just to make myself clear—Neki, I do not approve of it. I won't have it. It hampers work. Work colleagues are off limits, okay?'

I felt a rush of affection for Karan. He was obviously completely out of the loop as far as set gossip went. Imagine if I told him about Ranvir; he'd have a panic attack right here, I thought and chuckled. Aloud. It didn't go down well.

'Are you laughing at me? Listen, I don't know what's going on, but if there is something happening, it will stop. If something is going to happen, it won't, and if nothing is happening, I'm happy, okay?'

I nodded my head.

'Go and rehearse with Ranvir now.'

I shot PJ a murderous look and walked towards Ranvir, my

heart pounding. I didn't know how I was going to act with him. I passed by Sam who was busy handing out bags, hats, suntan lotions and mats to the background goras and telling them what to do. I noticed that he would lie down on the mat for a couple of minutes to rest his ass, on the pretext of telling them what to do. I saw him lying down next to a gora and I threw a towel at him. 'Do you mind?' Sam yelled. 'I am working very hard here under the sun!'

I continued to march towards Ranvir. Right behind Sam was Kriti. She was actually applying suntan lotion on her arms and legs. Her head was covered in a huge fancy hat and she was wearing dark glasses.

I reached Ranvir. I knew he had been watching me all this while through his dark glasses. He smiled at me. 'Hey. What's up?'

I simply handed him the scene and began explaining the sequence.

Ranvir stopped me half-way. 'Neki! I don't get it! What's wrong . . . and the least you can say is hello.'

'Why? You've had Minty saying hello to you repeatedly the whole morning.' Without giving him a chance to respond, I picked up where I'd left off in the sequence. After I finished explaining the scene to him, I paused and then turned to walk away.

Ranvir, with a deadpan expression, said, 'I'm sorry, I didn't get the scene.'

'Perhaps you should try reading it?' I replied.

'Perhaps you should try reading it out to me with a smile?'

'Perhaps I should send Minty over?' I retorted. And this time my voice was suspiciously heavy. I could feel a slight lump in my throat. Damn! I did not want him to see how upset I was.

But he must have, because his tone softened. He stepped forward and said, 'Neki, that won't be necessary. Minty wanted to rehearse her scene before coming on the set. I was just helping her out. Whatever people are telling you or whatever you think is wrong. I was looking forward to this outdoor so I could spend some time with you. Don't do this, okay? Please.'

'I hope your session with her helps her act a little better,' I said nastily.

Just then David stepped in from behind. 'Hey Neki, can we rehearse the scene once?'

I smiled at him, relieved. 'Of course. I'm done rehearsing with Ranvir here!'

I left with David and out of the corner of my eye saw Ranvir stiffening his jaw and shoving his hands in the pockets of his white trousers. He gave me a look which clearly said, 'This is not over yet.'

After I rehearsed with David, I went over to Fiza and told her the actors were ready with the scenes. She looked at me a little absent-mindedly and then did something that seemed, to me, a milestone in my career. She handed me the very sacred 'shot breakdown'. That meant I would be responsible for giving the number of the shot and telling the entire AD team which shot was being taken. In short, I was going to lead.

It was pretty clear by now that I'd left Kriti behind in the AD hierarchy. But getting the shot breakdown from the director was a big one! It was usually always with the first AD. I was flying! I looked up to see Kriti, Shivani, Sam, PJ and Karan all glaring at me. My hand was trembling as I looked at the paper. The entire scene had been divided into shots and numbered. Right now we were taking a wide shot of Minty and Ranvir strolling on the beach.

I spoke into the walkie. 'Guys, shot number three. We are taking a wide with Ranvir and Minty. David can enter from left of camera.'

Silence. I knew everyone had heard; why weren't they responding? What were they all doing? I could see that Fiza was expecting action immediately. The ADs should have started placing the people according to the frame, but they were just standing still, staring at me.

Finally Karan walked over to me. He pointedly took the paper from me, looked at it, and spoke into the walkie. 'Guys, shot number three. We're taking a wide with Ranvir and Minty. David can enter from left of camera. Neki, can you go and do background action please and get that guy there to move back a little bit? You're not required near the monitor. Oh, and one more thing, just because you've accidentally been given the shot breakdown, it does not mean you can call the shots here.'

Karan walked over to Fiza to discuss the placement of the actors in the frame. Would Minty and Ranvir be holding hands? Would they be smiling and laughing? Or should they look pensive and gaze into the sea?

I left them to it and walked over to where the guy in the neon pink shorts was standing. The same guy I'd been asking to move back in the sea. I could see his paunch hanging and his bald head sweating. He was clearly upset. Just then Sam came up to me. 'Babe, never step on Karan's toes. He is the first AD, he'll let everyone know what to do.'

I snapped, 'Fiza gave me the sheet. And he said the exact same thing I'd said in the walkie. I gave the right instructions!'

'Even if the instructions were right, it was wrong of you to give them. You went too far. Go and apologise.'

'No way. Fiza gave me the sheet, and I knew what I was doing.'

I saw Shivani going over to Minty to tell her that Fiza wanted her to look up happily at Ranvir. Then she came up to Sam and me and said, 'You know Neki, Fiza gives the papers to Punjabi the spot boy as well, does that mean he calls the shots? Ask Punjabi what he does with the shot breakdown paper if he finds it somewhere.'

I looked at Punjabi who was standing there, sweating in the heat, holding a tray full of soft drinks. He smiled, 'I give it to Karan sir. If he's not there then Shivani madam, if she's not there then PJ sir, then if he's not there Sam sir, and if he's not there then—'

'Doesn't matter after that!' Shivani said. 'If all these people are not there, it means the shoot isn't happening!'

Shivani moved back towards Minty to adjust her dress, pulling it down a little lower for some more cleavage to show.

I saw Karan and PJ staring at me. They had clearly heard the entire conversation. Just then Punjabi offered me a drink. 'Ma'am, tea, coffee, biscuits?' I knew Punjabi and I had a karmic connection. I was sure I'd given him poison and killed him in my last birth, because this time round, I only wanted him to give me poison whenever he offered me a drink.

Karan's look told me that things were different now. Earlier, he wouldn't pay too much attention to me; but now I knew I was on his radar.

'I think I told you to tell that guy with pink shorts over there to go further back into the sea,' Karan said coldly.

I don't know if it was the heat, Ranvir and Minty, or the shot breakdown fiasco, but I snapped back, 'I have. He cannot swim, he refuses to go any further!'

Karan replied angrily, 'Then convince him. I hope by now you can do a bit of your job instead of fooling around. I want him and only him to stand there, in the background. In the frame.'

I stood my ground. 'Why can't we get someone who is not scared of water to replace him?'

Karan looked at me with his eyes narrowed. 'We can't change him because I said so. And if you can't change your attitude I will be very happy to change you!'

Well this was it. The next level had started with the chief AD gunning for me. I am sure in some twisted psychoanalytical theory this was a sign of success, that I was making my presence felt, but this theory translated itself in real life as a nightmare.

And as usual I was playing the lead role in the nightmare.

## THE CLOWN

As Karan turned and walked away after his very loud, very public and very humiliating threat, I grabbed the mike from PJ's back pocket and called out for Aslam. That was the first time I had used the mike. My voice echoed on the beach. Karan, Kriti, Shivani and Sam turned sharply to where I was standing.

Aslam came running from one of the shacks, smelling of prawn, sweat and beer.

'Why did you get people who were scared of water for a beach sequence? How will they get in the sea?' I demanded, pointing to the fat, pink gora man.

'I had to beg half these goras to come here, Madam. Last-minute, cheap solution. If I ask for all these requirements, if they swim, dance or ride, I will have to take off my clothes, paint myself white and stand there in my chaddis!'

PJ spoke in the walkie. 'Karan, can we change the guy?'

'No!' Karan responded immediately. 'Fiza wants the splash of pink in the background. Can you all let Neki handle this? I gave *her* the job. Neki, either move the guy five steps back into the water or take his pink shorts and give them to someone else with the same paunch. And if you can't do that, please leave the set.'

I looked at Aslam. Aslam looked at me. 'Don't worry,' he said. 'I will sort out everything. Let's go and talk to the gora.'

Aslam and I walked over to the already harassed guy. Aslam called out to him confidently with a fake accent, 'John! Mr John!'

I was impressed. 'You know his name?'

Aslam shook his head, 'No, but they are all mostly John only.'

He walked up to 'John' and started chatting. 'Good afternoon! Having fun? Can you take off your shorts for the shot?'

John screamed, 'Nudity? What the fuck, I don't do nudity ... I'm off!'

I heard Karan shout on the walkie. 'Tell the guy to move to his left and five steps back, Neki!'

John was simply walking off the set. I ran to him, splashing in the water. I was soaked by the time I caught up with him and grabbed him. 'Please, Sir, there is no nudity. We just want you to move a little further back into the water. If you are scared, we will have to give your pink shorts to someone else.'

'Why should I give you my shorts? I'm not giving my shorts to anyone! I am out of here!'

'Okay, get out John!' Aslam said. 'I will talk to other John!'

'Shut up, Aslam! You're drunk!' I shouted.

This time Karan screamed on the mike. 'Neki! Can we take the shot anytime today? Place the guy and move out of the frame!'

The whole set was looking at me. I saw Ranvir and Minty also looking at me. Ready to walk in the frame on action. Their spot boys were standing next to them with umbrellas and juice. Ranvir had a concerned look on his face. Minty turned to Ranvir and said something, but he continued to look straight at me. He was worried for me. That made me burn.

I could see Sam running towards me all the way from the monitor. I had to do something before he reached us. I had to resolve this on my own. I whispered to the JA, 'Please John. If you don't move five steps back I'm going to lose my job. I promise, I will not let you drown.'

John looked at me and saw how desperate I was. Finally, he said, 'If I slip in the water you have to come and save me. I'm counting on you! Can you swim?'

'No, but Aslam can,' I said, looking over at Aslam.

'Of course, of course!' Aslam said, beaming. 'In my hometown there are only rivers and we used to be in the water all the time. I used to sit on buffaloes!'

'That's enough Aslam, thank you John.' I waved at Sam, gesturing that everything was all right.

John moved back to where I'd asked him to stand, and Aslam and I ran out of the frame. I spoke into the walkie, 'You can have your shot Karan. Anytime today.'

'Roll camera!' Fiza shouted as I heaved a sigh of relief.

'If he slips go there quickly, okay?' I told Aslam.

'Are you crazy?' Aslam said. 'Who will save *me*? I can't swim!'

'But you said . . .'

'I said I used to sit on buffaloes in the river. You don't need to swim if you are hanging onto a buffalo! I don't see any buffaloes here; I'm not going in there to save anyone! I just said that to get the work done. That's how films get made here!'

Through the shot, I kept my eyes on John. The poor guy was splashing in the water, pretending to enjoy the waves, but

I could see he was petrified. Thankfully the shot went off okay. Nothing happened. No one drowned. I went over and congratulated John.

'Am I done?' he asked hopefully.

Just then Karan said on the walkie, 'One more wide. This time David will shoot into the crowd, and Neki, we will need the pink shorts guy in the same position for the shot.'

I was explaining the situation to John when David walked up with a gun in his hand.

'Hey, just wanted to find out if someone has checked this gun. Maybe the gun technician? Because Sam gave it to me and rushed off before I could ask. On my last shoot, a fake bullet literally went through a guy's stomach!'

This whole gun business was freaking me out.

I looked at Aslam. 'Aslam, just call the gun technician here quickly!'

Aslam looked at me blankly, 'Who is that?'

David butted in, 'The guy who got the gun here and knows how to work it and all ... with safety procedures.'

'That's me,' Aslam said happily. 'I am your man and technician! Ask me, what do you want to know?'

David looked at him dubiously, 'Is this loaded, has anyone checked?'

'Of course it is not loaded! Shoot away!'

Aslam walked off and I ran after him. 'Aslam did you really check the gun?'

'Of course not! Arrey, we are making a film here. Let me do my job!'

Worried, I ran to PJ. 'Did *you* check the gun?'

By now, David was in position, holding the gun up for the shot.

'Yes I did,' PJ said in an offhand manner. 'I think it had

some fake bullets—I told Aslam to check it. He hired the gun. Aslam said it's all taken care of, so don't worry.'

My heart stopped beating. PJ's story about Brandon Lee getting hit raced through my mind. Before I could say anything, I heard Fiza call for action and saw David moving into position.

What I did not see was the look and the wink David and PJ shared.

A gunshot was fired, and I saw John fall down.

I ran. Right into the middle of a rolling camera. 'There was a bullet! He is hit! Cut! Cut!' I shouted. Everyone on the set began running towards John, except Aslam, who ran in the opposite direction towards the safety of his shack. Punjabi was holding a first aid box and right next to him were Ranvir and Karan.

Behind me was PJ, yelling, 'Neki, stop!'

'I told John I would keep an eye on him,' I shouted back. 'He cannot even swim!'

I jumped on John who was waist-deep in water, half-sitting and half-lying. I was literally sitting on him. He was screaming, so was I. By now everyone was there.

'John, are you okay? You got hit by the bullet?'

John looked at me and started screaming, 'I did? I got hit by a bullet?! Oh my god! Where?'

And then like ice cold water it dawned on me. PJ whispered in my ear, 'Get up, Neki. It was a joke. I made sure there were no bullets.'

Stunned, I sat there in the water. Evidently I was a sitting duck for everyone on set to attack.

Someone cleared her throat. Fiza had gone back to the monitor. In an agitated tone, she said over the mike, 'Karan, I need to take this shot now! I don't have time for stunts! And only *I* say "cut" on my set. Is everyone clear about that?'

Everyone around me smirked. Ranvir looked at me and stretched out his hand to help me up. I looked down at the water. Ranvir still stood there, his hand outstretched. I ignored him. Shivani stepped in and said, 'You guys carry on. We will get her.'

People started dispersing. Punjabi stood there, smiled at me and asked, 'Hot coffee?'

Just then Karan barked into the walkie, 'Someone remove Neki from the set now and I don't want her back! Get her out!'

Wet and shivering, I got up and began walking toward the cottages. I heard PJ whisper, 'Sorry, it was supposed to be a joke.' I did not reply.

Shivani barked on the mike, 'PJ, check the background now please!'

PJ left me to finish my walk to the gallows alone. I walked with my head down straight into the very silent and very cold cottage.

I changed, crawled into bed and simply passed out into a dark, dreamless sleep.

They say about one-third of your life is spent sleeping. The good news was, at least I was getting one-third of my life right.

I'd heard somewhere that when ducks are at risk of attack, they balance out the sleep and survival needs by keeping half their brain awake while the other half slips into sleep mode. Well, I was clearly under attack, but I slept dreamlessly, with both half of my brains switched off. That just proved that I was not even as smart as a duck—or anyone on the AD team for that matter.

∼

Aslam came by the cottage in the evening, saying he had been sent to call me out.

I changed into my favourite blue sundress. I needed all the beauty and dignity I could gather for my court-martial. I was ready to be given my marching orders.

When I walked out, I saw people sitting around a bonfire. Everyone was there: Minty, Ranvir, the ADs, and Fiza. 'Dear god! Please let her not fire me here in front of everyone,' I thought.

Just then David stood up. 'Here comes my beautiful heroine!' he said. Everyone laughed. It was a joke. It was funny. I was funny. Everyone was laughing except Karan, Shivani, Kriti and Ranvir. The moment Ranvir had seen me walking towards the little group, he had stood up. Now, he was walking towards me. I ignored him and went up to Fiza.

I cleared my throat and said, 'I am so sorry, Ma'am. I was not thinking clearly.' My hands were clammy and my voice was croaky. My eyes had welled up.

Fiza looked at me and smiled. 'That's okay, as long as you are not on a rescue mission tomorrow! Oh by the way, I wanted some great shots of bloopers and behind the scene action for the "making of the film" sequence. This is by far the best footage! Very funny! Well done!' Fiza laughed. Everyone joined in, including me. Ranvir was standing a foot away from me, looking at me. Waiting patiently for me to go over to him.

Suddenly the fire was brighter, the night darker, the moon more luminous. I looked at Karan. I realised I was laughing and crying at the same time. He looked back with a blank face and then turned away. PJ grinned at me and winked. I smiled at him and walked a little away from the party to a secluded spot to compose myself.

Somebody had a sense of humour up there. I was staying on. I think somewhere down the line, this film had chosen me to be a part of it.

Just then I realised Ranvir had walked up to where I was sitting. We were practically alone. I looked at him and simply said, 'Thanks.'

My anger had subsided somehow.

Ranvir knelt next to me and said, 'I'll be waiting for you later.'

I looked at him for a few seconds. Taking in the smell of salt water on his skin. 'I'm not coming,' I said.

Ranvir lightly brushed my cheek with his thumb and said, 'I'll be waiting.' He got up and walked away.

I sat there for a long time, just taking in the beach and the waves and thanking God for small mercies. Suddenly I realised PJ was standing in the shadows. He cleared his throat and said, 'So, quite a day for you, huh?'

I shrugged.

'Neki, I'm sorry about the joke.'

'I'm not. Goodnight PJ.' I got up and began walking towards Ranvir's cottage.

I realised Sid was right, again.

After time has passed, pain does become funny. You do laugh it off. There is no need to dwell on it.

There was still time for time to make my pain funny for me. In the meantime, I hurt. And I think it is okay to be in pain.

I understood Sid now when he said, 'To know that we need to keep fighting to keep afloat in the water, we need to know what it is to drown and hit rock bottom.'

I entered Ranvir's cottage and saw him pacing in his suite. I could taste the sand in my mouth, on my tongue, clinging to my dress. I walked towards Ranvir's bathroom and stepped into the shower. I wanted to wash the dress along with the snickering, the humiliation, the smell of beer and prawn and fear and the imagery of a clown.

No wonder clowns sometimes have a teardrop drawn on their cheeks. It's painful to be the clown.

The bathroom door opened and Ranvir came in. He looked at me, as I stood under the shower in my blue dress. He was still wearing the same white attire from the shoot. He quietly stepped into the shower and stood behind me. I stared at the stark white tiles of the bathroom wall as I felt the heat radiating from Ranvir's warm body. The water pouring down from the shower head, my blue dress clinging to me like hope, I let myself lean back so my head rested on his chest. I closed my eyes and let go.

I knew it was a mistake. I knew I was going to regret it the next day.

But today, tomorrow seems far, far away. There is still time.

~

*Dear Mom,*
*I went on my first outdoor shoot. We shot at a beautiful beach with foreigners. I was given the hugest responsibility that can be given to an AD—the shot breakdown. I was great. The other ADs were amazed. I saved a guy's life today as well. He almost drowned. Did I tell you? Fiza loves me. In fact, Fiza told me today I had given her the best moments for a blooper video. That means, after the movie is over and the end credits roll in the theatres, you can all watch me on the big screen, making a public fool of myself. I will be hilarious.*

The thing about hilarity is, it cannot exist without somebody else's misery. And the thing about misery ensuing from hilarity is, there is only one way to express it. Laughter.

No wonder people laugh and cry at the same time, when they see something funny. Though sometimes they are crying just a little bit more than they are laughing.

Love,

Neki

P.S: If anyone asks you what kind of a girl Neki is, tell them she is a funny girl. That will say it all!

## THE BRINK OF GREATNESS

My cell phone was vibrating again, flashing blue and green like it had been for most of the last six hours. Once again I ignored it. Suddenly the whole world had questions for me. All the news channels I had grown up watching were pursuing me with a vengeance.

Oh, did I mention that by now the whole country probably knew my name too? Some would say a big achievement for someone so young.

And I would say, well, I'd rather die than face another day.

There was a faint sound from the street again. In fact, I was quite sure I had seen a figure dart across the road and hide in the shadows.

There was one logical explanation for this: maybe the street was haunted by the ghost of a young drug peddler who had frequented this tiny by-lane, and maybe died from an overdose before he saw his first hair turn grey and before he could awkwardly pull his grey hair out, standing in front of a tiny bathroom mirror. One night he is listening to rave music and the next morning he wakes up with a heavy head and is invited to his own funeral. Scratching his head, he wonders, how did the party end last night.

This imaginary ghost reminded me of a very special ghost

in my life: the ghost who played cupid in my love story.

I flipped through the pages of Nano and stopped at:

~

1 January 2009. 3:00 a.m.
Dear Nano,
It's the new year, and what a way for it to start.

We just gave Rosh some sleeping pills because she wanted to rush to the bathroom every two minutes to take a bath. She's leaving tomorrow for her hometown, Dhanbad. It's a small town in Bihar. She won't even stay back to see her new hair oil advertisement on TV. This is the one where she is the main girl's friend who has split ends.

I feel pretty much like Rosh's hair in the ad—split in two different directions. One path leads to fulfilling my dream and the other to being a true friend.

What have I chosen? Like any sensible person, I've chosen me. And like any sensible person, I am trying hard to tell myself I've made the right choice.

It all started with Rosh today.

Sometimes when you get lost in a story it makes sense to start from the beginning. Rosh is a bit lost in her life story, and she needs to go back to the beginning. I know it's very difficult for her. In fact, every person who comes here from a small town has one fear. That she'll end up having to take the train back home without having achieved much.

In Rosh's case, the decision was taken by us, not her. We felt she needed some time to get over what's happened. Shikha with her overseas event, Zoya with her animation project, which would get her the elusive promotion, I with my film—none of us have the time to help Rosh heal. Not only that, somewhere deep down we all felt guilty about Rosh's situation. After all, we'd been the ones who told her to go for the assignment.

Last night, her coordinator had called, saying she had a simple assignment for Rosh. There was no shoot, all she had to do was wear a glamorous dress, go to this party in Juhu, get pictures clicked with the other guests, and come back. Quick money. Apparently the organisers wanted the party to look hip and happening, so to 'up the glam quotient', they were hiring glamorous guests. A group of ten girls would be going for the event, the coordinator said.

It was New Year's Eve, and we were all at home for different reasons. I wanted to recuperate from the hectic film schedule and I guessed Sam hadn't made definite plans with either Shikha or Zoya. I wish we had advised Rosh to stay home with us.

Rosh wasn't sure whether she should do the assignment or not. Shikha argued, 'Babes, you can go to the party and make contacts—and you are getting paid for it!'

I didn't know how I felt about it, but I told her that I'd overheard Minty do the same deal.

'Oh, by the way, Minty is going to be there too,' Rosh said excitedly. 'My coordinator works for her and she said I could meet her at the party as well!'

'This Minty runs a huge nexus,' Shikha interrupted. 'Deep pockets. She knows people in the ministry, in the police, in the business world, not to mention producers.'

'But why can't she get films for herself then, why does she only get second lead roles?' I asked.

Shikha rolled her eyes, 'Simple, she is making a lot of dough. Your waistline decides the length of your career. Now if Minty is in the business of casting others, she will continue to do so even after her face is wrapped in wrinkles and she puts on reams of fat. Long-term planning.'

Zoya, expertly rolling a joint, muttered thoughtfully, 'The thing about keeping a high-profile clientele is, you need to keep a low profile. Enough for people to know your name and not enough for media to hound you and know your every move and client.'

Wow, I thought, Minty 'the side actress' was a genius.

'Anyway, coming back to your problem Rosh, they are giving you twenty grand. I would go, if I were you. You have ten girls with you. What can go wrong?' Zoya said.

'What does your instinct say,' I said. 'Listen to it.'

'My instinct says go and take the money and buy the new iPhone so I can upload everything in a second, send pictures and be in touch with my coordinators all the time!' Rosh laughed.

Shikha giggled. Zoya blew a swirl of smoke my way as I pointedly opened the window for her. 'Very soon! I am waiting for you to come over to this side of the fence,' Zoya told me. 'We are in different worlds, you know!'

She passed the joint to Shikha who took a drag as well.

Rosh glared at them. 'It's bad for your skin and makes you put on weight. Neki Brar, promise me you are never going to cross the fence!'

I smiled at her and told her to get ready.

While Rosh was getting ready, Sam dropped in for a visit. Zoya went completely quiet, but Shikha did not notice. She was busy making plans with Sam for the night. She told him emphatically that she wanted to bring in the new year with him—alone.

Suddenly I needed some air so I went to the little balcony next to the kitchen. Sitting there, I could hear the strains of

Shikha's conversation and the strains of Zoya's silence. Then Sam and Shikha went into her room and Shikha shut the door.

I wanted to hit Sam.

Zoya came out and sat next to me in the balcony. We sat there for an hour. It was soothing. At some point Rosh said a hurried good-bye and left for the party. She looked stunning in a green dress. I forgot to tell her how pretty she looked because I was thinking of something to say to Zoya. She was pale and quiet. And she seemed focused on listening to every sound, imaginary or real, coming from Shikha's room.

After what seemed like another hour, we heard a loud thud and a door opening. We both heard Shikha scream, 'Get out!' I looked at Zoya. She was ghostly white. The main door slammed shut. Obviously Sam had left.

Just then I got a message from Ranvir on my phone. He was coming to pick me up for a quick drive in his car, he said. Since the outdoor in Manori, things had been better. The Minty episode was buried deep inside my brain, and the only thing on the surface was Ranvir's lovely messages and our clandestine meetings. Anyway, I was thrilled—he had thought of me at this time, New Year's Eve. It meant something to him. Would I need to change? I caught sight of myself in the glass: I was wearing a white sundress and a red plastic flower in my hair that Zoya had put in my long braid. I thought I looked fine and decided against changing. Suddenly, I realised Zoya was looking at me. I felt awful: I was sitting next to one of my best friends. Her heart was breaking, she was scared witless, and I was worrying about my hair and a red plastic flower.

Were we all made like that, or was it just me?

I heard Shikha crying in the living room. I knew I had to

go to her. Zoya and I exchanged a look and then I got up and went in. I was sure Sam must have confessed to Shikha that he liked someone else. Zoya came in and stood next to me. Shikha looked at us and started walking towards Zoya.

Was I supposed to intervene? Would she hit Zoya? Would she claw Zoya's eyes out or simply push her from the little balcony?

As I was going through these options in my head, a horn tooted outside three times. Ranvir.

Perfect timing.

I had the choice of seeing one of my best friends kill the other, or run down into the arms of my secret lover. Well, I was too late to avoid the murder as Shikha had pounced on Zoya.

Zoya covered her face and then realised at the same time as I did, that Shikha was not hitting her at all. She was hanging on to her, crying her heart out and abusing the girl who had stolen the love of her life. So Sam had not revealed the girl's name. God bless him.

All Zoya kept repeating was, 'I'm sorry', as she soothed Shikha. She caught my look and then said, 'It's not worth it Shikha. No one is worth destroying yourself over.'

I quietly slipped out the door, hoping the rest of my New Year's Eve would be better than it had so far. I ran down the stairs and saw a huge gleaming black Lexus by the side of the road, its headlights blinking on and off. It was parked in our back lane and I wanted to tell Ranvir it was not safe there. That drug peddlers and college kids with habits were in and out of there all the time. I ran up to the gleaming car, opened the door and got in. As soon as I saw Ranvir's handsome face, all coherence disappeared and I forgot about the advice I was going to give him.

I could smell something weird in the car. The same thing that Zoya had been smoking upstairs. Well, Ranvir was obviously on the other side of the fence as well.

'I was missing you,' he said, smiling. 'I have to go for Ahmed's party but I thought I would meet you before I leave.'

Like a starved puppy, I was happy with the crumbs he was throwing at me. In fact, I could see some strawberry jam on the crumbs as well. Ranvir had thought about me. He cared about me. After all, how many women would he make an effort to meet on New Year's Eve?

Ranvir passed the joint he was smoking to me. I was about to refuse when suddenly I felt an urge to be a part of what he was enjoying. One drag would not hurt. I tried to take one and ended up having a coughing fit. Five drags later, though, I was great at it.

'I'm not feeling a thing,' I complained. 'You think I'm immune to grass?'

Ranvir laughed. 'Let's see if you feel anything now.'

I found myself lying flat in his humungous car seat. Ranvir was on top of me, his hand pushing my dress all the way up. He used his other hand to push the seat further back. I lost all sense of place and time. Ranvir kissed me all over with an urgency that was intoxicating. I completely surrendered to his hands and his plunging mouth. His mouth tasted of mint and tobacco. I did not notice that my dress was now almost completely off, as was Ranvir's shirt. The only thing I could hear was my heartbeat. And it was getting louder. In fact, it had become a soundtrack to our lovemaking. Just then I realised that the soundtrack was not of my heart beating, but someone knocking on the window of our car. I pushed Ranvir, grabbed his shirt and covered myself. Ranvir and I looked up—it was a cop. Ranvir opened the dashboard and pulled out a pair of glasses and a cap to disguise himself. His zipper was open, his jeans were half down, torso bare, and he was wearing a cap and dark glasses. I wanted to laugh and cry at the same time, looking at him.

Ranvir rolled the window down and handed the cop a heavy wad of notes. I was trembling, and hurriedly buttoned up my dress. We waited for the cop to leave, but he took his time, deciding to give us a little lecture about bad conduct. He duly warned us about the immorality of public displays of affection in the country, duly informed us that he could put us behind bars, duly reminded us that we are from good families, and duly pocketed the crisp notes.

He turned around and left.

The atmosphere was as awkward as it had been intense just a minute ago. Ranvir buttoned up his shirt awkwardly and turned the car around. Before I slid out, he hugged me and said, 'Happy New Year, Neki.' He reached for something in the back of the car, and handed me a beautiful, slender wine bottle.

I stood outside the car for a second longer, unable to come up with something relevant to say. Finally, I simply said, 'Have fun and thank you for this.' I raised the wine bottle, shut the door and turned around. Ranvir drove away.

As I headed towards the apartment, I saw a taxi pull up in front of the building. It was Rosh. She was getting out very slowly, like she was drunk. I called out, but she didn't seem to hear me though I wasn't very far away. She continued walking towards the door. I called out her name again, and then I saw her face. She looked like she was in a state of shock. Her eyes were wide open. Unblinking. I touched her shoulder gently. She brushed my hand away and began climbing the stairs. I was right behind her, thinking the worst, the episode with Ranvir and the cop wiped out of my mind. She almost stumbled on a step and balanced herself. I did not attempt to help her. I could sense that the distance between us was important to her.

Rosh stood outside our door, simply staring at it, not attempting to reach for the handle. I reached from behind and opened it quietly to let her in. Zoya was giving Shikha a cup of coffee. Both of them looked up as Rosh walked in. She headed straight to the bathroom. Nobody said anything.

We all stood outside the bathroom for a long time. Roshni finally came out, practically white from being in water for more than an hour. When she saw us, she turned and walked back into the bathroom. This time Zoya barged in behind her, wrapped her in a towel and brought her out. Shikha, forgetting everything about Sam and heartbreak, held a glass of rum to Rosh's mouth.

After downing the rum, all Rosh said was, 'There were two Roshnis on the coordinator's list. The other Roshni was an escort; I was supposed to be there only for the photographs. But they confused me with the escort, and the guy I was with wanted his money's worth.'

None of us wanted to ask her what he'd done, how far he'd gone. We sat around her quietly till she fell into a deep sleep. Wondering if we should involve the cops. Zoya told us it was up to Rosh. A few minutes later, firecrackers went off outside. Mumbai was ushering in the new year.

Rosh got up several times in the middle of the night. She kept saying she wanted to leave the city. When we brought up going to the police, she got into a state, saying this was what her parents had warned her about, that they would never let her do anything again. Finally we had to give her some sleeping pills. During one of the times she was asleep, Zoya said, 'She needs to go back home.'

Shikha snapped, 'What about her work? She *just* shot an advert, it will take her ages to get back and make contacts when she returns.'

Zoya snapped back, 'She has to be in her senses, in control. It's a tough place. Let her go home and recover. Because I can't take days off and nurse her, you can't and I am sure Neki can't either. If one of you can, then okay, it makes sense for her to stay.'

Silence. In movies, this would be the time when the heroine steps up and says, 'I will sacrifice my career and my job and look after my friend.'

In reality, the moment is filled with awkward silence. In reality, we are all side-kicks, standing on the sidelines, bogged down by our jobs and desires.

Sometimes a dream can be the heaviest burden you carry in life. Mine was to make Technicolor films, and for that I was sending my friend back.

And all we had to offer our friend was a moment of silence. Where we knew we had a choice between being ordinary and great, we chose ordinary.

Rosh asleep, Zoya standing by the windowsill smoking, Shikha lying down staring at the ceiling, me sitting in a chair, looking at Rosh. That's how we brought in our new year.

At the brink of greatness.

## THE MISADVENTURES OF
## SHELLY THE GHOST

2 January 2009. 7:05 a.m.
Dear Nano,
Rosh left yesterday for Dhanbad, by the evening train. We all went to drop her off at VT station. The same station they show us in all the films, when the hopeful hero arrives in this city, Mumbai. This is the imposing structure that the hero sees. The structure that signifies Mumbai and everything else that follows. That assures him this is the city for him. This is the city that will help him get his place under the sun.

I stared at the beautiful building for a long time; the huge clock, the domes, the Victorian arches, the air of age and time, as if it knew the fate of every single person who arrived here. I wondered if it knew about Rosh. And if it knew what was in store for me in this city. I wondered if it knew what the city could give me, and more importantly, what it would take out of me.

I went for my shoot straight from the railway station. I was half an hour late. It was a night shoot and we were shooting a hospital sequence. The location was a real hospital—an old wing of Bhabha Ram Hospital, a municipal hospital in Bandra. They rented out this section sometimes for night shoots only. As I reached the hospital, my mind still on Rosh, the first person to greet me was Punjabi.

'Madam, tea, coffee, biscuits?'

I ignored him and walked in. Karan was briefing the rest of the team about the scene. We all knew the scene by heart and scene number, but Karan insisted on this ritual of explaining the whole thing anyway. He gave me a pointed look as I joined the group. Then continued, 'The scene we are shooting—Ahmed Khan is almost dying. Minty and Ranvir will rush down the hospital corridor with Ahmed on a stretcher. He will be operated on in the operation theatre as Ranvir and Minty wait outside teary-eyed. We are going to shoot the corridor and the operation theatre scene. Two scenes for the day. Neki, hope you have read the scene?'

'Scene number 28A and 28B. Page 32,' I muttered.

Karan paused and then looked at the others, 'Let's do a final check. Equipment?'

'Check,' Shivani said.

'Doctor's ready in costume, JA as nurses and ward boys?'

'Check.' That was PJ.

'Two main nurses?'

No one spoke. And then, Kriti said, 'Check for one, not for the other.'

Karan gave her a look and turned to Shivani. 'Make sure it's sorted out. I want the actors on set ready. First shot in the corridor of Ahmed coming in. Neki, I hope you can make sure at least Ranvir is on time.'

Before I could react, Karan left. As soon as he did, PJ erupted. 'What the fuck, dude? This is not cool!' He was glaring at Sam.

I noticed then that Sam looked a little odd and his eyes were red. Shivani was looking at Sam angrily too, and then she said, 'One mistake and I go straight to Karan and tell him you are high and tripping on acid on a SHOOT! And if that happens, you are *so* gone!'

Sam looked at her with a blank expression on his face. Shivani shook her head and left in a huff. Sam, still with that dazed expression, followed. Of course I knew why he was on drugs. Zoya had called and broken up with him before going to the railway station to drop off Rosh. And then the memory of Rosh and her face as she looked out of the train window came back to me. I had a horrible feeling in my stomach; that sinking feeling you get, like you want to throw up after eating too much ice cream in winter, is what I call regret.

I shook myself mentally and asked PJ, 'How come Karan hasn't figured out yet that Sam is high?'

'Because Sam has wisely kept his mouth shut in front of him, so Karan has not really noticed him yet. By the way, you better be careful before running off into deep dark corners with Ranvir—this place is haunted. And it's not a myth, it definitely is. And just for the record, I am not coming to save you.'

'PJ can you stop making my life miserable, please. Don't tell me this nonsense. And we both know you'll come and save me, even if I don't want you to.'

Just then Kriti came running up to us. 'Ahmed Khan has to leave early for a party, so we're taking the operation theatre shot first. Neki, get into the nurse's costume—one nurse has not turned up and you're the same build as her.'

'But so are you!' I said.

Kriti stared at me incredulously. 'I'm going to make my debut as a Hindi film heroine. I can't debut as a nurse! You can! You are never going to debut as anything, ever!'

Reality check. Not only was I a side-kick in real life but,

amongst these side-kicks making the film, I was the lowliest side-kick.

'No. Get some other nurse. PJ, I am going to check on hair and make-up.'

I walked off in a huff and bumped into Sam. He was looking at a ward boy's cap. I recognised the ward boy. It was the JA, Voltage. Sam seemed to be trying to fix Voltage's cap at a proper angle. Except he was lifting the cap and then putting it back on again. Then lifting it and putting it on himself. Voltage looked ready to hit Sam any minute. I grabbed Sam, smiled at Voltage and took Sam with me to the make-up room.

Oblivious of what he'd been doing, Sam suddenly decided to talk. 'Hey! Have you heard? PJ told me so far five light men have been killed in freak accidents on this floor. It's *haunted*. Somebody is gonna get hurt very, very bad!'

'Shut up, Sam!'

Just then I heard Karan scream in the walkie, 'Neki, change into the nurse costume now and report back on set. You are taking care of background action, so being a part of the action will help.'

I looked at my walkie, turned it on mute, and abused for the first time. Loudly and clearly. And then I heard that deep sexy voice. 'And hello to you too.' I turned around and saw Ranvir. My heart leapt. And then I saw Minty next to him. I wanted to throw up. She smiled at me and said hello. I ignored her and walked off with Sam to change into the nurse's costume.

I emerged from the changing room wearing a dress that barely covered my thighs, and white stockings. The hair and make-up artists began working on me as Karan shouted on the walkie for me yet again. He had taken it upon himself to make my life miserable. I got up and Sam, sitting by me, looked at my legs and whistled. I walked out and realised I had left Sam in the make-up room. I went back to get him. He was still staring at the place I'd been standing. Whistling. I gave him a pair of dark glasses and spoke to him slowly, 'You have an eye infection—okay?'

Sam looked at me and laughed. I sighed and dragged him along with me.

The frame was set. Ahmed Khan would be on the operating table surrounded by the doctor and two nurses, including me. In the scene, his life is hanging by a thread. He would die on the operating table—but of course (helped by Ranvir and Minty's prayers in a nearby temple) he would come back to life to avenge his killers.

'Neki, let's go for rehearsal before the actors come,' Karan said. 'Sam, stand in for Ahmed.'

'I am standing only,' Sam said with a stupid grin on his face.

'What's with the stupid glares?' Karan asked.

Before Sam could say anything, I spoke in the walkie, 'Eye infection.'

'Oh great, that's all we need. Neki, tell everyone what to do. The action is urgent—you guys are doing an operation.'

I looked over and saw Karan discussing something with Fiza behind the monitor. I turned to the doctor. 'You know how to play a doctor saving a life?'

The actor looked at me and smirked. 'I am from theatre, Madam. I can play anything!'

I was relieved. Sam had settled himself on the operation table. I whispered to him, 'Sam, pretend you are dying.'

Sam moved his head and began muttering over and over like a chant, 'I am dying, I am dying.'

'Going for rehearsal, action!'

We all moved at the same time. The doctor rushed to the table to look at Sam, as did I and the other nurse. Then we all stared at Sam, who was practically having a fit saying, 'I am dying, I am dying!'

We all stood there gawking at him till Shivani hissed in the walkie, 'Use the instruments; you are operating on him—not watching him die. And Sam is supposed to be in coma, not having an epileptic fit!'

I turned around and saw a kidney-shaped tray with gauze, a scalpel and cotton, which I handed to the doctor. Who handed it back to me, saying, 'I am not supposed to hold this.' He picked up an injection and loomed over Sam who started screaming looking at the needle.

Shivani ran up and snapped at all of us, 'What the hell—you guys! This is not a circus. Neki, there is no blood bottle and glucose bottle, get them! Karan, I will set the action, give me two minutes.'

I was glad to let Shivani take over. I went to look for PJ. He was busy putting fake blood on the sheets and other props. 'Where are the rest of the blood bottles?' I asked him.

'They are in the room at the end of the corridor. Listen, be careful—this place is haunted.'

I snapped, 'You are such a negative person PJ; just because you are not happy you want others to be sad and scared as well! You need a doctor. You are all mad here.'

'My doctor says the same thing. You know why my dad was not able to make the sequel of his film? Last day of the shoot, there was a freak accident. He fell from the building they were shooting on. Out of all the two hundred people, why was he the only one who tripped? You think it was a coincidence? I think it was predestined. He was in bed for a very long time. But you know what keeps him going? The dream of this sequel. So yes, each one of us here is mad—more or less. In fact, it's a prerequisite to be here.'

As PJ narrated this story, the entire world around me seemed suddenly black and white, like a sad film from the '40s. But that was PJ's life.

'You are all crazy,' I burst out. 'These spot boys running around, the light men, the ADs the costume people, the junior artists—shooting in the middle of the night in a haunted bloody hospital, all mad, including me in these ridiculous tights.'

PJ suddenly smirked, 'Exactly my point!'

Just then Aslam came and joined us. Nodding his head. Next to him, I saw two faces smiling and nodding their heads. As if they were very much a part of our conversation. Kamalji and Charu-di. Kamalji asked eagerly, 'Where should we sit? We are the patients!'

Aslam cut in, 'Nekiji, is everything okay? Anything production-wise you need today?'

PJ looked at Aslam and then me. Both of us knew that Aslam was never like this usually. I'd realised over the last few days though, that Aslam was hoping that Ranvir and I being a couple would get him a job as line producer on Ranvir's next film.

Kamalji interrupted again, 'If you could tell us what we are supposed to be doing in the scene and where we can place ourselves correctly?'

Aslam snapped at him. 'Which country you people live in? China? It's a municipal hospital. No rooms. No doctors. People die waiting for doctors or a room or a bed right here in the corridors. Just find any spot and pretend you are dying.' Kamalji and Charu-di glared at Aslam and walked away.

Aslam's assistant came up then and told him that Minty wanted Chinese food from China Garden. Aslam and his assistant rushed out to get it organised.

PJ muttered, 'What's the point of Aslam rushing for Chinese food. What if Minty trips and falls on a scalpel that tears her stomach, then all the food will go waste. I love Chinese. I'd hate to see it getting wasted.'

I didn't know what to do with PJ. I wanted to hug him and murder him at the same time. I chose to go fetch the fake blood bottles from the room PJ had told me they were in. The room was empty except for a few props lying around. Suddenly, I felt very weak, the sick feeling of guilt overwhelming me again. I sat down on the floor in the middle of the room holding my stomach. The door opened and Ranvir walked in.

'Why are you walking around alone in this place? You know—'

'I know it's haunted, thanks for the concern. I don't believe in ghosts!'

And then it happened. Chaos. Screaming. We both ran out. There were sparks everywhere; there must have been a major short circuit. We were all trapped in the corridor. There was only one way out and people were running towards the small exit that was at the other end of the corridor from where Ranvir and I were. I could see Fiza standing at the exit, yelling for everyone to move out. I saw Karan herding actors and crew from the operation room and pushing them towards the exit. PJ was helping the setting dadas from the art department, who were trapped in a big ventilator shaft they'd been trying to fix. PJ was the only one who remembered they were there. Kriti was screaming and running for the exit. Ranvir held me close and tried to navigate through the chaos.

Just then the sparks stopped—as suddenly as they had started. Someone had switched off the main power. The small flames on the set were put out hurriedly.

They said the whole thing lasted for about thirty seconds. I say, Bullshit.

How could it have taken me only thirty seconds to answer the question that all of us want to ask: 'Why do some people make it big and hundreds don't?' I realised that Fiza Kareem had made it big because amidst all the wrong things around us, she'd got the most important thing right. Her standing at the exit and ushering everyone to safety had given me the answer.

I could feel a pair of strong hands holding me. That was Ranvir. He kissed me repeatedly on the nape of my neck. Keeping me very close to him. Trying to keep the danger and the hysteria away. This was my 'moment'. The moment I would remember, sitting alone by the windowsill, watching a laughing couple saunter by hand-in-hand. This was the moment I would go running back to when I was alone. It was precious. Even though it happened in the middle of a dangerous situation, with sparks flying and people screaming and dark ash menacingly covering the entire corridor. It was perfect.

And I knew with time, a lot would be added to this moment. Maybe the murmur of a beautiful song in the background, or the fragrance of a wilting rose.

The dust settled. The chaos subsided. The cause of the fire remained unknown. Whispers started. It was the ghost.

Soon Aslam was telling everyone (and making them promise not to share the 'secret') that a light man had fainted just before the fire broke out, claiming he saw a woman, clad all in white, who screamed for everyone to leave this place alone. She'd said her name was 'Shelly'.

I was impressed that the ghost had introduced herself as well.

Aslam said he was personally going to sit next to the main generator and switchboard to see no ghost tampered with anything for the rest of the shoot. He turned towards me and added, 'Shelly was very beautiful too! In fact, if I get her talking, I will ask her if our film is going to be a hit and how much opening it will get—you want to know anything else?' And then he looked at Ranvir and laughed.

Obviously I wanted to strangle Aslam, and obviously no one believed him, but strangely no one was too keen to ask a very reasonable question as to how the fire started in the first place. Not to mention that it was comforting to know that Aslam was guarding us against the misadventures of Shelly.

I made sure Sam was okay—he was back on the operation table, in a state of shock—and then walked a little further to a secluded area to get some fresh, non-sooty air. And then I felt something around me as I was thinking of Shelly. Goose bumps. Aslam's nonsense was getting into my head, I reprimanded myself. A slight ruffle, a faint footstep. Maybe Shelly existed, maybe she was here. Well, there was just one question I had for her if she *was* here: what was Ranvir all about? I wanted to get to know him more. Just then a huge chunk of cardboard fell right next to my feet. I yelped. PJ saw me looking scared witless and ran up to me. It did not help my state of mind that he was laughing at me as he approached. Obviously Shelly did not approve of Ranvir.

Later, Ranvir and I sat in his van while the area was being cleared of ash. Ranvir was very quiet to begin with, as I mentally cursed Shelly for scaring the living daylights out of me. And then Ranvir started talking out of the blue—and went on for two hours. He told me how he had come to Mumbai from Ferozpur, with the dream to become a filmstar, just like everyone else. How he met up with coordinators. Went to parties. Hung around at all the 'cool' spots hoping to be noticed. Dated women much older than him. Used them to get more contacts. Got to know about political aunty, Prateeksha Devi. Wooed her. Started having an affair with her. She got him a role in his first film. Otherwise, he would have been out there, one of the many millions who had not succeeded. Who were more talented, more handsome and more deserving than he. He'd never believed in luck, so the only way Ranvir knew to fulfil his dreams was to use what he had and use it well. He had many casual flings but he stayed at the beck and call of Prateeksha Devi, and still is. He confessed that the situation would continue till he was sure his films would sell. That distributors would pick up his films. That his films would make money. He would keep this equation going till the numbers in his life made sense. He had no regrets, he said, and then asked me, 'You think what I did was wrong?'

I looked at him, and then I heard the whistle of the train. Saw the green dress Rosh wore. My discarded yellow pumps. Kamalji's photo on the wall. Punjabi's smiling face asking me if I want coffee.

Ranvir looked at me, 'You think you can live with all this—given my situation?'

'Yes,' I said.

Ranvir reached out for me and kissed me.

I had, without any hesitation, committed my heart to a person who had nothing to give me in return. In effect, Ranvir had asked me if I could live with him and his infidelity, his unapologetic need to have that third person in his life. I had said yes to both. But I felt better knowing that all wise men have to be foolish sometimes to gain their wisdom. If only Shelly could tell me what the foolishness will cost me.

## STICK JAW

Karan's voice on the walkie interrupted us. 'Okay everyone, let's move. We're all sorted. We need to finish the operation theatre scene today.'

'On my way,' I said into the walkie and walked out of the van. Confidently. I walked straight to Karan. There was no trace of the chaos from a couple of hours ago. Each and every person on the set was back at work. Shelly must be pissed, I thought.

Things started off smoothly. Shivani had given everyone clear instructions on what needed to be done and when to pick up the injection, the kidney tray, the AED.

The AED, automated external defibrillators, is of course the most favourite prop in Bollywood hospital scenes. It brings back most of our heroes to life. All the doctor has to say is, 'Charge—charge—clear', and the actor will move his body once or twice. When I played 'doctor doctor' as a kid, I had the same thing. Sam was using it like a telephone right now, sitting in a corner. 'Hello, yes, yes,' he was saying into one pad, 'we are making a commercial Hindi action film, where the hero Ahmed Khan and another hero Ranvir will save the Bank of India from getting robbed, which will save the world. We also have the famous heroine Kashish Kapoor in a guest role, who is very beautiful but unfortunately does not have a big role in the film so we don't get to see her much on the sets . . .'

Everyone was looking at him weirdly. I snatched the AED from Sam and told him to shut up.

I went back to my position.

Dharmesh sir suddenly shouted, 'What the hell is happening? Why are you moving over and over from your position? Do we want to take this shot or not? Who is that stupid nurse?'

Obviously that stupid nurse was me.

I looked towards Fiza who walked up to Dharmesh and said something.

Kriti whispered in the walkie, 'Fiza said to Dharmesh sir that the nurse is her assistant. This is her first film. She is doubling up as an actor and doing background action. Cut her some slack . . .' Kriti chuckled and continued, 'Can someone please tell Fiza the truth?'

Shivani laughed, 'I wish I could!'

To which Karan added, 'Lovely conversation people; now if only Neki would let us take this shot.'

To which PJ contributed, 'I think the ghost has gotten into Dharmesh sir. It's Shelly speaking and she will soon attack us!'

'Shut up PJ!' everyone screamed in unison.

I simply stood there on the sidelines of this conversation, furious. I vowed not to move an inch from my spot. The rehearsal began. I played the nurse perfectly. It was easy. I didn't need to have any expression on my face; just hand over equipment on cue. Sam was given the simple task of sitting out of frame and handing me the second kidney tray with some more instruments. I was not comfortable with him handling this task given his current condition, but the only person I could see around to help me was Punjabi. Obviously I let Sam handle it.

Fiza was about to say 'Action' then stopped and said, 'Shivani, set the sheets on Ahmed properly. I want the green one more visible and the red and white one tucked in.'

I continued to stand in my position, holding a tray. Shivani walked towards Ahmed with a strange expression on her face. She started pulling at the sheets. At the same time, Sam started whining, 'I hate blood. I hate violence. I want world peace!' Whatever drug he was on seemed to be working overtime.

The whole unit watched Shivani as she fumbled with the sheets. I could see her hands trembling. Sam carried on, 'You know, PJ told me during the break that in Steven Speilberg's film *The Twilight Zone*, two little kids and an actor died on the set because of a helicopter that was flying too low.'

I wanted to strangle PJ for feeding all this into Sam's head now. I could see tears welling up in Shivani's eyes. Her back was towards the monitor and Fiza.

'Hurry up, Shivani!' Karan called out.

Sam continued, 'The funny part is, in the crash everyone inside the helicopter survived. But these three did not! Now, how unfair is that? I hate choppers. I love world peace! Shivani will keep crying there, she is colour blind. I know the secret . . . only I know on the set that she can't tell between green and red. You know what that means? That means she will never be able to see the national flag of Bangladesh. I usually help her with colours, but right now I just only want world peace . . .'

Dear god! I pushed my tray into Sam's hands, rushed to Shivani and started helping her with the sheets. 'Sorry, they are tucked in very tight,' I said. Shivani looked at me, her eyes filled with tears.

Dharmesh sir shouted, 'It's that nurse again!' This time I did not pay any attention. The humiliation was less painful than before. I realised by now that I was an expert on public humiliation. And my verdict was that it is all in your hands. I could decide how humiliated I wanted to feel. Right now I could not be bothered, so the comments and the stares and the sniggers flew right past me. At least I had *something* in my control.

Shivani squeezed my hand. I looked up surprised, happy for that flash of gratitude. I needed it badly—the train's whistle from that platform was haunting me.

If pain is an antidote for pain and dreams an antidote for dreams, what is the antidote for regret? Acts of kindness, one would presume. Unfortunately, no. The gratitude remained for the acts of kindness—but so will the whistle of the train, I know.

Shivani composed herself and walked away. I caught Ranvir looking at me with a smile on his face. Fiza called for action. The actors began moving when, suddenly, Sam walked into frame. 'You have to live for world peace!' he shouted and lunged at Ahmed Khan, hugging him and crying at the same time. Ahmed Khan gaped at him, too shocked to do anything. Sam blabbered on, for some reason referring to Ahmed Khan as Stalin. If I'd known this drug evoked history lessons in your subconscious, I would have taken it in double dose before my history finals!

The shot was cut. The shades had to come off. The lie was exposed. Sam was out. The shoot was over.

The last AD meeting, at dawn, after Sam was packed off in a Sumo van with Aslam, was only about one question. Who all knew Sam was under the influence of drugs. Well the answer was, of course, no one. After braving the fire and the accidents and all the things in various shapes and sizes that one sacrifices to be here, who was going to admit something for the sake of honesty and get thrown out? So deceit won hands down.

Oh, and I was told at the meeting that I had officially moved up the AD ladder. I was the fourth AD now, Kriti was the fifth, and a new person would be the sixth. Kriti had an ADHD attack and, as usual, I was the one who triggered it off. (Though I still refuse to believe that ADHD is a recognised medical disorder.)

~

*Dear Mom,*

*Today I was immortalised on screen! I made my debut on film as a noble nurse. I get to save Ahmed Khan's life and am turning the entire plot of the story around. I looked really good. So much so that they refused to cast the other AD, Kriti, the wannabe heroine, for the role. Sam has left the team for another film. So, today, in my nurse's stockings, I move a step up the ladder. I am not the last AD anymore.*

*Rosh has gone home for a vacation. We all wanted her to stay back and celebrate the success of her promotion at work, but none of us stopped her. Now we all regret it. And regret reminds me of that sweet you got for me from a bakery in Dehra Dun—stick-jaw. Because I remember I'd brushed my teeth over and over again, but that stick-jaw remained stuck in my teeth. I think it will remain with me for years after I am gone! When I die, and my corpse reaches the skeletal state, my teeth will live on for a long time. That means so will the stick-jaw.*

*Love,*
*Neki*

# THE OBJECT OF ONE'S DESIRE

5 January 2009. 10:02 p.m.
Dear Nano,

After Roshni's train left the platform, it took away a lot from our Rose Mahal too. Our Rose Mahal with beautiful coloured windows was filling up with secrets and remorse. I had some confessions lined up already and I was sure Zoya was waiting for the right time to come clean as well.

We sat in the living room with Zoya lighting one cigarette after another, sitting on her favourite spot next to the window and hoping all her guilt would blow away in the smoke puffed out of our window. Shikha sat on the same spot for over an hour, punching away furiously on her cell, ostensibly playing a game, but to us the incessant tapping of the keys on the phone key pad was equivalent to her pain-filled cries, reminding Zoya and me of the role we'd played. I sat on the floor looking at both of them, with an old Kishore Kumar song playing in the background, his trademark yodel-oo-ing reaching our living room from a neighbour's blaring TV set. I was thinking about the train, Roshni, Shikha, Zoya and, of course, Ranvir.

After the talk with Ranvir, thanks to Shelly's intervention, I wanted to hear it being said aloud—that Ranvir and I were together. I wanted to say it in front of some people so that this association with Ranvir was not just a cerebral affair, which only existed in my head. In the language of Freud, only my conscious and subconscious mind knew about this affair. But now it was living, it was breathing, so it needed to be said when someone was listening—and then I heard myself saying aloud: 'I am seeing Ranvir Khanna. No one knows on the set, but everyone suspects.'

Shikha stopped punching buttons and Zoya's cigarette stopped mid-way. There was a question in that pause.

'Yes *the* Ranvir Khanna, the hero of my film, and yes I know there are lots of rumours about him.'

Shikha looked at me squarely and said, 'An actor, an AD, a film set—it does not even sound right.'

I closed my eyes to shut out the disapproval. I knew Zoya was of the same opinion even before I heard her say, 'Don't, Neki.'

I shut my eyes tighter and the murmur of their dissent continued for ages, with examples and arguments to show why I should reconsider my falling in love with an actor, till Smita rang the bell and asked in a high-pitched tone, 'What should I cook today? Rice, sugar and dal are over—you girls have not even ordered anything.'

None of us answered her.

Finally she made some eggs and toast and left them on the kitchen counter for us to eat later.

The eggs and toast were thrown away, untouched. Eventually, the flea-ridden dog frequenting our lane enjoyed it.

Talking about dogs, I read the other day that someone had interpreted Freud's theories in an interesting way. The person said that, according to Freud's theories, a dog's urge to bite is derived from its sexuality. That beneath the surface of both sexual and aggressive urges is an overpowering drive to connect with the object of one's desire.

Of course, knowing that the dangerous dog down the road had sexual urges behind his bark and bite did not help my phobia at all; hence I have decided to stop reading up on dog phobias.

## THE 'POODLE' LUMP

I reached behind and picked up the magazine I'd brought up to the balcony with me. *The* magazine. It was all crumpled up now. I turned it around to look at the cover page. It was the latest edition of *India Tomorrow*. And I'd made it to the cover.

A bad story needed a good face to sell it, and this one had mine on it.

Well, time to plunge back into the Nano—hoping to find some salvation. I did. In three words. Shah Rukh Khan.

~

8 January 2009. 3:42 a.m.

Dear Nano,

I would never have imagined that a person could see such highs and such lows in one day. And because I cannot bear to think about the low right now, I'll start with the high.

Today I completed a part of my journey to reach somewhere in the industry, for I met the man who rules it.

I met SRK. For forty-five minutes. Out of which forty-three were spent looking at him from a distance of twelve feet, thirty seconds from a distance of two feet and a glorious thirty seconds right in front of him. If I were to measure it with a ruler, it would be roughly twelve inches.

I reached the set at 7 a.m. sharp. It was a beautiful day.

Early mornings on the set are suspended time zones; the real world is far, far away, and the make-believe world is yet to begin. The set looks untouched, vulnerable.

Sipping a glass of hot tea, sitting on the plastic table outside the shooting floor, I watched the cleaners slowly sweeping the area. I could almost sense the huge floors yawning and stretching, waiting for the day to begin. Before the generators started, the cameras rolled, the lights were switched on and the film stars descended. It was peaceful and deserted. The huge brown gate of our set, with the number six hanging crookedly on it, stared at me.

It was the same feeling one got after pack-up, once the swanky cars left, and the generators and lights were switched off.

The beginning and end were always the same here.

Everything in between, though, constantly changed. The people, the cars and the stars. It reminded me of Siddhartha's journey once again. He had said, 'Learn from the river, it will teach you a lot. It teaches you that life is changing all the time'. I'd understood what he meant here on the set. My father would be happy I was finally finding meaning in the book he loved so much! The only thing was, I was discovering these meanings sitting on a plastic chair next to a rickety table, watching a spot boy scratching his balls.

I thought about the work lined up for me that day. The new boy—the new last AD—was a mystery to me. His confidence and attitude had been admirable. Before I could admire him anymore, he stopped coming—sick leave is what the other ADs told me. I was surprised to see how tame they were with this new guy; when I had joined, I'd been walked all over. Maybe I'd started off on the wrong foot with those yellow shoes.

Karan was still upset with me, but I did not mind. I was too happy with my elevation to fourth AD. Shivani and I were still in the 'menopause' phase of our relationship: hot and cold flushes. PJ and I were in a strange in-between zone: more than friends, less than lovers; more than colleagues, less than a couple; more than unimportant, less than the most important. Right now, PJ was one of my 'could-have-beens'.

Kriti and I were still toddlers, fighting over a toy that Kriti did not even want. Namely Ranvir's attention.

And the main hero in my story, Ranvir, was busy hiding our affair from anyone who might want to know: the actors, the crew, the godmother/girlfriend. Just then, in my drowsy state of mind, someone took advantage of me. 'Thinking about Ranvir?'

I smiled and, without thinking, said, 'Yes.' My smile vanished when I opened my eyes and saw who had asked the question. Aslam. In the same breath I said, a bit too loudly, 'No.'

Aslam grinned from ear to ear. 'Good morning Nekiji.'

He reminded me of an evil goblin with a split personality. One day he would distribute sweets to kids, and the next he would eat those kids as an after-dinner sweet dish.

Today I was the dish. I could tell from his smile.

'I hope Ranvir's driver dropped you safely to your place? After all, it was three in the morning. How do you manage to come so early to the set after such a late night?' he asked. He was practically glowing with the happiness of knowing this little secret. Secrets could anyway be so dangerous in the hands of people who would use them to their advantage, and here was mine, revealed to Aslam; a master at manipulating a secret and making a grand debut of it.

I looked at him angrily, 'Aslam stay out of this, you hear me?'

'Of course—I am just very happy for you. In fact we are all going to be working together in Ranvir's next film right? Me as the executive producer, you the chief assistant director, Prateeksha madam, the financier. It's all in-house!'

I knew Aslam was ambitious, and that he could be dangerous. Unfortunately, he was putting too much stock in my supposed influence. Plus he had evidently decided to promote himself from a line producer; he wanted me to tell Ranvir to hire him as an executive producer. It made me want to laugh. I was definitely not doing that! 'Aslam,' I started, 'I don't think—'

Just then Shivani broke up our little party by announcing, 'Neki, I am going to be looking into the background with PJ for today's shoot, we have a huge crowd today. You will be taking care of Kashish. Her hair, make-up, look, lines. Today you will be dedicated to her. The rest of the shoot we will manage.'

I was shocked. 'But you always look after the artistes. Isn't that a second AD's job?'

Perfect timing, as always, for Karan to appear. 'Your job, Neki Brar, is to do what I decide. You are being promoted for the day. Congratulations,' he said dryly.

'What is Kriti doing?'

'Kriti is unwell—the nail on her little toe got chipped, so she is not coming today,' Shivani said sarcastically.

They both left as PJ walked up to us. He was dressed all in white, as in fact was I. PJ smiled at me sheepishly. 'Wow! We look like a colour-coordinated couple!' He handed me a walkie. 'Heard your punishment for doing well and standing up to Karan is looking after the lovely, numero-uno actress in the country, Kashish Kapoor?'

I smiled. 'Actually, I'm glad. I have read a lot about her. And she's so glamorous and elegant. I mean, I am curious to see if she really is as beautiful as she looks on screen.'

Hearing me gush, PJ's smile disappeared. 'I don't want to burst your bubble kiddo, but if you get through today okay, I will take you out for dinner. And dessert. And some much needed vodka!'

'Stop exaggerating!' I laughed and began walking towards Kashish's make-up van. 'Besides she is only shooting with us for the next ten days! How bad can it be? And how horrid can she be? We should give everyone a fair chance—I don't believe in stereotypes.'

Shaking his head, PJ looked at me with a pitying expression on his face. 'Whatever novel you are reading these days, please burn it! Stereotypes exist for a reason.'

I made a fake smiley face and walked up to Kashish Kapoor's pista green van. A paper was stuck on the door, on which was scrawled 'Kashish Kapoor'. Suddenly, a hand emerged from inside the van, plucked the paper and tore it to shreds. Long, pink manicured nails were at the end of each finger—one of those fingers was now pointed towards me. 'Yes . . . who are you?' a nasal voice demanded. I looked at the person who belonged to the hand. The person had blonde, waist-length (fake) hair. Was wearing flowing linen pants under which I could see a pink thong peeping out cheekily. And had a man's face.

'Let's not be tacky here,' the person continued, pointing to the shreds of paper. 'Use a nice font, make the name bigger, get the paper laminated and then stick it back on the van door. Make sure you make it capital K!'

Before I could respond, Aslam—who had somehow materialised next to me—piped up, 'Will be done, Ginniji. There are chocolates and flowers, compliments of Show-Bizz Productions. Hope everything is comfortable?'

Ginni obviously thought it beneath her to reply. Instead, she asked, 'Is that tart and a half ready? I want her hair, make-up and costume details on my table before Kashish comes in. Got it?'

I realised the tart and a half here was Minty.

Aslam, unsurprisingly, acted like a saviour again—that is, he saved himself and offered me up as the lamb to slaughter. 'That Nekiji will be taking care of. Any information you want regarding the creative aspect of the shoot today, or Minty, just ask Nekiji. I will take your leave.' And he darted off.

Meekly, I mumbled, 'I will leave with him and be right back with the creative information you asked for ...' and scampered behind Aslam, who was scurrying away in his ridiculous white pants and bright orange shirt. He was a walking blot on the landscape and very hard to miss.

I caught him inside the set floor. Just before I could start in on him, Karan said over the walkie, 'Neki, Minty's assistant is coming over—can you explain the sequence we are going to shoot today?'

In what seemed to be less than a minute, Minty's assistant was in front of me, staring at me with her beady eyes. Aslam skipped away again and I rattled off the scene to her. 'It is a pre-climax dance sequence. Parts of the pre-climax song and scene are being shot today. Kashish and Minty are getting engaged to their respective heroes in the party when they realise their boyfriends are involved in a crime. Then there is the confrontation scene where they realise the boys are actually undercover agents.'

The girl stared at me for a second and said, 'And?'

'Uh, and this is where it all happens,' I said, waving my hand around to indicate the huge hall decorated with exotic flowers, peach and pink satin drapes.

'I know the story of the film! All pre-climax song and dance sequences are the same—but what is Kashish wearing?'

'Oh! Okay . . . umm . . . I am trying to figure it out. I will touch base with you as soon as I know.'

The girl's mouth stretched in what I supposed was a smile and she said, 'Of course, take your time. You have twenty minutes.'

The day was not turning out well. On the bright side, I saw PJ, Shivani and Karan running around, getting the JAs in costume, getting the dancers ready, checking equipment. I had escaped all the hard work.

I spotted the bright orange with streaks of white having a cigarette in a dark corner. I marched over to him 'Okay! Out with it . . . what did that man in a thong want? What is the scene with him or her or whatever?'

'It's simple. Kashish wants to know what Minty is wearing. Minty wants to know what Kashish is wearing,' Aslam said innocently.

I knew Aslam too well to believe that was all there was to it. 'Thank you very much Aslam, but I have figured that out already. What are you not telling me?'

'Well, basically, you have to be tactful and not annoy either of the heroines, and make sure they reach the set on time.'

This was ridiculous. This was not what I was here to do. I loaded off on Aslam. 'But they teach all this in public relations courses. Diplomats need these skills; ADs are not trained for this. We are supposed to help the director in telling the story correctly.'

Aslam gave me that perfect smile again. 'That's what you are doing! And very soon you will be telling your own story, with your own ADs!'

I looked at him squarely in the eye. 'Aslam that film you are thinking of is not happening. I don't care what you tell to whom, but you will have to talk to Ranvir if you want to do his film. It's not fair to ask for favours. You know it's his film and his money. But when I make my film, I promise I will take you as the executive producer,' I said smiling, expecting him to jump with joy. I had given him my word.

Aslam simply jumped on the butt of his cigarette. Obviously my words meant nothing to him. He looked up with a smile, 'That's fair. And I'll also be fair and tell you to be careful when you two do things in a car. Mumbai police can make a case against you for indecent public display of affection. P dot D dot A, Madam! That cop is very much in touch with Dohaji—after-sales service after all.'

It felt like a tight slap on my face, the kind that leaves angry red marks. I had to talk to Ranvir and convince him to give his hundred-year-old driver Dohaji the boot. Ranvir had told me that the cop had recognised him and gotten in touch with his driver Dohaji for more money. It was definitely time for Dohaji to retire. His tongue along with his asthma was getting dangerous for himself and people around. I felt bad for the driver, but he was giving out personal details about Ranvir. It was dangerous, I told myself.

As Aslam was getting into his air-conditioned production room to sign the bills for the day, I called out to him. 'Aslam, last question—is that a girl or a boy? What should I call him or her—Ginniji?'

Aslam stopped, turned around, and came all the way back to where I was standing. 'You look very nice in your white overalls. Ginniji likes cute girls, she will like you. She is the number one hair and make-up person in the industry. She knows all the secrets of the stars. Means they all respect her. So treat her with respect and don't call her Ginniji, call her Gajendraji. That was her name before the sex change operation. When you get close to Gajendra, close enough to be in the inner circle, is when you call her Ginni.'

I smiled at Aslam gratefully. 'I owe you one.'

Aslam looked at me and smirked. 'Yes, you do.'

I realised Aslam and I had a warped affiliation—the kind that cannot be measured, labelled or relied on. It was like a daily weather report. Some days reported thunder showers and some days boasted of warm sunshine. And one could never accurately predict what it would be like the next day. We were enemies. We were allies. We had no emotional ties with each other. In some crazy way, it could be called pure and uncomplicated too. I trusted Aslam the most on the set, to get me information; and I mistrusted Aslam the most on the set. We were in this relationship owing to mutual need and we did not have to pretend otherwise; that was the beauty of it. If someone were to ask me if disliked Aslam, I would not be able to say an emphatic yes; and if someone were to ask me if I liked Aslam, I would not be able to say no either.

As I stood there, wondering how to handle the two actresses, I saw Ranvir's spot, Inder, waving at me. Ranvir was here! I ran into his van to greet him.

He was gulping down some coffee as I entered. He got up and hugged me tight. The day was looking up again. 'Are you coming over in the evening?' he asked. 'I could press your feet if you get tired!'

I laughed. 'I'll think about it!'

Just then I saw a face peering at us through the van door. It was Ginniji, aka Gajendra Singh. Ranvir ended the hug awkwardly. Ginni walked in and gushed over Ranvir. And then she turned towards me, her face transformed into an expressionless mask. 'Honey can you get me the details I asked for? I can't start work. Actually, we can talk in that van, this hunk has to get dressed here!'

I knew I had to follow Ginniji out to the other van. I started walking behind her, wondering what Freud or Sid would say about the peek-a-boo thong. At the van, she turned and ordered, 'Wait here till you are called in,' as if she were addressing her pet dog. And I bet it would be a poodle.

I swallowed a lump. It was not a teary lump, nor was it painful, it was just a cold lump. Generally a lump can have various meanings—irregular shape or mass, a small cube of sugar, a collection or totality—but on a film set, this cold 'poodle' lump only meant one thing: humiliation. And this was handed freely and happily to one and all in different shapes and sizes—till you managed to race ahead of it all.

I braced myself for more as I stared at the van door, waiting for my orders to walk in.

## THREE LETTERS, ONE WORD—SRK

The van door opened and a spot boy stepped out. He had a funny Charlie Chaplin moustache. I smiled nervously and he grunted. It was a sign that I was being summoned in. I stepped into the van, wondering whether to call this person Ginni or Gajendra, like Aslam had recommended. But the moment I looked up, all thoughts flew from my mind. Kashish Kapoor was in there. Two things struck me. First, her pale beauty. She was half-sitting half-reclining on the couch in the van. Every detail on her face was familiar, but she was not the same beauty one revered on screen. There was a difference. Right now boredom and haughtiness were writ large on her face and she seemed to have the same beauty one saw in a cold, expensive glass vase. The problem with that is, if the vase breaks from a careless push, there is always another one to replace it.

The second thing that struck me was Ginni's anger. Furiously, she said, 'Kashish has been waiting for ten minutes! What have you got?'

In my head I knew this was a sensitive moment. I did not know what dress Minty was wearing. I was not supposed to look into the main actors' costumes for the day and I was given this job last minute. Shivani was in charge of this. I should tell Karan or Shivani to handle this.

'Gajendraji, please give me ten minutes.'

Gajendra's eyes widened. 'What did you say? What did you call me?'

I continued my babbling, 'Gajendraji, I will get Karan to tell you all the details.'

And then I saw, for the first time in my life, a person practically frothing at the mouth. She was so overcome with anger, even Kashish moved into a sitting position.

Ginni stared at me with bloodshot eyes. '*Gajendra*? How dare you call me *Gajendra*? You brainless whoever you are! I am Ginni, and all you can call me is Madam. And tell me the details of the dress now or—'

I had to say something. I was sure she was going to hit me. I blurted, 'Minty's dress is pink with orange shades.' I vaguely remembered the outfit from one of the trials.

'What?' shrieked Kashish. 'That's my colour!'

'See this conspiracy . . . that slut Minty is trying to steal the show in your joint performance. But we are prepared for it—we have another costume. Thank god we insisted Mohnish give us another option for the song. Anyway I liked this one better than the other,' Ginni said as she picked up a dress. It was blue and green and it was stunning.

I was about to leave, wondering if I needed to tell anyone about this change in costume when I heard another commanding question.

Ginni was staring at me suspiciously, traces of anger still on her face. 'What is her hair like?'

For some reason I was feeling guilty, as if I actually *was* part of some conspiracy. 'Long and wavy . . .'

'That's what I was going to do, but it's okay, I can go for the bun. It accentuates my cheekbones,' Kashish said. 'Use shade three to cut the face today. If the costume is blue use shade two for body tinting. The back is very low so we'll need to cover that. And my legs will show in the cut. They are not as toned as I want them to be, get me tie-ups to go with these. Also my arms are looking big today . . .' Kashish was looking in the mirror with utmost concentration.

I wondered if I'd ever woken up in the morning to find my arms bigger than the night before. And I was convinced this was not the Kashish Kapoor I admired on screen. She was someone who was trying hard to be *the* Kashish Kapoor fans loved and admired. But she didn't come close to it. I knew this because, all this while, she hadn't acknowledged a living, breathing, croaking human being standing two feet away from her. In her films, people fell in love with her because of her warm, light green eyes, her humanity, her warmth, her effervescence. In reality, Kashish Kapoor was a fraud.

Ginni turned to the actress and said, 'You don't need any make-up. You are stunning from the time you wake up!'

As I stood there looking at Ginni fawning over Kashish, I realised this was like a piece out of an exaggerated article in a bad gossip magazine. Except it was happening right in front of me. This was a performance I assumed Ginni had to repeat every single morning. It was a sad, sad job.

'I will have to inform my seniors about the changes—the looks are decided beforehand with the director . . .'

Ginni looked at me disdainfully. 'I know and I will inform whoever needs to be informed.' Before I could say anything else, two well-dressed girls with pretty, elfin faces walked into the van, holding some accessories. I was pushed into a corner near the toilet cubicle. I felt like an ugly showpiece standing in the middle of a tastefully-done living room. I was spoiling the décor. I suddenly remembered where I'd seen the fashionably-dressed girls. They were the famous designer Mohnish Singh's assistants. He exclusively did costumes for all the top actresses in the industry.

I decided to sneak out of the van. I held my breath, praying no one would notice my exit. It was easy. They had stopped noticing my existence precisely five minutes ago.

As I left the van, I saw Kashish plonk down on the couch. 'Girls, please be darlings and get me out of this. Need to try the blue one out.' I caught Kashish's eye. She was looking at me, giving me a once over. I was sneaking out of her van like a criminal, and she was basking in attention. I was cringing, and she was feeding on my discomfort. I made her feel like a star. The sad part was, she needed me to feel like a star.

Just then I saw PJ rushing inside the set with a prop. He saw me and winked, 'What do you say about the vodka now?'

I looked at him with a straight face. 'I'd like a bottle please. And if I happen to see any of Kashish Kapoor's movies, please just shoot me.'

PJ bowed, 'The pleasure will be all mine!'

'I feel cheated!' I cried. 'All these years, going for a film only because she's in it. What a waste of emotion!'

PJ laughed, 'Relax, Neki! Don't be in a hurry to give up on your star idols. Wait till you meet the *real* star.'

'What? Who?' And then it dawned on me. Of course. He was coming on the set today. The man himself—Shah Rukh Khan. He was doing a cameo appearance in the pre-climax song.

'Also, there's a message from Karan—he says if you are going to swoon when you meet SRK, it would be better if you take the day off.'

'Ya right, I'm not leaving this set even if ten wild horses tried to drag me out today!'

PJ chuckled as I turned around. I saw Ranvir's van and I remembered I had to tell him something urgently. His make-up was being applied when I walked into his van. 'Can I have a word with you?' I asked. My tone was a clear indication for Ranvir's make-up guy to step out of the van. Half of Ranvir's face was smooth and done up with make-up, and the other brown and bare. He looked weird, but handsome. I looked into his chocolate brown eyes. Ranvir instinctively knew there was something wrong. He touched my arm gently and came closer.

'What is it, Neki?'

Ranvir's closeness, his hand and his tone gave me confidence. I said, 'You know your driver, Dohaji? He's been telling stuff to people, about us. That I come over to your place, what time I reached home, even about that blackmailing cop. I think you will have to change him if you don't want stories about us floating around.'

His hand left my arm and I realised the handsome face had hardened considerably. He took a step back. I felt a direct blast of cold AC hit me; there was space between us now. Ranvir looked at me and simply said, 'No.' Then he turned to face the mirror and started dabbing his face with the soft white muslin cloth lying on the dresser.

I was confused. 'But you always get paranoid about people knowing about us, no? Now Dohaji has been telling stories to Aslam and god knows who else. Suddenly it does not matter to you?'

Ranvir looked at me in the mirror and said, 'You do know my first solo film is releasing next week? And Prateeksha Devi is signing a big budget film with me as the lead soon. This Fiza Kareem's film is being considered a super-hit already. The buzz in the market is that I am the next discovery in Bollywood.'

'What does that have to do with you firing your driver?'

'You know who Dohaji is? He has been in the industry for forty years!'

I still did not get his point. 'Okay, so maybe it's time he retires because he cannot see the traffic signals any longer. You need to hire a driver to drive your driver around!'

Ranvir threw down the muslin cloth and turned his chair towards me. He grabbed my arms and pulled me. I almost stumbled onto his lap. I could feel the raw anger radiating from Ranvir's body. There was something I was missing here.

'Neki, you don't understand these things!'

I heard some noise coming from the van door. I knew the make-up guy had left it open. This little scene was going to go all the way back to the senile old Dohaji. I had made an enemy.

'What is there to understand?' I said, trying to find answers in Ranvir's face, which was inches away from mine.

'That Dohaji has been part of the industry for four decades. Whichever actor he has worked with has become a superstar. You know why people hire Dohaji? Because he makes them a star. Understand?'

I started laughing. I shrugged his hands off me and laughed till tears came out of my eyes. This was beyond ridiculous. I realised that Ranvir was as crazy as the rest of the lot. I could see he was feeling a little sheepish now. He simply caught my hand and kissed me to stop me from laughing anymore. After a minute I pulled away and moved back but Ranvir continued to hold me. 'I know you think I am mad. The whole industry knows about this legend. And this legend is on my side. I don't want to take a chance. He is writing my success story. I am not letting him go. You can see how everything around me is falling in place.'

I scoffed at him. 'You are saying all those people became superstars because they had the same driver? Why don't they keep Dohaji in a museum and get people to pay to look at him? You believe in all this? That your success has nothing to do with your hard work and passion, but with your driver?'

And then Ranvir finally said something that made sense to me. 'When the stakes are high, and nothing is in your control, the only thing you have is your belief. And mine is unshakable.'

I saw that look in his eyes. He was desperate for me to understand his desperation. I simply hugged him. There was no point rationalising with Ranvir. Because beliefs can't be rationalised. They define the wise, they drive the fools, they steer the leaders, they bundle the followers. All you need to live a long lifetime meaningfully, is a small belief. If Ranvir, the star of tomorrow, believed his future would be better because of his driver, then so be it.

Just then I heard PJ on the walkie, 'Neki! Ginni and Minty are both looking for you. Urgently!'

I ran towards the door, then turned around, 'You know, maybe you are right. Dohaji may be an antique, but he is special . . .'

Ranvir laughed as I headed towards Minty's van. When I entered, Minty was busy working on a crossword, partially hidden behind a haze of cigarette smoke. She did not acknowledge my greeting. I cleared my throat and said, 'Uh, your assistant wanted—'

Minty cut me off. 'So what is Kashish's costume going to be for the day?'

'Well, she just said it's supposed to be orange and red, and her hair wavy and loose, but . . .'

Minty's phone rang and she stopped listening to me. Just

then the walkie crackled. It was Shivani. 'Fiza is calling for you on set now!' she said.

I ran out of the van and into the set as fast as my legs could carry me. PJ and Karan were already standing there. Shvani was whispering something in Fiza's ear. Fiza looked at me, 'All okay? Kashish's make-up has started?'

'Yes Ma'am, she will be on the set in the next forty minutes.'

Fiza smiled and nodded. I had impressed her with my competent response. And I did not want to spoil it by adding any details. I pulled Shivani away and told her about the costume fight. Shivani looked at me angrily, 'Is there one thing you *can* handle?'

'I'm sorry. Can you let Fiza know that Kashish is wearing blue?'

'Fine, whatever, just get her out of that make-up van within the hour.'

Then something happened that seemed to change everything on the set. A buzz slowly started and spread quickly: Shah Rukh Khan was due to arrive any minute. I tried to breathe normally. I had prepared myself not to gape or faint. My mother had emailed to say she was going to the temple to celebrate this landmark day of my career, and she would be expecting a picture of me posing with Shah Rukh Khan, to say the least. Also that my bai had asked for an autograph which she said she would show to the slut her husband was having an affair with because the old hag loved Shah Rukh too.

I have to confess, I'd grown a bit immune to stars after working on the set for over four months. Many had dropped in on the sets to say hi to Fiza—all the Khans and the Kapoors—but this was different.

I knew there was a difference because, after I'd got back from Ranvir's place, I'd stayed up to charge my camera battery for my picture with Shah Rukh Khan. The plug point in my room is loose, so I'd had to sit down next to the outlet, holding the plug in a particular position for the forty minutes the battery took to charge.

I walked out of the set to tell Kashish she had to be ready in forty minutes, and I saw a van standing at a little distance from all the others. It seemed like a regular van, but it was majestic. After all, it had three letters stuck on the door.

SRK.

The words were crooked, the font was small, but it looked grand. I wished I could show Ginniji it was not about the font or the size of the letters.

Just then Aslam came up to me. 'You know, the industry is a family. Dohaji knows everything and he is very upset. You need to go and apologise.'

'Are you mad? I am not apologising for anything. And Aslam, why did you tell me to call Ginni Gajender?'

Aslam smiled, 'Come on Nekiji, that was a joke.'

I realised that for Aslam and me, the weather report for the next few days would only show thunder showers with hail storms for additional suffering.

'You played me,' I glared at Aslam, still reeling from the realisation that Aslam had set me up so ruthlessly.

Aslam looked down for a second, I thought perhaps guilt flitted past for a second, but I realised it was a sarcastic smile.

'I am allowed some fun too. You people will go ahead and make films, become friends with stars and producers. I have been in the business all my life and I still struggle to get projects as a line producer. I have seen many actors and directors grow in front of me, but even now, every time, I have to go to *you* ADs to get a call sheet paper signed. You think just because you know the creative you know everything. I know the mistakes you make before you even make them!'

'What's your point Aslam?'

Aslam realised he had revealed something he should not have—his resentment towards the system and the established way of working in this film set-up.

'The point is, I have spent all my life here and I am still taking orders from flunkies half my age to humour them—so sometimes *they* humour me. Like it was a funny incident today Nekiji . . . it was a joke. Like I said, I am allowed to have some fun.' Aslam was still smiling but his shifty eyes were hard.

I glared at him, but was reluctant to press the issue further. I needed Aslam as an ally. And Aslam knew that. So I just turned and walked away.

When I think about it, I can't believe the mistake I made that day. I ignored and pissed off the small fish on the set. And then I landed in the frying pan. Towards the end of the day I was being served with tartar sauce on the set, and I hate the smell of that sauce.

The next hour passed in a whirl of activity. While the actresses were getting ready, I ran errands for Ginniji. Ahmed and Ranvir had given two shots already. Now, the pre-climax song blared in the background. In between placing the junior artists, ordering the tea and snacks for the actresses, fighting with Aslam yet again, I heard snippets of conversation—how SRK had made it in Mumbai.

Everyone knew the story, but it continued to be told. It wasn't a story anymore; it was a fable.

While I waited for Punjabi to give me a glass of water, I heard SRK had come to Mumbai with only his convictions.

While I waited in the scorching heat for Ginniji to open the van door and tell me how long Kashish would take for her make-up, I heard how SRK had struggled. He had known no one in the industry. He was not an insider like the star kids were.

Listening to Shah Rukh Khan's success story, the heat was bearable, the glass was less dirty and the tepid water was cold and refreshing. Ginni's attitude towards me was bearable because there was something warming my heart. It was hope. I did not mind this at all.

I started rounding up the JAs for the party scene inside. We had been promised two hundred JAs and fifty were missing from the set. They were all dressed up in formal party attire, but most of them were hiding in corners, taking a nap. The older women had taken off their uncomfortable high heels and were fanning themselves with makeshift fans. I looked at the tired swollen feet and guilty smiles. I ignored them and took the other lazy ones back on the set.

A few glasses of champagne were handed around and I instructed the JAs to laugh and talk to each other. They glared at me, annoyed about being hauled back on to the hot set. Karan screamed for a rehearsal, and as if a button had been switched on, the JAs smiled and turned to each other like long-lost friends.

Kamalji called out to me. He was smartly dressed and held a glass of coloured liquid in his hand. 'I heard SRK is coming on the set?' he asked. I nodded and moved away to help Shivani place the JAs. Kamalji followed me like a shadow. He told me how he and his family went almost every Sunday to look at the house SRK lived in at Bandstand. All the way there just to look at where the star lived. He wanted an autograph, he said, if I could get him one. I was wondering who was going to get *me* an autograph. But I nodded.

That was it. A part of the puzzle, a small reason for the big phenomenon called SRK. He represented a dream. His story made people believe in Santa Claus and in wishing fountains. It was the fantasy we needed to live our reality.

What a crushing burden for a man to carry.

I heard Fiza shout on the set, 'We are running an hour late! Where are the girls?'

I was just telling Fiza that Kashish and Minty would be on the set and ready to shoot in the next two minutes when the whole set crackled with energy. Fiza immediately moved towards the entrance. It was as if the whole room shifted.

SRK had arrived on the set.

## THE ENCOUNTER

I could barely see through the throng of people surrounding him. My first glimpse of the real Shah Rukh Khan. I knew why he was a star: he commanded attention and you had no choice but to give in. I was at the other end of the set, but I could not move. I saw him say hello to everyone. He hugged many people and greeted them warmly. And then he went to his van to get ready.

The whole set was charged. My hands were clammy.

Fiza disappeared and returned ten minutes later with SRK, dressed in a dapper suit. I stared at him from a distance. Not daring to go too near. SRK and Fiza sat behind the monitor. The on-set photographer had gone berserk taking pictures and everyone from Punjabi to Kamalji and the immobile me wanted to be in that photograph. I *had* to go up and get a picture with him taken with my camera. I was forcing myself to start walking when I heard Fiza call my name. I froze. 'Neki, please tell Shah Rukh his lines for the song.'

My heart stopped. I walked towards the figure sitting next to Fiza. My throat was parched. The paper in my hand with the lyrics was shaking. I saw him lean over to me as I sat down next to him. 'Hi darling,' he said.

And I said—nothing.

Absolutely nothing.

It seemed the whole set had disappeared and all I had were these lyrics dancing in front of me. And they refused to come out of my mouth. Finally I managed the first line, fumbling over it like an idiot. He waited patiently for me to form the words. I guess he was used to people reacting to his presence in strange ways. I felt like I understood the real reason behind the superstardom this man had seen. I can't wait to tell you. But let me finish writing about the encounter first.

So there I was, fumbling with the lyrics, which said a million things about my hyper state of mind. I knew Shivani was waiting behind me, ready to kill me. I was a stuttering fool. Those were the thirty seconds I was close to SRK—and they were over before I knew it. I looked at SRK politely after I was done. I knew I had merely mumbled the lyrics of the song he was supposed to sing. He simply smiled.

Just then Ahmed Khan and party surrounded him. I needed some fresh air before I fainted, so I walked towards the entrance of the door. I stepped out into the bright sunlight, desperate to call my mother and tell her that I'd finally met SRK. As I fumbled for my phone, I heard a voice.

'Neki, what the hell is this?'

It registered. I turned to look. And then I kept looking. Minty and Kashish were finally ready. They were two hours late. They both looked breathtakingly beautiful—and IDENTICAL. Both were in blue and green outfits and had their hair up in buns. If I'd been allowed into their vans even once, I could have seen what was happening and raised an alarm, I could have averted this disaster, but I'd been shooed away by Ginniji and Minty's entourage every time I'd gone to check if they were ready. That was the thing about being the fourth AD—I could be shooed away easily. And I had a feeling that in the next few minutes I was going to be shooed off the film set—forever.

Fiza stepped out of the set and stopped short. 'Neki ... what the hell happened?' she asked sternly.

Immediately there were accusations and counter accusations. By now the entire crew on the set was surrounding us. They had all smelt a disaster and they were here to savour it.

I looked at Shivani, who was red with anger. She had forgotten to tell Fiza about the change in the costume as well—and now both the actors had turned up in similar costumes! Ginniji had said she would inform people, but I could not blame her either. Fiza had given *me* the responsibility and I had fallen short—I should have rung the alarm bells that the actors were not wearing the pre-decided costumes to avert a disaster like this: turning up on the set after hours of make-up, looking like Siamese twins. In another universe and another era, I would definitely have found it funny, but right now, staring at various shades of shimmering blue reflected from both the designer gowns, I was only frightened. I realised two things: one I would never wear a blue gown, and two, that no matter what, the actor is *never* at fault on the set. And by extension of this rule, anything that does go wrong in *any* department on the set is an AD's fault. The lower on the ladder, the more the blame. I had to quickly come to terms with the fact that it was *all* my fault. Fiza was screaming at me. And when she stopped, Karan took over. The whole set was quiet and watching. I didn't register the angry words coming out of his mouth. Then Ginni joined in and launched a fresh attack on me, my incompetence and my 'preoccupation' with the male actors.

This was getting big and this was getting ugly.

Just then Ranvir walked up. By now Kashish had walked

back to her van after threatening to leave altogether if Minty did not change in the next five minutes. Minty, of course, had refused, and in between all this everyone was blaming me.

From the 'funny' girl on the set, I was the 'idiot'.

It takes no time at all for your title to change here.

I heard Ranvir say, 'Come on guys, just sort it out.' He walked off too.

Aslam cleared his throat and said, 'We need the floor empty by 11 p.m. There is another booking.'

That started a fresh spate of yelling till someone said, 'We will just get Minty ready in the next twenty minutes.' That was PJ.

Then someone said, 'I will call you Fiza; it'll finish on time, don't worry.' That was Karan.

Fiza stomped off in a huff.

Then a voice said, 'I'm sorry. We will sort it out.' That was Shivani. She was handing me a tissue paper. I had not realised that tears were streaming down my face.

Then a sympathetic voice said, 'Ma'am, tea, coffee, Pepsi?' This time I knew exactly who it was. Punjabi.

That was it. I heard myself say loudly, 'I quit.'

Karan glared at me. 'You can't just quit like that. Wait till the end of the day. You need to hand over information and responsibilities. Nobody quits as per their own sweet will!'

I looked at him, my nose running. Tears still streaming down. 'I quit,' I said again.

'Fine,' Karan barked. 'But quit after pack-up, you hear me?'

Just then Ginni butt in. 'They all quit. So many girls like you come and go ... this place is not for everybody. And by the way, I need another wig. The wavy one. In two minutes.'

Maybe she was right, I thought. This place was not for me. I started walking out of the set. I heard Shivani tell Ginni that she would get her the wig she wanted. PJ ran after me. 'Neki, relax and sit in the van. Cool down, okay. I'll just be back. I'll hand over the walkie to Karan and be right back okay?'

I nodded. PJ turned around. And so did I. PJ walked inside the set and I walked out the main gate and kept walking. I hit the road. I passed all the parked make-up vans and the main gate which said 'Dadabhai Phalke Film City'. Leaving the lights, the cameras, the set, the action and the accusations far, far behind.

# MY STAR IN SHINING ARMOUR

I continued to walk, cursing all the spiritual and motivation gurus and theories that existed, cursing our family astrologer Dubeyji who had predicted my success. I passed the green fields, the huts, the meadows and the barns till I reached a long, winding, narrow road. I sat down by the side of the road, my sense of utter failure numbing everything else, along with common sense.

I drew circles in the mud with my hand. It was comforting. I tried to make plans for my life ahead. It was blank. I cried for all the things I'd thought I could do; Ginni was right, I was wrong about me. They had all decided that I was not good enough.

What hurt the most was—they were right.

I realised it was dusk already. I had to go back and apologise and quit gracefully. But to quit I had to find my way back to the sets first. I was lost, I realised, and then another feeling settled in the pit of my stomach. I could smell it. It was getting stronger by the minute.

The lonely road, the desolate open jungle, the casual conversations over a glass of wine about leopards being spotted in Film City, and the fading light replayed in my mind.

That feeling I could smell was gut-wrenching fear.

I started walking back in the direction I thought I'd come from. I took my shoes off so I could walk faster. After fifteen minutes, I was ready to give up.

Just then I heard a noise. The whirring of a tired old two-wheeler. And then I heard a familiar voice. It was Kamalji and PJ, sitting on a rickety scooter. I looked at them and this time I knew I was crying.

PJ leapt off the scooter and hugged me as Kamalji said, 'We saw you leave. I know this area like the back of my hand, we just grabbed someone's scooter and we were looking for you. I told him I have lived all my life here, I know the roads like the back of my hand. Oh and this is the place where they spotted the leopard by the way.'

As Kamalji was rattling on in his stylish but crumpled black suit, I sobbed in PJ's arms. A strange emptiness seemed to be filling me. We stood in that narrow road hugging, with the dark valley behind us and Kamalji holding the scooter, talking about the leopard, for a long time.

Kamalji was uncomfortable. I knew this because he was chatting non-stop and when people are awkward, they hide behind incessant talk. 'We are at the helipad area of Film City,' Kamalji was saying. 'This road climbs all the way up to a muddy plateau. One song from that film *Main Hoon Na* was shot on that helipad. I was one of the JAs in it.'

Finally PJ knew I was ready to go. The ride back was memorable. I was sandwiched between PJ and Kamalji. PJ held me tight, as if scared that I would jump off the scooter. By the time the ten-minute ride ended, I was sore but calm.

I got off the scooter and told PJ and Kamalji I would come inside after a few minutes. They left me standing on the pavement looking at Floor no. 6, where we were shooting.

I was bidding a silent goodbye.

I heard a click, and then a flash hit my eye. It was blinding. I looked. It was the guy who had been clicking continuity pictures on the set. He clicked another picture of me and smiled. A sign—my moment of defeat marked and documented on camera.

I turned away.

As I was finishing my very long and very silent adieu, I saw a silver BMW with tinted windows approaching the exit gate.

The whispers around me said, 'He is leaving.'

So God had been kind enough to give me a chance to say bye to him as well. SRK.

As I watched the car go by, it stopped. Right in front of me.

The black window rolled down, revealing the stunning profile of this demi-god. He looked out the window, straight at me. Then he gave a small wave and said, 'Thanks darling. All the best.'

I was stunned.

I lifted a limp hand in a wave.

He smiled.

PJ was right, I had to meet the real star before I gave up my faith in them.

With a final wave, the window slid up, the car went away and what was left behind was—euphoria.

In the huge crowd of hundred-odd people, he had stopped for me. And said those words, to me. When millions were looking at him, his eyes had stopped and looked at me, even if only for a second.

It all meant one thing and one thing only. My dream was not over yet. And no one could ever tell me otherwise.

I wiped my tears for the last time and walked back to the

set. Seconds ago, I'd been ready to move on and now, I was ready to die here. It takes that long for lives to change. A second. And obviously, a star.

I heard PJ say in the walkie, 'Guys, Neki is here, I'm taking her to the costume room.'

When we were there, Karan walked in. He looked at me for some time. Trying to figure out his next move.

Karan put my walkie in my hand and adjusted the frequency slowly; then he spoke into his walkie, his eyes not leaving my face. 'Neki, can you get Kashish on the set please?'

Shivani, PJ and Karan waited with bated breath.

This was the moment when we stopped being colleagues and started being friends.

My answer would give Karan his answer. With this question, he was giving me a chance to stay on.

I lifted the walkie to my mouth and said, 'Sure thing, Karan.'

I walked out confidently towards the van to call Kashish on the set. A couple of minutes later, I walked back on the set with Kashish. She was all dolled up. She resembled the actress the nation loved. But I knew it was not her. Like diamonds, if you work very closely with the stars, you get to know who the real ones are. Their brilliance is unmatched.

We neared the monitors. Fiza turned around. I knew I would find out in the next two seconds if I was staying on.

'Go to your mark darling,' Fiza told Kashish. The actress went off in that direction. Fiza looked at me and said into the mike, 'Can you please get Minty out of her van, for heaven's sake! What is taking her so long? Is she doing her make-up or is she doing plastic surgery in there?'

I almost jumped with joy because I knew Fiza had practically said, 'Everyone makes mistakes, I forgive you!'

I nodded, turned back and walked out.
Fiza Kareem definitely had a big heart.

~

*Dear Mom,*
*Today I know why Shah Rukh Khan rules.*
*Because he remembers the face of a nondescript girl who met him for less than a minute on the set. Because when he sees her standing on the pavement, he does not zip by in his swanky car, but he remembers to stop and thank her. Because even though he has reached very far in life, he still knows where he started from. He knows what it means to be special, most importantly, because he knows what it means to be ordinary.*
*P.S.: Did I mention I spoke to him for a full ONE minute?*

## THE HAIR OIL SESSIONS

Most had left the set, as I sat on the pavement mulling over the moment with Shah Rukh Khan and replaying it repeatedly in my mind. I realised my head was hurting. I'm sure that image was tired of being played in different frame rates and motion multiple times. I was elated and exhausted at the same time. After PJ's many attempts to take me home, he eventually understood I needed this time alone here to take stock. He left reluctantly. Aslam was still hovering around. I finally walked out and saw that there were three taxis parked outside the main gate. I picked the most dilapidated and shabby one, because of what was written behind it in creamy white paint.

'Keep distance'.

I got him to take me all the way to Marine Drive.

As I sat there alone, looking out into the sea, I wondered why people did this when they were unsettled. I have seen it in movies too, several times. For me, sitting there by the sea was not helping at all. And it was ruining my hair. My mother always said that salt water was bad for hair and coconut oil was good. It was soothing to remember the sharp smell of the warm coconut oil she would vigorously rub into my scalp, recounting the benefits of the miracle oil which had made my grandmother's hair thick, long and black till she died.

I'm sure if I'd suggested that Nani had access to hair dye it would have ruined the moment.

I'd dreaded those hair-oiling sessions then, but they were important to me now, to validate that my world was all right.

Mundane, routine things are so conniving. Just like a creeper in the garden, they twist their way into your daily life and cling to your memories, so much so that it becomes difficult to live without them. You crave the chill of morning walks down the same path with the same crooked signpost. You listen out for the familiar sound of the milkman's sharp bell at 8 o'clock every day. You yearn for the taste of tea and two Marie biscuits with the smell of crisp newspapers and the disastrous news before you in your little balcony. You long for weekly hair-oiling sessions.

Before we know it, these mundane things become life.

As she massaged the oil into my hair, my mother would jog her memory for old tales. It was just like her trunk full of precious silk sarees. She would tell me stories about her mother, in which there was always a lesson in every laugh, there was a moment in every joke. There was a sense of a life lived happily.

I longed for an oil massage session. That sharp sea water made me uncomfortable.

Just then I heard a voice from behind me, saying my name. I turned. Ranvir. 'Aslam heard you telling the taxi guy to take you to Marine Drive,' he said. 'I've driven along the entire stretch, looking for you.'

I looked up at him and then turned back to the dusky sky and the waves. Ignoring him standing behind me, and deciding whether or not I wanted to go back with him just yet.

Ranvir waited patiently. I knew he was still standing behind me because I could smell his tangy, lemony aftershave.

'Would you mind if I wait in the car?' he asked hesitantly. I did not respond. I heard him walking back to his gleaming Lexus and opening the car door.

Immediately, I wanted to run behind him. I knew he was the perfect remedy to forget the mistakes I'd made today. And, I couldn't help feeling happy that Ranvir had come all the way here to get me.

I stood up and walked over to the car, opened the door and sat inside. He was on the phone. There was something else in the car apart from Dohaji's disapproving looks and Ranvir's agitation.

It was a familiar smell. Almost odourless, but if you paid enough attention, you'd know it was the smell of an impending disaster. I shrugged it away, blaming Shikha and Zoya for putting those ominous warnings in my head about 'getting involved with actors on a film set'. They were both united in their disapproval of Ranvir and I was determined to ignore them.

I could hear traces of a familiar voice from the other end of the phone. Then Ranvir hung up and we sped away to his house.

~

I woke up groggily, as if I were still dreaming. I looked up at the pristine white ceiling of Ranvir's bedroom; muted lights cast a soft glow in all the nooks and corners. I turned—Ranvir wasn't there. The sheets were rumpled and there was pulsating warmth coming from his pillow and the crevices of the blanket.

The ticking of the clock caught my attention. It was two-thirty in the morning. Almost five hours had whispered by softly.

And then I could smell it again. The sharp smell was creeping in, filling up the room.

Suddenly frightened, I got out of the bed and pulled on Ranvir's shirt lying by the bed. I could hear someone talking softly outside. I started walking towards the voice. The shirt was cool against my skin. It smelt of Ranvir.

I walked to the living room. Ranvir was sitting on the couch, talking on the phone. His back was towards me. I went up and hugged him from behind. He reacted sharply. Almost like a hunted animal. I found myself sprawling on the floor.

That smell was becoming stronger. I was right. This was it.

Ranvir looked at me with a glazed look and said, 'Neki, I'm sorry but you have to leave. Prateeksha is coming over now . . . we need to discuss a story. She's almost here. You'll have to leave now. I think she suspects something. Please. Understand.'

As he spoke, he walked towards the bedroom. I got up and walked behind him, trying to hear all his hurried words. He was straightening the bed. Removing every ripple, every dent and every trace of our lovemaking.

Erasing it completely with his hands and words.

I stood there dumbfounded. Just when he was about to straighten the pillow, something snapped. I wanted to do this myself. I straightened it, plumped it up and kept it as it had been.

Pristine. Untouched. And wrinkle-free.

The doorbell rang as I was putting on my shoes. Ranvir's urgency was driving me. His words had stopped sinking in.

I was being driven out. I ran towards the back door. I tripped and fell. A beautiful crystal vase hit the floor. One bit struck my forehead and fresh, warm blood slid down my cheek all the way to my neck. I was still being rushed out urgently by Ranvir. The door closed behind me. I tasted my own blood on the outside of my lip.

That was when I realised it. I was the 'other woman' in this scene. So *that's* what it felt like.

As I held my forehead with my hand, I saw a familiar hill, a familiar stone rolling down the hill and a familiar face looking at me from the airport.

My father.

By the time I'd reached the road, I knew what I was supposed to do hereafter.

Be the best that I could be.

## THE TRACE OF A MARK

13 January 2009. 9:31 p.m.
Dear Nano,
It's been a week. Ranvir has been asking for forgiveness for that night. The mark on my forehead is fading. I want it to stay forever because whenever I see it in the mirror, it shows me the way. It makes me run away from Ranvir and closer to my work. I spend every waking hour thinking about this film. As a result, the last week has been disaster-free. Fiza Kareem even told Ahmed Khan that the only AD who knew the script by heart was me.

## ANY GIVEN FRIDAY

18 January 2009. 8:07 p.m.
Dear Nano,
This Friday the equations and the numbers proved that Dohaji needs to retire. Ranvir's solo hero film flopped. One of the critics called the film a 'joke' and another called Ranvir a 'mistake'. Shikha marked the word *mistake* for me in red ink after reading the review and Zoya underlined the word *joke* for me with black ink. The colour of ink may differ, but the message was the same.

## WHY SO SERIOUS

21 January 2009. 2:30 a.m.
Dear Nano,
My roomies threw a small party for me to celebrate my being Ranvir-free. Zoya has stopped cussing and calling Ranvir names finally, and Shikha has thankfully stopped giving me that 'I told you so' look.

The underwear model was at the party too, making an appearance in our flat after a long time. To cheer us up—it was obvious that we were all feeling down with our own problems and Rosh's absence—he told us stories that he thought were funny. Like one about his latest ad shoot for another underwear brand. Apparently they had to shoot for an extra day because half the first day was spent putting bunched up socks inside his trunks as the ad director wanted the right effect, and the other half was spent perfecting the 'buttock pads' for the butt shot.

None of us laughed. I didn't think it was funny at all. Zoya is guilt-ridden, so nothing is funny to her anymore. And Shikha is still heartbroken, so nothing makes her laugh. The underwear model was the only one laughing. He stopped after a minute when Zoya stubbed her cigarette and walked out of the room.

## QUESTIONS

24 January 2009. 11:09 p.m.
Dear Nano,
Fiza Kareem and I were chatting in the production office today. I was eating a sandwich and Fiza reached out, took the sandwich, and had a bite. Does it mean anything? That she likes my work? That she likes me? Or that she was hungry?

# THE COAT

31 January 2009. 2:56 a.m.
Dear Nano,
Reputations are amazing, I've realised.

Your actions lead to a reputation, and then your reputation dictates your actions. You wear your reputation like a coat, a coat that never comes off. The colour of this coat may change with weather and time, but the coat remains. Luckily for me, my reputation as 'the girl with the memory of an elephant' was spreading far and wide. It was well known by now that I remembered the shots, the lines and the actors' clothes from every scene. First page to the last. The whole set marvelled at my talent.

I knew it was a trick. The trick was, I played a memory game. I kept my brain occupied with memorising every bit of activity on the shoot to shut out Ranvir and the staircase and the rumples in the white satin bed sheet.

If somebody congratulated me on my talent, I smiled shyly and thanked them. I let them think it was natural gift from God.

My success saga has continued happily. Today, on the set, I told Shivani how to aesthetically place cutlery on the table for a dinner scene. It was impressive: I could tell from the nod that Fiza Kareem gave, the glint of appreciation in Karan's eyes and the lack of resentment in Shivani.

PJ stood proudly after I was done setting the table.

Later, he whispered in my ear, 'The table looks fantastic, and you look scary. Look at the dark circles under your eyes!'

I whispered back, 'Either the table looks fantastic or me, and right now I prefer it to be the table!'

I had stayed up the whole night pulling up pictures from the Internet on 'setting beautiful tables'.

## GINGER CONQUERS ALL

2 February 2009. 8:25 p.m.
Dear Nano,
Today I glanced at the production report—the film's logistic details—before it was put away by Aslam. The report stated that we had finished two shooting schedules of the film already. And that the total number of days we need to shoot is a hundred and one. But the report did not state the things we ADs have done between the shooting schedules. For instance, apart from location scouting, we also evaluated the mistakes from the previous schedule that each of us made; conducted costume trials with difficult actors; stirred coffee sitting in our cosy office and exchanged stories and juicy rumours to update each other on the emotional quotient of the people on set. Since EQ is much more important than IQ here, this is really crucial information. Apart from reporting for rehearsals with actors for dance sequences, action sequences or scene sequences, we also bonded over cold leftover pizza late into the night. Apart from chasing after celebrated designers for costume fittings, we also chased away our ghosts and fears, resolving to perform better in the next schedule and outshine our peers. I, of course, had an additional task other than the ones mentioned above: to avoid Ranvir Khanna at all costs.

Some things were covered in the production report, and some were left out. The production report did not mention that the beginning and end of every schedule felt like the beginning and end of an era. As film-makers, we grow at the rate of a virus, exponentially, in terms of experience, skill and determination—if given the right environment. But like a virus, if we don't get the environment we need to thrive, we are inert and inactive. Another interesting thing to know about viruses is that they can lie low for months, even years, just like film-makers and talents that are dismissed and written off, but then suddenly erupt.

If Freud had heard my analogy between aspiring film-makers and viruses, he would have enlisted my name amongst his star subjects to observe. And if my mom were to analyse it, she would take me for a blood test and then make me eat a plate of raw ginger because she truly believes ginger can set the world right. From the common cold, to a disturbed mind, ginger conquers all.

## THE CITY

4 February 2009. 12:01 a.m.
Dear Nano,
I am in between schedules and had a day off. Days off are dangerous, because there is no fear to keep your mind occupied. No fear of forgetting to check the prop list. No fear of messing up the lines while rehearsing with an actor. No fear of being in the bathroom when Fiza Kareem or Karan or Shivani or the actors need me on the set. The day loomed empty and dangerous for me; if stress and fear do not fill it up, Ranvir does.

I was sitting by the window, staring out. Looking at the entire city framed from my little window.

Zoya came and stood next to me, smoking her cigarette. When she finished it, she stubbed it out forcefully. 'If you always look at the view from only one window, you will be fooled into believing that's what the world looks like.'

I looked up but did not respond. Zoya was in a sleeveless T-shirt and I could see her butterfly tattoo.

'Are you coming?' Zoya asked, on her way to the door. When I didn't move she continued, 'You've been stuck to the window for two hours. You can stay there the rest of the day if you want, I don't care, as long as you don't jump out of it.

After a whole day of walking around, I'll be too tired to take you to the hospital.'

I looked at her tattoo carefully now. It was not a butterfly. It was a scorpion with wings. The sad part was, Zoya meant every word of what she'd said to me.

She walked out of the apartment. I followed. I did not want to ask her where she was going. I did not care. As long as I was not left alone with my thoughts, I was fine.

I was glad I went with Zoya because she had nowhere to go. So we went everywhere. Every nook and corner Mumbai has to offer, that Zoya remembered.

We saw the huge serpentine line of people queuing up for Haji Ali. While we stood at a distance, simply watching. Thankfully neither of us was talking.

Our search had consumed us.

We knew we had to find it.

They say Chor Bazaar has something to offer to everyone who goes there. We found a huge collection of antiques and used furniture in the narrow, crowded lanes. We found huge blocks of incense that pervaded our senses; we found the most beautiful pieces of handicraft; we found dilapidated cars, old coins, brand new silver utensils.

We found a piece of everything in Chor Bazaar, but neither of us found what we were looking for.

We continued our search standing at the flyover in Dadar and saw Mumbai whizz by. It was momentary peace. Everyone was in a hurry as we watched them.

The search took us to the colonial structure of Crawford market. The yellow and green of fruits and spices welcomed us.

Sitting next to the pigeons and the tourists and the hawkers, we looked at the Taj Mahal Hotel and marvelled at its beauty. We soaked in the charm of Flora Fountain and got lost in the rows of markets around it.

We lost and found each other many times during the day, but did not find what both of us were looking for in our own ways.

Atonement.

As I looked out of my little window that night, framing Mumbai through it once again, I knew what makes this city very special. Outsiders usually talk about exploring a new city, but, Mumbai, instead of waiting to be explored by the curious, hesitant stranger, will offer itself to you, saying: Take whatever it is you want from me. If you want to be found, this is the place to be. And if you want to be lost, this is the place to be.

I also now know why the scent of the city is so addictive. It's enveloping and all-consuming. It smells of a pregnant cloud, promising that first burst of monsoon rain, when the leaves are brown and souls are parched.

I know the scent of the city is addictive because it smells of promise.

## WHITE LILIES

6 February 2009. 10:07 p.m.
Dear Nano,
Ranvir sent a bouquet of white lilies home yesterday. I threw the flowers, all of them, in the bin. They lay there the whole day. I could sense them rotting through the night. I heard our front door slam shut this morning and I knew the bai was taking the trash out to empty it in the main garbage dump down the road. I knew she had taken the first few stairs with the bin and the white lilies.

I lay awake, counting her every step.

And then I found myself running, barefoot, down the stairs. I stopped Smita, who screamed. She was startled. I rummaged in the bin and took one lily out.

Smita stared at me. I looked at her sheepishly as she shook her head.

I went back to bed.

The scar on my forehead is almost gone. I can smell the dried lily tucked away under my mattress.

I was ready for a new scar all over again.

My phone beeped. Another message from Ranvir. Another apology.

And finally I sent a message back. 'It's okay'. It was the first in weeks.

On the set the whole day, Ranvir tried to catch my eye, look at me, talk to me.

He was miserable. I was happy.

## THE SECRET

8 February 2009. 1:17 a.m.
Dear Nano,
While I was busy becoming an AD to reckon with on set, I made a huge mistake. I forgot I had a secret—a secret which had just been waiting to reveal itself.

Finally it happened accidentally. Shikha pulled out dal and rice from the fridge and then had a sudden urge to eat chicken biryani. She wanted to tell Smita to pick up the necessary ingredients on her way to our place but didn't have the bai's new number. 'Call her from my cell,' Zoya said and chucked her phone over to Shikha.

Just as she was scrolling though the numbers, looking for Smita's, Sam decided to reiterate his love for Zoya in a long, heart-felt text message which Shikha accidentally opened and then couldn't stop reading.

This could be called bad timing or a coincidence. I choose to call it the manipulations of a secret. This synchronisation of moments and planning of human urges to achieve a coordinated sequence of events which is almost like a perfectly designed symphony of actions, to make a grand debut and destroy our perfect world, is what a secret is capable of. Of course no one called Smita about the biryani, and I walked in to see Shikha and Zoya fighting. Zoya's cell was lying in two pieces in a corner. The bearer of bad news more often than not has to bear the brunt.

Shikha was screaming; she was livid. Betrayal is hard to take. I wonder which is the difficult part: is it difficult to swallow because it proves that you are a fool? Is it our vanity that makes it unbearable, or is it our loss of faith?

I held her close till she'd stopped crying. And all the time I held her, I wondered if she was ready to know that I betrayed her too. I'd known about the affair and hadn't told her. I comforted her, wiping her tears and fighting my demons and sudden nausea at the same time.

I decided to betray Shikha a little more and not tell her about my role in the whole affair. Sometimes doing the wrong thing seems like the only right thing to do.

And that's where the folly starts.

The nausea hit me suddenly. I had to rush to the bathroom. I stood at the miniscule white sink with the water dripping from the tap for a few minutes, but nothing happened. When I returned to the living room, I saw the dal on the wall where Shikha had evidently flung it. As soon as I saw it, I was relieved. There was something I could do besides hold Shikha, battle with my guilt in my little bathroom or hear the intermittent shouting. I could actually do something in this situation. Clean the food stains on the wall.

Mom was always telling Shivshankarji back home that haldi stains can be removed with lemon juice, so I squirted half a bottle on the wall. It helped. The tangy smell, the feel of the cloth, the repeated cleaning action soothed my senses.

I scrubbed the wall for what seemed like an hour. My hard work paid off. The splattered haldi and oil stains became one giant stain. People with a creative bent of mind would even call it the outline of a space ship.

I rubbed at the stain a little more because I've heard someone say the difference between success and failure is to hang in there for that extra five seconds, just when you are ready to give up. I was inspired. I would not give up.

The giant mark refused to go away. Inspiration should come with a warning—conditions apply.

And while I was giving up on inspiration, I was also losing hope in my ability to decide what the right thing was to do. Call the landlord and tell him to fix the wall, or buy a huge painting and hang it over the stain. So I simply sat and rubbed the wall, and listened to the accusations. Zoya was dealing with all this erratically: from being quiet, to apologising to Shikha, to finally screaming back at her and blaming Shikha for everything. I'm sure Zoya herself was puzzled at what she was saying. The bottom line, after all the scrubbing and accusations, is that we are splitting.

Shikha wants Zoya to leave the house. Rosh and I need to make a choice: either stay with Shikha or go with Zoya. Having given that ultimatum, Shikha walked out of the house. She is staying at a friend's place till we make a decision. Roshni and I have to choose.

Zoya sat down on the floor next to me and burst out crying. Instead of dwelling on the situation or the spaceship that I had created on the wall, thankfully my mind was on what the next step should be. It was a good distraction. Rosh would need to be told about the situation. She hadn't been taking our calls since she'd left. The only information we had was through her mother, who had called and told us she was returning in a couple of weeks. She was not sure of the exact date. I guess we would have to wait for Rosh to return and then speak to the landlord about leaving the house and settling the deposit money.

Just then I saw a message from Ranvir flash on my cell. It simply said: 'Sorry'.

Smita, who had quietly been cooking through the entire drama, was about to leave. She rubbed her hands on her pallu and looked sympathetically at Zoya. She switched on the TV in the hall and gave the remote control to Zoya. 'Here baby, watch TV,' she said.

Zoya pushed her hand away, picked up the remains of her phone and walked into our room.

I took the remote control from our now scared-looking Smita. 'Don't worry. She is in a bad mood.'

Smita smiled sympathetically. And then she said excitedly, 'Your film's hero. Look!'

I saw Ranvir's handsome face fill up the TV screen. He was smiling at the shutterbugs; next to him stood Prateeksha Devi. I looked at Smita and firmly pressed the button on the remote to switch the TV off. Ranvir continued to beam into the cameras. The remote was not working all of a sudden! I cursed as I pressed the button harder. In the background a reporter recapped Ranvir's story, mentioning how Prateeksha was the force behind his career. But that unfortunately, even with a godmother, God was not on his side as Ranvir's first solo hero film had flopped miserably. Dohaji could not help him either this time I thought. Of course I had not bothered to watch the film. I walked up to the TV set, switched it off and threw the remote control out of the window.

Smita stared at me, shocked.

She left without even telling us what time she would come the next day, as she usually does.

Later Sam came over with a friend and a vodka bottle to console Zoya. The plan was for Zoya to drink enough that she would sleep. As it happened, Zoya did not drink but she managed to sleep out of sheer exhaustion. I, on the other hand, was dead drunk after several vodka shots and practically licking the lime off the wall.

My head ached in the morning; my mouth tasted like sawdust and I also tasted disaster. I always did have excellent tastebuds, so it was no surprise that I was right about the disaster. I found out later that Sam's little friend, Oshi Tiwari, who sat in one corner like a lost puppy, is a journalist.

Sam had called later, and told me what a bad idea it was to let everything out in front of Oshi.

'Why did you get your friend to my house in the first place?' I'd snapped.

'If I knew you were going to act out your very own version of Psycho Part 4, trust me I would have never stepped into your place!' he'd snapped back.

## A DEFINITION THAT DEFINES

10 February 2009. 7:27 p.m.
Dear Nano,
Shikha is still staying at her friend's place. Zoya is in the house with me, but she is in a space where I cannot reach her. Sam has stopped visiting after that night—Zoya has told him to stay away. I think it's out of guilt. I looked up the definition of guilt and found that 'guilt is an affective state in which one experiences conflict at having done something that one believes one should not have done or conversely having not done something one believes one should have done'. Zoya is suffering from the first half of the definition, I am suffering from the latter half and sadly it is defining our friendship. We are barely talking.

There have been some positive developments too. After that horrible night of being so drunk and remembering every detail of my stupidity in the morning, I was not scared of humiliation any more. I had outdone humiliation. Beyond this, there could be nothing. I was free. It helped me in my work on the set. I was not scared to do things, to be shouted at. To ask questions.

The vodka bottle, the mousy journo, Sam, Shikha, Zoya and even Smita, they were instrumental in the accolades I was earning at work. We don't realise that sometimes things we need to be grateful for come disguised as disasters.

So that summed me up for this week more or less. Hopefully it gets better hereafter.

## CERTIFIED PSYCHO

12 February 2009. 1:49 a.m.
Dear Nano,
I can proudly write that I have taken on all the job responsibilities of the third AD. PJ and I are partners and we are doing a great job. So much so that Fiza Kareem gives me the responsibility of checking the frame. Which means that, just before the shot is taken, I look at the monitor and see if everything is in place just the way Fiza Kareem wants it.

I still avoid Ranvir, and the whole crew knows about it now. Thankfully I've been relieved of the duties of calling him from the van and rehearsing his lines with him. Shivani covers for me.

We've now got a new runner in the AD team since the guy we hired after Sam was fired never returned. I found out later that he is the son of an airline mogul. No wonder he was treated better than I was! Karan told us that he may drop in again if he wants to pursue film-making. The point I am trying to make here and which gets me on the verge of hysteria is that the runner can *'drop in'* when he wants. Anyway, there's now a new flunky to replace the runner who ran away.

There's some good news. I knew I was finally a respected

member of the AD team when Shivani invited me, along with Karan, Kriti, PJ and to my surprise Sam, to her house for an AD bonding and bitching session. Finally I felt like I had made my place here. I was truly one of the ADs. I guess Sam was invited for old time's sake and I have a feeling he may be brought back into the game too—Karan could work his magic.

Shivani's apartment is quite bare. She has lovely printed curtains and silver and golden cushions strewn around the living room. Floating candles in various nooks and corners and tiny twinkling fairy lights make up for the lack of furniture.

'You don't live with your parents?' I asked Shivani, as we nursed our drinks.

Shivani shook her head, her mass of tumbling curls bobbing around her. 'Mom passed away, dad remarried, so he lives with his family. I live on my own. Of course on weekends I go there. But lately I've started ditching the deadly lecture sessions—they want me to settle down and give up working in the industry. They think my life will be unstable till I work here.'

'So do you think they are right? That life is unstable because we work in this industry?'

Shivani winked, a little high on her wine. 'Of course not! It's just that working here means giving up the usual things sometimes . . .'

I could see Shivani had given up a lot of 'the usual stuff'. And she was still struggling.

We forget while hating the people we dislike that they are people to begin with, just like us. She had a story just like mine. She had good days and bad days. She had a hero and a villain. A dream and a nightmare. Just like me.

Like Shivani, I was ready to give up a chunk of my life and work my heart out too, but I wanted something in return. Recognition.

That night, everything about the shoot and film was discussed, apart from my unacknowledged fight and unacknowledged affair with Ranvir. Although I knew it was the most talked about thing on the set when I was not around. However PJ did pass me a wine glass with a message in a hushed tone, 'It's all for the best Neki—good riddance to bad rubbish.' I snatched the glass from him, knowing he was referring to the Ranvir situation and took a long painful sip.

Out of the blue, Karan looked at me and said, 'You are doing good for a girl who wears yellow shoes, Neki.'

I paused, my glass stalled on its way to my mouth. It was now or never; I'd been thinking about this for a while. It was a gamble—it could mean starting from scratch, going back to square one, or it would mean taking a leap. But sometimes, to take a huge leap, you have to take a few steps back. I was ready to take the steps. The words came tumbling out before my rational brain had a chance to stop them.

'Then give me credit for it, Karan, I don't want to be the last AD in the film credits. I want a suitable credit for my work.'

All the glasses went down. Awkward silence. It was expected. Thankfully, Kriti did the honours of breaking it. 'What a bitch,' she said.

I ignored her, and kept my gaze on Karan. I was not going down without a fight. 'If this appreciation is well deserved, forget the yellow shoes Karan, and remember the girl who worked hard all these months, just like everyone else, and give me the credit I deserve, according to the work I do.'

I could sense the anger building up in Karan. I had

cornered him in front of everyone. Karan replied tersely, 'That's not how it works. The rule is that you get the same title that was promised to you when you were assigned the job. And that's what we were all told when we started out!'

'I don't think that's fair, Karan.'

Karan shrugged. 'Too bad. This is not a free-for-all buffet where you can pick whatever you fancy.'

I stood up, angry that he was treating my legitimate request so dismissively. 'If it were,' I said, 'I would be going for your title.'

There was a shocked silence, and then Karan said, 'Neki, you're drunk.'

The party was over. I had ruined it for everyone.

I looked at PJ, Shivani, Karan and Sam. 'Look, I'm ready to work hard. But I want the credit—so I know I belong here. So I know I did well, so I can measure how well I did.'

'We'll talk tomorrow Neki—you're drunk,' Shivani said, returning to her cold self.

Karan simply turned his back to me and went to the balcony.

PJ took me home. There was silence in the taxi at first. As if I had violated a sacred code, asking for a higher credit. But the point was, to me, credit was much more than just that. It was certified proof to my spiritually-enlightened father that this was not a worthless pursuit. It was a validation for the choices and mistakes I'd made from my father's perspective. The credit was most important because no matter what I achieved, till I saw it reflected in his eyes, it would never be enough for me.

I tried explaining this to PJ. He heard me out. Looking out of the taxi window all the time. The cab turned into my lane. PJ finally turned to me. 'Goodnight Neki, don't think about this too much. When your dad sees you, he will know—you have learnt, and you have grown. This credit, certificates are mere tokens.'

I laughed at PJ's confidence. 'No, sometimes these certificates of excellence are more important than excellence itself.'

I slammed the taxi door shut and the driver gave me a sour look. 'Your door is still there, still attached to the taxi, okay, I am not running away with it,' I snapped.

The cab driver gave me another weird look and sped away. I recognised that look, it was familiar to me now. It said, 'Psycho Part 4!'

## HAPPY VALENTINE'S DAY

14 February 2009. 1:02 a.m.
Dear Nano,
Today after pack-up, Ranvir's driver Dohaji came up to me and said, 'Sir is waiting to have a word with you. He is in the car.'

That was a smart move by Ranvir. He knew my history with Dohaji and that I would be reluctant to outright ignore him. Dohaji was old and disapproving and I was intimidated.

I went to the car, my anger building up. I encouraged it. I needed a shield.

Ranvir's window slid down, his handsome face was smiling and his eyes were pleading. 'I could give you a ride home and we can go over the scene for tomorrow on the way.'

I clenched my teeth. 'Thanks, but no thanks.'

Ranvir stared at me. I could sense him trying to make up his mind. He made his decision. Suddenly he smiled and said, 'Okay I can tell Fiza I don't remember the scene. That you refused to rehearse the lines.'

I handed him the scene. 'I am sure you can still read.'

'I can,' Ranvir said, took the paper, and tore it up, 'but not from a shredded piece of paper.'

Before I could say anything, the car zipped away. The

pieces of paper he had thrown out the window were carried away in the wind.

Behind me, I heard Aslam clear his throat. 'Nekiji, meet my wife. Herself, Mrs Aslam Sheikh and yourself, Miss Neki Brar. You know she is a very important AD on the set,' he told his wife. 'Fiza is looking for her all the time. So is Ranvir sir,' he added with a wink and walked off.

His wife seemed like the kind of woman who said nothing but saw everything. She went and sat down in the waiting production car. The smelly Sumo.

In the middle of Aslam's sarcastic introduction, I'd realised it was time to end this madness. Aslam was near the Sumo as well. He went and sat in the front, next to the driver. He turned and waved at me.

A message flashed on my phone. Ranvir. 'If you want to rehearse, my terrace at 9. Else I come unprepared! And happy Valentine's Day'.

That was it. It was time.

I marched up to the car, opened the door and sat next to Aslam in the front seat.

Aslam was shocked, his wife scandalised. I looked at the driver with a murderous glint in my eye. 'Drop me to a taxi on the highway. Now!'

Mrs Aslam leaned between Aslam and me, as if trying to protect her husband from me. Aslam was now looking a bit nervous, probably worried that his wife would be suspicious about us. So that's how the four of us left the set, practically sitting on top of each other in the front seat because by the time we reached the highway, Mrs Aslam was almost in the front seat as well.

The driver stopped near a taxi and I got out without a backward glance. I could hear Aslam telling his wife apologetically, 'She is the crazy one on the set I keep talking about! She needs a doctor!'

His wife replied angrily, 'You come home every day and tell me they are all crazy . . . no wonder you are also going crazy. And no wonder your petrol is always empty in your car. You are running this highway service for girls on the set I am sure . . .'

Mrs Aslam's verbal attack was the one nice thing I'd heard in a long time.

They moved away and I got into the taxi. The vehicle sped down the road, and we passed under huge hoardings of films, stars' faces emblazoned on them. A couple had Ranvir as well on the poster of his flopped film. Before its release, the same poster had been grand, impressive; now it had dust and pigeon shit all over it. And that was the truth of it all.

I realised I had given this film six months of my life already.

In six months I'd moved from the last AD to being the third one, but I knew I had to run faster.

With a squeal of its rubber tyres, the car stopped. I was outside Ranvir's building. I paid the cab guy and stood there for a while. My phone flashed. It was PJ. 'Sam is back in the AD team. He said sorry and Fiza has taken him back. We're all going to celebrate. You could have waited to say bye before leaving the set. We're going to Tito's. Try and come'.

I ignored the message. The phone beeped again as I entered the lift. It was Shikha. 'Choose who you are going to stay with, Zoya or me. I need to know soon, till then am staying at my friend's place'.

Shikha's message suddenly reminded me of the huge stain on the wall that I had rubbed at endlessly. I'd hung a painting over the stain: a poster of the Mona Lisa. With those eyes and a smile full of secrets, she seemed the perfect choice.

I got off the lift at Ranvir's floor. He opened the door before I rang the bell. 'I'm sorry,' he said. 'What do I need to do for you to forgive me?'

I walked past him and sat down on his couch. It was aquamarine—the only splash of colour amidst his wooden floors and stark white furniture.

I opened the paper that had the scene on it and started reading aloud. Ranvir came and sat on the floor in front of me. He tried to interrupt me, but I just read louder. I was determined to show him I was not interested in anything he had to say to me.

'Scene 28. Interior. House. Day,' I read out. This time he was quiet. Then suddenly he reached out, took my feet in his hands, and began massaging them.

I continued to read, but I was fumbling with the lines now. Ranvir continued to massage my feet, his breathing uneven. He liked to take photos of my feet and legs; he had quite a fetish.

Finally I stopped reading. I could not utter another coherent word. Because I realised I was deeply in love with him, despite the fact that he was destroying me. There was no escape and there was no hope and that sometimes is true love.

Ranvir started talking, his voice hoarse. 'I can't think like this, can't act.'

I needed some support to fight him; I had almost given up to his touch. I began reading the scene again. 'Scene continued, interior house, we see the sunlight filtering in as Ranvir walks into a room. The walls are streaked with blood. He sees a mutilated body lying face down.'

Ranvir got up and held my shoulders. I continued to look down at the paper. 'I'm sorry! It's stressful for me. I am relying on this film too much: it's a make or break film for me. You know what happened with my last release. Please understand. If Prateeksha does not give me a film, I'm finished.'

I continued, 'Ahmed walks in behind you and takes in your stunned expression. He has a smile on his face as if he was expecting you.'

Ranvir caught hold of my hair, it hurt. Instinctively, I slapped him. I could not see his face clearly; it was blurred with my tears. I realised Ranvir had picked me up and had taken me inside his bedroom.

I had no fight left in me. Ranvir just held me and let me cry for some time. I woke up to find myself in Ranvir's arms. He was awake. I'd slept for over two hours. He pulled me under. I went, happily, into the momentary oblivion.

My cell beeped again. Later I read it. It was from PJ: 'I'm waiting for you at Tito's'.

## EITHER/OR

10 March 2009. 10:06 p.m.
Dear Nano,
Things were much better with Ranvir and me, and work was going well too, in this schedule. Ranvir and I were spending most of the time off the set in his house. Dohaji did not approve and so the house staff hated it as well. But Ranvir wanted me there and I wanted to be there too. Slowly, my stuff had started creeping into his house and drawers.

At work, his eyes sought mine the moment he stepped on the set till the time he left it. The entire set was talking about us. This time, though, the talk was not upsetting. The rumour was, this time, Ranvir had 'fallen hard'.

And at the apartment, Mona Lisa was doing a great job covering the stain on the wall. I'd been thinking of telling Shikha that I knew about Zoya and Sam's affair. She would be devastated. But then I'd tell her that I'm choosing to stay with her instead of Zoya. My confession and my redemption all rolled in one.

So life was relatively rosy, and I was keeping my fingers crossed that this phase would continue, that the days to come would be as they are now: predictable, ordinary and fulfilling. How foolish I was.

We had a lot of child artistes on set today. The scene setting was that of a kid's birthday party. The set was done up with balloons, cut-outs of cartoon characters and huge polka-dotted cups and saucers for kids to sit in.

All the kids were ready in their party gear. The part of the main kid was being played by a boy called Prince.

Prince is very fair, has light eyes and soft, brown hair. If you saw his parents gushing over this eight-year-old boy, you would know they have decided to help Prince in every way possible to spend his entire childhood on the sets of a film.

In the film, Prince plays David Brown's son. (Thankfully he had an Indian wife on screen, else we would have had to cast a European kid who is allowed to work only six hours a day, has a child minder on the set with him constantly and a teacher who is supposed to teach him in between breaks. But an Indian child can stay on set endlessly! No rules—no restrictions.) He is abducted for a hero-like trade-off by Ranvir and Ahmed. I was in charge of the JAs and the background action.

The status on the AD battle was that I was now stepping on PJ's toes—and he was letting me. But with work being so hectic, no one really had time to think about these things. And so the awkwardness with the other ADs had gradually faded away. But I still wanted the title.

There were two ways of moving up a crowded ladder, either someone lets you go up or you push them out. I had found a third one. What you lack in talent, opportunity, ability and destiny can be made up with sheer hard work, so at least you could die trying. I was proud of the third way, but it was a recipe for disaster. I was overworked, sleep-deprived and on the edge of collapsing.

I was jerked back into reality with the walkie crackling.

Fiza wanted Prince on the set; David was already on the set and waiting. This was the child's first shot for the day. I ran up to his van where I found that the child was in no position to act. He was wailing about something, and he needed to be in a cheerful mood for the scene.

'What's happening, Neki?' Karan said over the walkie. 'Prince needs to be here in five minutes!'

'Um, Prince refuses to come on the set. He is crying about something. But I'll get him,' I added quickly.

Karan heaved a sigh of relief, 'Thanks Neki.'

Prince's mother was trying to console her son, promising him the game he wanted, the toy car he wanted, the sweets he wanted. But Prince was inconsolable. His tummy hurt, he said. His father looked at me helplessly.

'If he can't come, we'll have to use someone else,' I said. I felt bad, but we couldn't hold up the shoot for the kid. Also, I wished his parents would just let Prince be.

I stepped out of the van and called Aslam. Sam was hanging around outside.

'What have you decided?' he asked, when I'd put down the phone.

'To get a replacement. Prince doesn't look like he's going to stop crying. I've asked Aslam to get another kid to play the part.'

'No, I mean who are you going to stay with? Rosh is supposed to get back anytime now. Zoya is devastated, she is not talking to me either; she needs you; you have to stay with her.'

'Don't you dare tell me what I need to do, okay?' I snapped.

Just then Aslam came up with a little boy. The boy was cheerful, he was sweet . . . he was happy. This kid usually did background roles. This was his first opportunity to be right in front of the camera.

PJ came towards us, talking on his walkie. 'What's happening? They're all waiting on the set for the kid.'

Sam smirked, 'First Neki has to decide who the baby lead is. Only then can we take the kid inside.'

I gave Sam a look. I told Aslam to get the kid changed into the birthday outfit, to see if he looked as cute as Prince.

Aslam took the kid away.

PJ lit a cigarette. 'Okay that means while the kid changes, it's time for a cigarette break. I have a story to kill time. You know that movie *XXX*. Harry L. O'Connor, Diesel's stunt double, he died on the set. His death was caught on camera.'

Sam and I rolled our eyes. 'Please can you not tell another morbid story? For a change a joke would be nice, PJ!' I said.

PJ continued, 'But I am coming to the joke. The joke is that the stunt double had done the stunt successfully once, but requested the director Rob Cohen for another take. He felt the first wasn't good enough. He was killed during the second take. You know what the cruel part of the joke is? His family had arrived from Prague just before the accident to watch his stunt and were there when he died.'

'Where do you get these disaster stories from, PJ?'

'The Internet.'

'You actually sit in front of your computer and hunt down these miserable stories? You know, you make *me* look good. In fact, you make *any* crazy person look good! Why do you do it anyway?'

'Maybe so I can freak you out, and maybe to remember that worse things have happened to people here.'

Before I could reply, Prince's parents emerged from the van. They were smiling. 'Prince is ready to shoot,' his mother announced. The boy was standing next to them, his eyes red-rimmed from crying.

Aslam arrived then, with the new boy in Prince's costume. Problem of choice—who deserved the chance. The worst thing was, I had to decide. The kid who came first, I kept repeating in my head, I was going to stick with him. That was fair.

Sam popped in my head as well. Zoya or Shikha? What was fair?

As I approached Aslam, I looked at the kid next to him, all dressed up. His eyes dancing with excitement and anticipation. My step faltered but, in a stern voice, I said, 'Sorry, we will be using Prince after all.'

I was expecting anything from tears to a tantrum, but I was not expecting the smile that came my way. The little child smiled at me with trusting eyes. This was the most beautiful kid there could be. 'Thank you, Miss,' he said sweetly.

The dress dada quickly jumped in and yanked the kid. 'Come quickly, take this off or the suit will get spoilt, I have to give it back to Prince.'

The child was ushered towards Prince's van. I followed with a heavy heart. Inside the van, his shiny bow tie, shirt and pants were taken off and handed to Prince. But something remained on that child's face. Dignity. He put on his jeans and blue T-shirt, looked at me and again said, 'Thank you Miss.'

Then he walked out of the van, taking tiny steps in his overused black canvas shoes. He had left behind the shiny new ones. I remembered there was an extra pair lying under the chair. I picked them up and held them out to him. 'Hey, here, keep this,' I said.

He smiled and shook his head. He walked out of the van to join his parents. I followed him.

'What's your name?' I asked.

'Vaibhav Sherma. The Sherma is with an E.'

I smiled and said, 'I'll remember that.'

I watched as Vaibhav took his parents' hands and led them away. I realised that, in the middle of this circus, surrounded by jokers, ringmasters, and a make-believe world, the brilliance of the human soul revealed itself every day, momentarily.

I felt someone watching me. I turned my head. PJ. He had been around all this while. 'You want to go out for dinner tonight? I can tell you more disaster stories,' he said.

Finally, he was asking me out. Without thinking I blurted, 'You know I'm dating Ranvir.'

PJ looked at me with an expression on his face that said he pitied me. 'You're finally admitting it?'

'I've practically moved into his house. He really likes me ... you know that.'

'You really think so Neki? There is a thin line between naïveté and stupidity.'

'Why can't you just be happy for me?' I said, angry with PJ for the first time. He had to approve of Ranvir and me. It was important to me that he believed Ranvir loved me. I was seeking approval, I realised. I wish I could lose that vice we all succumb to.

PJ looked at me with anger of his own. 'Because I just heard Ranvir on the phone. I heard him say your name and call you a slut.'

I stopped breathing. 'What? I can't believe you would lie to me ... stoop so low, make up stories ...'

'I'm not lying, Neki. Give me some credit.'

'You're really sick, you know that! And you know why? Because you knew about this the whole while and you're busy talking about disaster stories you downloaded from the Internet. You're pathetic!'

PJ took a few steps closer to me and this time it was sheer rage I could sense. 'I was on my cigarette break, and I did not want to ruin it by being a messenger of some trashy gossip in a bad love affair.'

'Consider it ruined.' I pushed him and stormed away.

I heard PJ mutter, 'Considered!'

I ran towards the set looking for Ranvir.

At the same time chanting over and over again in my head that there was no truth to PJ's accusations. But whatever my head was chanting, in my heart I already knew the truth.

## SITTING IN A CUP AND SAUCER

As I hunted desperately for Ranvir, I was stopped by Karan: he wanted me to set up the people in the shot with the other ADs. The scene on shoot was hectic. The talk with Ranvir would have to wait.

Ranvir finally came on the set with a sullen look on his face. He was biting everyone's head off. He did not even look at me once. Well, finally it was here. It always sends you messengers in various shapes and sizes before making a full appearance. Then it wears its most elaborate costume and makes a grand entry in your life. It likes to dress up and make an entrance. It was definitely inspired by a woman. But we usually call it 'Trouble'.

Ranvir finished his shot and immediately stalked off to his van. I had no time to go after him. Prince was acting up again and I had to calm him down.

Fiza announced a two-minute waiting period as the camera lens was being re-adjusted. Dharmesh sir was in a foul mood.

I had to get to Ranvir. It was killing me. I ran up to his van but I was stopped outside by Dohaji. He was standing and smoking with Aslam. 'No one is allowed inside. He is on a very important phone call,' Dohaji said dismissively.

I looked at Inder who politely said, 'Ma'am, he is on a

phone call but I will tell him you were here.'

Fiza called out for the next shot.

I ran back to the set. At least everything was perfect there. Prince was doing a great job. Fiza called for Ahmed and Ranvir to be brought on the set.

PJ said, 'I will go and call them. Neki, you handle Prince and David.'

Kriti barged in and hurriedly started checking David for his costume continuity. She tugged at his shirt saying, 'I think it was slightly out on the left, the last time we shot. Let me double check with the continuity pictures.'

We had shot part of the scene a month ago, and David had to wear the same costume. I looked at Kriti and said confidently, 'His shirt was tucked in.'

Kriti glared at me and looked at the continuity pictures. I knew I was right. She made a 'whatever' expression and walked off.

I saw Ranvir come on the floor with PJ and Ahmed Khan. Again, he did not look at me. He was definitely avoiding me, and I could tell that he was furious about something.

Just then Sam cornered me, 'Zoya is here on the set. She is hysterical. She needs to speak to you.'

The shot was set. Karan spoke on the mike, 'Neki, Fiza wants you to make Prince blow his birthday candles on the count of five and on the count of six he is supposed to jump off the stool and run towards David.'

I nodded and got ready with the mike.

'Zoya wants to know your decision now,' Sam said urgently. 'Are you staying with Shikha or with her? She needs to know, and you know this is not just about sharing a flat—whoever you chose to share your flat with is the one you choose as your friend.'

I ignored him. I had to focus on giving the cue to Prince. I had to fade out the chaos and the noises around and concentrate, because if I messed up, it would mean going for a retake. Sam realised the futility of trying to get a reaction from me and slithered away.

Just then I felt Ranvir's gaze on me. I turned. Our eyes met. I saw something there. Disgust. It was so strong, it was so crippling, that I almost dropped the mike.

I heard Fiza's call for a final rehearsal.

I looked over at Aslam who had come to give Sam the message that his friend was getting hysterical outside. That was Zoya. And then he whispered in my ear, 'Thought I'd warn you—there was a story that was going to come in the newspapers. About you and Ranvir. All the details. It was squashed by Prateeksha Devi. She knows about you and him. Oh, and you will have to sign the requirement sheet for tomorrow. You have called for ten junior artistes and five cars. Please confirm.'

Aslam turned around to leave when Fiza screamed at him on the mike, 'Can you get out of the frame, Aslam?'

'I am trying very hard for you to see how beautiful I am Madam, my inner beauty, so you can launch me one day!' The whole set burst out laughing. Aslam was a shark.

Fiza called for action. Ranvir looked at me again. I held his gaze and counted purposefully. One, two, three, four. Prince blows the candles. Five. Jumps off the stool. Six, jumps into David's arms.

Perfect timing. Perfect shot. My life was a disaster.

Ranvir walked off the set. I followed him. He shut the van door and Dohaji stood in front of it. I knew I wouldn't be able to go in.

I was looking for Aslam when Sam came up to me, 'Zoya is uncontrollable—you need to speak to her now.'

Just then the little boy Vaibhav came up to me with his pictures. 'Miss, I am leaving. Please keep my pictures with you.'

I said a hurried okay, snatched the pictures from his hands and ran towards the AD van. Zoya was sitting there, smoking a cigarette. The van reeked of smoke. I coughed. Zoya got up and asked, 'Decide now. Are you with Shikha or me?'

I coughed a little more. My eyes burned from the smoke.

I should have stayed with Vaibhav for a couple of minutes and given him some promise and hope. I should have stepped up for Roshni. I should not have pushed PJ away. I should call my mother more often and tell her the truth. I should go up to my father and admit he was right—this is tough. I should break up with Ranvir.

I should tell Shikha the truth.

'I am staying with Shikha,' I heard myself say to Zoya.

In this whole mess, I had a chance to do *something* right and I was going to take it.

Zoya looked at me. I had failed her. I knew I was losing a friend. 'I need you,' she pleaded. 'I need you to not judge me and to stand by me.'

I stood there, not saying anything. Finally Zoya picked up her bag and left. I stood in the van, coughing, the smoke a welcome pain.

Just then there was a knock on the door. It was Aslam. He was standing there with a call sheet. He came inside the van and handed me the pen. 'Please sign the requirements on the call sheet for tomorrow.'

I took the pen and stared at the paper.

'Why is Ranvir angry with me? What have I done?'

'Because it's some friend of yours, Oshi, who wrote the article. Apparently he got all his information from you only.

Are you sure you need only ten JAs because it will be difficult to ask for more at the last minute.' Aslam seemed very amused with the situation. I gave him a nasty look and walked away to look for Ranvir. I had to speak to Ranvir. I had to go over and tell him it was a huge mistake.

But before that I had to kill Sam.

Outside, I realised there was chaos because Prince was having loose motions. Everyone was panicking. Karan barked, 'Neki you are in charge. Take him to the loo in between takes. We need to finish these five shots today.'

So there I was, rushing Prince to the bathroom in between takes and calming his parents down. There was chaos outside Prince's van.

'Has he finished pooping? Fiza is calling for you!' Aslam smirked.

'Shut the fuck up, Aslam! Get lost!'

Aslam handed me some Eno, 'In case you have acidity.'

I gave him a filthy look. He looked at me with a smile and added, 'You know, I will make a great executive producer. In case you and Ranvir get back together again.'

Just then Sam came up. 'I expected more of you! Zoya is devastated.'

Prince screamed from inside, 'Ma, I am done. Ma?' I ran inside, wondering why his mother wasn't responding, only to find her swaying a bit; she looked like she was having a dizzy spell.

Sam had followed me inside the van. I turned to him and yelled, 'You—your friend, that Oshi, has ruined my life ... he was going to publish a horrible story about me!'

'Who told you to tell him everything? Thank God you didn't start climbing your walls and ceiling. I was scared to death what you would do next. Don't blame me. If you can't handle your alcohol don't drink with strangers!'

Prince's father came up, 'Sorry my wife has a BP problem!'

'Can you get your kid off the pot?' I barked at him. Just then I spotted Ranvir from the glass window. He was outside his van. He was talking on the phone. I ran towards him, leaving Sam in charge of the potty situation.

Before Ranvir could walk back into his van, I screamed, 'I did not know okay? I did not mean to tell that guy anything. I was drunk. He took advantage. Can we please talk?'

Ranvir's face hardened. He opened his van door and gestured for me to get in. He walked in behind me and shut the door.

'You have ruined everything. Leave and please do not talk to me ever again,' he said bluntly.

I looked into his face. For something to give me hope. There was nothing. I was looking for emotion, but I just saw the face of a man who could have been a stranger.

'That day at the hospital shoot you asked if I could be with you despite your equations with other women to get your numbers right, and I said yes.'

'Get out Neki.'

'You asked me to accept you and understand you despite you throwing me out of your house—I did.'

'Get out.'

'And when I ask you to overlook a mistake—'

I could see Ranvir's eyes were glassy by now. He had gone away. A second—that's all it took to make or break a connection. All I could register in the van was the garish floral curtains and the cold. It was chilling.

'Neki, just go.'

He opened the door and I walked out.

From this van into the next van where Prince was sitting on the pot, crying. His mother was still giddy, unable to stand. I went in, took the jet spray attached to the pot and handed it to the harassed dad. 'We need him on the set—NOW!' I said loudly. Prince stopped crying, and his dad, looking a bit scared of me, sprayed Prince's butt. I looked at Prince and muttered, 'You have to smile. Wipe your face with tissue now.'

Prince did as I told him. I took his chubby hand in mine and led him out. I sharply instructed his parents to stay away. Prince rubbed his eyes with his other hand. I could see his lips trembling. It was hard for him, he was in pain and scared of me. And I was going to put him in the spotlight.

As we walked towards the set, I saw him rubbing his eyes again. I switched off my walkie and led Prince to one of the discarded polka-dotted cups lying outside the set. Prince was excited to sit in the cup, distracted from his fear with the bright colours and dots. I bent down and held his sweet chubby hands. I said sorry over and over. Then I hugged him. I needed the hug more than Prince did and he obliged. I tickled him. His chubby fist was still tight as a ball but he laughed. His laugh was infectious. Looking at Prince's face, so excited to be sitting in the cup, I realised it was a beautiful day. Sid was right again; look at the world like a child and you will see the most amazing things in the most beautiful way.

I sensed someone standing behind me. Aslam. His phone rang and he turned away. 'I don't know where Neki is, I'll try and find her.' I sat with Prince in that cup for two minutes till I saw Prince's fists opening up. In those two minutes, as I saw the tiny fingers letting go of fear, I decided I was going to let go of Ranvir. It was over. It was not meant to be.

Prince looked at me and smiled. He was ready to go back on the set. I wasn't so sure whether I was, but I took his hand and he led me all the way to the set.

PJ came up to me after pack-up and said, 'You need a ride to shift your stuff from Ranvir's place?'

I shook my head. I hailed a cab and went to Ranvir's apartment. He was not there. I picked up all my stuff and walked out of his house. The lift doors opened up and Ranvir came out. He looked at me, and the stuff I had in my hands. He walked past me and into his house. He made it a point to shut the door.

I got into a cab outside and told the driver to take me to Marine Drive. When we reached, it was dark and everything was lit up. People were walking up and down the beautiful promenade. I walked for a long time and finally sat down. I could smell the salt and feel the waves crashing on the promenade.

I took my laptop out from my bag, and after a long time I wrote to my mom.

It was time.

*Dear Mom,*

*Mumbai's Queen's Necklace is magical. You can taste, smell and hear the sea as you walk along it.*

*We shot with a kid today. I made him get up from the pot and got his butt sprayed for the first time by his dad—in return he made me open my fist and let go. I rejected another kid today, Vaibhav Sherma—he reminded me that Sherma is spelt with an e and also that when we choose one thing, we have to let go of something else. I sat in a polka-dotted cup and Aslam the horrible line producer gifted me Eno. (Don't worry, I don't have acidity, and if I did, I know I am supposed to have freshly prepared buttermilk with roasted cumin seeds, some rock salt and some black pepper.) Aslam is running after me to get him his next project. From sitting in a polka-dotted cup to refusing jobs, we cover a lot of roles on the set—all in a day's work and so far it's turning out perfect.*

*And do see a movie called XXX. I've heard the action and the stunts in that film are to die for.*

*Love,*
*Neki*

## THE ANT TRAILS

15 March 2009. 4:43 a.m.
Dear Nano,
Today we were shooting a big action sequence. It's meant to continue for three days. The first stunt for the day was that Ahmed, Ranvir and Kashish jump off a tall building just when David Brown is about to shoot them. They jump only after Ahmed Khan gives a heroic speech, of course.

Ahmed Khan, Ranvir and Kashish were working very hard to prepare for the jump sequence—in their respective make-up vans, applying make-up to look like they're bruised.

So did three other people in the tent outside. The stunt doubles, who were actually going to do the jump. Kashish Kapoor's stunt double is someone called Alisha. Of the two guys playing Ranvir and Ahmed's doubles, I knew one, Hassan, because I had seen Shivani talking to him in the nooks and corners of the sets, sharing a joke or two.

I was supposed to be coordinating between the action department and the direction department today. It was a very hot day, but suddenly I shivered. Ranvir's gleaming car had come and screeched right in front of me. Ranvir got out and looked directly at me. I could sense the people around—the driver, Aslam, Punjabi, Karan, Shivani, the stunt doubles—

looking at us. Perhaps I should have looked away, but I played to the gallery. I stared straight back. Ranvir finally turned away and walked into the van. I found myself staring into a pair of beautiful, compassionate brown eyes. Alisha. She had positioned herself in front of me, blocking my face from the curious on-lookers. This was the first time I was seeing Ranvir after I'd taken my stuff from his apartment.

Surreptitiously, she handed me a tissue. I had no clue what I was supposed to do with it. 'You have something near your eye,' she said, seeing my puzzled expression. I dabbed at my eyes. The tissue was wet.

'Come on people! An hour to go before we start the show!' Karan shouted.

Alisha looked at me and smiled, 'I need to warm up before the jump.'

'Are you scared?' I asked her, sniffling. I looked up at the ten-storey building she was supposed to jump from. There were inflatable safety landings positioned below, but it still looked like a very scary thing to do. Even though the stunt doubles were harnessed for safety, there were many things that could go wrong. Alisha smiled confidently, 'No, because I am concentrating on the jump and the shot. How will the shot look? How can it be done seamlessly? I am not looking at the height or the fall or a mistake. If I don't look at it or think about it, it doesn't exist.'

I looked at her and smiled. 'You know that huge car there?' I pointed to Ranvir's glossy car. 'It does not exist!'

Alisha laughed.

Just then Shivani bumped into me, rattling out instructions for Sam and Kriti and the new AD. Shivani's nose looked a bit red, like she'd been crying. I wanted to ask her if she was all right.

Like I wanted to ask Sam if Zoya was doing okay.

And PJ if we could go out for dinner.

And then I saw her, walking towards me. She was looking pale in a white shirt and blue jeans. Rosh. She was finally back. She had taken longer to return than the couple of weeks her mom had mentioned. But we knew that even though Rosh was finally here, her actual coming back to us might or might not happen.

When I looked at her, the first thing that came to my mind was an ant we met on a lazy Sunday afternoon. In a frenzy of cleaning, we'd swept away an entire ant trail. When we'd put our legs up on the couch, satisfied with a job well done, we spotted one small ant on the white marble floor. A tired forlorn ant who'd escaped our onslaught, making its way somewhere. Looking to start over. Rosh reminded me of that ant. We had named that ant 'ant-zilla'. You just had to look at it and grudgingly admire it.

I started walking towards her, but was stopped by David Brown, the script of the upcoming scene in his hand. 'Neki, can you explain what Ahmed says before he jumps, please?'

I gestured to Rosh that I would be with her in a minute and took the paper from him. Rosh looked strange: the same, but different too.

I started reading Ahmed's dialogue aloud. He was supposed to recite some lines from a poem by Harivanshrai Bachchan. I looked at the poem and laughed. Today definitely was an 'ant-day'.

'When you are about to kill them, Ahmed turns to you defiantly and says:

Nanhi cheenti jab dane le kar chalti hai,
chadti diwaron par sau bar phisalti hai
akhir uski mehnat bekaar nahi hoti;
koshish karne walon ki haar nahi hoti.'

I was just going to explain what the lines meant when I noticed David Brown's incredulous expression. 'He says all that? While I'm about to shoot him? Why is it mandatory to do this in Bollywood films?'

'Well, the hero has to say something important which will give meaning to his sacrifice. The intention will make the action big or small, not the action itself.'

David nodded his head sarcastically, 'Nice speech Neki . . . so what's he telling the people now?'

'Basically he is quoting excerpts from a poem which goes like: If you try hard enough then you are always the winner. Just like the diligent ant who makes its way time and again for that one piece of grain.
Falls and stumbles but never once fumbles.'

'Great, so when the hero is about to die, he is talking about ants? Impressive.'

That made me laugh. 'There's more,' I said.

David rolled his eyes. 'What? You're kidding me!'

I heard Karan call me aside on the walkie. Promising David I'd be right back, I went over to where he had called me. Karan was in a hurry and without wasting a moment, said, 'Neki, I have spoken to Fiza. You will get the credit you asked for—the third AD. After all, you have taken the responsibilities of that title, and we all agree on that.'

Suddenly, I felt dizzy. I wanted to throw up. That was a strange reaction to good news. Karan looked at me concerned and asked, 'Are you okay?'

I nodded. 'Thanks . . . but why?' I mumbled.

Karan shrugged, 'When I started out on my first film, I was given the title of a production assistant, but eventually I did the work of an AD. But I finished with no title at all, because I gave my chief AD a choice, either to give me a suitable title, or not give me any title at all. He told me the rule was that you get the same title promised to you when you are assigned the job, so he chose the latter. Probably also because there was no space on the screen for the name of an extra AD. The title song was only sixty seconds long, out of which the director wanted his name to stay on the screen for at least ten seconds. I watched that entire film for the first time in the theatre, sitting with my team. But the only thing that played in my mind constantly was that my name was nowhere on the screen. I remember the feeling I had sitting in that preview theatre, watching for agonising hours, my sweat and toil and hard work brutally eaten up in the film. I threw up repeatedly after the film. In fact some of it spilled on my first AD.'

I looked at Karan, narrating an incident which perhaps had changed his life, like he was discussing the weather. 'Thanks Karan.'

Karan shrugged. 'I've never been asked for a promotion before so I reacted instinctively, but now I think I want to wear a new shirt at the screening of the film and I just don't want anyone throwing up on me, that's all.'

I laughed.

I saw then that Rosh was three feet away from me, patiently waiting for me to finish my talk with Karan. I started walking towards her.

'Neki!' Karan called me back. 'You know friends are not allowed on set. On real locations, especially, if we are doing a dangerous stunt!' He glanced at Rosh, came up to me and said softly, 'Sam told me about her. It's horrible, but we are on a film set. You leave the baggage outside. Someone could get hurt, okay?'

'We never leave the baggage outside Karan, we only pretend it's not there.'

Karan looked at me concerned, 'Are you really okay? You are looking weird and talking weird. Are you up to being on the set? Otherwise we can send you back—'

Just then Karan's walkie crackled with a voice; it was the new girl, panicking. 'Karan, Dharmesh sir is screaming here and he has already hit a light boy and he is saying the direction department is directionless, the art department is a useless antique and the production is—'

'Thank you for this update on the walkie, for everyone to hear. I will be right there,' Karan said sarcastically and switched off the walkie. 'I don't have time for this crap. Handle your shit, report back and better chat with all the other ADs about your promotion. I've spoken to them about this of course, but if I feel there is a problem or somebody is uncomfortable, it may not happen.'

I was shocked. 'Karan, you're telling me I have to take their permission to get a title I deserve?'

'I think you can answer that question yourself. And Neki, I need you on the set soon,' Karan looked at Rosh and added pointedly, 'and without that girl.'

I turned around and walked to Rosh. I hugged her. She let me.

We walked together to a tent which had been set up near the location for crew members. I called for Punjabi.

As soon as Rosh had sat down, she said, 'I have come here to tell you: I don't want to stay with either Zoya or Shikha or you, Neki. I'm going to be taking my own place. I'm moving out today.'

Well so Rosh was not coming back at all.

I searched for a reply to that statement. There was none.

I could feel the heat beating down on the tent. The table fan whirred slowly and was a much-needed reprive in the silence and the heat. Nausea was hitting me fast and hard.

'Can I sit here for some time before I go? I need to meet my new landlord at four,' Rosh muttered.

I nodded. Just then Alisha walked into the tent. She wanted to know how many shots they were taking with her before lunch. I told her the action sequence and then, turning to Rosh, introduced her to Alisha.

Rosh stared at her and then said, 'Why do you do it? When no one even knows you do it?'

I moved away to another corner to slow down the buzz in my head as Alisha answered that often-asked question.

From the corner I could see Shivani dashing behind the tent, stabbing at her tears. The stunt guy Hassan followed her.

'I can't believe you are breaking up with me! I got you so many jobs!' Shivani was saying.

'That's the reason—you are a great girl . . . I don't want to fool you, you deserve someone who loves you,' Hassan said.

'They all leave because they all think I am a great girl! I hope you fall from the building today and break your neck!'

I saw Ranvir walking up to the tent. He was coming to talk to me, I thought, wanting to hug him and cry.

But he walked up to Hassan and started chatting with him.

He could have called Hassan to the van; he must have come out of the van to see me, I was sure. And he did start walking towards me. A warm feeling spread all over. He came up to me and took out something from his pocket. It was a piece of paper. I could see a heading which read: 'Star-AD hook-up'.

'You are disgusting,' he hissed. 'I will make sure this does not come out in the papers. You will have to shut your mouth. Please.' Harsh words, and there was desperation. Ranvir left.

Punjabi came up, 'Madam, tea, coffee . . .'

Aslam came into the tent and said, 'She will have water.'

I knew I had to follow Aslam outside.

Aslam started talking immediately, 'It's Ginniji. You pissed her off and she is talking to everyone about you. Even the journos. She is on the set today. Make up with her. Ranvir is trying to do Prateeksha's film and this can't reach the press again.'

I looked at Aslam: his white shoes, white pants, floral shirt. His perfume was strong and revolting. 'How do you know all this?'

Just then the third stunt double came up us. 'Aslam bhai ... thank you so much, my kids send salaam.'

Aslam patted him on the back. The stunt double walked away as Aslam said, 'You know they work hard, very hard; get hurt, get scratched, get up in the morning everyday to stay in shape. I don't even give them insurance. If they get hurt, break a leg, break a hand, I give them some money. I don't do much for them. I give them work, they know me, they work for me, they call me Aslam bhai. I fix jobs for them and fifty other people on this set. If they break their arm I do what I can and then I move on ... to get Chinese food for someone, to get a better room or better hotel for someone else. My job is not a job, it's a sentence. Ginniji knows people. She helps me with getting these people jobs. And if she asks something, I tell her. I told her about you too. You better fix things with her Neki. This article is not coming out, but Ranvir cannot stop all of them.'

I saw what Aslam was trying to say with those hundred words. Sorry. His face had beads of sweat and traces of guilt.

'Apology accepted, Aslam,' I said. My walkie came to life. It was Karan. 'Neki, please tell Alisha to be on standby.'

I looked at the crumpled article, printed out on a faded yellow A4 paper. My first thought was, who prints gossip articles on yellow stationery? I decided not to read the article. I crushed it and slumped down on a chair nearby. Just then I saw a familiar pair of shoes standing next to me. David Brown.

There was a moment of blackness. The alarm bells should have started now, but they didn't.

David Brown thrust the scene towards me. I took the paper and said hurriedly, 'Oh yes, as you point a gun at him Ahmed continues his poem,

Man ka vishwas ragon mein sahas bharta hai:
chad kar girna, gir kar chadna na akharta hai,
aakhir uski mehnat bekaar nahi hoti,
koshish karne walon ki haar nahi hoti.'

David rolled his eyes, 'What am I supposed to do while he continues talking?'

'You keep holding the gun.'

David's eyes were as wide as saucers, 'And what does it mean?'

'It means:
Your belief is all the strength you need;
To stumbling and falling you pay no heed;
Hard work is never in vain;
Because people who try never lose the game.'

I paused.

David looked at me for a full moment. Then, looking almost scared, he asked, 'There's more?'

I nodded.

He shook his head. 'I don't want to know . . . let me speak to the action director!' he said and walked off.

I went to Alisha to call her. I could hear her talking to

Rosh. 'I have done almost five hundred stunts so far and have been a double for all the top Bollywood actresses. I usually go for stunts alone, but Hassan is always with me, like a shadow. My mother feels better that there is someone looking out for me when I jump down from the sky. I go for his stunts too. We need to fight for better protective gear and equipment to minimise risks; it's better to put your point across as a team ...'

Rosh was staring at Alisha. Her eyes blank. There was no emotion there. In fact, Rosh had not shown any emotion for the last one hour.

Fear, deep and cold, was squeezing my gut. We were losing her for good this time.

Alisha continued. 'Before doing a stunt I just close my eyes and say a little prayer; if it goes well, everyone claps. If not, well, it's a retake or an ambulance.'

'Alisha, you need to go near the building; the action team is waiting for you. Rosh, will you be okay?' I asked. She nodded.

Alisha and I walked to where the stunt was to take place. Through my dizziness, thoughts of Ranvir, Aslam, Rosh, the AD team swam in my head. I had to talk to each one of them. Shivani had been treating me like an equal lately, and Kriti hadn't given me one caustic remark for ages ... was there a chance that they would agree to my promotion? Was there a chance that Ranvir would altogether disappear from my life? Was there a chance that Alisha and Hassan may not land on the safety balloon spread like a bloated blue and yellow mammal in front of us on the ground?

Alisha looked at me, winked and went inside the building to go all the way up only to jump all the way down. We all waited with bated breath.

## A JAW AND A LEG

Three cameras had been set up to cover the fall. Dharmesh sir was losing it in the heat yet again. Screaming and shouting at anyone who had ears. The shot was for all the three stunt people to jump together. And land, hopefully, without mishap.

The monitor was set; the stunt guys were being briefed by the action director—a portly guy who was constantly sweating and whose shorts always seemed to be on the verge of falling. I was nervous about him being responsible for three lives. If he could barely handle his shorts, what was he going to do about three people? But they said he was the best in town.

Shivani was sitting in one corner and the rest of the AD team was next to the monitor. Ahmed Khan was on the set to watch the stunt. His dialogue portion of the scene was going to be shot later in the day. Ranvir and Kashish were inside their respective vans.

It was time to have that chat with Shivani. I walked up to her. 'I hope it's okay that I'm getting credit as third AD?' I asked.

Shivani laughed. 'You stupid, stupid girls . . . you see that twit running around in her Gabbana pants?' That was Kriti; she was wearing fuchsia designer pants. She and PJ were standing to the side of the monitor, in the middle of what looked like a tense moment. She seemed to be pleading with PJ for something. That was new for Kriti. I was intrigued.

Shivani continued. 'God has given her so much and she is miserable. Begging PJ to give her some important work in the stunt shot. She wants to impress her father. You know he's coming on the sets today?' I shook my head as Shivani continued her monologue. She was definitely distressed today. 'But Neki, who do I impress? I have a father who wants me to marry someone and settle down, but for me that would mean I have failed. Maybe I have. I have the experience, I have learnt, I can tell stories, I know how to take shots, I know how to run a set, how can I fail? How can Hassan leave me again? After all that I've done for him? Oh God! And yes it is okay for you to take the title! I don't care; even if you take the *producer's* title, I won't care!'

Shivani was losing it. We all do at some point or the other. This was Shivani's point for sure. She was clutching her stomach, and that made me think that either she was having acute stomach cramps or she was acutely in love with Hassan. If it was the former, I had a solution my mother swore by: chamomile tea. I instantly blabbered. 'Shivani, can I get you some chamomile tea? You can even use the mug as a hot compress for your lower abdomen while you are drinking it.'

Shivani stared at me as if I had lost it. Her tone changed drastically, 'Neki you are weird. Please disappear from my line of vision and go far, far away from me.'

I gladly obliged.

I turned around to see the action director pull up his shorts for the hundredth time. He was about to call for action. The three were readying to jump. I sent out a little prayer ... it was dizzying to even watch them do this. Just before action was called, there was a moment of silence. I think it was respect for the risk these people were taking for a two-second shot in the film.

They jumped—perfectly, and landed safely. One shot okay. Everyone clapped. As I was marvelling at the quickness of the fall, Karan thrust a sheet of paper in my hand and walked away. It was the details of the second stunt for the day—a shot of a bomb blast.

I turned back to Shivani, who had tears rolling down her cheeks. Before I could stop myself, I blurted, 'I think Hassan might be in love with Alisha . . .'

There was an awkward silence. 'You don't know that for sure, so stop butting into my life . . . please leave,' she said harshly.

Today was not a good day.

I looked up and saw that it was probably going to rain. It was cloudy and I could sense the birds were unsettled. Nature has its own language and meaning; in the flock of birds fleeing, in the sudden silence of the crickets, in the heaviness of the wind, in the trembling of the leaves.

The signs are everywhere.

I saw Shivani walk up to Hassan. They looked like they were having another argument, Alisha standing a few feet away from them.

I spotted PJ dashing towards the direction room and stopped him mid-way. 'Zoya said Rosh would be better when she comes back from home—she isn't. People said being in love is great—it sucks. What is happening PJ? You think we should have dinner tonight?'

PJ stared for a second, obviously stumped by my sudden question. Then he said, 'That was weird, very weird, but I think I'm going to say yes.'

I was relieved.

Just then a very distinguished looking man walked past us. 'That's Kriti's dad, the guy in the suit.'

'PJ, are you okay with me sharing credit with you, for third AD?' I asked without thinking.

PJ looked at me and smiled. 'Only if you keep the dinner date.'

I smiled back. The day was looking a lot better.

And then I saw her, walking towards us. Actually walking towards Ranvir's van. Wearing jeans and a pale pink chikan kurta, her hair tied in a bun, not an ounce of make-up on her face. Prateeksha Devi really was a very attractive woman.

Aslam was escorting her like a puppy dog. It might have been my imagination, but I thought she looked at me. There was no expression on her face. She reminded me of Rosh in some way. Instead of lipstick, eye shadow and rouge, she had beauty, tragedy and strength written all over her face.

I liked her instantly.

I could sense the bile rise up my throat and taste it in my mouth. I liked the woman who was stealing the love of my life. My state of mind must be delicate, to say the least.

My grandfather often said, 'We all learn who we are everyday. Let's just hope we like the discovery.' My discovery about myself could be summed up in one word: lunatic.

I needed some fresh air. I walked further away as PJ was called inside by Karan.

I found a secluded corner and sat down to calm my nerves, away from it all, before the madness started. I could hear the action director some distance away, rehearsing the next stunt with his team. There was going to be fire and a controlled explosion. The action was simple. Stunt double 1 was supposed to pull the trigger and shoot a ball of fire. Simultaneously, stunt double 2 would pull the lever on the harness so that stunt double 3, who was connected to the harness, would be lifted up enough to jump over the fireball. Stunt double 3—Hassan—was supposed to leap with perfect timing so it coordinated with what 1 and 2 were doing. And then the fire would hit the fake wall, leading to a semi explosion. Thermocol balls, paper and cardboard would be used for the 'explosion'.

I saw Hassan rehearsing his moves and Alisha standing to the side, watching to make sure he was okay. A little beyond, I could see Shivani staring at Alisha, watching every interaction between the two.

~

The shot for the blast was set. There was mild tension in the air. Kriti's dad was sitting behind the monitor with Fiza Kareem, the action director and the rest of the team. The ADs had taken position to cordon off people and keep them away from the stunt team.

Two things were out of place.

Kriti was practically hysterical with her dad on the set, and Shivani was livid about the Hassan-Alisha discovery. The estrogen levels were drowning the set, not to mention my own queasy stomach, which flipped over when I saw Ranvir come out of his van and sit behind the monitor.

We were minutes away from the action stunt. I crossed my fingers. Just then I heard a yelp. Aslam had stepped on the tail of a stray dog by mistake. Whining, the dog ran away. It seemed like the dog was cussing at us from a distance. Something was not right.

I was meant to keep a watch from the south direction, so no one would pass in the frame in the background. Kriti was complaining because she wanted to stand where PJ was so her dad could see her clearly.

I closed my eyes, my nausea hitting a new level all together. When I opened them, I saw Ranvir staring at me. I turned away to see Shivani standing next to Kriti and PJ. 'You can't do serious work in those fuchsia pants,' she said to Kriti. 'And besides, I am standing at this spot.'

Kriti glanced at her father and said, 'No way, I'm standing here.'

I knew why Shivani wanted to stand there. That spot happened to be closer to Hassan. Closer than Alisha, who was standing far away in one corner.

I crossed my fingers more tightly. And opened them with a start. A massive thud had come from somewhere. A mirror, placed by the cameraman to reflect the light, had fallen because of a sudden gust of wind. People ran over to clear it away.

My mother always said the breaking of a mirror was a good omen, because the mirror takes all imminent mishaps and ill luck upon itself.

It was a good sign.

I heaved a sigh of relief, until I saw one of the setting department guys being rushed off to see the medic. A shard of glass had cut his right hand deeply.

This stunt should not happen.

I saw PJ walking away to take over Shivani's position at the other end. Both Shivani and Kriti had got their way.

The action director called for stand-by. I saw Kriti standing on some ropes, her eyes glued to her father, to see if he was watching her or not. Sheer desperation reflected in her eyes.

I could feel it rising again. Was it the bile, was it tension or was it disaster.

I saw Shivani was five steps ahead of her mark, and she was staring at Hassan. Love- and hate-struck. I was hoping to God she was not asking for Hassan to break his neck.

I saw Kriti had changed her position as well; she was now right next to the first stunt double.

I did not have the energy to speak or talk.

The action director called for action. The count was called out. One, two, three, GO—stunt double 1 pulled the rope with a sharp tug and his elbow smashed into something.

It was Kriti's beautiful, delicate face. She had moved closer to the stunt double so her father would see her standing next to the man pulling the rope.

A few production people ran towards Kriti to help her instinctively, without realising the danger. They ran in from my side, oblivious of the fact that Hassan was running, and the fireball—let loose by the tug of ropes—was heading straight towards him.

It all happened in a split second, but it seemed like a few hours. 'Don't move!' I screamed at the production people running in from my side. My hysterical screams made them stop.

I could hear the crew running towards Kriti from other directions too. They stopped as well.

PJ and Karan cordoned off the area, acting fast.

If this went wrong, Hassan was going right into the fire. I saw Alisha praying quietly in the corner.

No one tried to rush in except Shivani, who ran into frame to help Hassan. Her foot caught in the ropes lying around and she tripped.

The camera kept rolling. Hassan—blocking out all the noise and confusion—jumped beautifully over the ball of fire.

The director called out 'cut'. The shot was okay.

It had only cost us a jaw and a leg.

Kriti had a broken jaw.

Shivani had a fractured leg.

## NOTHING MUCH HAPPENED

As both Shivani and Kriti were being taken to the hospital, I saw Rosh walking out of the tent quietly. I had not given her any time today. As she left, she turned and waved at me.

Karan called me over next to the monitor, 'That was good thinking Neki. By the way, with Shivani injured, you and PJ will be acting as second assistant directors now.'

I swayed and I knew the moment was here when I was going to fall and hit the ground and crack my skull. But someone caught me. It was Ranvir. I could smell his cologne. The bile was rising. Finally the moment was here—I could let it all out, at once. I threw up all over Ranvir.

I had water in my eyes and nose. It was getting dark and I couldn't really see his face. I only felt him gently touch my forehead.

~

I opened my eyes. Someone was sitting next to me, holding my hand. PJ. I was shivering. I wasn't feeling cold, but I was shivering. There was this bad feeling in the pit of my stomach.

The doctor wanted to have a word with me alone. PJ and

Ginniji exited the van hesitantly. Once the doctor was done, he called them inside. Ginniji stood in one corner. She gave me a pleasant smile. I saw she was wearing a long white skirt, under which I could spot the straps of a yellow thong. She left the van with the doctor once again. They were friends it seemed.

PJ held a glass of water for me to drink, made me wear his jacket and took me out of the van and studio from the back entry. He knew I could not bear to see anyone right then.

We reached his house in silence. I lay down on his bed and slept again.

It was three in the morning when I woke up. PJ was watching me. The feeling in my stomach was still there. PJ lay down beside me and held me. I had to tell him something, the words were not coming out. My throat was parched. I needed some water, and I was drowning.

PJ was kissing me. I was crying. I needed to pull away. PJ needed to hold me more.

And then it hit me. Finally. What the doctor had been trying to hint at. I knew it in my gut. PJ was lying peacefully next to me. Breathing softly. I knew that I should tell him. I should tell him now. He was sleeping lightly. I woke him up. I looked at the time. It was important to look at the time so that I could say it aloud and document this moment in my head.

At 4.03 a.m. I told PJ I was pregnant with Ranvir's baby.

At 4.04 he asked me 'Are you sure?'

At 4:05 I told him I had missed a month of my cycle already. But I'd just realised it a few minutes ago.

At 4.06 PJ walked out of his own room.

At 4.10, I realised Ginniji knew I was pregnant too.

*Dear Mom,*

*Not much of consequence happened today. The only*

*important thing that happened was that Shivani broke her leg while running up the stairs and Kriti broke her jaw while playing volleyball in our lunch break (don't worry I stay away from all these dangerous games). Everything else was fine. Rosh is back in town finally. You will be happy to know that I am now promoted to second AD on the film.*

*Love,*
*Neki*

*PS: It rained heavily in Mumbai today. The weatherman said the rain and thunderstorm was unexpected. But I knew about the thunderstorm—I knew it was coming. It did.*

## THE PIED PIPER

Sitting here on the parapet, I realise this might be the darkest hour of the night. They say the darkest hour of the night is just before dawn. But then, they say that in the movies.

My phone is flashing again. I need to read my last diary entry before I succumb to the pull of oblivion and push myself off this ledge. Ironically, I was sitting at the same spot four months ago, when I'd made a promise, looking down at the treetops, the bright sun coating the green leaves with a golden hue.

I'd been sitting in my room, filing my nails, when the music had first whispered in my ear teasingly. I ran to my living room window, but could not see who it was. I ran up to the terrace. It was a flute vendor, playing a haunting tune as he walked down the quiet street on a Sunday afternoon. He had about twenty flutes stuck on a pole, which he carried on his shoulder.

I stood at this parapet, looking down at the flute player. A couple of dragonflies chased one another with wild abandon, dancing to his tune; their wings reflecting rainbow colours. I had stolen this magical view from an otherwise plain Mumbai street, thanks to the flute player.

I had decided at that moment that I had to experience the

magic of making music. Weaving sounds that enchant. I promised myself I was going to learn to play an instrument.

The promise would have to wait for another life. For now, it was time to read the last entry in my diary.

## THE STAND-IN GIRL

17 March 2009. 8:01 p.m.

Dear Nano,

PJ was really quiet after that night, not mentioning our conversation or my condition at all. Not that I wanted him to. I just wanted to focus on getting through the day and working hard. But today had other plans for me. Minty had a cramp in her foot, and I had to be her stand-in. A 'stand-in' is a person who 'stands-in' for an actor while the director of photography lights them for the shot. For one brief moment the stand-in gets to be in the middle of it all, with the lights, the camera, the world revolving around them.

The moment the real actor comes in, the stand-in steps aside, to be another face amongst many.

I was always taught that everybody is dispensable, but in the world of a film set, the actors are not. And, perhaps, therein lies the allure and the pull of stardom. Eventually, though, supple youth moves along and age sets in, the body is tired, but the mind is a traitor. It keeps them going, teasing them, refusing to understand that it's all right to be dispensable. That it's time to hang up your boots. Even if they are Italian custom-made.

Today, as Minty's stand-in, I was supposed to be in

Ranvir's arms and deliver romantic dialogues with him. This was the climax scene of the film, where Ranvir is supposed to take Minty in his arms and leave the burning hall. (So my story gets a happy ending after all—even if it is just in a rehearsal.) The hall explodes the minute we, i.e. Minty and Ranvir, step out of it. Yes, I know we've seen that too many times in Bollywood. As in real life, in Bollywood the stories always remain the same. Originality is overrated. For it's not the story that is unique, it's the person reading the story that makes it so.

It was the last week of our film shoot. Just the four of us were left in the AD team: Karan, PJ, Sam and me. The new girl had quit after seeing Kriti and Shivani turn hysterical.

I have to confess, there is a reason I never told you the new girl's name. Her full name is Neki Chopra. And the reason I refused to call her by her name is because, all my life, I believed I was unique and different.

The more I see the world, though, the more I realise that everybody is unique and different. So everybody ends up being the same.

Originality is definitely overrated.

I saw PJ walking over to me, a call sheet in hand. This is a paper listing requirements for the next day's shoot, which is circulated on the set. I was standing in front of the camera. Dharmesh sir had marked a place for me and I was not supposed to move from there. He was in one of his bad moods and, as usual, I was right there at the wrong place at the wrong time with an itch to sneeze. But Dharmesh sir, adjusting the lights on my face, glared at me if I so much as moved to scratch my arm. I was not allowed to breathe, let alone sneeze. When Dharmesh sir was in this kind of mood, it meant only one thing for the rest of the crew. Hide. He has a nasty temper.

I saw Aslam standing right behind PJ with a cup of tea in his hand. Both of them were looking at me.

'Nekiji? Tea?' Aslam asked, with a fake smile. I knew Aslam was here to tell me something and I had a feeling I was not going to like it. I ignored him, my mind focused on not thinking about what was happening in my body. Instead, I concentrated on a light-man standing on a seven-foot rickety ladder in the middle of the set, fixing a light on the breathtaking chandelier, to the background of Dharmesh sir cussing him and telling him to hurry up.

PJ broke into my trance-like state. 'Neki, why did you write in the call sheet that we need twelve band guys in uniforms?'

I looked at him, confused. 'As if you don't know, PJ. Fiza wants a fully-dressed band playing outside the entrance for the shot, to lead in to the party.'

'The twelve band members are ready and in uniform,' PJ said with a straight face.

'So what's the problem?' I asked.

PJ cleared his throat, and came closer to me. Fortunately for me, Dharmesh sir was busy abusing the light-man and, at the same time, swatting an unsuspecting light boy with a mike, or I would have been in serious trouble for talking while being a stand-in.

'Nothing much, just that the band members are here without any instruments.'

Aslam's smile grew wider. 'You did not put in the call sheet that the band members require instruments, so the production guys did not order any. Actually, this production guy is new, but I don't blame him; if it is a requirement it should have been in the call sheet.'

I was furious. 'It's obvious, Aslam, that band members are

not invited to a party to socialise. The band is there to play, so they need instruments! It's so obvious!' I almost screamed. I was ready to hurl a camera or a light at Aslam's face any minute.

Aslam pointed to the call sheet again. 'If it's so obvious, then why did you not put it in the call sheet Nekiji? Anyway, I am trying to procure some instruments . . .'

'And if I don't get the instruments on time, what is the band going to play with?' PJ asked.

I muttered through clenched teeth, 'Tell Fiza that the band will be playing with Aslam's broken head.'

PJ took the cup of tea from Aslam and held it out to me. 'Relax Neki . . . Have some tea; you need to rest as much as you can . . . in your condition.'

I stared at him open-mouthed. 'By your condition, I mean as a stand-in girl, opposite Ranvir,' PJ smirked. 'In the movies, I mean.'

I looked at PJ; he was mocking me. I realised he was angry. He was angry at me for getting myself into this situation. He was angry because he believed I deserved better. His anger was the most comforting thing around.

But his mocking statement had, in some way, summed up my life.

Maybe I was Ranvir's 'stand-in' girl. Not just in rehearsals, but in real life too.

Softly, so Aslam wouldn't hear, I said, 'I swear when the next wave of nausea hits me, I will find you. I will dig you out from wherever you are and puke on you.'

I could see Aslam was trying to eavesdrop on our conversation.

PJ looked at me intently. And then I saw it coming—his master device to distract me, a random hypothetical scenario.

'What if Aslam were to have a heart attack here and die with that call sheet in his hand? Would he care if the band members were playing instruments or not? If they were playing in their band uniforms or underwear? Would he care if he managed to get the Chinese food and the Iodex? How does it all matter, when he is lying on the floor? His mouth half open, dead.'

Aslam squealed, 'What?! Why would I have a heart attack with my mouth open?'

PJ turned. 'It's an example.'

'Choose someone else for an example. In the unit of two hundred people you could only find me as an example for a heart attack victim?! And even if I did have one, I will make sure the band players are fully clothed and the Iodex and everything that is asked for is arranged. I am the greatest line producer there is, I won't even die till I provide you with things you have asked for!'

Just then Karan barged in on our little party, looking harassed. Before he could say anything, PJ butt in. 'Karan, I was thinking, can you excuse Neki from being a stand-in today? She has fever and as a stand-in she will have to rehearse with the actors the whole day.'

Karan put his walkie down and stared at PJ for long uncomfortable seconds. And then he spoke in a calm voice. 'Sure . . . tell me PJ, which one of us here can stand in for Minty and rehearse with Ranvir? Let me guess, Shivani, hopping on her broken leg? No. Maybe Kriti with her dislocated jaw? The new girl who has run away? Or wait! Maybe *you* can do it; or me with my beard. You think Ranvir will appreciate lifting me in his arms and gazing into my eyes as he walks out of the hall?'

Karan and PJ glared at each other. The spot was getting heated up, and not just because of all the lights around.

'If Ranvir were a good actor, he could rehearse with a broomstick and make it look romantic!' PJ said angrily.

Karan clenched his teeth. 'Come on guys! Last week of the shoot, pull it together. We have three hundred junior artistes, we have a stunt to complete, we have a scene with the hall on fire and we have a heroine with a sprained ankle. No one gets to complain today. And Aslam, you need to pitch in as well.'

'Of course I will have to help out. Your team has serious health concerns,' Aslam promptly replied, looking at me. There was a glint in his eye, which could mean only one thing. 'I just wanted to make sure you know, Neki, that your health concern is now a very public issue,' Aslam continued.

'What is he talking about? Karan asked with irritation, probably thinking that he had just lost one more AD. When he didn't get an answer, he shook his head and walked away.

PJ and I looked at each other and back at Aslam. PJ was about to say something when Aslam interrupted. 'It's spreading like wildfire,' he smirked, looking at something in the distance. We turned. He was looking at Karan, who was standing about ten feet away from us, under a beautiful bouquet of white and lilac flowers tied with huge pink satin bows that were fluttering in the wind from the fans that were whirring all over the set. But the most striking thing was the expression on Karan's face. Dumbstruck.

Ginniji was standing next to him with a smirk on her face. A green thong peeped out from under her very low pants. I could see she had just given Karan the good news.

I had to tell Ranvir before somebody else did.

PJ was called away by Fiza who asked him to get the other actors on the set. Before going, PJ whispered in my ear. 'I am around.'

I could feel the moisture in my eyes. I took a step towards

PJ and Dharmesh sir yelled, 'Neki, can you just stand in your position correctly?'

I froze and went right back to my mark.

'I need everyone to clear the frame right now. NOW!'

Everyone started running helter-skelter. I was left alone on the spot, marked under the harsh lights. I was in the spotlight, and not just literally.

Before leaving, Aslam hurriedly said, 'I just came to tell you, don't worry. Even if people like Ginniji leak the information, it won't come out—I have just told Prateeksha Devi. I have warned her so she can stop it from reaching the press!'

Aslam had told Prateeksha about my pregnancy? I could feel hysteria build up in me. I knew it because the tea that I had been holding a minute ago was now all over Aslam's feet, and he was hopping around and screaming, 'Why did you do that? Are you crazy?'

'I am going to do a lot more, Aslam!! I am not done with you ... how could you?' I asked, angry tears flowing down my face.

Just then all the noise around us came to a halt as Dharmesh sir screamed, 'What the hell is happening on this set? Aslam, what are you doing?'

I could sense everyone looking at us. And then, on the mike, Fiza said hesitantly, 'I know Minty is supposed to cry in the shot, Neki, but you are supposed to be a stand-in only, not actually do the heroine's role yourself!'

Just then Sam ran up and handed me a crumpled tissue paper, with stains of some mango pickle on it. 'Don't worry I can stand in for you.'

Dharmesh sir blew up again. 'I don't need a stand-in for a stand-in. Why is this AD standing in for an AD?!'

'Sam! Off the floor, now!' Karan yelled. 'Get tomorrow's call sheet ready!'

Fiza spoke in the mike again, 'What is happening on my set today?'

Before he left, Sam quickly whispered in my ear, 'Zoya is waiting outside; she wants to meet you one last time before she moves her stuff and hands over the keys of the flat to you.'

That meant I was going to be all alone in the flat. Everyone was leaving. I wasn't even sure any more if Shikha was coming back from her friend's place. Slowly my world was moving away, while I was still standing at the same spot.

Dharmesh sir screamed again, 'Can you look this side, Neki? How many times are you supposed to be told this? Can't you do your job properly?'

'I am doing the best I can,' I replied in a high-pitched tone.

I could see Dharmesh sir's face flushing. 'You are going to be the stand-in for the entire week, you understand? What do you think . . . ?'

Just then I heard a voice, 'Sir . . . I'll take my position. I saw your film yesterday, what stunning lighting! You make a dirty rock look like a painting.'

Dharmesh sir calmed down. Ranvir had just rescued me.

I noticed his black suit, black waistcoat, crisp white steam-pressed shirt, and bow tie—he was looking perfect. I needed to tell him that he looked very handsome today, and maybe also mention that I was pregnant in the same conversation.

Fiza began giving out instructions. 'Ranvir, the camera will follow you all the way to the door as you pick Neki up and walk out. Dharmesh sir, I want all angles covered.'

Dharmesh sir mumbled grumpily, 'I *have* them covered. I've put one camera on the track, one camera hand-held, it will all be covered.'

The handheld was a heavy camera which the cameraman would carry on his shoulder and follow the actors.

'Record this rehearsal,' Fiza announced on the mike.

Just then Ranvir's spot boy Inder came running to us, panicked, 'Prateeksha ma'am has called five times.'

'I will talk to her after the rehearsal,' Ranvir replied curtly.

'She said she will hold the line. It's urgent.'

Dharmesh sir had the camera on his shoulder and he shouted, 'Ready!'

The stage was set. I knew this would be the only chance I had to tell Ranvir before Prateeksha did.

Ranvir picked me up like a child. This was it.

'Action!' Fiza called out.

I whispered in Ranvir's ear, 'I'm pregnant.'

Ranvir froze.

Dharmesh sir went all the way to the door, assuming we would start walking out, but Ranvir just stood there. Dharmesh sir came back, lugging the heavy camera on his shoulder. We were still standing on the same spot. Dharmesh sir, struggling under his camera, screamed at us to move forward. Fiza screamed cut—and then finally Ranvir moved. He put me down and simply walked out. Out of the door, out of the set, out of the main gate.

A second later, Fiza followed him out of the set.

I stood there. I had nowhere to go.

Just then a meek voice asked me, 'Ma'am, tea, coffee, water? I have even got a chair. You need to sit down.' A searing pain in my stomach made me clench the chair for support. My vision blurred with the pain as I heard some muffled screams and some figures rushing towards me.

Out of focus shot.

In the movies, sometimes they use 'out of focus' shots to

show that the main character is about to faint or a big twist in the story is about to follow. Well, movies are not too different from real life after all. In the real world too, there is an 'out of focus' moment, when your focus in life changes forever. And in the movies, just after the out-of-focus shot, usually the screen goes blank for a split second before the next chapter begins.

I passed out.

The screen blanked out.

I was in my split second.

But people say it lasted a day.

## MY SPLIT SECOND

There was no one in the room when I woke up. I could tell I was in some kind of clinic. The room was stark. Small. The bed I lay on was narrow. I could see a tiny window from where I was. The faint hum of traffic filtered through. I registered a tube in my arm and a glucose bottle next to the bed.

The clock was prominent. I could not see it but I could hear it. I wanted to raise my head and look at the clock so I could tell what time it was. I was disoriented. Somehow, knowing what time it was would comfort me. It always does—you wake up in a strange place, you look at the time.

I had lain there with my eyes open for some time when Shikha and Zoya walked in. I wasn't ready to talk, and they could sense that. So they just sat by my side quietly. It helped that they were not talking to each other. There was complete silence in the room. Rosh came into the room as well, but the silence did not leave.

The doctor came and said something to the effect that I was very weak and I needed to stay in the clinic for two more days; that there was a miscarriage.

I was alone at night—I'd insisted that the girls leave. PJ came in. He talked. I was quiet. He told me the shoot had resumed after I was rushed to the hospital. That it was all under control. I should rest and come back to work and put everything behind me. He did not talk about Ranvir. What was Ranvir's reaction to the news? Did Ranvir know I was here? Was he coming to see me? Did he hate me? Did he love me? I thought I would find out the answer to the last two questions for sure. This was my chance. This was my last hope.

'Where's Ranvir?' I asked.

PJ got up very slowly. All he said was that he would drop in the next day after pack-up.

The next day was the same. Rosh, Zoya and Shikha sat in silence. To distract myself from my thoughts, I observed the three girls through half-closed eyes. They had all changed. Their faces had lines and marks I had not seen before. Rosh's face was more beautiful and ravaged. There was strength in those cruel lines.

Zoya's was burnt a little bit near her nose, as if she had taken too much sun. There was regret in those tiny dark patches of skin.

Shikha had wrinkles near her eyes. There was distrust trapped in those tiny lines.

They were all so stunning.

Today they were all making an attempt at polite conversation to distract me. No one spoke about Ranvir. I was informed that Karan had called twice on my cell, to check on me. He said Fiza was very concerned and wanted an update every hour from the doctor.

'She needs to talk to her parents,' Zoya said. They'd told me earlier that my parents had not been informed yet.

Rosh looked at Zoya and said firmly, 'No.' I had never heard Rosh use that tone before. Zoya stared at her for a second, and then nodded.

Rosh handed me a note. 'Minty dropped by while you were sleeping,' she explained.

I looked at the pink paper and took in its heady flowery smell. It was so typically Minty. The paper had three words scrawled on them: 'Hang in there'. I stared at the piece of paper. Minty was a scheming sidekick, a conniving businesswoman, a vain person—who came to visit me when I needed people to stand by me the most.

Who was she?

She was neither jet-black, nor pearly white. She was grey. And grey, it seemed, was the colour of life.

## A FINE MAN

On that note, my last diary entry ended. I shut the book.

I'd been sitting on my white hospital bed this afternoon, my things packed in a small bag next to me, which Zoya had brought over. I was waiting for PJ, who'd said he would pick me up in an hour.

The doctor had come in then, with a couple of nurses. There was a sympathetic look on her face. The nurses had a look on their faces too. Not sympathetic, not hostile—just strange.

The room felt like a museum and I, the *objet d'art*.

'Is something wrong?' I finally asked.

The doctor looked at the nurses and curtly asked them to leave the room. When they were out, she said, 'Actually, Ranvir Khanna visited the hospital last night and asked about you. He took care of the hospital formalities and all that. They are just curious.'

So the nurses disapproved of me.

The good news was Ranvir had come. He'd been here. He did not meet me, but he'd been here.

I needed to go meet him. I blurted, 'Can I leave?'

'You can, but I think it's best to have someone escort you. I have signed your discharge papers.'

The doctor wished me luck and walked out. On her way, the doctor reprimanded another nurse who was peeking in to take a look at me. Ranvir had certainly made me a celebrity in the hospital.

I could not sit there a second longer. I picked up my bag, walked out of the room and hospital, and hailed a taxi. I could not wait to reach the set.

PJ had taken my cell away this morning—so I wouldn't be disturbed, he'd said and I'd been too tired to argue. He was looking hassled and was in a rush.

I wished I had my phone now: I needed to call my mom. I had to see Ranvir. I needed to get my phone back and my life back.

I settled in the back of an old taxi and gave him the address. The taxi driver stared at me in the rear-view mirror.

Calmly I said again, 'Film City.'

The taxi driver seemed to do a double flip and looked at me again. There was recognition in his eyes. Maybe he had taken me somewhere before, I thought, and looked out the window.

He lit an incense stick. Actually, two.

This time I did not open the window. Or stick my nose out. This time I took in the fumes of the rose-scented sticks. I was not scared of being robbed anymore, because Ranvir had looked me up in the hospital.

All the way to Film City, I made plans.

I was going to apologise to Fiza and come clean.

Meet Ranvir and then go back home, for a while.

It was time for me to start a new story . . . all over again.

I just needed to know the end, before I had a new beginning.

I needed to know why Ranvir had come to the hospital.

The taxi driver pulled up in front of Floor no. 6. I saw the familiar vans, generators, cars, spot-boys running around. Punjabi came running towards me and asked if I was okay.

I was glad.

The smell of the sets was familiar, the potholes were mine, the overgrown shrubs were my friends, the plastic chairs were my comfort, the discarded, stained yellow glasses on the tables were a part of my routine, the rusty metal doors were welcoming.

This was my place under the sun.

The make-up assistants sitting outside the set saw me and stood up. They were not even gossiping or whispering. They were simply staring. I smiled at them.

No one smiled back.

I walked into the studio. Punjabi ran in front of me, to inform someone that I was here, I assumed. The polka-dotted van was there and so was Goku. The dwarf. My dwarf. He made me miss my mother all over again.

Goku jumped up. 'Ma'am remember me? You said you would try for me, if my stories work, if there is any role? I saw you in the magazine today and thought I will come and check again. My daughter is diagnosed with jaundice, and it's getting worse.'

'Magazine?'

'Yes, you are on the cover of *Waqt Aaj Kal*, with Ranvirji, no? I have not read the story—I have been shuttling between hospital and house, because of my daughter. But I saw this magazine and thought of you. Please, you have to help me,' he said, handing me a folded magazine that had evidently seen a long bus ride and a hot sweaty day. I straightened it out, my heart beating so fast I thought I would collapse. Again.

On the cover was a picture of Ranvir Khanna, all handsome and glistening body. And beside it, another picture—of me. A palm-size picture, six by four inches.

It was the same measurements I would give out to aspiring actors and models looking for a role, hoping for a chance. I would rattle off, in a mechanical voice, without even looking at them, 'Send your picture. Make sure it is six by four.'

So many of those hopeful six by four pictures were lying in my drawer, discarded in my bag, forgotten in my files.

My picture on the cover of the magazine was the same size. My six by four was right here. Staring back at me.

I was in white overalls, my hair bundled up with a dirty yellow rubber band. It was appalling.

I read the headline—'Bollywood Ka Ashleel Chehra', the ugly face of Bollywood—and then quickly went through the article. Apparently I was supposed to be this stereotype of a girl who comes to Bollywood, and instead of working with the actors gets involved with one, instead of getting accolades at work gets an unwanted pregnancy. It was the story of an ambitious, scheming girl who ends up in a mess; a good warning and a bad example for all the hopefuls.

Well my grandfather always did say lead by example.

I stood right there and read the entire article. I could sense people running around me, getting things ready for the shot happening inside, and quite a few just standing there and watching me read the article.

Someone running past me was screaming on the walkie, 'Karan wants a red mug in the shot now. I am running as fast as I can to get it from the kitchen!' He stumbled in his rush, got up again and started running again. Someone yelled at him on the walkie, 'Are you an idiot? Stop running like a headless chicken and get the mug from the art department!'

The guy was definitely a new AD.

I heard Karan scream on the runner's walkie, 'Minty's button on her dress has popped, fix it now!'

I continued reading the article. It was well written, I had to say. I looked at the author's name. It was not even familiar.

I realised where the picture had been taken. It had been when I was standing on the pavement that day, thinking about quitting the industry.

I heard Aslam behind me. 'Sit down Neki,' he said.

'You said it would not come out.' My voice sounded strange even to myself.

Aslam sounded guilty. 'I thought so too, I was wrong. The media is hounding Ranvir now for interviews. He is all over the place. It is a scandal to beat all the little stories on TV right now and Ranvir is supposed to give a statement in the press saying he is concerned about your health but it has nothing to do with him and that he helped you out with the clinic etc. on humanitarian grounds.'

'Humanitarian grounds' echoed over and over in my head like an unending loop. Something snapped. I don't know for sure what body part inside the human body snaps: our liver, kidney, heart, our stomach or intestines. But something does snap and a molten slick cold liquid spreads all over your limbs, making you feel numb. It is comforting; pain beyond a level becomes comforting. I was glad something had taken over, because Freud's conscious and subconscious mind had failed miserably.

As I was coming to terms with the newfound numbness within, I realised that Goku had given up on his crumpled magazine and me. He was walking off the set, his small frame hunched over with disappointment.

I started laughing. There—I knew why Ranvir had come to

the hospital. Ranvir had to do what he had to do as well. He was being the Good Samaritan, he was promoting his film, he was promoting himself. It had nothing to do with me. It never had.

Or maybe he did love me just a little bit. But the beauty was, I would never know.

I saw PJ running towards me. He took the magazine from my hand and threw it in the bin. 'I was supposed to come and get you. Fiza wants to meet you, she is very worried and she is furious about this whole thing. She is going to—'

'I need my phone.'

PJ looked at me for a second and then silently handed it to me.

'I'm going now; please *none* of you follow me.' I marched towards an auto that was leaving and hopped into it.

Someone was already sitting in the back—Goku.

'Can I come with you?' I looked at him.

'Till where?'

'Wherever you're going. Can I come with you? I won't get in the way.'

'But ... I am going to the hospital first then I have an audition at three in the afternoon, then another at five, then I have to go to my homeopathic doctor to get medicine for my girl ...'

I looked at Goku pleadingly. He sighed and then instructed the auto driver to head to Bhabha Hospital in Bandra. I sat outside the hospital, waiting for Goku.

I sat outside the seedy little production office that Goku went to in Oshiwara. He was auditioning for a tiny role in a comedy caper. All the while in the auto rickshaw, he practiced a few jokes he would say in front of the camera for the audition.

He rehearsed as if his life depended on them. They were good jokes. Goku told me he had written them. He was talented. He was funny.

I knew the jokes by heart by the time we reached his audition.

I took the local train with Goku from platform number two from Andheri station. We got off at Churchgate for his doctor's appointment. In between writing out Goku's prescription and making the medicine for Goku, the old doctor asked me, 'Are you okay? You need some medicine? Do you feel hot more or cold? Your motions are normal? Do you have pain during your menstrual cycle?'

I stared back at him. He was expertly putting tiny white balls in a bottle and marking it with a black pen. Goku's medicine. Goku believed these would cure his little girl.

I saw a few of the sweet balls roll down and fall on the floor. Each sweet white ball was hope. I sat down on the floor to pick them up.

I saw the doctor and Goku's panicked faces. They thought I had gone cuckoo. It made them nervous.

I roamed around the streets with Goku. We bought groceries for his wife. Goku haggled over the cheapest deals. I could feel he was keeping one eye on me, as if I would suddenly start running naked on the street. His nervousness amused me. We reached a filthy bus stop. It had a digital advertisement with a bare-chested man in briefs looking at a well-dressed woman. 'Calvin Klein.'

Goku noticed the naked man and almost blushed. Then looked at me again. He wanted to say something. I knew what it was, he wanted me to leave—but I needed to hear it. I needed to be told today. He finally looked at me and said, 'Ma'am, I have nowhere else to go today.'

'Okay,' I replied.

Goku smiled gently, 'Thank you Ma'am for helping me for the day. It was very kind of you.'

That's when I knew, Goku was a fine man—a very fine man indeed.

## A BEAUTIFUL NIGHT

When I got back home, to Rose Mahal, it was practically empty, naked. The only thing left behind in the living room was Mona Lisa. She was still smiling, the way she had been when things were fine. She was still covering the secrets she was supposed to. Everything else had been taken away by Rosh and Zoya. Shikha had still not shifted back in.

I touched the painting. It brought a smile to my face.

My phone was ringing non-stop.

I opened the fridge and saw a bottle of wine. It was the bottle Ranvir had given me on New Year's Eve.

The landline rang. I walked towards it and picked it up. It was someone from ISDI insurance. I politely said I was not interested. The person on the other end insisted that this was the best possible deal I could get on life insurance. I told him I did not want any life insurance because my life was not unpredictable. I knew exactly how, when and why it would end. The person was quiet and then he hung up.

I went to my room. Most of my stuff was gone. Rosh had taken it with her. She had announced at the clinic that I would be staying with her. No one had argued.

A few things had been left behind. I had a warm bath. Washed my hair with a lovely smelling shampoo. I applied nail paint on my toes. And then I walked out of our apartment. Locked the door behind me and climbed the flight of stairs to our terrace—my diary in one hand and the bottle of wine in the other. It was a perfect night, clear skies, twinkling stars, crisp breeze and a beautiful moon. The first thought that crossed my mind was, what a beautiful night to die.

∼

The time was right. The dogs were sleeping peacefully. The sky was preparing for daybreak. My cell blinked again. This time I looked at the name flashing on it. PJ. I waited. I knew people were looking for me everywhere and I knew this was the last place they would look. The door was locked and as far as the others knew, our terrace was out of bounds for tenants.

I saw other names in the missed calls list. Aslam. Karan. Shivani. Kriti. Zoya. Shikha. Sam. Rosh.

I saw Fiza's name.

A warm rush of tears spilled from my eyes.

Then my mom called; her name flashing urgently. And before I could answer her call, I jumped.

## AN END BEFORE A BEGINNING

I hit the ground. Something cracked. Maybe my skull or could be the pavement. Something hammered in my head. I saw the white light; that brilliant flashing light at the end of the tunnel. And then I saw her, a beautiful lady standing, smiling. Somehow she seemed familiar—a friend. I couldn't place her though, and then she disappeared. Another burst of light, maybe an angel was coming for me. But in my case, he was dressed like a hawaldar, the same hawaldar who had caught me with Ranvir in the car. Oh Lord . . . not him! He was dead too! Please send anyone else to take me to heaven but not that hawaldar.

But whoever had come to take me away, the time had come—I was facing death.

I was petrified, and then I remembered. My mom reading out something about life and death one quiet afternoon, while stirring a pot of dal makhni in the kitchen. That during our life, around five lakh cells die each second, and each day about fifty billion cells in our body are replaced. So during our life, body change is constant. We are living and dying at the same time, each day, each minute, each second.

Finally I understood that my mother's incessant ramblings had a reason. I smiled. I was not scared of death any more.

And then I saw Aslam with PJ. If Aslam was here, I knew I hadn't made it to heaven.

My dream broke.

As usual I'd been at the wrong place at the wrong time.

The shadows I had been watching, sitting on the terrace, had not been a figment of my imagination after all. They were actually policemen waiting to nab a junkie selling a few grams of weed to make some extra money.

As usual, I had upset everybody's plans that night.

I had landed on a plainclothes policeman; he had broken my fall. In return, I broke his hand and dislocated his shoulder.

The crack I'd heard was neither my head, nor the pavement, it was this hawaldar's shoulder. He was the same hawaldar who had beaten our bai and was scared when I'd threatened him. Turns out he was right to be scared of me.

~

So there I was, back in a hospital. It had a peculiar smell. Then I realised the smell seemed peculiar because it was odourless. The hospital had no smell at all. Or my nose was seriously damaged.

There was a crowd of strange people gathered around out of curiosity. Curiosity is defined as an emotion related to natural inquisitive behaviour such as exploration, investigation and learning, evident by observation in human and many animal species. I wondered if the crowd *explored* the reason why I was lying limp on the stretcher, or *observed* my perfectly painted pink nails and *investigated* into the reasons for my jump. Lack of facts were happily filled in by assumption and conjecture, and of course the magazine article helped.

Thankfully the police and the doctors shooed them away.

I could see Aslam's face clearly. Head bent, guilt chasing shock and remorse from his face. Before I could look at the other familiar faces around me, the beautiful lady reappeared. The familiar feeling; like I had never seen her face before but that I knew who she was. I could see her standing at the end of the corridor. She was standing with the nurse. Looking at me.

～

The media had gathered outside. News of my jump had travelled far and wide.

The entire AD team was there, from Karan to PJ, to Shivani, hobbling in a cast, Kriti with a bandaged face, Minty the side actress and, much to my surprise, even the new girl Neki Chopra. And of course there was Rosh, Shikha and Zoya.

Amongst all these faces, there was one that was expressionless. PJ's blank face expressed his utter shock and disbelief at what I had done. I felt a tiny prick, no it was not the nurse's needle, it was a reminder of the colossal mistake I had made.

I looked at PJ and pleaded, 'Can you take me somewhere else, please?'

No one paid any heed to my incoherent mumblings. They had decided to keep me in the hospital till my parents arrived. I was not ready to go yet.

There was still time.

～

Despite the hospital ordeal, the tears, and my parents' anguish, I stood my ground. I was not ready to leave Mumbai just yet. My parents eventually left. Post the incident my parents went on a trip together. Travelling often helps people find themselves. It turned out well for my parents. After the trip, for the first time in their entire wedded life, Mom stopped her compulsive reading aloud from newspaper cuttings and Dad stopped hiding behind Siddhartha. They actually had conversations with their coffee.

As I looked out of the living room window of Rose Mahal, I heard someone enter. The door opened and I was surprised to see PJ there. He walked in. He did not even acknowledge me. He just stood and stared at my smiling Mona Lisa for a long time. Maybe he was still very angry with me. I decided to stay quiet. I walked into my room and shut the door. PJ yelped as the door banged shut. He seemed startled. He was edgy; I was sure he was so upset with me that this time round he would throw me from the balcony himself.

I heard him talking on the phone. I listened carefully. He was talking to my parents and apologising to them that he had not been there to prevent this. He was telling them how wonderful I was on the sets. PJ was definitely going overboard, painting me like the Virgin Mary. But I needed good public relations at this stage so obviously I did not whack him. I let him be. I walked towards the balcony. I could feel PJ's gaze following me closely.

I looked out from the balcony, beyond the crowded market, looked up and saw the sky. It reminded me of the first day I had come to Mumbai. It was a beautiful bright day again and it exposed the ugliness of my yard. I could hear water dripping from the drain. I could see the unkempt, overgrown shrubs. A bright day kept no secrets. It was cruel, stark and real. The shadows of darkness were kinder. I could pretend this was my little palace in the darkness and the shadows would let me. But daylight showed no mercy.

'Why did you jump?' I heard PJ's pitiful croak.

'I didn't want to jump. I was drunk. It was a mistake—a slip. I regret it, PJ,' I pleaded.

I could see the anger building up in him. I looked at PJ's grief-stricken face.

'You are a coward. You deserve everything you got Neki Brar,' he said softly. He walked away, shaking with anger. I stayed in the balcony.

I saw the sky chasing away the sunny noon and embracing the purple evening. Change was constant here as well. And very soon the sky was going to chase the pale evening away and wear the inky hue, disappearing into the dark night.

I went into my room and shut the door.

PJ came in after a while and looked at me intently, but I pretended to be asleep. He stood there in my room for a long time. And then he left. His silence had said everything that needed to be said.

I knew I was never going to see him again. He had bid his final adieu.

∼

I was alone in the flat again. I looked at Mona Lisa on the wall. Once again she was the only one left, thankfully with her smile. And she was the only one who knew *my* secret.

∼

I was sitting alone in my balcony when I heard someone walking in. It was Rosh. She came and joined me quietly. So did Zoya and next to her Shikha. We sat there, our feet tucked in, huddled together. This time the silence was there, but it filled the distance between us.

A tragedy is violent; it can rip you apart or bind you. Mine was enough for my friends to come together.

~

Finally, I was ready to let go, of this city and the most important thing that comes with it, its promise.

But before that I wanted to see Ranvir one last time. I knew there was a huge party being held at Prateeksha Devi's house. They were launching a film together. I'd heard Aslam say many times to all my friends how bad Prateeksha was feeling about everything. I decided to go to the party. Thankfully a lot of my old teammates were working on this film as well, including Aslam.

Ranvir was behaving very strangely at the party. Everyone noticed that. He was like a man hounded by his shadow. When he spotted me, his eyes went wide and glazed.

He watched me from the balcony as I mingled with the cast and crew of the film, his gaze never dropping for an instant. Ranvir did not smile. He looked at me, straight into my eyes, and then finally turned away, as if he could not bear to look at me.

The waiters were serving garlic chicken. My mum would have been happy: garlic was the only thing that came close to her favourite—ginger. I was telling the waiter that garlic could cure a cold, acne, cholesterol, and help even ear aches, but he looked through me and walked away. I heard someone laugh. I turned around. It was she again. My friend—the lady in white. Before I could roll my eyes at her, telling her to go away, I was distracted by Ranvir. I looked at him closely.

This was definitely not the handsome man with dimpled cheeks and twinkling eyes I knew. He just resembled him vaguely.

I walked up to the balcony. It overlooked the huge expanse of sea. Clouds were building in the sky. The whole city had taken a black and white hue. My yellow pumps were the only splash of colour I could see.

Ranvir was nursing another glass of whisky. Out of the blue, he whispered, without even looking me in the eye, 'We need to talk, Neki. I need to explain . . . we need to . . . I need another chance—just one chance, please.'

I remember it was at that moment that the rain started. The heavens opened and it poured. I moved closer to Ranvir so he could hear me over the howling wind and the pounding rain. 'A thunderstorm in November,' I said. Ranvir jerked away startled. He was a troubled man. One could tell. 'It's not supposed to rain now. It is supposed to rain in the monsoon and you are supposed to move on, just like I will.'

Ranvir moved closer. 'Neki . . .'

Just then Aslam joined us, wearing shiny white pants and a shirt with DKNY across it. He was holding a glass of champagne. 'Beautiful weather, isn't it?' he said, breaking the moment. Aslam stared at Ranvir. 'Are you okay? Looks like you've seen a ghost.' And then he followed Ranvir's gaze and looked in my direction with a questioning look. In answer to Aslam's unspoken question, I shook my head. I knew Ranvir was not well, and he was not going to be either.

A couple of phones beeped in the room around the same time. Aslam squealed, 'That must be the BMC messaging "Heavy showers in Mumbai—do not step out of the house today because you will drown"!'

People in the vicinity laughed. I spotted her again. She was standing on the beach in the rain. Waiting for me. I had to go. I waved to Ranvir, hoping he would forgive himself as I had forgiven him.

On my way out, I saw the whole AD team sauntering in. Sam introduced a scared-looking girl clutching a handbag with an airport baggage tag tied to it. 'Guys, please meet Jasmine. She has just come from Dehradun and she will be joining the AD team.'

Shivani made a face. 'Sam, shut up and pass the whisky!'

'Karan told me to introduce her—she has come through his reference!'

'Can she even breathe in those clothes,' Kriti said to Shivani and smirked, pointing to the orange cardigan Jasmine was wearing. The others laughed as Jasmine stood in the middle of it all, her eyes glued to the floor.

Near the door, I turned around and winked at Jasmine. She smiled tentatively.

I turned around one last time and caught Ranvir's eye. There was a question in his gaze. There was a longing in his look. There was remorse. It was over for him too. I could tell. The truth was, when I jumped, I had taken many lives with me—and Ranvir's was one of them.

On the brighter side, I knew what I had to do now. I had to meet Freud and tell him that his theories were outdated, and I had to meet Sid and tell him—well done.

I walked out of that party, towards the glistening sea.

I spotted her standing there on the beach waiting for me, dressed all in white, reminding me of the most beautiful painting I had ever seen—Claude Monet's 'The Lady in the Garden'. Actually, I had only seen a poster of the painting. A distant cousin had gifted it to my mother, and Shivshankarji had put it up in the kitchen, next to the refrigerator. He liked to look at the English lady, he said. The red flowers and the parasol reminded him of his village back home. It made me laugh.

I ran all the way towards the vision in white. And this time there was no one to stop me and ask if I could run in my yellow shoes.

The lady turned. I finally knew who she was. Aslam had been right as usual. Shelly, my cupid ghost definitely existed, and she was beautiful. She had a dimpled, mischievous smile that made me remember the fire on the set.

'You're late, Neki,' she said.

'I was at a party,' I replied, grinning.

'You had more time here,' she said softly.

'It was a mistake—a mistake that I have to live with all my life now!'

Shelly gave me a pointed look.

'I mean a mistake I had to die for! I was drunk, and I didn't mean to, and I ended up dead! I need therapy!'

Shelly made a face. 'I'm sure you do,' she said, and then added wickedly: 'If you impress the right people, you can choose your next life.'

I looked back one last time. I knew I couldn't fully understand the pull of the Bollywood dream—this great obsession driving thousands of us to try our luck in it; but I also knew that if I came back, I would want to do the same thing all over again. I would choose this, again.

Shelly smiled as if she knew what I was thinking, as if she'd expected it. Shelly, after all, had been a dancer in Bollywood. She had died in an accident while shooting: her long hair had gotten caught in a storm fan, which a careless technician had switched on when she was right next to it. Shelly had been sucked into the furiously whirring blades. But at least she'd died happy: she was one of two girls shortlisted for a film role, and had been looking forward to the final auditions the next day. Unfortunately the storm fan had taken the decision in its hands—and it was in the other girl's favour. But Shelly died believing her life was going to change the next day, and she is still waiting for that change. Like every struggling aspirant, Bollywood promised Shelly that dreams do come true—and tomorrow could be the day that your life changes. The beauty was, like Shelly, it failed most of them, but the belief remained. And eventually it becomes more than a belief, because they find their spirituality and their reason for living in it.

Shelly cleared her throat.

It was time. Shelly knew I could still make a choice and stay here with her. Amongst the things I love.

I could hold on to all this. I had to choose again. It was at the juncture of this momentous ghostly decision that I realised the biggest lesson I had learnt from Siddhartha; we can find our spirituality in the things that surround us if we find a meaning or a purpose in them. My mother found it in ginger and garlic, my dad in his solitude. I found it every day of my life too—on the set, in my AD struggle, in the apple-feeling, in the poodle lump, in those hair oil sessions, in a costume trial, in a stunt mishap, in a stand-in rehearsal, under a small shiny shoe, sitting in a polka-dotted cup, hanging up Mona Lisa, in my nurse costume, in an auto ride with a dwarf, in my fall from a balcony. And now I need to seek my spirituality in my death. Finally (unlike my repeated failed attempts sitting at the parapet), my whole life flashed by in a second, like a giant film passing though the light of the projector in the projection room. I was not a sidekick any more. In my life, I played Juliet. But regret remains for how it ended, for my parents.

Shelly whispered in my ear, 'They are happy.'

That meant only one thing. My mother was looking at the last letter that I had written to her, along with all my pictures that were taken on the set. She had made an album.

Sometimes the most important thing to know is *when* it's all over. And I was not going to get stuck in between like Shelly was, just to hold on. I was dead—I needed to accept it and move on to the next journey. I needed an end to have a new beginning.

I was happy to know though, while I walked into the water with my yellow pumps, that my mother was reading my letter—again.

~

*Dear Mom,*

*It was a good life. Remember, I am not going with disappointment but with a will to come back and do better.*

*I hate my dirty yellow hair band and that photo in the magazine is distorted. If you were to see me now you would know—I am beautiful. The way you want me to be. And everything I wrote to you was me.*

*There is no truth or falseness in it.*

*Because that was my reality.*

*You will always find me in the letters I wrote to you . . .*

*Not in the magazine, not in the article, nor the talks or the whispers.*

*Love always,*
*Neki*
*P.S.: I finished as the second AD on the film.*

## ACKNOWLEDGEMENTS

I have many people to thank—people who have helped me in my debut novel and also those who help me become a better person every day.

I would like to start with thanking someone who was the very first person in Mumbai that I worked with and who welcomed me as a part of the amazing company Red Chillies Entertainments—Sanjiv Chawala, aka Bobby, and to many of us here, simply Bobs. Bobs, you are a part of every celebration and success in my journey. You have taught each one of us here at Red Chillies many a thing about living and dreaming; and we are all waiting for you to wake up and be there with us through all the mistakes we are going to make. You are terribly missed. Come back to us soon.

Red Chillies has been an integral part of my journey, as have my colleagues and friends there. A special mention to Vaibhav Misra, Ketki Samant and Ruchira Sehgal, who had to hear about the novel endlessly. Thank you for doing it with a smile and taking out time for the feedback I demanded, in various shapes and sizes.

I owe a very special thanks to my first publishing house and their entire team, for encouraging first-time authors and giving me this opportunity. It all started with Paul Vinay

Kumar at Westland, so a huge thanks to him. Of course, a heartfelt thanks to my editor Deepthi, for being so patient and making my first experience of writing a novel extremely memorable and wonderful.

A very special thank you to my family who has always encouraged me through all my hairbrained schemes! Especially my sister. I love you the most and you make me proud every day. My little brother for his unconditional love, my father for his unwavering support and my mother who inspired me to be a writer to begin with, with her Shakespeare and her Keats and her poetry books surrounding me all the time. She made us all fall in love with the delights of turning the page of an interesting novel. She was also the one who told us, the only way you can make your world better is when *you* go out there and make it better; there is no one else who can do it for you. I remember that Mom, and strive to make my world better every day.

A very special thanks to David for making this journey so wonderful.

A big thank you to Farah Khan for being one of the most amazing people I have had the privilege to work with. She continues to inspire me with her persona, her indomitable spirit and her generosity.

And as always, I owe a very special and heartfelt thanks to Mr Shah Rukh Khan for being a mentor, guide and the most wonderful and charming boss in the whole wide world! He has not only motivated me in my stories, but he motivates me every day in every way by being the person he is: gracious, humble and incredibly wise. He gave me my first job, my first film and my first title as a screen-writer. He is largely responsible for making many dreams come true, and mine is just one of them.

297

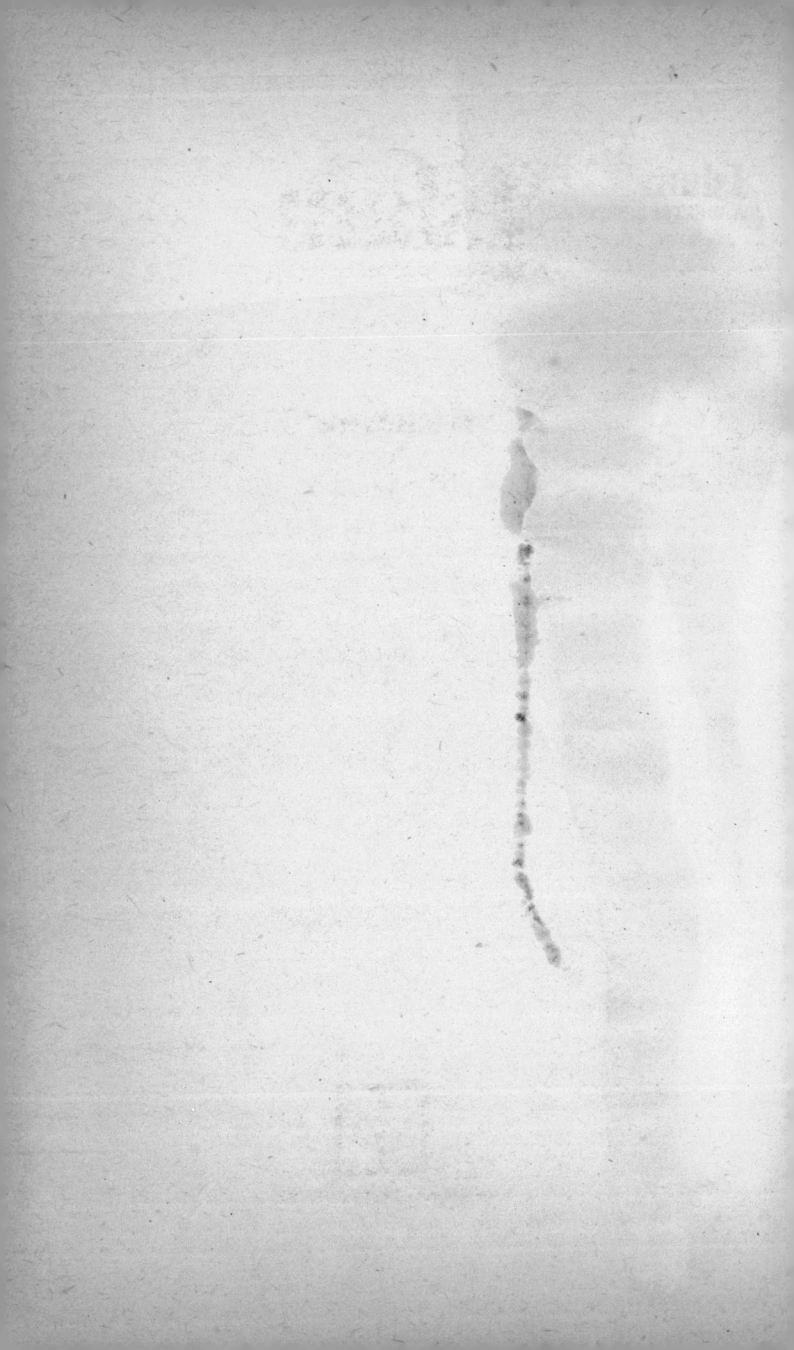

# Islam
## A WESTERNER'S GUIDE

**D S Roberts**

Hamlyn Paperbacks

ISLAM
ISBN 0 600 20346 8

First published in Great Britain 1981
by Kogan Page Ltd
Hamlyn Paperbacks edition 1982

Copyright © 1981 by D.S.Roberts

Hamlyn Paperbacks are published by
The Hamlyn Publishing Group Ltd,
Astronaut House, Feltham,
Middlesex, England

Printed and bound in Great Britain
by Cox & Wyman Ltd, Reading

This book is sold subject to the condition that it
shall not, by way of trade or otherwise, be lent,
resold, hired out, or otherwise circulated without
the publisher's prior consent in any form of binding
or cover other than that in which it is published
and without a similar condition including this
condition being imposed on the subsequent
purchaser.

*Author's Acknowledgements*

I am grateful to my daughter Hannah Roberts for the help and criticism she has given in the writing of this book, and the suggestions she made for its organization and form.

My thanks are also due to the following for permission to refer to source material: Abacus (Sphere Books Ltd) — *The Arabs* by Thomas Kiernan (Abacus, 1978) for material in the chapter on Society and Politics; Oxford University Press — *An Introduction to Islamic Law* by Joseph Schacht (OUP, 1964) for material in the chapter on Islamic Law, and *The Koran Interpreted* by A J Arberry (OUP, 1964) for all quotations from the Koran except those contained within other quoted texts.

# Contents

| | |
|---|---:|
| *Introduction* | 1 |
| **1. The Prophet Mohammed: His Life and Times** | 5 |
| Arabia in the Seventh Century *5*, Mohammed's Life *9*, The Prophet's Successors *29* | |
| **2. The Message** | 35 |
| The Five Pillars of Islam *36*, The Koran *39*, *Hadith* and *Sunna* *41*, *Jihad* *42*, Sacred Places *43*, Sacred Days *43*, Sin *44*, Death *44*, Resurrection *45*, The Hour *45*, Judgement *45*, Paradise and Hell *46*, *Kalam* (Theology) *47*, Muslim Sects *50* | |
| **3. Islamic Law** | 54 |
| The *Sharia* *54*, The Basic Features *55*, The Concepts of Islamic Law *56*, The Schools of Law *58*, Procedures *60*, Punishment *62*, Property *66*, Ownership *67*, Contracts and Obligations *68*, Marriage *70*, Divorce *70*, Legitimacy *71*, Inheritance *71*, Law Reform *72* | |
| **4. Society and Politics** | 77 |
| Islamic Principles: Theory *77*, Islamic Principles: Practice *80* | |
| **5. Social Behaviour and Customs** | 101 |
| Traditional Hospitality and Courtesy *101*, Ritual Ablution, Bathing Shaving *102*, Food and Taboos *103*, Drink and Alcohol *105*, Greetings *106*, Mosques *107*, The Prophet's Tomb *109*, Dress *109*, Charms *109*, Names *110*, Entertainments *111*, Sport *113*, Animals *113*, Deportment *114*, Vices and Virtues *115* | |
| **6. Family and Domestic Life** | 116 |
| Family Structure *116*, Fathers *117*, Mothers *118*, Children *118*, Collective Responsibilities *123*, Respect for Elders *124*, Neighbours *125*, Houses and Homes *125*, Death and Burial *127* | |

## 7. The Status of Women         130
The Status Defined *130*, Property Rights *132*, Marriage *133*, Prostitution *137*, Unlawful Intercourse *137*, Divorce *139*, Seclusion of Women *140*, Sex *143*, Employment and Public Life *145*, Women Saints *147*, Swiss Civil Code in Turkey *147*

## 8. Commerce and Trade         149
The Traditional Role of Commerce *149*, The Example of the Prophet *151*, Associations and Combinations *152*, Customs in Business *153*, Making Contracts *156*, Usury *157*, Debt *159*, Insurance *159*, Decision Making *160*

## Conclusion: The Oil Factor         162

*Appendix 1: The Islamic Calendar*         169
*Appendix 2: Modern Islamic States*         170
*Appendix 3: Mohammed's Wives*         176
*Bibliography*         183

# Introduction

To the ordinary Western mind the world of Islam seems incomprehensible. Its attitudes appear bigoted and uncompromising, and its actions harsh and arbitrary. Nor is this only a modern judgement. As far back as the Middle Ages the propaganda of the Christian church presented the Muslims as savages, and throughout Europe men flocked to the banners of the Crusades to restore the Holy Land to Christendom. Yet even then the propaganda sometimes proved self-defeating, for on making contact with the enemy the Crusaders found them to be, as often as not, quite gentish knights. Indeed, for some the discovery was so startling that they began to question their own cause. In the 14 centuries that Islam has been with us, both it and its founder, Mohammed, have been subject to all manner of denigration and abuse, and although scholars from East and West alike have laboured to modify this unsavoury image, they have met with little success.

After languishing in a historical backwater for hundreds of years, Islam is now once more on the rise and its image in Europe and the West is little changed. This is not because works on Islam are not published in the West. There are voluminous works in every European language examining Islam and its ways in the minutest detail. But for the most part these are scholarly and academic works, or works actually promoting or interpreting the faith. There are also a few recently published books analyzing, from various points of view, the current political situation in the Middle East. What is conspicuously missing, however, is a popular work setting out clearly the beliefs, attitudes and customs of Islam in a way that is readily understandable to the Western reader but is not viewed through a veil of Christian values.

The author's purpose in writing this book has been to avoid the two common mistakes of seeing Islam either as uncompromising and uncivilized at worst or as mysterious and inexplicable at best. It does not seek to justify the Muslim faith nor gloss over the harsher aspects of the Islamic code; nor does it attack or pass moral judgements on the religion and its faithful. In a word, the intention is not to examine Islam through a telescope made in Christendom but to try to see Islam as it sees itself.

It is impossible to understand the most elementary things about Islamic life without knowing something of its religion; but, although the main features and basic beliefs of the faith are described, this is not a book primarily about religion. Islam, it is true, is a way of life based upon the will of God, which is known through its holy book, the Koran, and the sayings and actions of its prophet, Mohammed. But many of its characteristics have been inherited from the traditions of the society into which Mohammed was born, and this combination, together with the different interpretations put upon its teachings in different places and at different times, makes up 20th century Islam.

The first difficulty in attempting to gain some insight into the Muslim mind and setting it down on paper is one of presentation. It is more likely than not that the average Western reader is the product of an educational system which has set the qualities of clarity, order, logic and sequence high in the list of educational virtues. Traditional Islam, however, does not pursue enlightenment in this way. Every aspect of life is seen as part of an indivisible whole, literally inseparable from all other aspects. Sequence is not important. On the contrary, the more man attempts to order existence the more likely he is to stumble into error. For a Muslim, life as it was created by God is complete by definition. The task of man is not to rearrange or order it, or even to understand it, but to obey the laws laid down for him.

How, then, does man know what those laws are? For Muslims the answer is simple: they are laid down in the holy Koran. Yet for the Westerner this often obscures the question still further. The qualities of the Koran are discussed in greater detail later, but it is fair to say that, however good the translation, no recognizable 'structure' would be apparent to the average Western reader. It is a work which can be read from the beginning or from the end or from any point in the middle with no difference to the Message contained within it. In a fundamental sense the Koran has no beginning and no end. Because of this, and although modern Muslim scholars adopt perfectly recognizable forms in their work, there is, underlying all Islamic culture, an element that, notwithstanding the repeated calls that the Koran itself makes to logic, ultimately undermines communication with outsiders.

This point needs emphasis because, in an attempt to achieve a comprehensible balance and form for this book, the chapters and headings have been divided into distinct subject areas. The only reason for choosing these chapter and section headings, however, was to provide familiar points of reference for the Western reader. To a conservative Muslim it would seem strange to attempt to separate law from religion, and bizarre to separate the status of women from either.

In a system seeking to control all aspects of a believer's life it is sometimes difficult to distinguish between what is fundamental law and what is merely tribal or social custom, allowed or even encouraged by Islam, but not actually required by its law. As a result there are many important issues where theory and practice are confused. And even when the law is clear the outcome is often not. For example, the Koran is uncompromising in its declaration that the penalty for theft is amputation, as it is that a man has an absolute right to take up to four wives if he treats them equally. But this clear-cut authority is not uniformly accepted throughout Islam. Few countries allow amputation; and, even in countries where it is not statutory, monogamy is becoming increasingly common.

Another temptation to be avoided is the association of everything Islamic with Arabia and vice versa. Arabia has a special place in the fabric of Islam because it has its roots there — the language of the Koran is Arabic and Mohammed himself was an Arab. Yet the Arabs represent no more than a third of all Muslims, and, furthermore, not every Arab is a Muslim.

The range of the subject has made it difficult to know not only where to stop but also, often, where to begin. There is common agreement that the Koran is the supreme authority in directing the life of a believer. If a clear precedent cannot be found there, the next level of authority is the *Sunna*: the sayings and actions of the Prophet Mohammed. Human interpretation is heavily involved at this stage, as the various schools of law adopt their positions. If we add to these considerations the tribal and social customs of both pre-and post-Islamic times, and allow for the regional variations which are to be found in Islam from Spain to China, there is clearly considerable scope for oversimplification in any book of manageable length.

The object of this book, then, has been to set out the main features of Islam against the general background of relevant world events and ideas and to sketch in what Muslim society is actually like — the sort of thing a Westerner can expect to find in an Islamic country, or the attitudes he or she will encounter if dealing with Muslims at home. For, despite the differences readily observable between Muslims, it would be a mistake for an outsider to see such disagreements as anything more than family quarrels. In the heat of the moment it is often easy to miss the underlying hard core of human unity. It is this unity which underpins the faith of every Muslim, and if you find yourself discussing Islam with a Muslim anywhere in the world, you are likely to be asked 'Why do you have all these questions? Become a Muslim and you will have answers.'

4 *Islam*

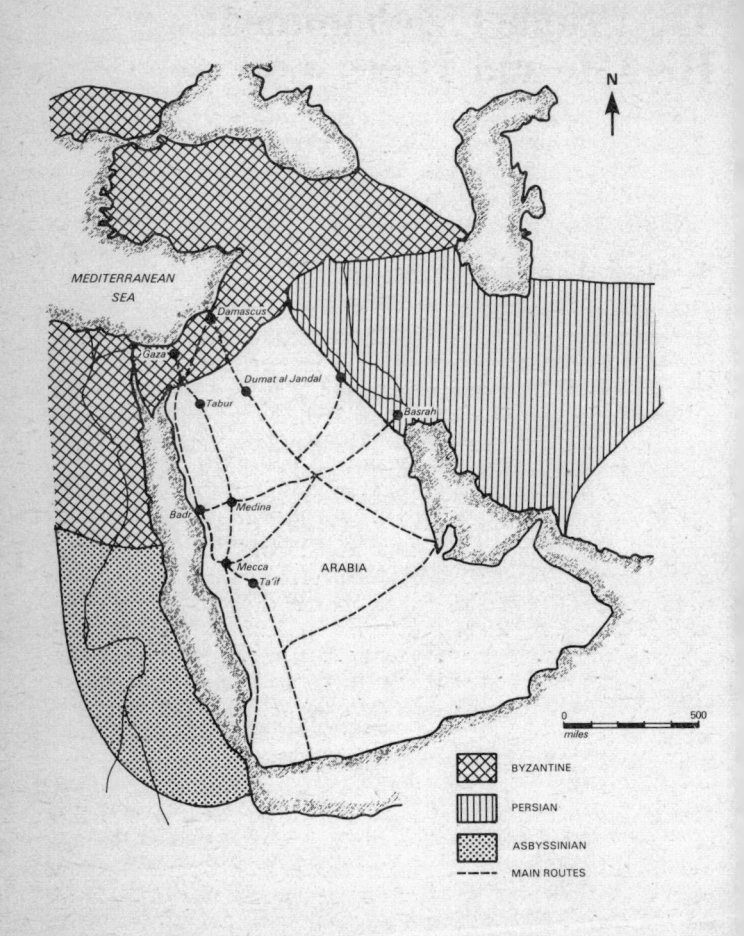

*Arabia and Western Asia c AD 630*

Chapter 1
# The Prophet Mohammed: His Life and Times

## Arabia in the Seventh Century

The prophet of Islam was Mohammed ibn (son of) Abd-allah. He was born in the town of Mecca in Arabia about AD 570. The exact year of his birth is not known and the details of his early life remain obscure. His father died before he was born and he became the ward of his grandfather, Abd-al Muttalib, but it is believed that he spent most of his early years with his mother, who belonged to another clan. It was the custom among Meccan families to send their children away for a year or two from the town to the hard but healthy life of the desert, and the infant Mohammed was sent to a Bedu[1] tribe to be wet-nursed by one of their women. When Mohammed was six his mother died and he came directly under the care of his grandfather until he too died two years later. He then passed into the care of his uncle, Abu Talib, the new head of the clan Hashim.

From this obscure and unpromising beginning grew the man who was to found a new religion, unite under its banner the previously hostile tribes of the Arabian peninsula, and lay the foundation for an immense empire which, 100 years after his death, stretched from Spain to the Punjab. To be both an orphan and poor in seventh century Mecca were crushing handicaps for even the most gifted and able man. Mecca was a commercial town, an oasis, mid-way between the Indian ocean and the Mediteranean. It controlled the caravan routes between Yemen, India and Abyssinia, and the markets of the North. Thus the popular idea that Islam sprang from the nomadic way of life in the desert needs revision; the first homes of Islam — Mecca (the place of Mohammed's birth) and Medina (the place in which he sought refuge from persecution) — were both towns.

### Arabian Society before Mohammed

In pre-Islamic Arabia communities took the form of a number of

---
1. Bedu or Bedouin: desert nomads, living off herds of camels, goats and sheep.

groups or tribes who were held together by loyalty to a leader or by descent from a common ancestor. The family units that made up the tribes were equal in status to each other. The head of each family had power to select the tribal chief or *sheikh*[1], who could theoretically be anybody, but in practice normally came from certain families. Such families held positions of great importance within the community at the time of Mohammed, and the major factor in a man's authority was his birth. Moreover, the test of superiority was family purity, and no family tainted with ancestors of servile or negro origin was eligible for high office. Society was stratified into a self-perpetuating class system in which careers, opportunities and social position depended very largely on the circumstances of birth. Slavery was commonplace and persisted throughout the centuries almost to the present day. Before Mohammed's time slaves were either prisoners of war, or taken in raids in hostile territory, or the offspring of slaves. In those days it was still possible for Arabs to enslave their fellow countrymen by capture, or to sell themselves for a gambling debt.

Outside the towns the way of life was dictated by the land and what it would support. Apart from a few oases and trading centres the peninsula was desert, and the way of life nomadic and pastoral. Desert life was harsh and uncompromising, and was often accompanied by grinding poverty. There was a strong temptation to lay hands on the possessions of others who were apparently more fortunate. This took the form of raids (*razia*) in which there were strict rules laid down by tradition. Where possible, goods were seized without loss of life. Manslaughter carried severe penalties according to the tradition of the desert. The free Arabs were bound by no written law, and no authority existed to enforce statutes. Therefore, the only protection for any man's life was the certainty, established by custom, that it would be dearly bought. Blood must be paid for by blood, a life by a life. the tribe protected its own under all circumstances, and undying shame attached to the man whom tradition designated as the avenger if he allowed a murderer to live. Retribution or vendetta (*tha'r*) was one of the pillars of Bedu society, and this made Mohammed's survival possible during the early days of his Prophethood (see page 13).

Tribal society was not rigidly structured. Leadership was not inherited but was conferred upon the man most able to command prestige and respect. Although selected by popular will, the leader could use only his moral authority to command obedience. He had no power to lay duties or inflict penalties on others, and he led through

---

1. In modern usage the title *sheikh* might still signify the leader of a tribe, or might be used by those claiming descent from the first two caliphs or from Abbas, the Prophet's uncle. More common, however, is its use as a courtesy title, designating respect.

sensing and directing the climate of opinion. A member of a tribe had a singularly independent position and offered his services voluntarily. He conformed to the minimum rules concerning the rights of property, and observed traditional practices concerning marriage, in return for which he could claim allegiance and protection. Otherwise he was free to do as he wished (including, in the last analysis, withdrawing from the tribe) without invoking any penalties.

The fortunes of the nomadic tribes varied with the circumstances of plunder, trade, war or drought. In the towns commercial stability, such as it was, made the fortune of tribe or family somewhat less vulnerable. In terms of culture the Arabs admired men of eloquence and persuasion, who could argue their point of view well in the tribal council. Wise men were highly esteemed, but poets were valued still more. They were both respected and feared because they were believed to be possessed by spirits, and their work was considered to be of supernatural origin. The poet sang of love, grief, joy and sorrow, but also played an important part in public affairs. Contests were held at which each contestant boasted of his own tribe and satirized those of his rivals.

The Bedu had religious beliefs but these were not necessarily central to their social life. They believed that the land was peopled by spirits, the *jinn*, who were often invisible but could appear in animal form. Offerings were made to them, and cairns of stones were erected on their graves. Certain trees and stones housed spirits and divinities. The number and names of divinities varied from tribe to tribe, but there were some common denominators. One was Allah, creator of the universe and keeper of sworn oaths. In addition there were three goddesses who were the daughters of Allah, and other gods were worshipped in various places. Certain places became sacred, within which no creature could be killed. These became places of asylum where the pursued could take refuge. Some sanctuaries were the object of pilgrimage (*hajj*), and rituals were performed within them. Notable among these rituals was the ceremonial procession around the sacred object. Prohibitions, such as abstention from sexual relations, had to be observed during these rites. Boys were ceremonially circumcised. Superstition prevailed and magic was practised. As Maxime Rodinson[1] has pointed out, these tribes were evolving their own concept of morality in the formation of which religion played no part. What was important was courage, endurance, loyalty to the group and social obligations, generosity and hospitality. A man strove to conform to these ideals out of a sense of honour (*ird*).

But the unwritten rules followed by the Arabs were often broken.

---

1. *Islam and Capitalism*, Allen Lane, 1974.

The savage excesses which appeared on certain occasions prompted some devastating comments from their more civilized neighbours. A Syrian soldier, Ammianus Marcellinus, said in the fourth century: 'I would not wish to have them either as friends or as enemies'.

By contrast, the settled and relatively civilized people of southern Arabia lived a life of comparative wealth and luxury in organized states of some complexity. These southern states employed the wandering Bedu as mercenaries in their auxiliary forces, each state favouring its own tribe. It is possible that they acknowledged some distant kinship, and some northern tribes claimed later to have come originally from the cultivated regions of the South. After the triumph of Islam under Saracen leadership, the southern Arabians were rapidly assimilated, and the inhabitants of the peninsula as a whole embarked on the conquest of the world. But the memories of their superior civilization did not fade at once for the Yemenis in the Muslim ranks; they stuck together and set themselves apart from the northern Arabs, and knowledge of their old tongue and writing persisted in some places for several centuries.

## Mecca and the Caravan Trade

Little is known about the commercial life of Mecca during Mohammed's early life. It is clear, however, that it was a prosperous commercial centre, whose power and influence was growing. Although tribal structure and authority still dominated society, the settled way of life and commercial organization demanded by the caravan trade to some extent modified the grip of traditional values. The demands of trade made Mohammed and others aware of new worlds outside their own experience, and brought them into contact with new ideas about the way the affairs of men should be ordered. The influence of the clan in the towns was waning, but it remained the only structure available to organize affairs; no other semblance of regional or local authority emerged. Commercial interests needed to be defended and the clans were not slow to form the so-called League of the Virtuous, an alliance to keep out foreign interests and to preserve the Meccans' monopoly of the caravan trade. Although there were tribal conflicts within Mecca, the town had by legend the reputation for self-control when its best interests were threatened.

Once the Bedu tribe had settled, they formed themselves into trading companies to finance caravans. The transportation of valuable goods gave rise to large profits, and the commercial structure dictated its own forms of organization, not only in Mecca but in the whole of western Arabia. The town of Ta'if, south of Mecca, did a prosperous trade in fruit, vegetables and wines. In the string of hill towns near

Medina, Jewish settlements created a flourishing agricultural life. The mercantile economy encouraged the use of money rather than barter for trade. In this process the Bedu often borrowed from the rich, got into debt, and were either sold into slavery or reduced to a dependent status. Success became vested in personal achievement, and no longer in the well-being of the whole tribe. The bond of kinship became weaker and gave way to others based on common commercial interests. As people became aware that new values were beginning to replace those of tribal tradition, they became more susceptible to the idea of a religion based upon individual salvation rather than group survival. Judaism and Christianity were known, if not properly understood, but these were foreign faiths associated with powers that were fighting for the control of the Arab peninsula. What was required was a man who could provide a focus and an inspiration, and into that situation Mohammed was born.

## Mohammed's Life

### Origin and Background

The Koran makes frequent reference to the rights of orphans, and this is no doubt some reflection of the difficulties Mohammed experienced in his early years. Traditionally the clan was responsible for the welfare of its weaker members, but the old ways were changing under the commercial pressures generated by the caravan trade in Mecca. Although he was clothed and fed, not much attention was given to Mohammed's education or interests. He had to be satisfied with the trade of camel driver, and make what he could from the experience of travelling to Syria with his uncle, Abu Talib.

Almost nothing is known about Mohammed's youth, although numerous stories and legends were supplied by subsequent generations, who were keen to present the early life of the Prophet in an idealized way. The oldest collections of historical narratives date from 120 years after the Prophet's death. These stories are fragmentary and contradictory, and Muslim scholarship has been content to repeat these contradictory traditions, one after the other, quoting the source for each and adding 'but God knows best'. Yet many facts can be established, as there is wide agreement about the main features of the Prophet's life.

Of major importance in Mohammed's life was his marriage to Khadija in about AD 595. Although few details of this period are recorded, the young man clearly took full advantage of his new situation and quickly established himself in the commercial life of Mecca. As his business flourished he lived in reasonable prosperity for the next

15 years, and consolidated his reputation for straightforward and trustworthy dealing. He was able to betroth his daughters to quite prosperous men, who were all in some way related to either himself or Khadija.

His marriage to Khadija relieved him of the daily pressure of earning a living, and provided leisure to contemplate other matters. Great changes were taking place, but they were not changes he liked. The upheavals in the north represented the death throes of two enormous empires, the Persian and the Byzantine. Nearer home, the dislocation caused by the pursuit of commerce was accompanied by a decline in moral standards and an abandonment of traditional values.

In seventh century Arabia, as elsewhere, religion fulfilled much more than spiritual needs. It also embraced and defined social and political relationships. By all accounts the pagan Arabs were not particularly interested in religion, but some, including Khadija's uncle, had adopted the Christian faith, and there were established Jewish communities throughout Arabia. The extent to which Mohammed was familiar with either religion is not certain, but he would certainly have come into contact with their ideas when travelling in pursuit of his trade.

## The Call

At the age of about 40 Mohammed was used to retiring to a rocky hillside near Mecca and spending time there alone in meditation and seclusion. He sometimes spent several nights in a cave, and on one of these occasions began to have extraordinary experiences. He had vivid dreams and visions, and in one of these a mighty being appeared high on the horizon and began descending towards him until he was 'only two bow lengths away'.

The voice spoke a command in Arabic which was to change the world:

> Recite: In the Name of Thy Lord who created,
> created Man of a blood-clot.
>
> (Koran 96:1)

The effect on Mohammed was traumatic: 'I was standing but I fell to my knees and dragged myself along while the upper part of my chest was trembling. I went to Khadija until the terror had left me.'

This and subsequent experiences convinced Mohammed that he was formulating ideas and expressions that were not his own. He perceived these words and ideas as recitations by God — Koran (Arabic *Qur'an*) literally means recitation. Slowly Mohammed became aware that he was the Messenger of God. The realization was so stunning that he was wracked by self doubt. He, a modest merchant of humble origin in the obscurity of Arabia, had to convince the people of Mecca, who had known him from a boy, that he had been chosen as the Messenger of God. He was so overwhelmed by the burden that for some time he kept these events secret, confiding only in his wife, Khadija. On occasions the measure of the task seemed so great that he was tempted to take his own life. Stories are told of how on such occasions inspiration would always return to him, and he would be reminded of the importance of the task he had to complete.

It is important to understand that for Mohammed, and for all Muslims, the revelations which began so dramatically and continued over a period of 20 years, came from a source outside the Prophet. He was merely the human mouthpiece through which the messages were conveyed, and this was quickly recognized by his followers. In his own lifetime he became known, even to his wives, as the Messenger of Allah. Neither Mohammed nor any of his followers ever claimed that he had any direct relationship with God. It is perhaps the fundamental principle of Islam that God is alone and unique. Even in making His will known to Mohammed, he used an intermediary in the form of the angel Gabriel. It therefore follows that nothing must be associated with God, and there are many references in the Koran condemning 'associaters'. Mohammed was clear that he could distinguish between his own thoughts and opinions, and the revelations that came from outside his own experience. The revelations are therefore literally the speech of God. It is probable that most of these were written down during the Prophet's lifetime, either by him or under his direction, but in any case the Koran in its present form was finalized about 20 years after his death, in AD 650.

The organization of the Koran reflects the fragmentary nature of the revelations and the fact that they came over a long period. There is no recognizable time sequence, and each *sura*, or chapter, deals with a variety of subjects and incidents, even though it is given a single name by which it is generally recognized. This is an important matter when trying to understand the Muslim mind. What is important about the Koran, and therefore important to a Muslim, is meaning and not sequence. Clearly, the Message, if it was to be comprehensible, had to be related to the conditions and beliefs prevailing at the time in Arabia. From the first revelation in about AD 610 it took Mohammed some three years to understand the nature of his future work: and it is a historical fact that in about 613 Mohammed began preaching in the streets of Mecca and publicly claimed the title of Prophet.

## The Message

When Mohammed stood up for the first time in public there was nothing revolutionary in his message: at least not at first sight. In his first revelations he did not attempt to deny either the existence or power of other divinities. The monotheism of the Jews and Christians was not unknown, and Mohammed was after all relating his message to the same God. No disquiet was caused by the thought of mankind being judged since this was not a new or unfamiliar idea. Criticism of the rich and their declining moral values was accepted in moderation. The idea of almsgiving had a pedigree which stretched back to the old tribal ideal of putting generosity foremost among virtues, although it had subsequently rather fallen out of favour. Making sacrifices to pacify the divinity was common practice. So in the beginning Mohammed's method was to win men over to his ideas by persuasion, and he was not challenging established authority outright by presenting a radically new way of life. What was unique was the way in which those ideas were made available to him in order to be passed on. The individual was to be judged without reference to class, position or tribe, and some basic Judao-Christian ideals became acceptable because they were presented in Arabic through the personality of an Arab Messenger. At the beginning, then, Mohammed posed no great threat to the Meccan establishment, and the new movement seemed indistinguishable from others that were thriving in western Arabia at the time.

The first Muslim was the Prophet's wife, Khadija, and the second was either his freed slave, Zayd, or his teenage cousin, Ali. Apart from these, converts numbered about 40, who for the most part were either very young, uninfluential or slaves. But what they lacked in influence they made up for in independence of mind.

## Opposition from the Meccan Ruling Class

No doubt the class consciousness of the Meccan ruling council played a part in postponing recognition of the threat that Mohammed posed. If God was to make His will known and point the community in a new direction, surely He would make it known through them and not through a minor citizen preaching in the streets. The conflict came into the open only after Mohammed attacked the pagan cult of goddesses, *jinn* and spirits that had served the Arabs from time immemorial. This had deep religious significance, for it condemned the ancestors of all the worthy Meccans to damnation and hell fire. It also had political significance. The pagan Arabs had shown that they were not afraid of the ideas of a monotheistic religion as such. There were thriving Jewish and Christian communities living among them, and no-one became anxious if a few Arabs were converted. But these religions were foreign imports; Mohammed was preaching to the Arabs in their own language and offering them their own religion and ideology. The leading citizens of Mecca were not slow to see the implications of this. They themselves believed in God as the Creator, but they did not concede his uniqueness. If the new movement gathered strength and Arabs came to believe that God was giving them a new creed by which to live their lives and reorganize their society, then political as well as religious power would be taken from the ruling council and priests of the old system, and passed into the hands of God's Messenger and his followers. The Meccan ruling class had to defend not only an ideology but also commercial and economic interests, and when they realized the true nature of Mohammed's mission they reacted violently against him.

For the most part there were strict limits to the persecution that Mohammed and the early Muslims had to endure, because of the system of kinship and the protection offered by the clan to all its members, even the most wayward. All members of a clan could rely absolutely on physical protection unless it was specifically withdrawn by the leader. If a member were harmed for any reason, the clan was honour bound to avenge the injury and seek retribution, whether or not they thought the victim deserved his treatment. Only slaves could not rely on this protection, and there are accounts of physical torture being used to make them renounce their faith. But if violence was generally ruled out, all other forms of pressure were not. The full weight of social pressure was brought to bear: the new Muslims were abused, castigated and ostracized, and merchants were boycotted. The conservative Quraysh tribe brought every pressure to bear on Mohammed's clan, the Hashim, in order to get them to withdraw their protection from him. No-one was to do business, or form marriage ties, with any members of the clan of al-Muttalib. The boycott lasted for about two years, although it was not always strictly enforced.

In the meantime the revelations continued and the new doctrine took shape. The little community in Mecca continued to gather converts, and in time totalled about 100. The Meccans were unable to suppress it, but at least it was being comfortably contained and, except for unforeseen events, might have remained a small and insignificant cult like many others. But in 619 Khadija and Mohammed's uncle Abu Talib both died within a few days of one another. The death of his wife must have been a great blow to Mohammed, but the death of Abu Talib had very serious consequences. He was succeeded as head of the Hashim clan by his brother Abu Lahab, who at first agreed to extend his protection to the Muslims because he was moved by Mohammed's

## 14 *Islam*

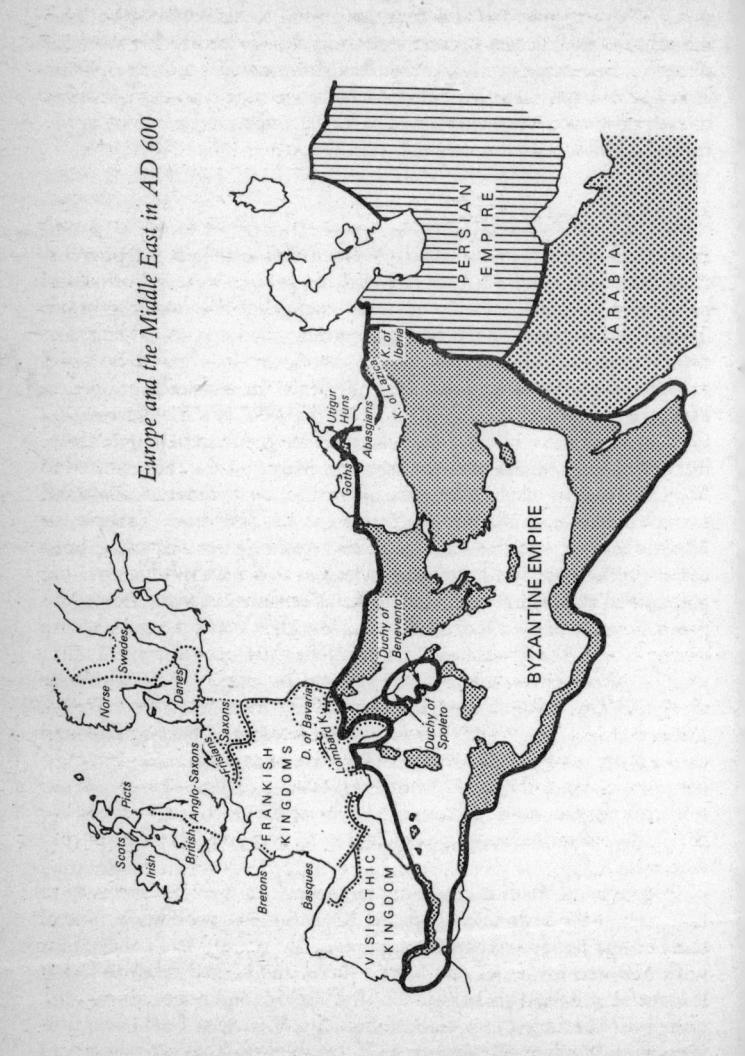

*Europe and the Middle East in AD 600*

misfortune and grief. But the Prophet's enemies persuaded him otherwise. They suggested to him that, according to his nephew, both his grandfather and the newly departed Abu Talib were suffering the pains of hell as unbelievers who had rejected Mohammed's message. When Abu Lahab confronted Mohammed with this suggestion the Prophet could only confirm it, whereupon his uncle, angry at the lack of family feeling, withdrew his protection on the spot.

## Hijra: Emigration to Medina

From then on the situation rapidly worsened. The insults and provocations increased, and Mohammed and his people were pilloried and physically attacked. The community seemed to be losing ground. There were no more spectacular conversions, and it is quite likely that the pressure caused some new defections. A new base had to be found for Mohammed's operations. He considered the possibilities open to him, first looking at Ta'if, a green hillside town where many Qurayshites had property. He spoke to all the prominent people there, but could persuade no-one to take in the Muslims, and he returned to Mecca a dejected man. After some hesitation, he cast further afield and saw possibilities in the city of Yathrib as his new base. Yathrib, or Medina as it became known, was strictly speaking not a city at all but a collection of oases with clusters of houses and fortified huts among plantations of palms and fruit trees. Relationships between the various groups there were at a very low ebb, although at that time there was an uneasy truce. The Arabs had inherited from their nomadic past a tradition of blood feuds which were continually erupting in wholesale slaughter, and it was clear to all sides that the war would be revived in Yathrib before long. This was a desperate situation for an agricultural community which depended upon relatively settled ways to secure its harvests. Eventually, good sense suggested to some that it was intolerable for the whole community to be drawn into wars because individuals had spilled blood which had to be avenged regardless of consequences.

People from Medina made frequent visits to Mecca, especially to take part in the holy rituals nearby. Mohammed spoke with some of these and at last found common ground. He already had connections with Medina; his father was buried there, and he had relatives living there whom he had visited as a child. Meetings and negotiations took place over a period of two years. Gradually Mohammed won over converts from Medina, and he sent one of his ablest followers to the city to recite the Koran and teach the people the doctrine. Eventually an agreement was made at a decisive meeting at Aqaba at which 75 Medinans, among them two women, were present. The Medinans were promised that God, through Mohammed, would arbitrate in any future disputes and put an end to the internal tribal conflicts. In exchange the Medinans pledged protection.

This movement of Mohammed and his followers from Mecca to Medina was known as the *Hijra*, and it secured the future of the Islamic movement. It is sometimes rendered as 'flight', but 'emigration' is a better translation, suggesting as it does the travelling of Muslims in small groups over a period and ending with the departure of Mohammed himself. The significance of the new era was such that, later, the Islamic calendar was designated from that date, and the Christian year AD 622 became the Muslim year AH 1. So it came about that this tiny group found sanctuary in an obscure Arabian town on the very edge of the civilized world. The conditions were right for a new community to take root and to develop its own laws and customs based on the new religion.

## Acceptance: the Followers

In Medina Mohammed let God decide where he should build his house and seat of operations by settling on the spot where his camel stopped. Once settled, he set about his work as arbitrator in disputes, thus establishing a new principle. He had become the leader of most of the Arabs in Medina by letting the will of God be known not only in spiritual matters but also in the things that affected men's day to day lives. For the most part his decisions were accepted and the only opposition that irritated him came from some pagan poets, who satirized the Medinans for accepting the decisions of a stranger.

The Prophet also had to face up to the potentially dangerous problem of the Jewish communities in Medina. At first he expected to gain their support, as the message he brought was substantially similar to that received long before by the Jews at Sinai. He was impressed by the antiquity of Jewish scriptures and the reliance on them of other religions, and he seems to have thought it possible to form a united front with these confirmed monotheists against the pagan forces surrounding them both. Before moving to Medina he had become acquainted with Israelite customs, and certain instructions to his followers suggest a willingness to cooperate wherever possible. These included facing Jerusalem to pray, organizing large prayer meetings on Fridays, (the day on which the Jews prepared for their festival of the Sabbath), observing the fast on the Day of Atonement, setting aside a time for prayer in the middle of the day as the Jews did, and even adopting Jewish modes of dress and hairstyles. An additional revelation gave the faithful permission to eat the food of the People of the Book (ie Jews and Christians) and to marry their women. He did not consider imposing the Jewish dietary laws in full, since he took the Christian view that these were God's punishment of the Jews' sins. But he did introduce a more limited prohibition: on the eating of pork or blood, or any animals that had died a natural death, had their necks wrung, or had been sacrificed to idols. Nor did Mohammed observe the custom of resting on the seventh day, for the very simple reason that God did not need a rest.

But on the whole the Jews did not respond to the call of Islam. They may have mistrusted Mohammed's long-term political motives, but it is more likely that they were unwilling to endorse the revelations claimed by the Prophet. From their point of view the Koran distorted the Old Testament stories, and they could probably see no reason to adjust their religious or social position in any way. This was a situation that Mohammed would have to face at some time, but first there were more urgent problems pressing for his attention.

## Attack on Meccan Trade

The first of these problems was simply a matter of subsistence. None of the emigrant Muslims had the means to buy land in the oasis, and without lands or flocks survival was becoming a desperate mater. In these circumstances the traditional Arab solution was that of the raiding party, and a suitable target was the Quraysh caravans from Mecca that had to pass within 60 miles of Medina. The Quraysh were obvious targets because they had forced the Muslims to flee in the first place, and attacking them rather than other tribes would avoid making unnecessary enemies. This was not such a violent solution as it might seem, since raiding was carried out by strictly observed methods designed to avoid bloodshed. The general principle was to send out a raiding party of such overwhelming numbers that the victim could run with complete justification and without losing face. The raiders would then help themselves to the booty left behind. The next stage was generally that the dispossessed would amass a party of even greater numbers and would set off in pursuit of their property. This kind of private war was an accepted custom and could be initiated by any chief who was so minded. If he were wise he would weigh the circumstances before setting out and be prepared to take the consequences if anything went wrong, such as someone getting killed, which would initiate a vicious circle of vendettas.

Under Mohammed's direction the Muslim raids on the Meccan caravans began in earnest, and in year 2 of the *Hijra* (AD 624) the inevitable happened and a caravan guard was killed. From then on what had been a religious and ideological struggle between the Meccans and the Muslims developed into an armed conflict that was to be fought to the finish.

## The Battle of Badr

Two months later Mohammed learned of a large rich caravan leaving from Mecca which was said to be worth 50,000 *dinars*. He had no difficulty in raising a party of 300 men, of whom only 90 were Meccan emigrants. They set an ambush at the well of Badr on the road to Syria and laid in wait. The leader of the caravan, Abu Sufyan, either anticipated or discovered the danger and sent word to the merchants of Mecca to come out and protect their property. As they were nearly all involved, they quickly raised a force of over 900 which must have been almost every able-bodied man in the town. Abu Sufyan diverted his caravan around Badr, whilst the Meccan army marched to engage and put down the Muslims once and for all. At this point the Muslims captured a young Meccan water carrier who told them of the relief expedition bearing down upon them. If Mohammed needed any excuse to retire without dishonour, the overwhelming superiority of the enemy provided one. But he decided to stand and fight, even though his original objective was now out of reach. At Badr he filled in all the wells except one and took up his position in front of it. The two sides began hurling traditional insults and throwing down challenges and the battle began with single combat of champions from either side.

After a while a pitched battle developed and the Meccans were startled by the fury of the Muslim onslaught. Mohammed had promised his followers certain entry to Paradise for all those who fell in battle, and this had its effect on the Muslim army. The Muslims also had a unified command, while the Meccans fought as individual tribes and made little use of their overwhelming strength or of their cavalry. Many Meccans were inhibited by tribal custom from killing men who were related to them, and shortly before midday panic swept their ranks and they fled. They lost over 50 dead, including two of their leaders, and another 70 or so were taken prisoner. On the Muslim side about 15 were killed.

The spoils were substantially less than those carried by the caravan, but were still considerable. 150 camels and horses and large quantities of arms and armour were seized, as well as some merchandise. Quarrels broke out as to how this should be divided. The Prophet settled the matter by ordering the spoils to be collected together and then distributed equally. Traditional custom laid down that the leader of a victorious side should have one quarter of the booty, but Mohammed as a general rule took one fifth, as prescribed:

> Know that whatever booty you take, the
> fifth of it is God's, and the Messenger's,
> and near kinsman's, and the orphan's,
> and the needy, and the traveller.
>
> (Koran 8:41)

The Battle of Badr is a landmark and had far reaching consequences. It sanctioned a concern for material existence and the use of force as a means of survival, and both were built into the foundations of Islam. The practical gains of victory were considerable, since the ransom paid for the prisoners was heavy, but the gain in prestige and influence was of greater importance. The Muslims had defeated a powerful city in open fight and had demonstrated that they had not only the Message but also the power to back it up. It confirmed and reinforced Mohammed's position in Medina; those who wavered rallied to his side, and the Bedu tribes came offering friendship. Above all, the effect upon Mohammed himself was remarkable. After all the doubt and despair of the early years, here at last was a sign that God's hand had intervened. Mohammed had not intended to do battle, but God had not only decided on confrontation but had also made the Muslims victorious.

The victory was interpreted by the Muslims as a sign that the city of Mecca would fall and that all Mohammed's opposition from Christians, Jews and pagans was in the wrong. Mohammed henceforth saw his task as overcoming all opposition.

Certain pagan elements were dealt with first, and the targets were the two poets who had irritated him most: Asma bint Marwan and Abu Afak. When it became known that the Prophet wanted them silenced, his followers responded by assassination.

Even before Badr Mohammed had doubts about an alliance with the Jews. Their unresponsive attitude caused him some irritation. Before the battle he was content simply to loosen his ties by decreeing that Jerusalem was no longer to be the direction of prayer, but it was noticeable that not a single Jew had volunteered support for the expedition, and afterwards the Prophet decided to make the break. The Jewish fast soon ceased to be observed, and the fast during the month of Ramadan was substituted.

Mohammed had shown the uncompromising side of his character for the first time when dealing with the pagan opposition, and this was underlined shortly afterwards when he turned against the Jews. Clearly at some point the Prophet realized that the Jews must be treated as opposition rather than as potential allies. Some sources say that the matter came to a head after some Jewish tribes made formal alliances with the Meccans against the Muslims, while others take the view that the mere presence of such an intractable religious and cultural body at the heart of Mohammed's operations was in itself a threat to his political stability.

In any event, the incident which brought matters to a head started casually enough. A Bedu girl who was married to a Muslim was selling some vegetables in the market when some young Jews began teasing her. They tried to life her veil, and one of them hitched her skirt in such a way that when she stood up it came off. A young Muslim bystander came to her aid, and in defence of the girl's honour killed one of the Jews. The Jews retaliated in kind and the quarrel was on.

The Jewish clan, the Qaynuqa, withdrew inside their fort. this may have been done to limit the conflict, as they had reason to believe that some of their Arab allies would intercede for them and that the matter would be settled with indemnities on either side. But Mohammed would have none of it and sent his army to blockade the fort.

After 15 days the fort surrendered, and Mohammed's first reaction was to condemn all its occupants to death. But at this point one of the Arab leaders, Ibn Ubayy, made a strong intervention, threatening to review his allegiance if the sentence was carried out. Ibn Ubayy was a powerful ally, and Mohammed relented on condition that the Jews left Medina within three days, leaving their goods for the victor. Ibn Ubayy and others renewed efforts for a more merciful decision, but Mohammed was adamant. The Jews departed to join their kinsmen in the North, leaving behind their considerable wealth.

## The Battle of Uhud

In the meantime the Quraysh were stirring themselves for further action. The news of the disaster at Badr had been greeted in Mecca first with disbelief, then with sorrow, and finally with a fierce determination for revenge. This determination was reinforced when Mohammed sent 100 men to attack another of the Meccan caravans bound for Mesopotamia, taking goods valued at 100,000 *dirhams*. The Quraysh prepared their retaliation carefully. Negotiations were begun with all the neighbouring tribes and an alliance was sealed which raised an army of 3000 men, many of them armoured, and a cavalry force of 200.

It took the army 10 days to reach Medina, whose inhabitants had plenty of time to withdraw into their fortified dwellings. At first the Medinans agreed that their strategy should be to stay where they were and fight off the attack. But some of the young men, eager for excitement, urged that they should go out and meet the Meccans head on. Mohammed was persuaded, perhaps believing that, as at Badr, numbers were not important, and his army prepared to leave its stronghold. But then his young followers approached him saying that they had changed their minds and that it might be better to stay where they were. By this time Mohammed had put on his armour, and he announced that, having gone thus far, he was not going to take it off until after the battle. About 1000 Medinans were assembled without cavalry. They marched out to face the Meccans, but on the outskirts of the oasis Ibn Ubayy turned back, taking about a third of the army with him. The next day, undaunted, Mohammed and his 700 followers took the field against the Meccan army.

This time the Meccans were much better organized. They used their cavalry to great effect, drove wedges through the Muslim ranks, and overwhelmed and cut down the isolated groups. The Prophet himself was obliged to fight, surrounded by his faithful bodyguard. At one stage he was knocked down and the rumour spread that he had been killed, causing further consternation and confusion among the Muslims. In fact he was only wounded, and had to be carried off to safety. The Muslims were comprehensively defeated, and the pagans celebrated their victory in the barbarous manner of the times. Their women mutilated the dead by making necklaces of ears and noses, and one woman is said to have carved open the man who killed her father at Badr and chewed his liver.

The Medinans had left about 70 dead, of whom 10 were emigrants, and the other side had lost about 20. The victors did not march on Medina to finish off their opponents, which turned out to be a costly mistake. They had noted that not all the tribes had joined Mohammed (particularly the powerful Jews) and they had seen Ibn Ubayy defect. Clearly, they were unwilling to antagonize anyone unnecessarily and retired in triumph. Almost immediately Mohammed rallied his forces and set out in pursuit of the Meccan army. He took good care to keep his distance, lighting as many fires as possible at night to exaggerate his strength. His purpose was largely to impress upon surrounding tribes that his situation was not as desperate as the Quraysh were bound to make out. This done, he returned to Medina.

This was a critical time for the Prophet, and his position was now seriously challenged by his opponents. Those still undecided argued that if victory at Badr had been won by the grace of God, defeat at Uhud must mean that God had changed sides. The crisis spread to the Muslim ranks when Ibn Ubayy and his followers said that their advice should have been noted and that in future experienced people should have more say in public affairs. Many of the most ardent Muslims saw this as an act of treachery, and Mohammed had to restrain Ibn Ubayy's own son from killing his father on the spot. The situation was finally resolved by revelation (Koran 3:119) and Uhud was interpreted as a test to distinguish the faithful from the faint-hearted. But the real significance of this period is that what had started for Mohammed as a purely religious issue was now taking on political and economic significance in which some of the issues were being settled by military force.

## The Jewish Opposition

But Mohammed never lost sight of his original inspiration. Although he was a Prophet and not a scholar, the presence of the strong Jewish community in Medina must have been a constant reminder to him of the intellectual strength of the faith he was challenging. For their part the Jews of Medina had enough knowledge of their scriptures to realize that the claims of Mohammed were incompatible with Judaism. Their argument was that the Koran was mistaken on a number of issues raised in the Old Testament. Therefore it followed that the Koran was not the word of God. This being so, Mohammed could not be His Prophet. Something had to be done about such fundamental opposition.

The Jewish settlements throughout Arabia were numerous and well organized. Their life was based on skilled agriculture, and their communities were exclusive and tightly knit. In Mecca, Jews seemed to have been comparatively rare, and were viewed with a mixture of curiosity (because of their strange habits and taboos) and apprehension (because of their energy and success). Both Christians and Jews viewed the Arabs with some contempt. They were seen as primitive and uncivilized, having neither moral values nor an organized church. Both referred to the Arabs as *hanif* (pagan or infidel), and it may have been inverted snobbery which eventually, after the triumph of Islam, led the Muslims to adopt the label of *hanif* as a badge of superiority.

Mohammed's attitude to both religions was not that their faith was intrinsically wrong or that their prophets, including Jesus, were mistaken. They were serving the will of the same God, but Mohammed's message to them was that his revelations superseded all previous revelations, and the preaching of all previous prophets. Yet he found an intellectual justification for his cause in the Bible itself: Ismail was the father of the Arabs, and his brother Isaac the father of the Jews. This being so, their father Ibrahim (Abraham) was, strictly speaking, not Jewish at all. He had faith in one almighty God, but, as he preceded both the Christian and Jewish religions and was the first to submit to the will of God, then surely he was the first Muslim:

> And they say, 'Be Jews or Christians and
> you shall be guided'. Say thou: 'Nay, rather
> the creed of Abraham, a man of pure faith:
>   he was no idolater'.

(Koran 2:129)

Mohammed was told that Abraham had settled some of his people in a barren valley near the holy Temple of God, and his son Ismail had built this temple and made it a place of pilgrimage and asylum. Furthermore, he asked God to select one of the future inhabitants of this place as a Messenger to tell people of his revelations and wisdom. At this point the Voice instructed Mohammed that the faithful should turn towards the *Kaaba*[1] in Mecca to pray, not towards Jerusalem. Thus at one stroke Mohammed formally and irrevocably announced his break with the Jews, and at the same time absorbed the Arab's ritual of the pilgrimage to Mecca.

This altered the status of Islam in relation to the other two religions. It was no longer an uncivilized and barbaric people being led by the untutored Mohammed, usurping the tradition of revelations given by Moses. It was the faithless Jews who were now accused of rejecting the Message which, according to their own tradition, had been addressed to their ancestors. They were accused of having neglected and persecuted their own prophets for preaching the Message, of having rebelled against Moses, of disobeying the commandments they had been given, and of continuing to do so. As the Christians had testified, they had failed to believe in Jesus, killed him and slandered his mother. This ideological conflict was given common meaning by focusing on the Jew's dietary laws. Was it not a fact that their law forbade them things that were perfectly good to eat? How could this be if it were not, as the Koran said, a punishment for their sins? It is interesting that the Christians had used the food issue to make their own break with the Jews 600 years earlier.

## The War of the Ditch

Meanwhile the Quraysh, under their new leader, Abu Sufyan, had no intention of letting matters rest. The threat posed by Mohammed and his Muslims to their position and power was now clear to them and they resolved to destroy the movement in Medina. To do this they needed an army much larger than the one at Uhud, and they set about recruitment of the Bedu tribes. Mohammed heard of these intentions, and retaliated with his new power and wealth. There followed a period of minor raids, assassinations and intrigue. Mohammed became convinced that the Jewish tribe of Banu n-Nadir were plotting his assassination, and he ordered them to leave the oasis. He gained the consent of the Medinans that the Jews' land should be divided up among the Meccan immigrants so that they would no longer be a burden upon the community. The produce would be used for the maintenance of the destitute.

---

1. Arabic for cube: the centre of the pilgrimage in Mecca.

The final confrontation with the Quraysh began when Abu Sufyan, at the head of three armies with a total strength of 10,000 men and 600 cavalry, marched on Medina. Mohammed had time to prepare for the assault, but as he could raise no more than 3000 men, there was no question of meeting Abu Sufyan's army in the field. Except to the North the oasis was protected by hills from cavalry attack. On their exposed side the Medinans dug a huge fortified ditch, and took up their positions behind it. The Meccans approached the ditch, halted, and did not seem to know what to do next. Tradition has it that both sides stood hurling insults and arrows at each other for two or three weeks (sic) with few casualties on either side. Abu Sufyan tried to resolve the matter by intrigue in urging the last Jewish tribe left in Medina, the Qurayza, to strike Mohammed from the rear. The Muslims responded by sowing dissent among the tribes in the coalition facing them. The siege dragged on and the attackers seemed reluctant to do anything that would involve too many casualties. When it became clear that nothing had been achieved, and little could be done about it, they went home.

For Mohammed it was a triumph. The eyes of Arabia had been upon him, and he had shown that he was not to be moved by force. If an army of 10,000 men could not shift him, nothing could.

## Massacre of the Qurayza

Immediately afterwards the Prophet took action against the last group in Medina to cause him any anxiety: the Jewish Qurayza. His supporters besieged them in their fortified village and called upon them to surrender. After 25 days they offered to depart on the same conditions as the Nadir. He refused and insisted on an unconditional surrender. After some hesitation the Qurayza gave in. Mohammed offered them their lives if they would submit to Islam: only one Jew agreed. Mohammed was besieged by them and their allies asking for mercy, but he had his answer ready. Would they accept that one of their own allies should decide their fate? If so, all must abide by his decision. When this was agreed the arbitrator from the Aws tribe pronounced that all adult males were to be executed, the women and children sold into slavery and their property divided. The next day the sentence was carried out and over 600 men were massacred. It was May AD 627.[1]

It has been suggested by some European scholars that Mohammed adopted this policy of clearing the Jews from Medina just because they were Jews, but this is inconsistent with his general policy of seeking

---

1. This traditional view of the incident has been challenged in the recent work of Barakat Ali.

allies wherever possible. Mohammed attacked them because they criticized the Koranic revelations, thus undermining the foundation of the whole Islamic community, and gave support to his political opponents. In the end he turned on them not as Jews, but as an opposition. It is significant that in places where the Jewish communities were too small to be effective, or where they did not generate hostile activity, they were allowed to live unmolested.

## Truce with the Quraysh

For some while after the siege of Medina, neither side took any military initiative. The Prophet changed his tactics and announced his intention of going to Mecca for the ritual of *umra* — the traditional ceremony connected with processions around the *Kaaba* — and he invited his followers to go with him. It was to be a peaceful expedition of several hundred men and a few women. The Meccans, believing it to be an attack, met the force outside their city, but after negotiations a treaty was concluded between the two sides which denied the Muslims access to the *Kaaba* on that occasion, but conceded access to Mecca the following year.

Many of Mohammed's supporters were disappointed by this apparent reversal, but Mohammed had obtained the diplomatic concession he wanted. In making a treaty with the Muslims the Meccans had recognized both Mohammed's authority and that his followers were part of the traditional cult associated with the city.

## The Jews of Khaybar

Having secured a non-aggression pact with the Meccans, the Prophet turned his attention to his other enemies, this time in the North. The Jews of Khaybar had broken up their alliance with the Quraysh and the Bedu tribes; thus there was an opportunity to move against Khaybar while the Jews were isolated. At the head of 1600 men, Mohammed attacked and beseiged the forts one by one. Each surrendered in turn and had to accept the Muslims' terms. Mohammed's task was made easier because there was no central authority among the Jews, and they had been abandoned by their Bedu allies. This time, apart from taking some prisoners, the Muslim terms concentrated on property. The Jews had to surrender the better part of their possessions, and hand over half of the date harvest. As, one by one, the Jewish colonies of the region surrendered, they were given better terms, and were allowed to keep their possessions on payment of a tax. All religious opposition was now crushed and the Jews would present no further obstacles to the spread of Islam.

## Fall of Mecca

The following year, sure of his position in Medina and clear of all other effective opposition, the Prophet fixed his eyes firmly on Mecca. At the same time the Quraysh, after a period of long and painful adjustment, faced up to the realities of the situation. Their leader, Abu Sufyan, had reached the conclusion that it was in their best interests to come to an understanding with Mohammed, and in the end the majority agreed with him.

The siege of Medina had shown that the Muslims could not be moved by force. Mohammed's victories over the Jewish tribes, his expeditions to the North, and his treaties with the Bedu had all increased his power. His activities were still seriously interfering with trade, which was the life blood of Meccan existence. The Muslim pilgrimage to the *Kaaba* had greatly impressed the Meccans by its discipline and intention. Clearly, Mohammed was not set on destroying their institutions, but on the contrary seemed to be trying to reinforce them, albeit with a different perspective and to the exclusive glorification of Allah. What is more, the religious and military success of the Muslims had been reinforced by material success and wealth. The Meccans were above all businessmen, and they recognized that a practical accommodation had to be found with the new movement and its ideology.

Abu Sufyan was sent to Medina to open negotiations. Ostensibly he was there to negotiate about the blood feud that involved the two sides and seemed irreconcilable. There are different interpretations of what went on during the negotiations, but it is undisputed that immediately afterwards Mohammed began preparations for an armed expedition. The story was circulated that the expedition was bound for the North, but when the Prophet had assembled an immense army of 10,000 men he marched them south. This was 10 Ramadan, Year 8 (1 January 630). On the way he collected recruits, including many of his old enemies from the city of Mecca itself. Two days from Mecca the army camped and lit 10,000 fires. The city panicked and sent Abu Sufyan to the Muslim camp to negotiate. Whilst with them he was formally converted to Islam and returned to Mecca announcing Mohammed's terms: the city was in no danger if it welcomed the conqueror peacefully. The lives and property of all those who surrendered would be safe. They must lay down their arms and either stay in their houses or take refuge with Abu Sufyan.

After allowing time for the terms of the ultimatum to be understood, Mohammed broke camp on Thursday, 20 Ramadan 8 (11 January 630). The Muslims entered the deserted city in four columns. There was only token resistance which was quickly put down with very few casualties.

Mohammed went straight to the *Kaaba* amid the jubilation of his supporters and, watched by the Qurayshites, he touched the Black Stone and pronounced in a loud voice the supreme exhortation of Islam: *'Allahu akbar'* ('Allah is greatest') and 10,000 voices took up the call. His second act was to have all pagan idols thrown from the shrine, and the frescoes removed, save, it is said, those of Abraham, Jesus and the Virgin Mary. He then made a speech urging the Qurayshites to acknowledge him as the Messenger of God, and to come forward and swear allegiance.

Mohammed stayed barely two weeks in Mecca, and the only people who suffered persecution were the propagandists and poets who had satirized his claim to prophethood. He took the opportunity to borrow some large sums from the wealthy Qurayshites in order to distribute compensation to the Muslim soldiery who had failed to gain any booty, and over 2000 of the most needy men were given 50 *dirhams* each. He had all idols destroyed, but otherwise seemed content to leave things much as they were. There were now considerable advantages to being a Muslim, and, having physically established authority over the two most important towns, he had created a climate in which the adoption of his religion could take its own course. Social pressures now worked in favour of Islam rather than paganism, and in a few years paganism in Mecca was a thing of the past.

## Unification of the Tribes

Mohammed had quickly to face a challenge from an unexpected quarter. A large confederation of tribes called Hawazin had risen against him. They were in alliance with other tribes centred on the city of Ta'if, and were old enemies of the Quraysh. They saw Mohammed's rise purely in tribal terms and saw his new power as a Qurayshite threat. Both sides raised huge armies which met at Hunayn. After a fierce battle, in which Mohammed himself took a major part, the Muslims were victorious. The defeated withdrew into their fortified town and, after a brief siege, Mohammed withdrew to divide the spoils of the battle. This almost turned into a riot, and after considerable difficulty Mohammed restored order, and shocked his old Companions by his generosity towards the new converts. Even the pagans were given something. He was now in a position to return to Medina where, eight years before with a few Companions, he had sought sanctuary from persecution.

Paradoxically, it was the almost simultaneous events outside Arabia that made the subsequent unification of the country swift and complete. The Roman Empire in the West had been overrun by barbarians. In the East it had survived under the style of the Byzantine

Empire with its capital at Constantinople, but it had fallen into confusion, partly because of attacks from without, and partly because of internal conflicts and inefficient rule. The serious rival to Byzantine was the Persian Empire of the Sassanids in the East, which stretched from Iraq to Afghanistan. Following 50 years of uneasy peace, a long and decisive war began in AD 602. For almost 30 years the conflict raged across the Middle East, first one side and then the other gaining advantage. The sack of Jerusalem and the carrying off of what was believed to be the true Cross caused consternation among Christians throughout the Byzantine Empire, and provided a rallying point for their forces. Eventually, the Persian resources were exhausted by the long struggle, and in June 629 Constantinople was occupied in triumph. The Holy Rood was restored to Jerusalem in March 630. To the civilized world the triumph of Christianity seemed assured. The defeat of Persia meant the decline of Persian influence in southern Arabia and the Persian Gulf. The political vacuum left the field open for the inspired sword of Islam.

In the years following, Mohammed made the most of this situation. There was a constant exchange of envoys between the Muslims and the tribes in the far corners of Arabia. The Prophet undertook a complicated diplomatic and military task. Alliances were made in which acknowledgement was given to the power of God, and through which peace, security and the benefit of trade would accrue at home. Spoils were to be generated from abroad. Each tribe had to embrace the faith, promise not to attack other tribes which had made alliances with Mohammed, and furnish troops when required. The system had proved itself in both effectiveness and prosperity, and converts flocked irresitibly to the creed which had set its sights on an Arab state with an Arab ideology. For all practical purposes Arabia was united.

Within a year of the fall of Mecca there was the last great expedition, to Tabuk in the North. Its purpose was to test the limit of the Prophet's influences, and treaties were signed with local princes, Jewish settlements and one Christian king.

## The Farewell Pilgrimage

Since his entry into Mecca Mohammed had been content to allow the ritual pilgrimage (*hajj*) to be attended by Muslims and pagans alike. In AH 10 (AD 632), however, he decided to remove all pagan influence from this ritual. Mohammed was accompanied by all his wives and the most eminent of the Companions. With a great crowd around him he performed the *umra*, the processions round the *Kaaba* and the seven journeys between Safa and Maraw. On 8 Dhu L-Hijja, the ceremonies of *hajj* began. He performed the traditional rites at Mina, Arafat and

Muzdalifa: the prayers, pauses, the casting of stones and the sacrifices. But he made it clear that the acts were dedicated to God alone and not to the divinities that had been associated with these sanctuaries. On the tenth day he had his head shaved according to custom and performed the ritual depurification. In the days of the *hajj* he made speeches and had dialogues with people. These were later collected into one great speech. In it Mohammed forbade usury and blood feuds for crimes committed during paganism. He laid down the organization of the calendar, the four sacred months, and its lunar structure. He defined the mutual duties of husbands and wives, urged the proper treatment of slaves, and preached brotherhood among all Muslims. With the ceremonies completed, he immediately returned to Medina, and he was never to see his native city again. The visit was to become known as the Farewell Pilgrimage, and from that day to this only Muslims have been allowed to enter Mecca.

## Death of Mohammed

Shortly afterwards the Prophet became ill. He was planning another campaign to the North which had to be entrusted to Usama, a negro youth who was his son by an Abyssinian freed woman. Mohammed was suffering from severe head pains and fever, and took to his bed. His illness grew worse and he began to suffer from fainting fits. Some two weeks later on 13 Rabi (8 June 632) he recovered enough to show himself to the faithful in the courtyard. His family and Companions were delighted and the word began to go round that the Prophet was better. But by that same afternoon he had to take to his bed once more as he became steadily weaker and delirious. Before nightfall Mohammed the Prophet, Messenger of God, was dead.

# The Prophet's Successors

Mohammed made no provision at all for a successor after his death, following the Arabic custom that the leader emerges according to the consensus of the community. In the absence of any revelation to the contrary, Mohammed allowed matters to take their course. According to tradition, Abu Bakr had been asked by the Prophet on his deathbed to lead the community in prayer as *imam*. As he was also the Prophet's father-in-law and a leading member of his following, it would have been easy for him to assume the right to succeed Mohammed as *Khalifa* (Caliph) or 'substitute'. But he did not take the initiative. In the confusion following the Prophet's death it was Omar, son of Al-Khattab, an outstanding personality in the Quraysh, who saw the need to resolve the question of the leadership quickly. He gave Abu Bakr the *bay's*, the clap of palm on palm, which for the first time was used to acknowledge sovereignty, and Abu Bakr became the first Caliph.

His role was naturally more limited than that of Mohammed. He had certain religious duties such as acting as *imam* at prayer, but any respectable Muslim can perform this function. It is God and not the Caliph who directs religious affairs. Nevertheless, the Caliph clearly had great political power, which increased in scope as the Empire of Islam spread.

The appointment of the Caliph without reference to the community was a significant departure from Arab custom, and this did not go unnoticed. When Omar himself became Caliph, having been nominated by Abu Bakr on his deathbed, he wrote a letter to the Governor at Basra:

> People have an aversion to their rulers and I trust to God that you and I are not overtaken by it . . . See to the execution of the laws . . . Strike terror into wrongdoers and make heaps of mutilated limbs out of them. Visit the sick among Muslims, attend their funerals, open your gate to them and give heed in person to their affairs, for you are but a man among them except that God has allotted you the heaviest burden.

Omar nominated a council of six to elect his successor. The council chose Uthman ibn Affan, a member of the Umayyad clan, who had been one of Mohammed's sons-in-law. By this choice, however, they passed over another of the Prophet's sons-in-law, Ali, who was also his cousin. Ali, and many other members of the community, considered that he who was nearest in blood to the Prophet had a stronger claim to be Caliph. This conflict was to divide Islam permanently. Ali was elected Caliph when Uthman was assassinated, but the Umayyad clan held Ali responsible for the assassination and refused to accept him as Caliph. One of the Umayyads, the governor of Syria, proclaimed himself the true Commander of the Faithful, thus precipitating the split of the Islamic community into two principal sects, the Sunnis (who accept the legitimacy of the first four Caliphs) and the Shi'ites (who favored Ali as nearest in blood to the Prophet).

Ali met his death at the hands of a group of purists, the Kharijis or Seceders, who considered both Caliphs usurpers on the grounds that neither had been raised to the leadership of Islam by the free choice that Arab custom demanded. These democratic tribesmen, detesting the family rivalries at Mecca and the struggle for political power in Medina, disputed the need for any *imam* or head of state so long as the divine law was carried out. They saw the struggle for power between the rival factions as irrelevant, and dangerous to the purity of Islam, and therefore vowed to assassinate both Caliphs. Their attack on the governor of Syria, however, was not fatal.

Under the first four Caliphs the unity of Islam was more or less maintained by a central leadership, but within the first 100 years of its foundation, the territory it controlled became too big to be managed by a central administration. As the pace of expansion increased, the driving force for controlling and administrating the new society became local in character. Various powerful families inside and outside Arabia embraced the new religion and became its champions by exporting it to new territories and founding new dynasties. The first of these was the Umayyad based in Damascus. After a thousand years in which dynasties flourished and foundered from Spain to China, the three great Muslim empires—the Ottoman in Turkey, the Middle East and the Mediterranean; the Safayid in Iran; and the Moghul in India—flowered in the 18th century. By the 19th century all three were either destroyed or seriously weakened by the imperial expansion of the European powers. However, it was only the power and wealth of these Empires that was challenged by Europe. The religious faith that underpinned them remained unchallenged, and has provided the foundation for the revival of Islam in modern times.

## Class Structure Under Islam

The unification of Arabia under Islam, and the organization required to spread it far beyond, brought about the structural changes in tribal society where a man's position was virtually determined by his birth. The Koranic revelations superseded the authority of the tribe which had previously determined its own beliefs and way of life. Islam substituted a detailed code of moral and social behaviour, affecting every aspect of a person's life. This code provided not only the cohesion of a new religion, but also the elements of an embryonic nation. Henceforth the authority for the doings of the community rested not with the chief or the collective voice of the people, but with Mohammed and, beyond him, with God. This introduced an idea foreign to the Arabs—that of a central authority.

The tribal aristocracy established by birth still persisted and continues to be important[1], but it exists, as it were, in parallel with the idea that all Muslims are equal within the brotherhood of Islam. In its early days one of the most subversive aspects of the new creed was the notion that any Muslim was not only equal to any other in the eyes of

---

1. See Koran 6:165:
  'It is He who has appointed you viceroys
  in the earth, and has raised some of you
  in rank above others.'

God, but also equal to the unbelievers who ruled society by right of centuries of established custom and tradition. The element of hope embodied in Islam is one of the main reasons for its spread (for example, in India where it offered a social refuge to the Hindu untouchables).

In Mohammed's Farewell Pilgrimage, when preaching brotherhood among all Muslims, he is said to have stated that all men are equal in Islam and that the Arab has no superiority over the foreigner, nor the foreigner over the Arab, save in fear of God.

Yet in spite of the Prophet's own preaching he has won a place in the hearts of the masses which has eclipsed even the most noble birthright. Since his day even the slightest kinship with his tribe, the Quraysh[1], has been held in the highest esteem. A Qurayshite would be honoured above the highest nobleman, and even an adopted member of the tribe would have precedence over the offspring of an old sheikhly family.

The question of class arose most sharply when marriage was involved. It was the responsibility of the father or guardian of the girl to become her *wali* (literally: protector) and it was his duty to see that the suitor was of equal birth and that the match was suitable in other ways. When Islam abolished distinctions of birth it became theoretically possible for a slave to ask to marry a girl from a distinguished family although this is unlikely to have occurred any more often than a serf asking for the hand of a lord's daughter in medieval England. People knew their places, and gradually society arranged customs to ensure that the ideas of equality did not get out of hand. The Quraysh became the new élite and the rest of the Muslims were in an equal class irrespective of their tribe. In marriage a non-Arab Muslim was equal to an Arab if both his father and grandfather had been Muslims before him, but even so he was obliged to provide an adequate endowment. Nevertheless, tribal tradition, directly contrary to Koranic doctrine, strongly discouraged the marriage of an Arab with a non-Arab woman in early Islamic times.

Although Mohammed made important reforms in tribal customs and brought about significant changes in the treatment and rights of slaves, like other religious leaders before him he took slavery as part of the natural order of things. Nowhere in the Koran is there any suggestion that it should be otherwise. Mohammed encouraged the humane treatment of slaves and urged their emancipation, and as Islam matured the stigma attaching to the status of the slave slowly

---

1. In modern Arabia the descendants of the Prophet are known as *Ashraf* (plural of *Sharif*). They are often large landowners, forming separate communities, and generally marry within their own clan. In no sense do they have authority as a religious community.

diminished. Quite early on the principle was established, even though it is not laid down in the Koran, that Muslims were not to be taken as captives or slaves.

Slaves might be acquired by sale, gift, inheritance or capture. As it became illegal to sell a free Muslim into slavery, parents were forbidden to sell their children, although this has not always been observed, even in modern times. Legislation provided for the sale and purchase of slaves as for any ordinary goods with certain restrictions in the case of females who had borne children by their masters, and of the children themselves. Slaves had very few legal rights, their labour and their bodies being the property of their master to do with as he liked. Household slaves were very rarely sold, and were often adopted as members of the family. In exceptional circumstances slaves had opportunities to acquire great wealth and power. There was a slave king of Delhi and the Manluk sultans of Egypt were originally slaves. A whole series of dynasties was founded in the Middle East during the 12th and 13th centuries by the Turks, whose original slave bodyguards were appointed to high office, and eventually became kings who founded dynasties.

The spread of Islam by conquest gave rise to a unique class. These were named Mawali, converted Muslims of the subdued territory outside Arabia. They became affiliated to one of the Arab tribes from among their conquerors, owing allegiance and receiving protection. They were not always well treated by their conquerors, were often made illegally to pay tax and suffered harassment and contempt. In Kusa they had to have a mosque of their own; and under the Umayyad régime, even when they fought for Islam, they were sometimes deprived of their share of the spoils. Nor was this poor treatment confined to backward communities. It was not long before the religious scholars of Persia and Turkey, taking their new faith seriously, became expert in its doctrines and traditions, and the most learned doctors in Islamic theology. But far from this gaining the respect of the Arab invaders, it simply encouraged them to regard the conquered people as inferior beings fit only for studying culture and science. This treatment of the Mawali led eventually to their adopting fabricated Arab identities, changing their names and inventing family trees. Eventually Persian political influence became strong in the middle of the eighth century, and both theological and political pressure redressed the balance.

## Chapter 2
# The Message

> Today I have perfected your religion
> for you, and I have completed My blessing
> upon you, and I have approved Islam for
> your religion.
>
> (Koran 5:8)

'Religion' is translated from the Arabic word *din*, but this does not convey the proper meaning to the Western mind. For *din* does not mean simply the spiritual fulfilment or enlightenment of the individual, it means all matters pertaining to a way of life. *Din* encompasses theology, scripture, politics, morality, law, justice and all other aspects of life relating to the thoughts or actions of men. For the Westerner, used to viewing religion as a matter of private conscience, this is the fundamental point to grasp in trying to understand Islam. It is not that religion dominates the life of a faithful Muslim, but that religion, in this comprehensive sense, *is* his life.

His faith is based on the belief that literally everything in life is the predetermined will of God, and that His will has ruled and does rule absolutely from always to eternity. Not only is every aspect of each individual's life predetermined but also 'not a worm weeps in the earth, not a leaf falls from the tree except by the decree and will of God'[1]. Giving unto Caesar that which is due to Caesar is an idea alien to Islam.

This does not mean that the Islamic faith has no structure. There are fundamental beliefs, 'pillars of faith', which form the core of the religion, and to which all other aspects of life are ultimately related. But first it is useful to consider a few basic definitions in order to establish a foundation upon which to build.

*Allah.* Allah is Arabic for God, the Supreme Being of the Muslims. The first article of the essential Muslim creed states *'La illah il-Allah'* — 'There is no god save Allah'.

*Islam.* Islam means submission to, and therefore being in the proper relationship to, God.

---

1. F A Klein, *Religion of Islam*, Curzon, 1972.

*Muslim.* Muslim means submitter.

*Prophets.* Prophets are recognized as Apostles or Messengers who are divinely sent for particular nations or communities, and who bear witness to the divine message. Noah, Abraham, Lot, Ishmael, Isaac, Jacob, David, Moses, Shu'aib and Jesus are among them.

*Mohammed.* Mohammed is the Messenger of God, to whom God revealed His word and His law in such a manner and in such detail as to supersede all other revelations and previous interpretations of his Word, and upon whom He placed the ultimate Seal of the Prophet. It was Mohammed who first called upon the Arabian tribes to submit to the will of God and to commit themselves afresh each day and each moment to His service. But no degree of divinity is conferred on Mohammed, in spite of the special place that the Prophet holds in the hearts and minds of Muslims; such a suggestion is considered blasphemous. God is unique and alone.

*Koran.* Koran means recitation; it is the sacred book of Islam. It is the uncreated and direct word of Allah and is coexistent with Him. It is a discourse on what God has uttered, and describes itself simply and finally as 'the best of histories' (12:3). It is held that the Torah of Moses, the Psalms of David and the Gospel of Jesus were all sent down by God, but that the Koran is the last and final word of God.

*Revelation.* The idea of revelation is central to Islam. It has been described as the flashing of divine light on the soul. The Koran explains that

> It belongs not to any mortal that
> God should speak to him, except
> by revelation, or from behind
>   a veil,
> or that he should send a messenger
> and he reveal whatsoever He will.

(Koran 42:50)

# The Five Pillars of Islam

The basic duties of Muslims towards Allah are known as the Five Pillars of Islam.

## Shahada

The first duty is recitation of the *shahada,* or short creed: 'There is no God but Allah, and Mohammed is His Prophet.' This profession of faith said in public is enough to gain recognition by the community.

## Salat

The second pillar is *salat*, the devotional worship. The usual translation is prayers, but worship or formal prayer gives a better indication of its meaning. *Salat* is essentially an acknowledgement of God's might and power, and does not consist of asking Him for favours. It is both an adoration and an act of submission, a physical act which is repeated at least twice and finishes with the worshipper touching the ground with his forehead. Muslims worship five times a day—at dawn, midday, mid-afternoon, sunset and after nightfall. The call to prayer is uttered from the minaret of the mosque by the muezzin (*mu'adhdhin*):

> 'Allah is most great,
> There is no God but Allah, and
> Mohammed is His Prophet,
> Come to prayer, come to salvation,
> Allah is most great, there is no
> God but Allah.'

And in the morning: 'Prayer is better than sleep.' The Shi'ites always add 'come to the best of work'.

Ritual ablutions must be performed before *salat*, including the washing of hands, face and feet. If water is not available, sand is used. The prayers themselves are ritualized and include recitations of the first *sura* and other verses from the Koran. Preferably prayer should be performed in congregation, although it is valid in private, and may be seen all over the Muslim world in airports, shops, offices, building sites and streets.

On Fridays congregational prayers take place at noon in mosques (*masjid*, or place for prostration). Prayer is led by an *imam* (president) with the worshippers standing in ranks behind him. At least 40 faithful are required to form a congregation, and it is obligatory for all adult males to attend. Hence Friday mosques, roofed or not, must be large enough to hold the whole male population. Women normally take no part in these proceedings.

Generally before the prayers, the *imam* delivers from the pulpit an address in which the teachings of Islam are expounded.

Friday is not regarded as a day of rest, and there is no prohibition on work. Particular emphasis is placed on the midday prayer on Fridays, but, this aside, it is not considered a special day.

The direction of prayer is called *qibla* and is generally marked in a mosque by a niche in a wall which indicates the direction of the city of Mecca in Arabia. More specifically it is the *Kaaba*, a black cubic shrine sited in the courtyard of the Great Mosque. By tradition the *Kaaba* had been established by Abraham, and was the centre of worship for the Arab tribes, but was subsequently usurped by idolators. Mohammed deemed that the *Kaaba* should be established as the direction of prayer, which had previously been Jerusalem.

*Imams* (and in some places *sheikhs*) are appointed to certain mosques and orders, but this does not confer on them any exclusive right to lead prayer. The leadership may be taken by any good Muslim if he is acquainted with the nodalities of worship.

In spite of the communal character of some Islamic institutions, worship for a Muslim remains essentially something that takes place between an individual and God. If it is convenient and appropriate to do so, Muslims pray together, but the duty of the prayer devolves directly and unambiguously upon the individual. Even if there were only one Muslim in the world, there would be nothing to prevent him from carrying out all the requirements of the Islamic faith, and every Muslim understands that on the Last Day he will be judged alone.

## Zakat

The third pillar is *zakat*, the obligatory tax for the needy.

> And what you give in usury,
> that it may increase upon the
> people's wealth, increase not
> with God; but what you give in
> alms, desiring God's Face,
> those — they receive recompense
>   manifold.
>
> (Koran 30:38)

In the days of Mohammed payment of *zakat* was possibly the clearest external sign of adherence to Islam and encapsulates the old Semitic ideas of sacrifice. Each believer is required to contribute a fixed percentage (usually 1/40th) of his income or property to the needy and wayfarers. Normally there are no formal arrangements for the collection of *zakat* and the custom has declined in many places. A notable exception is Saudi Arabia, where *zakat* is levied as a formal tax, and even foreign companies are not exempt from payment on behalf of their Saudi employees.

## Sawm

The fourth pillar is *sawm*, the fast during the month of Ramadan. The Koran commands that for the entire lunar month Muslims must refrain from all food and drink and other sensory pleasures during daylight hours. The fast begins with the red of the dawn and ends with sunset. By tradition, during the nights of Ramadan it is customary to sit in the mosque or at home praying and reciting the Koran.

Travellers, pregnant women, the sick and the aged and some others are exempted from the fast. When the month of Ramadan falls in summer it is especially difficult for people in the hot and humid countries of the Middle East and it is common for shops, offices and government departments to open restricted hours. This is generally considered a bad time for trade and business.

The start of Ramadan is determined by astronomical observations, so that the calendar date may be flexible within a day or two. The exact start is usually announced near the day. At the end of Ramadan there is a day of obligatory feasting followed by a festival of several days (*eid*) when people visit one another bearing gifts. In strict Muslim countries during Ramadan it is decidedly bad manners, if no more, for foreigners to eat, drink or even smoke in public.

## Hajj

The fifth pillar is the pilgrimage, or *hajj*, to the *Kaaba*, the holy shrine in Mecca. *Hajj* means 'to set out for a definite purpose'.

> It is the duty of all men towards God to come
> to the House a pilgrim, if he is able to
> make his way there.
>
> (Koran 3:92)

Thus every able-bodied Muslim is expected to make the pilgrimage at some time, and to many it is the climax of a lifetime. Only minors, slaves and the poor are exempted.

There are various ceremonies connected with the *hajj*, including wearing a special garment called *ihram*, circling the *Kaaba* seven times (*tawaf*) and kissing the black stone in the corner of the shrine. One of the pilgrim's important duties is to sacrifice an animal on the 10th day of the month. This sacrificial festival is celebrated at the same time throughout the Muslim world. The climax of the pilgrimage is the 'standing on Arafat', a hill and plain to the east of Mecca. The time for this is from midday to sunset on the ninth of the month.

The Prophet forbade access to Mecca for unbelievers and the interdict has generally been held to apply to Medina also. Very few unbelievers have penetrated either, and then only in disguise and at considerable risk.

The numbers of pilgrims are increasing each year, and in 1979 totalled over 2 million, the majority of whom also visit Medina to pray at the tomb of the Prophet.

## The Koran

The language of the Koran is Arabic, and because it is the uncreated work of God many consider that it cannot and should not be translated into other languages. When it is rendered into another tongue, however skilfully, the words are no longer those spoken by God, and therefore no longer the Koran. Certainly, most educated Muslims will have a working knowledge of Arabic, and even the illiterate are likely to know some words through learning passages by heart.

The Koran is not organized in any chronological or sequential manner. Although some of the text was written down under Mohammed's supervision, it is agreed that it was completed in its present form at the time of Uthman the Third Caliph (AD 644-656). Its contents reflect the manner in which God revealed His message to the Prophet over a period of 20 years. On close examination it becomes clear that there is a structure, which reflects an intention to demonstrate that aspects of life should not be seen separately, but accepted as a whole based on the divine will.

The fragmentation of the text also reflects the fact that those who collected Mohammed's revelations after his death were not concerned to preserve their chronological order.[1] Muslim historians agree that parts of the same revelation are sometimes widely separated in the pages of the book.

It seems probable that for some years the revelations were retained only in the memories of Mohammed and his followers, although some scholars believe that much of the Koran was written down by the Prophet himself. When early Christians and others challenged Muslims to point to any miracle of Mohammed's that would demonstrate his prophethood, the orthodox reply was that the Koran itself was his miracle, since he could neither read nor write. It is still widely held among Muslims that the Prophet was unlettered and that he recorded the Holy Book under divine inspiration. Some modern Western scholars argue, however, that there is no evidence to show that Mohammed could not write, and that, given his experience in Meccan trade, it is possible that he could write as well as the average merchant.

Reason plays an important part in the Koran. In it God is always discussing, arguing and appealing to reason, and it continually expounds the rational proofs of Allah's omnipotence. Christians are called upon not to exceed the bounds of rationality:

> People of the Book, go not beyond the bounds
> in your religion, and say not as to God
> but the truth. The Messiah, Jesus son of Mary,
> was only the Messenger of God.

(Koran 4:169)

---

[1]. The exact state of the Koran at Mohammed's death, however, remains uncertain, although it is clear that the revelations could not have been collected in any final form so long as the Prophet was alive and adding to them.

Repeated some 50 times in the Koran is the verb *aqala* which means to connect ideas together, to reason, to understand an intellectual argument. A reasoning passage is frequently followed by the phrase 'have ye then no sense?'. Infidels who are unconvinced by Mohammed's preaching are regarded as 'a people of no intelligence', incapable of the intellectual effort required to cast off routine thinking. It has rightly been said that Mohammed comes close to considering unbelief as an infirmity of the human mind. The Koran is peppered with exhortations to people to re-examine the beliefs of their fathers, to recognize and understand the signs which God is displaying through revelations to His Messenger. Those who will not believe are not only ignorant but wilful. Perhaps the ultimate appeal to reason lies in the fact that God has taken the trouble to send his preaching in Arabic so that 'haply you will understand' (Koran 43:1).

The Koran is roughly the size of the New Testament. It is divided into 114 *suras* (chapters), each of which bears the name of something contained in it. The *suras* are divided into *ayat* (verses). The *suras*, with one exception, are arranged roughly in order of length, with the longest first, and it is generally agreed that the shortest ones, coming at the end, date from the Prophet's earliest days. Reverence for the Koran is evident everywhere among Muslims. The book is never laid on the ground or allowed to contact anything dirty. There is probably no other book in history, including the Bible, that has been subjected to so much study and analysis. Commentaries (*tafsirs*) on it fill entire libraries. The best known of these is by al-Tabari (d AD 923) which is a phrase by phrase analysis filling 30 volumes.

## Hadith and Sunna

After the Koran the second foundation of Islam is the *Sunna*. This seeks to designate the sayings, actions and behaviour of the Prophet during his lifetime.

It was found after Mohammed's death that people faced problems that reference to the Koran alone did not solve. It was natural therefore that they should seek guidance from what people before them had done, and in particular from what the Prophet and his Followers in the ideal Muslim community of the first generation had said or done in comparable circumstances. Thus, the search for precedents became all-important.

Over the years, however, situations arose for which there was no exact historical precedent. Traditions began to be fabricated, and some believed that they understood Mohammed's mind so well that they could speak for him, perhaps because he is believed to have said 'Whenever someone says something true, it is as if I said it'. Eventually there was a reaction which resulted in systematic studies designed to sift the reliable from the fabricated. Such controversies were finally resolved by the jurist al-Shafii (d AD 820), who held that the *Sunna* of the Prophet alone is authoritative.

The *hadith* are literally oral reports going back in an unbroken chain to the Prophet. The nature, character and reliability of each witness in the chain was minutely examined by students of *hadith*, together with the action or saying in question. Eventually a vast body of biographical material was accrued to assess the strength and reliability of each *hadith*, and by the third Islamic century several great collections of *hadith* had emerged, which have since become recognized as second in authority only to the Koran. The collections are known as the Six Sound Books.

Controversy still exists about the *hadith*, however. In the last hundred years, disagreement about their reliability has emerged among Muslim scholars. Some still place full reliance on the historical accuracy of the classical method, whilst others reject the *hadith*, and seek guidance only from the Koran.

## Jihad

*Jihad* literally means an effort or striving. It includes a religious war against unbelievers with the object of converting them to Islam or subduing all opposition (see Koran 9:5; 4:76; 2:214; 8:39). It is the sacred duty of the Muslim nation to ensure that Islam triumphs over all religions. It is considered a general duty of the nation as a whole, not of individuals. Furthermore, it is a duty which relates only to religion. It has nothing to do with economic exploitation, political repression or imperialism in any form.

In his early career Mohammed spread Islam by teaching and persuasion: several early Meccan *suras* stated that he was sent only to preach. When, at Medina, he wanted to win Jews over to his side, he stated that there was to be 'no compulsion in religion'. This attitude changed on his flight to Medina, when he declared that God had allowed him and his followers to defend themselves against infidels, and later when he proclaimed that he had divine leave to attack them and set up the true faith by the sword. Mohammed himself fought in nine battles and ordered many more. It is still the duty of the *imam* to order war against infidels on every suitable occasion. If he neglects to do so he commits a sin, unless his forces are not strong enough to subdue the enemy. Detailed rules are laid down about such matters as the declaration of war, who can be spared the sword and under what circumstances, who may keep their religions, how taxes are levied and how the spoils of war are to be distributed.

*Jihad* is to be taken very seriously. It is one of the few areas in which the Koran criticizes the judgement of the Prophet:

> It is not for any Prophet to have prisoners
> until he make wide slaughter in the land.

(Koran 8:68)

## Dar al-Islam and Dar al-Harb

The world is therefore divided into two — *Dar al-Islam*, (the seat of Islam) and *Dar al-Harb* (the seat of war, which is inhabited by pagans, Christians and Jews).

# Sacred Places

The *Kaaba* is the most sacred place for believers. Much more than a mosque, it is believed to be the place where heavenly power touches the earth directly. The Prophet's mosque in Medina is the next in sanctity. The third is Jerusalem as the first *qibla* (direction of prayer before it was changed to the *Kaaba*), which, according to tradition, is the place where Mohammed made his ascent to heaven. For the Shi'ites, Karbala in Iraq (where Mohammed's grandson Husayn was martyred) and Meshed in Iran (where Imam Ali ar-Rida is buried)- are special places of pilgrimage. For the masses the Sufi shrines are particular objects of veneration despite the fact that this is against Islamic teaching. In Baghdad, the tomb of the greatest saint, Abd al-Qadir al-Jilani, is visited by pilgrims from all over the world.

# Sacred Days

The two festivals kept are: *Eid al-Fitr* (breaking the fast) which immediately follows Ramadan, starting on the first day of Shawwal and lasting three days, and *Eid al Adha* (sacrifice) which begins on the 10th of Dhu-l Hijieh, when the pilgrims perform their sacrifices, and lasts three or four days. The noon prayer on Fridays, with its accompanying *khofba* (homily) is a weekly event.

In addition to the Five Pillars, Muslims celebrate important religious occasions. On the Prophet's birthday meetings are held, speeches made and prayers offered. Shi'ite Muslims hold a great festival on the 10th of Muharram commemorating the martyrdom of Husayn, the Prophet's grandson, in the battle of Karbala (61/680). Parades are held with symbols of the slain Husayn, and the worshippers weep and flail themselves. There are also dramatic performances of a passion play to show the martyr's suffering.

## Sin

According to the Prophet, there are seven ruinous sins:

1. Associating anything with God
2. Magic
3. Killing people without reason
4. Taking interest on money
5. Taking the property of an orphan
6. Running away from battle when *Jihad* has been declared
7. Accusing an innocent woman of adultery.

Some sects add to these: disbelief, fornication, sodomy, cuckolding, refusal of alms, despairing of God's mercy, disobeying parents, disavowing of kinship, swearing a false oath, fraudulent measuring or weighing, drinking alcohol, postponing the *salat*, suppressing evidence, theft, bribery, eating pork, breaking the fast of Ramadan, treachery and fighting believers.

It is the duty of a Muslim to show repentence for sins immediately; any delay in itself constitutes a sin. There is no place in the system for discussion or ambiguity. Canonical punishment for sins is stipulated in the Koran, and such punishment, when administered, automatically confers forgiveness.

## Death

The sheer scale of the obligations set upon an orthodox Muslim's life and the difficulties that might be found in keeping them, are acknowledged by the rewards that await the faithful after death. Paradise, which offers unimaginable pleasure and fulfillment, is described in some detail in the Koran. There are also specific descriptions of Death, the Resurrection, the Last Judgement, and Hell, so that no one can be in doubt about their options in eternity.

Death takes place when men reach the age which God has appointed for them. After death each person will be asked by the examining angels: 'Who is thy lord, what is thy religion and who is thy Prophet?' If the person gives the satisfactory answer: 'God is my Lord, Islam my religion and Mohammed my Prophet' he is assured of the mercy of God and the delights of Paradise. If the answer is unsatisfactory, two angels beat him between the eyes and he is doomed to eternal hell-fire. Dragons will torment him to the day of Resurrection, and his grave will be made narrow to crush him. The infidel will suffer such torments forever, the disobedient believer for a period according to his sins. Prophets and martyrs are said to be not subject to examination. Angels are also exempt, but not the *jinn*.

It is written that obedient believers will go to Paradise and that infidels will go to Hell. Disobedient believers will also go to Paradise if they are penitent. If they are unrepentant God will pardon or torment them as He pleases, but He will not leave them in Hell forever because they are believers and must not be treated like infidels.

## Resurrection

The exact time of the Resurrection is known only to God. At the approach of the Last Day, the Hour may be known by certain signs such as the appearance of the Mahdi,[1] who will go from Medina to Mecca, the appearance of an antichrist who will ride an ass and be followed by 70,000 Jews, and who will finally be slain by Jesus, the descent of Jesus[2], near the Mosque at Damascus during afternoon prayer, the appearance of the barbarian nations Gog and Magog who will invade the Holy Land and proceed to Jerusalem where Jesus will request God to destroy them, the rising of the sun in the West, the destruction of the *Kaaba*, and other inescapable signals.

## The Hour

The sign of the imminent coming of the Hour will be the sounding of the trumpet which will strike terror into the hearts of all creatures; all buildings and mountains will be levelled, the heavens will melt, the sun will be darkened, and the seas will dry up. This will be followed by a second blast when all creatures in heaven and earth will die. Between the two blasts all creatures will be in an intermediate state between insensibility and death for 40 years.

## Judgement

At the sound of the blast of Resurrection all souls will repair to their bodies and mankind will go to the place of assembly for Judgement. The graves of the dead will open up and their occupants will join the assembly. God will appear and, according to tradition, Mohammed will rise first and place himself on the throne at God's right hand. All the other Prophets will then take their places under him.

All creatures will be questioned, and a balance will be set up to weigh the books of good and bad actions. Each man will be handed his

---

[1]. A ruler who will appear in order to preside over the earth's last days. The Shi'ites say he has already appeared as the 12th *imam*, and resides in some secret place until the end of the world. The Sunnis say he has yet to appear.

[2]. It is prophesied that Jesus will marry, beget children, die at 40, and be buried at Medina.

own account and will be asked to read it. A good man is said to be given his book in his right hand. After each account is rendered and each man's actions weighed, sentence is pronounced according to whether the good actions outweigh the bad. A bridge will then be spread over the midst of Hell and all will have to pass over it. All men without exception will pass through Hell. Believers will pass through quickly, while infidels remain there forever.

The judgement is passed on the individual and is not influenced by a man's position, kinsmen or wealth. Tradition has it that in earlier times whole communities went to Hell because they showed solidarity in rejecting the prophet sent to them. In the later passages of the Koran, however, the issue is belief or unbelief: man must not only fulfil the will of God, he must also believe in it.

## Paradise and Hell

The result of the Judgement is either everlasting bliss or everlasting torment. There is no intermediate condition. Some scholars have interpreted certain Koranic passages as implying that a state of Purgatory exists, but it is universally accepted that there are only two *final* destinations, Paradise and Hell.

There are many names for the place to which the condemned are sentenced — the most common is *an-nar*, the Fire. The torments of the damned are depicted with a wealth of detail. The overseers of Hell are angels instructed by God to administer punishment, and since all water is in Paradise, the damned of Hell must beg for it. The righteous, having crossed the bridge, will enter Paradise and enjoy all sensual and spiritual pleasures.

Paradise is described as abundance and luxuries of many kinds for the gratification and enjoyment of the blessed. The recurring image is that of believers reclining on silken couches, in surroundings perfect in every detail. There is an abundance of fruit and wine served by ever-youthful boys. The reference to wine is interesting in view of the prohibition on alcohol, but its quality is such that it does not befuddle the mind or pain the head. The setting is quite specifically a garden with rivers of pure water, milk and honey.

The imagination of both East and West has made much of the *houris* of Paradise, and there are several passages in the Koran describing the maidens who are to be companions of the believers. They are spotless but amorous virgins resembling pearls, ruby or coral, with swelling breasts unseen and untouched by men or *jinn*. Their eyes are cast down in modesty and they are perpetually enclosed in pavilions.

But Paradise does not consist only of bodily and sensual pleasures; it also includes spiritual delights. The believers experience forgiveness, peace and the satisfaction of the soul in God, and ultimately they receive the most precious gift of all — seeing the face of God.

The relevance of all this to men is quite clear. What is intended for women is not so clear. The Koran says:

> Whosoever does an evil deed shall be
> recompensed only with the like of it,
> but whosoever does a religious deed,
> be it male or female, believing — those shall
> enter Paradise, therein provided
>     without reckoning.
>
>                                                              (Koran 40:43)

Again, we are shown the faithful 'busy in their rejoicing, they and their spouses, reclining upon couches in the shade' (Koran 36:55). Dark eyed *houris* are promised to each man as brides and it seems likely that women, or at least those who survive the Judgement, will be transformed to occupy the place allotted to them in Paradise. Just as each man will be perpetually 36, so each woman will be a uniform but unspecified age, and will be endowed with considerable physical charm.

What is true of women in Paradise is true also of children. They are mentioned in the general scheme of things as 'immortal youths' (Koran 76:19) and the Koran states

> ...those who believed, and their seed followed them
> in belief, We shall join their seed with them
>
>                                                              (Koran 52:21)

It is not stated whether children are subjected to the Last Judgement, or at what age a person becomes responsible for his actions.

The eighth century scholar Abu Hanifa, founder of the Hanafi school of religious law, gave no answer to the question of whether the infants of disbelievers will have to answer for themselves on the Day of Judgement, or whether they will go to Hell or Paradise, and there are contradictory traditions. One tradition says that every child is born into the law of God, and therefore will enter Paradise. A follower of Hanifa has said 'I am certain God will not commit anyone to the punishment (of Hell) until he has committed sin'.

However, it is not sensible to seek a single consistent picture, as the images suggest what it is beyond man's capacity to conceive. The fundamental message is that Paradise holds the means to satisfy man's deepest relationships and most profound spiritual needs.

## Kalam (Theology)

There is no church in Islam, no hierarchy, and no central See directing affairs. *Kalam* literally means speech (of God) which is the Koran. It also has a technical meaning — the process of advancing reasoned arguments to support religious beliefs. A practitioner of *kalam* is called a *mutakallim*.

It is probably true that in Islam theology does not occupy such an important place as in, say, Christianity. Mohammed was, after all, a Prophet not a theologian, and he belonged to a people with no previous philosophical or intellectual tradition. Indeed, in early times the problems facing theology were political rather than religious, involving the leadership of the community. Following the murder of the third Caliph Uthman, the issue of political power took the form of religious discussions among the contending parties: the first problem was that of predestination and free will, and the second that of major and minor sins, and whether a sinner is excluded from Islam.

The question of predestination and free will is clearly raised in the Koran:

> Surely your Lord is God, who created
> the heavens and the earth in six days,
> then sat Himself upon the Throne,
> directing the affair...
>   Will you not remember?

(Koran 10:3)

> And beware a day when no soul for another
> shall give satisfaction, and no counterpoise
> shall be accepted from it, nor any
> intercession shall be profitable to it,
>   neither shall they be helped.

(Koran 2:117)

Embodied in these two verses are the twin teachings that God alone is responsible for conducting the affairs of the universe, but that every individual is personally responsible and personally accountable for his actions.

These matters were first raised in a critical sense by the establishment of the Umayyad family dynasty over the Muslim world in Damascus in 661. Their rise had been accomplished by the defeat of some of the most respected of Mohammed's followers, including his son-in-law and cousin, Ali. The Umayyads justified their rise to power by stating that all things happen according to the will of God. Against this government propaganda, factions arose to argue that man has free will and controls his own destiny; therefore to oppose a government was not to oppose God.

The arguments become more sophisticated as Islamic scholars met Christians in such centres as Damascus in the second and third Islamic centuries. Christian scholars, armed with a more developed theology, stimulated Muslim thinkers to attain a better grasp of their religious convictions in order to defend their faith. This, together with contact with Greek analytical thought, absorbed by a group called Mu'tazilites, gave birth to the *kalam*.

## Good and Evil

The Mu'tazilites claimed that human reason, independent of revelation, is capable of distinguishing good from evil, and that revelation confirmed the findings of reason. Man is therefore expected to do right even if there were no prophets and no divine revelation. Revelation must therefore be interpreted in accordance with rational ethics, and its function is twofold. First, God's aim is to aid man in making the right choice between good and evil (for which reason He sends prophets). Secondly, revelation is necessary to make clear the positive obligations of religion, such as prayers and fasting, which would not be known without revelation.

The most significant and lasting contribution to the *kalam* was made by al-Ashari (born 260/873) who marshalled sophisticated arguments in defence of conservative Islamic doctrines. His views with slight modifications represent the theological stance of most Sunni Muslims today.

## Free Will and Predestination

Perhaps the most subtle and difficult of these stances is the relationship between free will and predestination. Every Muslim must believe in God's absolute decree and predestination of both good and evil, and that God has from eternity predetermined and decreed literally everything — good, bad, belief, unbelief, and that everything that has been or will be depends on His will. At the same time Muslims believe that man is responsible for his actions and deserves reward or punishment for them. These apparently contradictory ideas are reconciled in theological distinctions between man's and God's spheres of power. Man's actions are of two kinds — voluntary and involuntary. Both are created and produced by God alone, and man has no influence whatever over them. But because God causes both power and choice to exist in man, man's actions as created are ascribed to God, but as produced are ascribed to man. In any event, no man can question that he will be judged by his evil doings, even though all is created by God, because, ultimately, no man has the right to question the doings of God.

## Muslim Sects

Although the Koran warns against discord and emphasizes that believers should not allow themselves to be divided into factions, no one leader emerged after the fourth Caliph to hold Islam together. After the death of Ali, differences in interpreting doctrine arose, largely as a result of political pressure, and differing groups appeared.

Mohammed is said to have prophesied that his followers would divide into numerous sects and the number of Muslim sects today exceeds even those of the Christians.

The four main divisions are derived from the schools of law, and these have produced an immense number of commentaries and other works, all differing on a variety of points but coinciding in general principle.

### Sunnis or Sunnites

The majority of Muslims are Sunnis — followers of the *Sunna*, the orthodox and traditional doctrine. The Sunnis recognize the legitimacy of the first four Caliphs as leaders of the community and upholders of the law. They used to see the Caliphate as the property of the Quraysh tribe, the tribe of the Prophet. From the Quraysh the man of the most profound faith and outstanding ability would become leader. But religious authority rests wholly in the Koran and the *Sunna* and on the interpretation based on the consensus of the community, the *ijma*.

### Shi'ites

After the death of Mohammed, one party (*shia* means party) contended that the succession should remain with the closest relative of the Prophet. They therefore favoured Ali, his son-in-law. Shi'ite is derived from Shiat Ali, the party of Ali. Although Ali eventually became Caliph, he was preceded by three other men and soon lost his rule to the Umayyads. A central religious belief fo the Shi'ites is that God has chosen a series of *imams* for the leadership of the community and endowed them with special knowledge providing a source of living guidance. Therefore the Shi'ites believe that true Islam cannot be known and practised without the guidance of the *imam* God has chosen. To the Sunnis this confers a degree of divinity upon leaders and is blasphemous. Similarly the Shi'ites do not recognize the *ijma* (consensus).

Some would argue also that the leadership conferred on the *imam* allows a more flexible attitude to social, economic and political change, as interpretation of the faith is given an emphasis which is not matched in the Sunni doctrine.

The Shi'ites are well spread throughout the Islamic world and are most numerous in Iran, Iraq, Southern Arabia and the Indian sub-continent.

## Ismaili

The most important of the smaller sects is the Ismaili, who hold that the Prophet will be followed by seven *imams* who will interpret the will of God to man.

## Kharijites

Another important group are the Kharijites (the seceders or rebels) who are strict conformists. They asserted that the Caliph could be any Muslim, irrespective of race or tribe, provided that he had the purity to make him the finest.

The Kharijites held that any who committed a grave error or sin and did not repent ceased to be a Muslim. The profession of faith alone did not make a person a Muslim unless his faith was accompanied by righteous deeds. This aggressive idealism was accompanied by the belief that *Jihad* was among the cardinal pillars of Islam and the Kharijites interpreted 'enjoining good and forbidding evil' to mean the vindication of truth through the sword. This inflammable combination resulted in almost constant rebellion against nearly every established authority and led to their virtual extinction during the first two centuries of Islam, although a moderate group of Kharijites have survived in the form of Ibadis, who retain the beliefs without resorting to the aggressive methods.

Although the differences between Muslim sects are often deeply felt and sometimes lead to conflict and violence, they should be viewed by the outside world as domestic quarrels. The overriding belief and faith is that Islam is true, monolithic and indivisible.

## Sufism

Orthodox Sunni Islam is a relatively austere intellectual faith. It lacks ceremony, authoritarian leaders and outward passion. Its sophistication has little appeal to the emotional needs of the rural masses far removed from the centres of learning and the great mosques. A subtle streak of mysticism has been present in Islam for centuries in the form of Sufism, which offers a new dimension to the religion of the mosque and the law courts. Sufism, or mystical Islam, named after the crude woolen garments (*suf*) of itinerant holy men, has appeared within all theological schools of Islam and is, in a sense, independent of them. It represents an alternative approach to the divine.

The highest point of veneration for the Prophet was reached among the Sufis. Many Sufis regarded Mohammed as the eternal manifestation of the very force which created and sustains the universe, and through which alone God may be approached and known. The effect of this piety was to confer on Mohammed supernatural qualities which both he and orthodox belief were careful to avoid.

As in other mystical sects, Sufi ascetics cultivated the ecstasy of intimate union with God through discipline and overwhelming love for the divine. They developed their philosophy of the faith from the eighth century through defining mystical experiences, and by the 12th century orders of Sufics were organized throughout the Islamic world. A Sufic order was known as *tariqa*, or way to attain union with God. Each order was headed by a *sheikh*, the arbiter of spiritual knowledge, who with his followers maintained an establishment similar to a monastery where members lived out their régime of discipline and meditation.

These were important social institutions because common people had access to them, not only for spiritual advice, but also for food, medical care and even financial assistance. Some orders became very powerful, notably the Safawid order, which became the nucleus of the Persian Safawid Empire, and the Baktashi order of Turkey. Each order was distinguished by the special ceremony of worship and meditation, perhaps the most famous of which is the dance of the Turkish Malawi order, the whirling dervishes. A later development of Sufism was the designation of saints and this aspect still appeals to ordinary Muslims. These Sufi masters are believed to possess spiritual power and the ability to perform miracles.

Great reverence is paid to saints and when one dies his tomb becomes a place of pilgrimage. Reverence for saints has led to some abuses in Sufism and modern Muslims seeking to purge Islam of superstition have caused a decline of Sufism among the educated throughout the Islamic world, but it retains its hold on the masses.

\* \* \*

The notion of love for one's neighbour, in a Christian sense, is not enshrined in the Koran. There are certain prescribed duties towards the disadvantaged, the poor, widows, orphans, slaves and the vanquished, but these are of a practical nature, and no emotional commitment is required or expected. There is also the concept of Muslim brotherhood. He who accepts the faith and becomes a believer is automatically accepted as a Muslim brother without question. This confers certain rights of treatment which do not apply to unbelievers.

This underlines the essentially practical nature of the Islamic faith. God's will is interpreted as a series of rules for all occasions, and either one conforms to them or one does not. Conforming to them has certain consequences, breaking them has others. This rigid simplicity is the underlying structure of Islamic thought, and will be present, whether open or hidden, in all circumstances, from international affairs to trivial domestic matters.

## Chapter 3
# Islamic Law

Apart from the status of women in Islam, nothing seems to excite a more hostile reaction in the West than what are thought to be the standards of its traditional law. In many ways the heart of Islam is its law, but this law includes much more than any legal system devised in the West. Not only does it deal with matters of religious ritual, it also evaluates every aspect of political, social and private life.

## The Sharia

The general term for law in Arabic is *sharia*, which can be roughly translated as 'the path in which God wishes men to walk', and every human deed without exception falls under the perspective of the law. There has been no more far reaching effort to lay out a complete pattern of human conduct than the Islamic *sharia*.

The general assumption underlying the *sharia* is that men are incapable of discriminating between right and wrong by their own unaided powers. It is for this reason that guidance was sent to them through prophets. God, who is all powerful, revealed a path for men, based upon his unrestricted sovereign will. His will is not to be judged by human reason, and it must be obeyed in total and without question. For a Muslim the *sharia* represents divine and eternal law, and is consequently completely trustworthy. It is the basic institution of Islamic civilization, and underpins the certainty that Muslims have always felt about the correctness of their way of life. Law is therefore linked in the Muslim mind with a comprehensive set of rules for life which, if followed, please God in this world and earn salvation in the next.

In all Western systems law is associated with the state, applies to all within its territorial boundaries, and is enforced by a police power. None of these facts holds true of Islamic law. It is binding primarily upon individuals who stand directly in a relationship with God, and it is not enforced by the state. Although there are some rules for non-Muslims, most of the provisions of the *sharia* apply to Muslims living in Islamic territory, and can become inoperative in foreign lands.

The limit of Western systems of law is generally to regulate man's relationship with his neighbour and with the state, but the *sharia* includes also his relationship with God and his own conscience. Usually, the first chapters in the legal manuals deal with basic religious duties and ritual practices. The *sharia* is as much concerned with ethical practices, and what man should or should not do in conscience, as with what he is entitled or bound to do in law. These acts are divided into those which are praiseworthy (and therefore find divine favour) and those which are blameworthy (and therefore bring divine disfavour) but in neither case is there any legal sanction or punishment, nor any reward.

Another major distinction between the *sharia* and Western systems is the Muslim belief that law expresses the divine will. On Mohammed's death God's revelations ceased, which meant that the form and content of his revelations were fixed and unchangeable. The result of this is that when the *sharia* law was crystallized and recorded in the medieval manuals it became a rigid and unchangeable system. In sharp contrast to the Western secular systems of law, which grew out of social circumstances and change in society, Islamic law moulds and fashions society itself.

## The Basic Features

None of the modern classifications or distinctions between categories of law exists in the religious law of Islam[1]; there is even no clear separation of worship, ethics and law in the Western sense. Consequently, although it is convenient for the Western reader to consider various aspects of the law under separate headings, the subject matter is in fact continually overlapping, and there is no sense of systematic distinction.

The fundamental principle underlying the whole of Islamic religious law is intent. Originally this applied to the ritual worship, which is not considered valid unless it is accompanied by pious intent. Silence cannot be taken to replace a declaration of consent, except in a few special cases. In theory, evidence in writing is accepted unconditionally only from a mute person, and from others with considerable reservations, but modern practice has considerably modified this traditional view. In matters of fraud there is little inclination to protect the victim. The effect of duress is given considerable scope, not only in removing the penal sanction but in making the act itself permissible. For instance, drinking wine or having illegal intercourse under threat of death or injury is permissible; indeed, refusal would be sinful.

---

1. See Joseph Schacht, *An Introduction to Islamic Law*, Oxford University Press, 1964.

Under the law all men's actions are divided into five categories: obligatory, recommended, indifferent, disapproved, and forbidden. Islamic law does not recognize institutions or corporate bodies as entities in their own right. Government is not recognized by the traditional law, and therefore the Ministry of Financial Affairs, for example, is owned not by the government but by the Muslim community, (ie, the sum total of individual Muslims).

The capacity to transact legally belongs to a person who is *rashid*. Technically this means of prudent judgement and is normally associated with reaching puberty. Both sexes are said to have reached puberty by the age of 15, but in no case can a boy attain puberty below the age of 12, or a girl below the age of nine. People who are not *rashid*, because of minority or deficiency, are placed under interdiction and their affairs are managed by a guardian.

A fully responsible citizen is a free Muslim who is sane and of age. Legally a women has fewer rights and duties from the religious point of view. In respect of blood money, evidence, and inheritance she is counted as half a man. In marriage and divorce she has fewer rights than a man. She is equal to a man in terms of the law of property and obligations, and may act as a *qadi* (judge) in certain matters. The legal rights of slaves are as carefully defined by the law as those of free men.

The legal position of non-Muslims in Islam relates to the law of war; they must either be converted (not by force) or be subjugated or killed (except women, children and slaves). By tradition, under a treaty of surrender Muslims may undertake to safeguard the life and property of non-Muslims who are called *dhimmis*. By this arrangement the non-Muslims live and work under certain disadvantages, but their freedom of religion is guaranteed and they are free to observe their own customs. A non-Muslim who is not protected by a treaty is an enemy alien and his life and property are completely unprotected by the law. In criminal law the *dhimmi* is liable to *hadd* (see page 62) and discretionary punishments as far as they are not specifically Muslim. Thus, a *dhimmi* would not be subject to *hadd* for drinking wine, but would be subject to discretionary punishment. Non-Muslims have complete legal freedom provided they do not interfere with the religious interests of Muslims. Freedom in matters of religion is explicitly guaranteed.

## The Concepts of Islamic Law

In spite of its divine origin, Islamic law does not claim universal application. Inside Islamic territory it is binding in full for the Muslim, but outside its application is more limited. For example, according to the Hanafi school it is legal for Muslims to indulge in *riba* (interest) with non-Muslims in enemy territory. Furthermore, the law takes for granted the decadence and corruption in contemporary society. It has an inbuilt, matter-of-fact view of human fallibility, and has not remained immune from such practices as the bribing of witnesses and *qadis*, or tolerating the abuses of corrupt governments, and highly placed individuals, over whom the *qadis* were powerless. Islamic law considers valid the appointment of a *qadi* who is not 'of good character', nor does it question a judgement based on the evidence of a witness who is not of good character, or even the appointment of a *qadi* by a political authority which is not legitimate.

As in the field of worship, obligatory acts are accompanied by others which are only recommended. For instance, heirs can be recommended, but are not obliged, to pay the debts of the deceased, and even the next of kin who has the right to demand retaliation for murder is recommended to waive it against the payment of blood money.

Joseph Schacht[1] has pointed out that it was the first legal specialists themselves who created the system of Islamic law; they did not borrow it from pre-Islamic sources, although these sources did provide many of its material elements. Similarly, the development of Islamic law can be distinguished from that of Roman law in a fundamental way. In Roman law it was the growing importance of commercial life which called for the creation of corresponding legal forms; in Islamic law it was the religious zeal of a growing number of Muslims which demanded the application of religious norms to all aspects of behaviour. If the Roman jurists were to be useful to their clients they had to try to predict the probable reactions of the magistrates and judges to each transaction; if the earliest Islamic lawyers were to fulfil their relgious duty, as they saw it, they had to search their consciences in order to know what good Muslims were allowed or forbidden to do. In Islamic law even the two formal legal concepts valid and invalid are continually pushed into the background by the Islamic concepts of allowed and forbidden. The aim of Islamic law is to provide concrete and material standards, not to impose formal rules on the interplay of contending interests, which is the aim of secular law. Consideration of good faith, fairness, justice, truth and so on play only a subordinate part in the system. The rules of Islamic law are valid by virtue of their existence and not because of their rationality. If, for example, a boy is mutilated accidentally on being circumcised, the full blood money is paid, but if he dies only half the blood money is paid. This is because half of the cause of death is attributed to the circumcision itself (because this alone may cause death) and only half to the mutilation. Only this second half creates liability because the performance of circumcision

---

1. Ibid.

(which is recommended or obligatory according to the school of law) does not in itself create liability. If the owner of a wall which threatens to collapse sells it after he has been asked to demolish it, and it them collapses and kills someone, neither the seller nor the buyer is liable; not the seller because he was not the owner at the time it collapsed, and not the buyer because he had not been asked to demolish it.

However it it not unknown for Islamic law to diverge from a formally correct decision for reasons of fairness or appropriateness. But according to some Western lawyers this principle, both in theory and application, occupies too subordinate a position for it to be able to influence positive law to any considerable degree. Further, although Islamic law possesses an impressive number of legal concepts, they are, generally speaking, derived not from the realities of legal life but from abstract thought. For instance, a finder may use found property if he is poor, but not if he is rich; if he is rich he is entitled to make it a charitable gift (*sadaqa*). Even this is not strictly applied however, because if the finder's parents or children are poor he is entitled to give it to them.

It is important to understand that public powers are, as a rule, reduced to private rights or duties, and the essential duties of the Islamic state are seen not as functions of the community but as duties to be fulfilled by a number of individuals. The whole concept of an institution is missing.

The idea of criminal guilt hardly exists and, apart from religious expiation and one or two other exceptions, there is no fixed penalty for any infringement of the rights of a human being or the violation of his person and property, only the exact reparation of the damage caused. Monetary fines are unknown. Also the execution of the judgement in this sphere is, in principle, a matter for the party in whose favour it is given.

## The Schools of Law

Although the basis of the *sharia* is the Koran, the holy book is in no sense a comprehensive legal code. A relatively small number of verses deal with strictly legal matters and these cover a wide variety of topics. Their main effect was to introduce many new rules and to simplify and modify the existing Arabian customary law. When Mohammed was alive he was the supreme judge of the community and resolved legal problems as they arose by interpreting the provisions of the Koran, as did the Caliph of Medina after his death. This served the community well when it was small, but it would not do for the vast empire that came into being shortly after the Prophet's death. An organized judiciary evolved with the appointment of judges (*qadis*) to the various provinces and districts. In the absence of a detailed documented legal code the *qadis* had considerable discretion in applying the law. Their decisions were based upon the rules of the Koran wherever these were relevant, but where there was no clear parallel or precedent they interpreted the law as best they could, very often absorbing elements from Roman and Persian law in the process.

Early in the eighth century groups of pious scholars began to debate whether the law was being administered in accordance with the religious ethic of Islam. These early jurists reviewed all current legal practice in the light of Koranic principles, and established an Islamic code as part of their ideal scheme of law.

The two most important schools of law were founded by Malik ibn Anas and Abu Hanifa, and became known as the Malikis in Medina and the Hanafis in al-Kufah. Because the early law schools wrote independently from each other and were subject to different influences and social pressures, it is not surprising that they came to different conclusions on certain issues. Perhaps the most important of these was the deep conflict of principle which emerged between those who maintained that outside the terms of the Koran scholars were free to use their reason to ascertain the law, and those who insisted that the only valid source of law outside the Koran lay in the precedents set by the Prophet himself.

The third school of Sunni law was founded by the jurist al-Shafii (died 820) who tried to produce a greater uniformity in the law by eliminating conflicts and defining the exact sources from which the law must be derived. He taught that proper knowledge of the *sharia* could be found only through the divine revelation either in the Koran or in the divinely inspired precedents (*Sunna*) of the Prophet as ascertained through authentic reports (*hadith*). Human reason was to be employed only in cases not specifically answered by divine revelation, confining itself strictly to arguing from the principles of closely parallel cases to be derived from the Koran or *Sunna*. Al-Shafii's reliance upon the importance of the *Sunna* triggered off remarkable and intensive activity to establish as accurately as possible all the sayings and actions of the Prophet in order to compile a complete catalogue of precedents covering as many aspects of behaviour as possible. As very little, if anything, was written down at the time of the Prophet, this immense undertaking had to be carried out by personally interviewing descendants of the Prophet, and his Companions and Followers. The character and reliability of each person interviewed had to be assessed and documented. Each facet of each story (evidence) had to be checked back through preceding generations, and at every point the character of the person passing on the information had to be investigated.

As a result of al-Shafii's work the legal process had crystallized in the 10th century into a specific procedure. The jurist must first consult the Koran and the *Sunna*. When a specific solution cannot be found from these sources, he must deduce precedents for the situation and take into account the public interest. The results of this process must then be evaluated against *ijma*, or the consensus (of scholars). The result of these deliberations could be either a tentative conclusion or conjecture on the part of individual jurists, or, if there was unanimous agreement, a certain and infallible expression of God's law.

The consensus view was originally permissive in the sense that it allowed the validity of different opinions in man's attempt to define the *sharia*. Later it became restrictive, because once the consensus had agreed on the variations that were legitimately possible, the subject was frozen and any further variations or opinions were bordering on heresy. Once the *ijma* had been concluded and the result recorded in the legal manuals, further individual speculation and interpretation ceased, and subsequent jurists were bound to follow the doctrine as it was recorded in the 10th century. This method of finding out the precise terms of the *sharia* is known as *fiqh* (understanding).

The division between the various law schools became geographically defined as the *qadis'* courts favoured the doctrine of one school above the others. In this way Hanafi law became predominant in the Middle East and India; Malaki law in North West and Central Africa; Shafi'i law in East Africa and the southern parts of Arabia, Malaysia and Indonesia; Hanbali in Saudi Arabia.

Apart from the four schools of Sunni or orthodox Islam there are the minority sects, the Shi'ites and Ibadis, whose interpretation of the *sharia* is considerably different from that of the Sunni. In particular the Shi'ite view that the *imams* are divinely inspired, and are therefore the natural rulers of the community, gives rise to a different balance within the law. Shi'ite law is applied in Iran and in the Shi'i communities of India and Africa; Ibadi law applied in Zanzibar, Oman and parts of Syria.

## Procedures

The rules of procedure and evidence in *sharia* law are quite different from any Western system. Traditionally the court is administered by a single *qadi*, who is the judge of the facts as well as the law. When confronted by a difficult issue, he has discretion to seek the advice of a professional jurist or *mufti*. There are no superior courts or systems of appeal. The court procedure is simple and without ceremony and is controlled by the *qadi* through his clerk. The parties usually appear in person, although legal representation is permitted.

The *qadi's* first responsibility is to decide which party bears the burden of proof. The initial legal presumption attaching to each case is that the accused is innocent, and the burden of proof rests with the prosecution or the claimant, but the burden of proof might shift between the parties in a case where counter-claims are made. The standard of proof required is a rigid one and basically the same in criminal and civil cases. If an admission of guilt by a defendant is not forthcoming, the prosecutor or plaintiff is required to produce two witnesses to testify orally to their direct knowledge of the truth of the charge. Circumstantial evidence or written evidence, even if overwhelming, is not normally admissible. Two male adult Muslims of integrity and reliability are required to give oral testimony. Women witnesses are allowed, but two are required in the place of one man. In claims of property one witness is often enough, together with the plaintiff's own solemn oath as to the truth of his claim. The prosecutor is given judgement if he produces proof in the required form. If his evidence is not substantial, the defendant will receive judgement in his favour. In cases where the evidence is not conclusive, or not properly given, a sworn oath by the defendant can win him the judgement, but if he refuses to take the oath, judgement is given to the other side. The importance of the sworn oath, and consequently the reliability of a person's word, can be gauged by the importance attached to it by the courts. Two witnesses are the prescribed number; no advantage accrues to the side producing more than two.

Stringent demands are made of witnesses in terms of qualifications and the content of their statements, particularly in the evidence on unlawful intercourse where four male witnesses are required instead of the normal two. They must testify as eye witnesses, and in order to qualify for the *hadd* punishment a confession of unlawful intercourse must be made on four separate occasions. A further safeguard lies in the fact that if the witnesses, or any one of them, are found to be false or there are discrepancies between them, they are all in principle liable to the *hadd* punishment themselves.

There is no official prosecution or punishment for murder, bodily harm or damage to property, only a guarantee of the right of private vengeance. In these cases pardon and amicable settlement are possible, but repentance has no effect.

In most cases the simple procedures of the *qadi* court give rise to an almost automatic process. In this traditional system, once the matter of the burden of proof is settled, witnesses are or are not produced, the oath is or is not administered and sworn, and the verdict follows automatically.

However, although the *sharia* doctrine was always the focal point of the legal system, it was never exclusively authoritative, and has always recognized jurisdiction other than that of the *qadis*. The *qadis'* courts have a cumbersome system of procedure and evidence, and did not prove satisfactory in all cases; very rough justice was often done, particularly in respect of criminal, land and commercial law. Accordingly, other courts were set up, known collectively as *mazalin*, for these purposes, and the jurisdiction of the *qadis* was generally confined to private family and civil law.

## Punishment

The penalities prescribed by Islamic law fall into two groups; private vengeance, and punishment of crimes against religion and military discipline. In Islamic law the first group has survived almost intact. Crimes against religion are: unlawful intercourse; its counterpart, false accusation of unlawful intercourse; drinking wine; theft; and highway robbery. The punishments prescribed for them are fixed and are called *hadd*. According to the offence, punishment can vary from death to flogging. There are no fines in Islamic law.

The *hadd* is the right of God, so no pardon or amicable settlement is possible. Prosecutions for false accusation of unlawful intercourse or theft take place only on the demand of the persons concerned, and the applicant must be present both at the trial and at the punishment. In the case of unlawful intercourse the witnesses play the major part; if they are not present (and if they do not cast the first stone) the punishment is not carried out. The religious character of the *hadd* punishment is shown by the part played by active repentance; if the thief returns the stolen goods before prosecution, or repents from highway robbery before arrest, the *hadd* lapses. In cases of unlawful intercourse and drinking wine it must be proved that the act was voluntary. Only one *hadd* is applied for several offences of the same kind. Proof for *hadd* offences is made difficult. Confessions can be withdrawn, and the *qadi* should suggest this possibility to the accused, except in a case of false accusation of unlawful intercourse.

Witnesses are recommended not to testify against accused people, and the judge is obliged to give full weight to all the circumstances extenuating the guilt of the guilty. By contrast, where punishment established by the law of *hadd* is concerned, the judge has no choice and must execute the prescribed punishment. In these cases even a plea for mercy by or on behalf of the accused is not allowed. However, in order to establish guilt, very difficult legal proof is always required, and the rules allow everybody the opportunity for escaping punishment. In cases involving *hadd* a confession of guilt is required before 'determined punishment' can be executed, and consequently punishment takes on the character of penitence.[1]

Preventive or punitive action may be taken under the law for reasons of public policy. Muslims who refuse to obey the *imam* are forced into obedience and are not subject to any special penal sanction. A male apostate from Islam is condemned to death, but he is normally reprieved for three days to give him an opportunity to return to the faith. A woman who commits apostasy is imprisoned and beaten every three days until she returns to Islam. There are no legal penalties for offences against religion, even for neglect of the ritual prayer. There is no punishment for perjury or for giving false evidence; it is simply given publicity, and in certain cases liability arises for any damage caused.

There exists no general concept of penal law in Islam. The concepts of guilt and criminal responsibility are little developed, and that of mitigating circumstances does not exist. On the other hand the theory of punishments, with its distinction of private vengeance, *hadd* punishments, *tazir*[2] and coercive and preventive measures, shows a considerable variety of ideas.

## Hadd Punishments

*Hadd* means an unalterable punishment prescribed by canon law which is considered a right of God.

There is no concept of marital fidelity in Islamic law. Married people are not required to be faithful *to each other*, and sexual intercourse outside the legal bounds is not a violation of the married partners' rights, but an offence against God. In unlawful intercourse (*zina*) a distinction is made between people who are *muhsan*, and those who are not. In the category of *muhsan* is a free person who has concluded and consummated a valid marriage with a free partner, or who is able to do so. Such a person, if convicted of unlawful intercourse, is subject to the punishment of death by stoning. The penalty for a person outside this category is 100 lashes (50 for a slave). Unbelievers cannot be *muhsan*, but strictly speaking they are subject to the Islamic law and the punishment of flogging.

The *hadd* punishment for drinking wine, and this includes being drunk and incapable for whatever cause, is 80 lashes (40 for slaves) though the application of this punishment is made difficult by the required proof that the act was voluntary. This means that the *hadd* cannot be applied automatically to a person found drunk and incapable, and further proof of intent is required.

---

1. This is not to say that these provisions of Islamic law have always been recognized by Muslim authorities. Arbitrary and self-interested punishment has been, and still is, inflicted under Islam as under any other code of law.
2. A punishment intended to prevent the culprit from relapsing, to purify him.

Theft is defined as taking by stealth something of the value of at least 10 *dirhams* for which the culprit has neither the right of ownership nor custody. Excluded from the category of *hadd* punishments are all those things found in Islamic territory which are not strictly speaking owned, such as wood, grass, fishes, birds; provided that ownership is not obvious, as in the case of wood in the form of a chair. Also excluded are easily perishable things like meat and unharvested fruit. It excludes also things which cannot be objects of property such as a free person, wine, and musical instruments, and things of which the accused is part owner, such as public property.

The stiplation of custody excludes theft from a near relative, from a house which the accused has been permitted to enter, and embezzlement. Property has to be removed from its legal ownership, therefore a thief caught, say, within a house, according to some, is not subject to *hadd*.

The punishment consists of cutting off the right hand and, in the case of a second theft, the left foot; in the case of further thefts, the thief is imprisoned until he shows repentance.

The crime of highway robbery is related to both theft and murder, and the penalties inflicted differ according to the facts of the case. If only theft is involved, and the value of the property when divided by the number of culprits satisfies the requirement for *hadd*, the right hand and the left foot are cut off; if murder alone has happened, execution with the sword is the penalty; if both plunder and murder have happened, execution by crucifixion is the sentence (Koran 5:33). These punishments are awarded to all accomplices regardless of their individual involvement, except that if one of them for any reason is exempt from *hadd*, for example because he is a minor, the *hadd* for highway robbery lapses for all, although each remains criminally responsible for his individual acts.

## Retaliation

Offences against the person from murder to assault are punishable by retaliation (*kisas*) in which the offender is subject to precisely the same treatment as his victim. However, this kind of offence is not technically regarded as a crime since it is not the state which has the right to prosecute, but only the victim or his family.[1] For this reason, these offences have been described as civil injuries and the victim's family may opt for compensation or blood money (*diyah*) in place of retaliation.

---

1. As retaliation is a matter for the next of kin, when there are several equally related in a family, the demand for *kisas* has to be unanimous among them, otherwise it does not apply. *Kisas* is not applied in the case of accidental killing.

For *kisas* to be applied certain conditions must be fulfilled. For instance, the killer must be a Muslim, adult and in full possession of his faculties. Other conditions are sometimes imposed, but these are disputed in various law schools. For example, when several people commit a murder, and one of them for one reason or another cannot be put to death, the others also escape *kisas*. In addition to these conditions, three of the law schools demanded that before *kisas* can be allowed, the murdered person is at least the equal of the murderer in respect of Islam and liberty, whilst the Hanafis take no account of this. *Kisas* can be applied only in Islamic countries, or in countries under Islamic control.

The penalties for murder vary according to the degree of culpability. A distinction is made between deliberate intent with or without a deadly implement and between killing by mistake and indirect killing. In cases of bodily harm, retaliation takes place for specific injuries. There are rules laid down when a murder is committed and the culprit is unknown. Where a body is found in an inhabited or occupied place, the inhabitants of a street, for example, must swear 50 oaths that they did not kill him. If there are less than 50 people involved then some must swear more than once. If a body is found in a mosque, the public treasury pays the blood money; if it is found in open country, his blood is not avenged.

Although it is the exclusive prerogative of the victim or his next of kin to claim retaliation, Islamic law recommends waiving it. In this case, penance by the culprit can take the form of the freeing of a Muslim slave, or fasting for two consecutive months.

The Koran lays down the principle of retaliation in two different ways. Referring to the Torah given by God to the Jews it reiterates:

> We prescribed for them:
> 'A life for a life, an eye for an eye,
> a nose for a nose, an ear for an ear,
> a tooth for a tooth, and for wounds
> retaliation'

(Koran 5:48)

And:

> O believers, prescribed for you is
> retaliation, touching the slain;
> freeman for freeman, slave for slave,
> female for female.

(Koran 2:174)

It is not surprising that difficulties have arisen in interpreting these two passages. For example, is it intended that a free man can be put to death for the murder of a woman? Although some jurists will insist that this cannot be so, general practice allows this form of retaliation. However, the life of a free Muslim cannot be had in retaliation for the death of a slave, nor can *kisas* be applied to any Muslim for the murder of an unbeliever.

*Kisas* can be applied only after deliberate proof of guilt is produced. The procedure of proof in a murder trial is the same as in any other case, and the *kasasa*, or solemn oath, plays an important part. The execution of *kisas* is open to the avenger of blood and takes the form of either beheading with a sword, or, within certain limitations, the murderer is put to death in the same way as his victim. If somebody deliberately and evilly inflicts a fatal wound, he is legally liable in principle to similar treatment. If *kisas* is not permitted, or the person entitled to it voluntarily forgoes his claim, compensation may be demanded for an unlawful injury; a form of blood money or *diyah*. A woman receives between one-third and a half of the man's rate depending upon the school of law. A minor or insane person is not liable to pay compensation in ordinary circumstances. The *diyah* for the latter is paid by the state. If a minor and a person of age together kill a Muslim intentionally, the latter is put to death, the former pays half the *diyah*.

Women and children are not liable to pay *diyah*. Employers are liable for injury to employees. Owners are responsible for their animals. People who cause accidents are responsible for the consequences.

## Property

Although Islamic law does not define property it recognizes several graded categories on which restrictions are placed in legal transactions.

There are things which by definition cannot be property, and the sale of which is null and void. These include a free person, animals not ritually slaughtered and blood. There are things in which ownership is not vested at all, such as big rivers and public roads; everyone is entitled to use them provided the public interest is not prejudiced. A third category is things in which there is no separate ownership, which means things that do not yet exist independently, such as flour from corn or milk in the udder. (This means that something that has a potentially separate existence, such as un unborn animal, cannot be sold or bartered until it has a separate existence). This includes constituent parts of a whole, such as columns supporting a building (but part of a building, like an apartment or suite can be owned separately). There are things that are defined as property, but on which there are restrictions concerning disposal.

# Ownership

Ownership is defined as the right to the complete and exclusive disposal of a thing and is called *milk*. The legal categories of ownership and possesion are numerous and detailed, and often differ from Western ideas. For example expectation can play an important part in acquiring ownership. If a man plants an orchard in order to harvest the fruit, and a bird nests in one of his trees, anyone who takes the eggs, the nest, or the bird for that matter, acquires ownership of them, even though he takes them from land belonging to another. Similarly the owner of land does not have exclusive rights to any minerals or treasure found in it. One fifth must be paid to the public treasury, as is the case for booty taken in war. Ownership can never be acquired by finding. If something is found, a public notice is posted, and if no claim is made the finder is entitled to make a charitable gift. Only if the finder is poor is he entitled to use the object himself, and even then he holds it in trust. If this intention is lacking the finder becomes a usurper. It is an assumption of the law that any property or treasure dating from Islamic times is not ownerless, and must be regarded as found property. In Arabia today articles can be left unattended in the towns for days, and in country districts, or in the desert, for years, the assumption being that one day the owner will return to collect his property.

The concept of public property is restricted in scope by a certain logic. A thoroughfare, for example, is public because it leads somewhere, whereas a blind alley is not, because it does not. To some extent use of public property is free to every person, either for its intended purpose, or sometimes for private use. An individual may loiter, sleep, or trade in the street, or even erect a shelter providing it does not prejudice the public interest. Similarly every person can sue for its removal. Land in the vicinity of an inhabited place is considered a common for the inhabitants.

Land which has no determined owner and is not put to use may be cultivated by anyone on obtaining a license from the *imam*. The license lapses if the applicant fails to cultivate it within three years. In real estate land can be sold, but the right to build upon it cannot.

By tradition the ownership of land seems to have been less important than the acquisition of money. This situation came about by the circumstances of the Arab conquests. Vast areas of cultivable land became available which the conquerers were either unable or unwilling to work themselves. Consequently they extracted revenues in the form of rent and taxes which were controlled by the Caliph who distributed funds among those with a right to payment; a proportion being reserved for the expenses of state and to provide help for the needy as described by the Koran. As a result the idea came into being that real property had to be cultivated or developed thereby generating an income. The right of ownership had to be deserved, and although the right of ownership was not lost through land remaining idle, it could vanish if someone else bought it under cultivation. Although this perhaps explains some of the traditional Muslim attitudes towards ownership it has to be said that custom varied from place to place, and since the 19th century most independent Muslim countries have simply adopted Western land law; in colonial countries reforms were carried out to the benefit of the occupying power.

The common right to water has always been an important issue in the Middle East and on this subject Islamic law has its origins in Iraq rather than Arabia. Big rivers are public property, and small water courses are the joint property of the riparian owners. The right to use water is separated from the land to which it belongs, and although a canal might be privately owned everyone has the right to drink from it, or to use it for the ritual ablution, but he must not trespass on another person's land except in cases of necessity. Water is only considered private property if it is in a container.

## Contracts and Obligations

Unjustified profiteering and unjustified risk are both rejected on ethical grounds, and these general prohibitions pervade the whole of the law. Islamic law provides for certain fixed types of contracts within which there is considerable scope for varying terms. Custom plays an important part in contracts, and transactions are allowed only in so far as they are customary. There is no general term for obligation; the nearest approximation to it is care as a duty of conscience. The conclusion of a contract is eesentially informal. The contract is a transaction that requires an offer and an acceptance, which are both normally made in the same meeting. An offer can be withdrawn before acceptance.

In a number of places the Koran prohibits unjustified enrichment, or receiving a monetary advantage without giving a counter value, and he who gains in this way must give the proceeds to the poor as a charitable gift. This applies in particular to reselling a commodity at a higher sum before payment has been made for it, or reletting a hired object for a greater sum (for example a house). The general prohibition applies in the first place to sale and barter, but also to exchange. It is directed against speculation in food and in precious metals.

Based on the Koranic prohibition of a certain game of hazard (*maysir*), Islamic law insists that there must be no doubt concerning the obligations undertaken by the parties to a contract. The object of the contract must be determined or known. This requirement is directed

Islamic Law 69

particularly at objects which can be measured or weighed; the quantity must be determined exactly even if the price of a unit of weight or measure is stated. For the same reason it is forbidden to sell unripe fruit to be delivered when ripened, or a house from the architect's drawings, because it is not known whether the fruit will ripen or the house be completed.

The elimination of risk or chance was aimed primarily at forbidding gambling which was a great passion in ancient Arabia. This general principle has been expanded to cover lotteries of any kind, and the award of prizes for any performance. There are only two exceptions to this rule; prizes are allowed for the winner of a horse race, on account of the importance of training horses for Holy War, and for the winners of competitions relating to the knowledge of Islamic law.

The definition of liability is complicated, but in general it arises from either the non-performance of a contract, or from tort, or from a combination of both. Liability is here distinguished from negligence.

## Negligence

There is no concept of negligence in Islamic law. The general principle is that it is a person's responsibility to look out for himself. If someone digs a hole and another falls into it, the person who dug the hole is not liable if he did it with permission of the land owner. If somebody erects a building on public property, and another falls through a faulty staircase balustrade no liability arises. If a wall threatens collapse, its owner is only liable if any person (like an adjoining owner) who might suffer has asked him to demolish it.

## Interest

All transactions in Islamic law are bound by the doctrine of *riba*. Strictly this is a prohibition on usury, but it was extended to preclude any form of interest on a capital loan or investment. Coupled with the law forbidding gambling transactions, *riba* law in principle does not allow any transaction or speculation the results or benefits of which cannot be forecast precisely.

## Waqf Foundations

A unique feature of Islamic law is that relating to *waqf* foundations. This is a procedure whereby an owner relinquishes his right to real estate property which henceforth belongs to God. The income or benefit accruing from such an arrangement is normally invested in some charitable institution, but might include the founder's own family.

## Marriage

The family is the only group based on affinity which Islam recognizes. Islam is opposed to tribal solidarity, because the solidarity of believers should supersede the solidarity of the tribe.

Marriage is a contract of civil law. The bridegroom concludes the contract with the legal guardian (*wali*) of the bride and he undertakes to pay a price (*mahr*) or dower directly to his wife, and the amount must be stated in the marriage contract. The contract must be concluded in the presence of free witnesses, two men or one man and two women: this has the double aim of providing proof of marriage, and of disproving unchastity. The contract is the only legally relevant act in concluding marriage. The *wali* is the nearest male relative in the order of succession; he can give his ward in marriage against her will if she is a minor, but when she comes of age she has the right to rescind. Some hold, however, that she does not have this right if her father or grandfather gives her in marriage. Similar rules apply to the bridegroom if he is a minor. A free woman who is fully responsible may give herself in marriage, but the *wali* has the right to object if the prospective husband is not of equal birth.

When the woman has been married previously her consent is necessary, but it is still her father or guardian who contracts the marriage on her behalf. In Shi'ite and Hanafi law only minors may be contracted in compulsory marriage, and adult women contract their own marriage, providing they do not marry beneath their social status.[1] Men may be maried to a maximum of four wives at the same time, but a woman is restricted to one husband. A husband is obliged to support the wife, provided that she is obedient to him in domestic and social matters. A wife who leaves the family home without cause forfeits the right to maintenance.

## Divorce

A divorce may be effected simply by the mutual agreement of the spouses, known as *khul*, in which case the wife pays a financial consideration to the husband for her release. In all except Hanafi courts a wife may obtain a divorce on the grounds of some matrimonial offence committed by the husband, such as cruelty, desertion or failure to maintain.

1. See also Chapter 7.

The wife's rights in divorce are strictly limited to the above situations. A unique feature of Islamic law is the right given to the husband unilaterally to terminate a marriage at will by repudiation (*talaq*) of his wife. *Talaq* is an extra-judicial procedure and is not subject to the scrutiny of the courts or any other body. A marriage can be finally and irrevocably dissolved by a repudiation repeated three times. After the first *talaq* a waiting period of three months begins, known as the wife's *idda*, which establishes whether or not she is pregnant. If she is, the *idda* is extended until the birth of the child. During this waiting period a single *talaq* may be revoked at will by the husband and the marriage remains valid.

## Legitimacy

A child is indisputably legitimate if it is conceived during the lawful wedlock of its parents, and the legal position of children in respect of inheritance, maintenance and guardianship depends on their legitimacy. There is no legal relationship between a father and his illegitimate child in Sunni law; but for all purposes there is a legal tie between a mother and her illegitimate child. For example, care and control of the person for the purposes of education and marriage, and the property of minors, belongs to the father or a close male relative; the right of custody of young children, if parents are divorced or separated, belongs to the mother of the female paternal relatives.

## Inheritance

The law in respect of inheritance is strictly laid down. Two-thirds of the estate passes to the legal heirs of the deceased under the compulsory rules of inheritance. An individual may dispose of the other third at his discretion.

There is a fundamental difference between the Sunni and Shi'ite systems of inheritance. Sunni law is essentially a system of inheritance by male relatives who trace their descent from the deceased through the male line. A share is laid down for each male relative according to class, degree and blood tie. The females among the relatives take half the share of the male relative of the same class, degree and blood and none of them can exclude from inheritance any male agnate, however remote. There is a complicated system of dividing the estate between those entitled to inherit, and the proportion each one receives is determined exactly by the rules laid down, but the system is designed to favour descendants through the male line. If, for example, the deceased is survived by his wife, his daughter's son, and a distant agnatic cousin, the wife will receive a quarter of the estate, the grandson will be excluded altogether, and the cousin will inherit the remaining three-quarters.

Shi'ite law rejects the dominance of the agnatic tie and does not distinguish between male and female connections. In this system the surviving spouse always inherits a fixed portion, as in Sunni law, but all other relatives are divided into three classes: parents and descendants; grandparents, brother and sisters and their children; uncles and aunts and their children. Any relative in class one excludes any relative in class two, who in turn excludes any relative in class three, and a fullblood excludes the half-blood. As a result, although in principle females still receive only half the share of a corresponding male, in general they are much more fairly treated. In the example mentioned above, the wife's position would remain unchanged, but threequarters of the estate would go to the daughter's son, or indeed a daughter's daughter rather than to the cousin.

## Law Reform

> There are two important changes of direction within the history of Islamic law: one was the introduction at an early date of a legal theory which not only ignored but denied the existence in it of all elements that were not in the narrowest possible sense Islamic, and which reduced its material sources to the Koran and the example of the Prophet; the second, which began only in the present century, is modernist legislation on the part of contemporary Islamic governments, which does not merely restrict the field in which the sacred law is applied in practice but interferes with the traditional form of this law itself.[1]

Modern criticism is directed against traditional Islamic law not as a religious law as such, but against the body of doctrine developed in the Middle Ages and regarded subsequently as unchangeable.

The *sharia* law is still applied in its entirety in the Arabian peninsula[2], but in other parts of the Muslim world it has been restricted from the beginning of the 20th century into family law, including the law of inheritance, and the singular institution of *waqf* endowments. But the criminal and general civil law in most Muslim countries is now based upon European models, with a system of secular courts to apply them.

Modern reform of Islamic law started with the Ottoman Law of Family Rights of 1917 which was later repealed in Turkey but remained in force in Lebanon, Palestine, Syria and Jordan.

From 1920 onwards the legislative impetus moved to Egypt where reforms have been enacted in family law, the organization of the *qadi* courts, the law of inheritance, legacies and culminating in 1955 in the

1. Joseph Schacht, *An Introduction to Islamic Law*, Oxford University Press, 1964.
2. The Shi'ite form has been applied in Iran since the revolution in 1979. See Chapter 4.

Islamic Law  73

establishment of unified administration of justice in the hands of secular courts. Other reforms on divorce and a code of personal status are in draft form. This activity has inspired similar movements in the Sudan, Jordan, Lebanon, Syria, Iraq and Libya; in some cases the laws enacted go further than those in Egypt.

Outside the Arabian peninsula even the *sharia* family law is not applied in the traditional manner. Throughout the Middle East it is now generally expressed in the form of modern codes and it is only in the absence of a specific code that recourse is made to the traditional manuals. In India and Pakistan much of the family law is now embodied in statutory legislation, and the authority of judicial decisions has superseded that of the legal manuals. The *sharia* as a central entity has been abolished in Egypt and Tunisia, and *sharia* law is administered through a unified system of national courts, as is the case in India since partition. The rules of evidence of the *sharia* have been modified in many countries. In the Middle East circumstantial and documentary evidence is now generally admissible; witnesses are put on oath and cross-examined, and the general procedure, whereby one side produces witnesses and the other takes the oath of denial, has been largely superseded. In India and Pakistan, the courts apply the same rules of evidence to cases of Islamic law as in civil cases generally.

In the 20th century, the dominant issue in the Middle East concerning the reform of the *sharia* has been the need for justification on a jurisitic basis. That is, given the social and political desirability of reform, the overriding factor has become the justification for change in terms of Islamic jurisprudence, so that the change appears as a new, but orthodox, version of the *sharia*. Reform has been effected by the secular state in some cases, without challenging or altering the *sharia* in any way. One example of this flexibility of the Muslim mind is the attempt in Egypt to prohibit child marriage. In 1931 a law was enacted that the court was not to entertain any disputed claim of marriage where the marriage could not be proved by an official certificate of registration, and no such certificate could be issued if the bride was less than 16 or the bridegroom less than 18 years old at the time of the contract. The effect of this law was not to say that a marriage contracted of a minor was invalid, but as it would not be registered all legal rights would be forfeited. Another example is that as traditional Hanafi law was enforced in Egypt, a wife was not allowed to petition for divorce under any circumstances. However, by substituting the Maliki law in this area a wife's right to the judicial dissolution of her marriage could be obtained through her husband's cruelty, failure to provide maintenance and support, and desertion. By contrast, the British administration in India met the problem head on, and in 1929 enacted that the marriage of girls below the age of 14 and boys below the age of

16 was illegal under pain of penalties, while the Dissolution of Muslim Marriages Act, 1939, was modelled on English Law, allowing a Hanafi wife to obtain judicial divorce for cruelty, failure to maintain and other standard grounds. The only two countries to abandon the *sharia* completely[1] are Turkey, which in 1926 adopted the Swiss Civil Code and Albania, which in 1967 made all religions illegal.

Since the 1950s, in parts of the Middle East, pressure for legal reform has been growing. Modern jurisprudence has claimed the right to challenge the interpretations of the medieval jurists placed upon the Koran and the *Sunna*, and to interpret for itself, in the light of new circumstances, the original texts, and to re-open questions that had in theory been closed since the 10th century.

One example is the Syrian law of personal status, 1953, which has reassessed the terms under which a man may take more than one wife. The Koran instructs a man to treat all his wives equally, and if for any reason he is not able to do this he has to restrict himself to one wife. Traditionally, this qualification has been left to an individual's conscience, but the Syrian interpretation insists that it is a legal economic requirement. Coupled with the requirement that marriages must be registered, this enables the *qadi* to withhold permission from a married man to take a second wife until he can show that he can support them both in equality. The Tunisian law of personal status, 1957, goes further and argues that the Koranic injunction refers not only to economic equality, but also to equal treatment in all other respects. Since under modern conditions total equality and impartiality is impossible to achieve, the essential conditions for polygamy cannot be met, and Tunisian law therefore prohibits polygamy.

Syrian law also challenges the traditional right of a husband to divorce at will, and subjects the husband's motives to the scrutiny of the court. The Koranic requirement that husbands should make a fair provision for divorced wives and retain wives with kindness or release them with consideration has by tradition been left to the conscience of the husband. In Syria the court is now empowered to order a divorced man to pay a maximum of one year's maintenance if he has abused his powers. But in this matter also Tunisia has gone further. The reformers here rest their justification on the Koranic passage which urges the appointment of arbitrators between husband and wife in the case of matrimonial discord. They argue that if a divorce is imminent there must clearly be discord, and arbitrators must be appointed. Who better to arbitrate dispassionately than the courts of the land, having, as they do, trained judges to sift evidence? The law thus withholds from a husband the extra-judicial right to divorce, taking this duty

[1]. This applies also to the republics of Southern USSR and the Muslim communities in China.

Islamic Law 75

upon itself, and declaring that divorce outside the court is without legal validity. Although the court must dissolve a marriage if a husband persists in his repudiation, it has unlimited rights to compensate a wife for damage she has suffered as a result. In Pakistan the traditional *khul* divorce, where by mutual consent a wife pays compensation to her husband, has been modified to give a Muslim wife the right to obtain a divorce by payment of suitable compensation, whether a husband agrees or not.

It would, however, be a mistake to give the impression that in modern times the reform of Islamic family law is a formality, or that it proceeds apace. Changes in the law in Algeria, for example, have been relatively rare and mainly concerned with the guardianship of minors and the formalities of marriage and divorce. In 1959 an ordinance was laid down that marriage is concluded by the consent of husband and wife, fixing minimum ages for marriage, and decreeing that the marriage can be dissolved only by a judicial decision on certain grounds at the demand of husband or wife, or at their joint demand. A final court of appeal was established in the Court of Appeal in Algiers. This court has on occasions diverged from the strict doctrine of Islamic law when it appears to conflict with Western ideas of fairness, justice and humanity.

In some countries like South Yemen, Somalia and Tunisia, the state has been able to break from the strict provisions of the *sharia* in issues relating to marriage, divorce, abortion, etc, and has promulgated new laws which have abolished polygamy, restricted a husband's right to divorce, legalized abortion, and provided women with the same share in inheritance as men. The Somali state has even gone so far as to exempt government workers from fasting during Ramadan, in order to keep up production.

In Saudi Arabia the *ulama*, who regulate religious practices, argue that the law comes only from God, therefore the government, through the king, issues decrees. In modern times justice is administered by a mixture of secular institutions and the traditional *qadi* courts. In the case of an industrial accident, for example, claims for compensation are decided by the Ministry of Finance, whilst the *qadi* gives judgement concurrently on the question of blood money. In the case of a road accident the police investigate and decide on the guilt, if any, of the driver, and the *qadi* then allots the blood money on the basis of their decision. Various decrees provide for fines and imprisonment as punishment, which, if it is considered appropriate, are imposed in addition to the punishment prescribed in the *sharia*.

A hard core of traditionalist opinion still adamantly rejects the process of re-interpreting the basic texts of divine revelations, and great problems of principle and practice still have to be solved. The traditionalists maintain that the function of law is to fulfil the will of God and not to suit the changing needs of society. By contrast, modern jurisprudence bases itself directly on the tradition of the early medieval jurists, who were interpreting the Koran and the *Sunna* against the social and political needs of the time. They argue that neither the Koran nor Mohammed forbade subsequent interpretation, and that much of Islamic law has social origins.

# Chapter 4
# Society and Politics

In the upheavals which have rocked the Middle East since the Second World War the conflicts seem to have been as violent between Muslim states as between any others. Yet there are threads of Islamic principle linking them together on a political as well as a religious level.

This chapter, rather than analyzing the political and military conflicts between Muslim countries, discusses briefly the extent to which the teachings of Islam are reflected in their political and social institutions.

## Islamic Principles: Theory

### Politics and the Individual

The function of Islamic society is to fulfil the divine will, not through the activity of the community or the organizations and institutions within it, but through each individual understanding his duties. There is an important distinction between being individually responsible, and acting in isolation. Muslims are expected to fulfil certain communal functions, as is shown by the importance attached to the Friday *salat*, the giving of alms, and the consensus of the (Sunni) community (*ijma*). However, these are not seen as communal responsibilities, but as the responsibilities of an individual acting with other individuals. The underlying theology is man's ultimate responsibility to God for all his actions.

In all Sunni communities the only social unit recognized by authority is the family, and a believer is discouraged from forming loyalties to any other group, including the tribe. In strict Islamic terms the only other body to which a Muslim belongs is the brotherhood of believers — in other words the Islamic nation. In this important respect, Islam has from its inception been not simply a religion, but also a state, and by definition has always had an inherent awareness of the political process. Furthermore, the Islamic state has within it everything required for life, its own assessment of what is important and what is not. The relationship between economic relationships and political power was recognized by Mohammed from the very beginning; he was not only Islam's founder and Prophet, but its first lawyer and statesman.

But the intellectual void left in society between the family and the state means that for historical and cultural as well as religious reasons a Muslim will not organize or associate with political parties as readily as his counterpart in Europe.

Thus, for the past 150 years, political development inside Islam has either been stagnant or, more recently, has developed quite differently from any Western model. This has to be explained not simply in terms of Islam's former colonial status, but also by its political image of itself.

It is useful to refer here to A Universal Islamic Declaration made in London in 1980.[1] It is the first document of its kind in modern times, and sets out some fundamental political aims:

> A universal order can be created only on the basis of a universal faith and not by serving the gods of race, colour, territory or wealth. The ideal of man's brotherhood seeks and finds its realization in Islam.
>
> Establishment of justice on earth is one of the basic objectives for which Allah sent His prophets and His guidance. (Koran 57:25). All human beings have rights on all that Allah has provided, and as such Allah's bounties are to be shared equitably. The poor and the needy have the right to share in the wealth of the rich. (Koran 51:19). It is the religious duty of Muslims to harness these resources and to serve the ends of justice, to promote goodness and virtue, and to eliminate evil and vice. (Koran 3:110). Allah's resources must not be allowed to become instruments of oppression and exploitation by any individual or section of society or state.
>
> It is only the mandate of Allah which confers legitimacy on governments, rulers and institutions, and legitimate power and authority can be derived only in accordance with the mandate laid down in the Koran and *as Sunna* of the Prophet Mohammed (Peace be upon him).
>
> Any system of government is Islamic as long as it upholds the mandatory principles laid down by the Koran and *as Sunna*. Apart from this mandatory requirement there is considerable flexibility in the form which an Islamic government may adopt. It is through this flexibility that Islam caters to the requirements of every age and place.
>
> The primary duties of the state are to establish justice in all spheres of life and to nurture and strengthen the unity of the *umma*[2].

1. *The Times*, 14 April 1980.
2. The community

> These objectives can only be achieved when the full expectations of people are fulfilled; and when differences in rank, power, wealth and family ties are not permitted to undermine the socio-political process of Islam.
>
> Islam aims at creating a model society. Its strategy is to mould the individual in accordance with the tenets of Islam, to organize and mobilize within a social movement for progress and development, and to establish an Islamic Order by building society and state, their institutions, and policies at national and international levels.

It is noticeable that nowhere in the Declaration is any mention made of individual liberty or political freedom. On the contrary, Islamic strategy is to 'mould the individual in accordance with the tenets of Islam'. This is consistent with the tradition which holds that man cannot attain the right path through his own unaided efforts, and the inference is that individual fulfillment is more likely to lead to vice and evil than anything else. Nor is anything said about abolishing poverty, or riches for that matter. In fact, the Declaration has nothing to say directly about altering the class relationships in society.

But if Islam does not subscribe to the ideas of liberty and equality, the same cannot be said for fraternity, and the first clearly identifiable political aim is brotherhood. The reference to man's brotherhood finding its realization in Islam is fundamental. The Prophet frequently discussed the question of why mankind consists of a plurality of *ummas* (communities) and has not remained a unit. He saw the ultimate reason for this in God's Message 'Mankind were only one nation, then they fell into variance' (Koran 10:20).

At first Mohammed regarded the Arabs in general as a closed *umma*. But in time his *umma* came more and more to consist exclusively of his immediate followers — the Muslims. One of the consequences of the spread of Islam was Mohammed's ruling that once a man embraces the faith he becomes a member of the community and must not be attacked by his Muslim brothers. This edict turned the tribal aggression of the Arabs outwards, which in the course of time brought together very different races and nations to form a Muslim brotherhood.

The second social objective of Islam is to uphold justice, which is seen clearly as part of the socio-political process. It is perhaps under this heading that the greatest scope is offered for discussion of changing political ideas in Islam:

> Indeed, We sent Our Messengers with
> the clear signs, and We sent down
> with them the Book and the Balance
> so that men might uphold justice.

(Koran 57:25)

Finally, the Sunni doctrine of *ijma* must be considered. Literally, *ijma* means 'agreeing upon'. Originally this was interpreted as agreement of those people who have a right, by virtue of knowledge, to form a judgement of their own. After Mohammed's death, these were his Companions; later it meant the religious scholars. But the idea is open to, and has been given, other interpretations. The fundamental tradition from which the *ijma* is derived quotes the Prophet as saying 'my people will never agree in an error'. In consequence, it is argued, there is in the consensus of the people as a whole a power to *create* doctrine and law, and not simply to stamp with approval that which has been handed to them. The *Shorter Encyclopaedia of Islam* gives two examples of the power of *ijma* expressed by the community. The first is that the cult of saints has become practically a part of the *Sunna* of Islam, in spite of its being disapproved by purists and religious scholars; and even stranger is the popular belief in the infallibility and sinlessness of Mohammed, in spite of clear statements in the Koran to the contrary. In these cases the *ijma* has not simply shown its flexibility on certain points, but has changed settled doctrines of the greatest importance. The idea therefore that the consensus of the community can be used as an instrument for political change has a respectable pedigree. There is some controversy, however, as to whether this means that the Muslim people can made Islam whatever they, as a whole, wish.

These, then, are some of the theoretical building blocks from which all modern Islamic societies are constructed. Just as the Western democracies have used, with varying degrees of conviction, the ideas of the French Revolution, liberty, equality and fraternity, Islam has generated from its own internal resources the alternative slogan of brotherhood, justice and the right of the community.

## Islamic Principles: Practice

### The Ottoman Empire

In spite of prohibitions, there is nothing new about Muslims fighting each other. Almost as soon as the Arab invaders broke out of Arabia in the seventh century their conquests became too extensive to be administered and controlled from a central source. The result was the rise of various Muslim dynasties that sought to extend their power and influence over the Islamic world by intrigue and conquest, until the expansion of the European colonial powers in the 18th and 19th centuries.

At the beginning of the 16th century, Arabia, Iraq and Syria, and Palestine lost their importance as the trade routes between Europe and

Asia, when Europe discovered an alternative route by sea round the Cape of Good Hope. Ironically, this was made possible by the Arab researches in physics, astronomy, geography and other sciences brought back by the Crusaders 500 years earlier. The medieval gloom from which Europe was emerging was soon to descend on the Arab regions because of their diminished economic importance, and the domination of their fellow Muslims by the Ottoman Turks, who were to rule the region until the First World War. International trade bypassed the Arabs for four centuries, and the Middle East was transformed from a cosmopolitan and international trading centre based on a capitalistic money economy to an insular and regressive backwater with a feudal political structure. Just as Europe was reconstructing the whole of its intellectual, economic, political and social life, the Middle East, under Ottoman rule, was embarking on a reverse course. Ottoman society, dominated by inflexible religious leaders, was encasing itself in a rigid code of Islamic law.

## European Imperialism

By the end of the 18th century the stagnation and corruption of the Ottoman Empire made it ripe for conquest by European imperialism, and all aspects of the Middle Eastern life were materially affected for the next 150 years. It is impossible to understand the development of modern Islam without understanding the colonial role ascribed to it by the European powers.

France made the first move when Napoleon sent an expeditionary force to invade Egypt, and eventually French influence extended along the North African coast and into Palestine and Syria. Initially, Britain's interest was to secure the sea route around Africa, and in order to control the Indian Ocean she set up, by various means, bases in Iraq, Persia and along the coasts of the Arabian peninsula. When the Suez Canal was opened in 1869, Britain expanded its imperial interest to the eastern Mediterranean. In putting down a minor Egyptian revolt in 1882, she took control of the Suez Canal from the French and occupied Egypt to become the dominant colonial power in the Middle East.

In the meantime Austria and Russia had cast covetous eyes on the Eastern European and Western Asian parts of the Ottoman Empire, and when Germany and Italy began to make their imperial interests felt, the Ottoman government had its hands full. The economic and strategic exploitation of the Middle East by Europe had other and equally important consequences for its people. Throughout the second half of the 19th century European dominance dragged in its wake cultural influences and technical changes which lifted the dead hand of the Ottoman régime. The most important and ironical consequence of this was that the conditions were created for the re-emergence of the Arab identity. The Ottoman Empire was no match for the tide of events, and out of its ruins the Arabs constructed a new sense of identity, based on their own heritage, but rationally supported by the political and nationalist ideas formulated in Europe.

The present day geographical boundaries of the Middle East did not exist under the Ottomans; the region was identified as provinces of the Ottoman Empire. But even more significant were the differences between the Muslim sects. The Ottoman Turks had imposed on Islam the rigid orthodoxy which became its official version, or *Sunna*. Those who accepted this view came to be known as Sunni, or Sunnite. However, there remained a large minority of believers who refused to accept this interpretation of Islam. They maintained the belief of the early Shi'ites, who had founded the Baghdad Caliphate. The Shi'ite stronghold became Persia, the birthplace of the movement, but others were scattered throughout the Arab world. They believed that the leadership of the Muslim world, and consequently the interpretation of the divine will, could only be assumed by the direct descendants of Mohammed, through his son-in-law, Ali. The Ottomans tried but failed to put down Shi'ite aspirations to justify their own power in the Muslim world, which was not descended from the Prophet.

There also arose in the 18th century a division within the Sunni movement itself. This was led by Abd'al-Wahhab, a religious scholar, and a local tribal warrior chief called Mohammed ibn Saud. They formed an alliance in the Arabian heartland to challenge and reject the Ottoman theology. The Wahhabis preached and practised a brand of Islam that was basically simple and harsh, and the movement gained control of central Arabia and shut off the routes of the pilgrimage to Mecca. These conflicts between Muslim sects were another factor affecting the political balance within Islam, and persist to this day.

But although the internal tensions within the Ottoman Empire had real significance, it was the rivalry between the French and the British from the beginning of the 19th century that was largely responsible for the turn of events, and still influences the course of Middle Eastern politics.

The first 40 years of the 19th century saw the internal struggle of Mohammed Ali, the viceroy of Egypt, who sought to expand his power and territory at the expense of the Ottoman Sultan. Britain and France intervened at various times and took sides to neutralize each other's influence. At the same time, Russia cast predatory glances at the accessible regions of the tottering Empire and the conflict of imperial interests subsequently brought about the Crimean War (1854-55). Although the Ottomans won the war against Russia, this was only done with the support of Britain and France, and the price paid for victory was the domination of their Empire by the economic and political interests of these two powers. Subsequently the Ottoman government fell steadily into decline and bankruptcy. After the British occupation of Egypt to gain control of the Suez Canal, the Ottoman régime no longer had the economic power, political will, or military strength to control its Empire. When militant nationalism, born out of the French Revolution, filtered into the consciousness of its minorities, from Greece to Egypt, its decline was complete.

Towards the end of the 19th century small but important secret Arab societies had sprung up in Egypt, Iraq and Syria, preaching political independence. At the same time a new political movement, Zionism, was being formed in Europe, based on the idea of a Jewish state. The Pan-Arab movement gathered strength, and in 1905 in Paris a book was published called *The Awakening of the Arab Nation*. It envisaged an independent Arabic speaking nation extending from the Fertile Crescent to the Suez Canal.

By the beginning of the 20th century France was already in control of the provinces of Algeria and Tunisia and was moving into Morocco. Britain was established firmly in Egypt and the Arabian peninsula. Italy had scarcely been born as a state before she wanted a share of the pickings and selected the North African province that became known as Libya. Italy invaded in 1911 and triggered off a local war with Turkey that eventually led to the Balkan Wars of 1912-13, and indirectly contributed to the tensions underlying the outbreak the First World War in 1914. The end of that war brought the dissolution of the Ottoman Empire.

## Arab Nationalism

In 1902 a revolt was launched in Arabia by Abdul Aziz ibn Saud, a descendant of the original ally of Wahhab, which was essentially directed at the corruption of the Ottomans. National independence movements were proliferating throughout the Empire, not just in the Arab regions, but also in its Eastern European and Western Asian territories. The repression of these movements by Constantinople had the effect of forcing them underground, and societies dedicated to revolution and national self-determination were formed in most major cities, including the Arab cities of the Fertile Crescent, but before full expression could be given to these new movements the war of 1914 erupted.

The First World War had some profound effects on Islamic politics and society. First, as a result of a series of big power manoeuvres, the Ottomans found themselves allied with Germany, and therefore on the losing side. Secondly, the waging of a modern war brought to the Middle East a military presence and civil support of a strength not seen in the region since the Crusades. The indigenous population came into direct contact with new ways: new organizations, new weapons, new transport and communications, and, above all, new social relationships. Furthermore, intervention by the allies was largely welcomed, rather than resented, by the politically conscious factions: the British and French were fighting the Turks who had become the primary target for emerging Arab nationalism.

The British took the initiative in the fight against the Ottomans and arranged a deal with the Grand Sharif of Mecca, Hussein ibn Ali. The arrangement was that in return for Ali organizing and leading an armed rebellion against the Turks, thereby helping the British war effort, Britain would be prepared to recognize and uphold the independence of the Arabs in the region consisting of the Fertile Crescent, excluding Egypt, and virtually the whole of the Arabian peninsula. In the meantime, France had begun to make proposals of her own to divide up the Ottoman Empire between the Allies, including Russia, at the conclusion of the war, which it was assumed they would win.

Britain, in order to maintain her allies' wholehearted commitment in Europe, was made to agree with their post-war expectations, and in 1916 the three concluded a secret agreement which totally ignored the British agreement with Sharif Hussein. To add to this duplicity, the Zionist movement had gained sufficient influence in British power politics for serious consideration to be given to the idea of setting aside part of the territory committed to the Arabs by London as a homeland for the Jews: namely Palestine. Upholding their end of the bargain, Hussein and his followers embarked on their revolt in a campaign that made famous the name of T E Lawrence.

Then came two events which were to have a shattering effect on Anglo-Arab relations, and which are still remembered with bitterness in the Arab world. The successful Bolshevik Revolution in Russia had unearthed in the Kremlin archives a copy of the secret agreement between the Allies. This was made public, and Britain's true position became clear to the Arabs. Shortly afterwards the Balfour Declaration was published by the British government. Although it was careful to stress the importance of safeguarding non-Jewish communities, it looked with favour on 'the establishment in Palestine of a national home for the Jewish people', and pledged Britain's best efforts to achieve that aim.

At the end of the First World War the Ottoman Empire lay in ruins, and the imperial vacuum was filled by the victorious European allies: Britain and France. For 500 years under the Turks the Middle East had had all its Islamic characteristics reinforced and entrenched by a conservative but increasingly corrupt Muslim régime. The exposure to the power politics of Europe brought new political perceptions to the region, and the geo-political processes of the West began to influence and modify the entrenched Islamic attitude.

The 20 years between the two world wars were dominated by the issue of nationalism, and the manoeuvering of Britain and France to contain it. Nationalism is a political, rather than a religious, idea, and for the first time since Mohammed's death there arose forces in the Middle East capable of ordering the course of its history but not inspired exclusively by Islam. It is still barely perceived in the West that, for example, Egyptian and Arab nationalism are not only different from each other, but are also not exclusively Muslim. Both have within them Christian minorities and even Jewish communities who regard themelves as Arabs: and it took President Nasser, at the height of his power, to convince the Egyptian people that they should not regard themselves as a separate nation, but identify with the Arab cause. Furthermore, under the Ottomans none of the geo-political boundaries which we now recognize existed, apart from the Egyptian. In particular, greater Syria consisted of what we now know as Syria, Lebanon, Palestine, Jordan and parts of Arabia, and the nationalist struggle between the wars was largely focused on the efforts of the Arabs to turn this region into a unified Arab state.

Britain and France prevented this by dividing up the Fertile Crescent, with France retaining control over Greater Syria, and Britain having the Southern part and Mesopotamia (Iraq). At the same time, Britain installed Prince Feisal, son of Hussein ibn Ali, as king of a provisional government of Syria, excluding the Syrian territories of Palestine and Transjordan (Jordan). Feisal had neither the power base nor the political programme to unite the nationalist aspirations of the Arabs. He spent his time in London and Paris, trying to negotiate the independence of Greater Syria. In the meantime, the nationalist groups at home had become increasingly restive and had organized independent guerilla groups. When sporadic fighting broke out between the groups and the French in 1920, and it became clear that Feisal was unable to control his people, the French overturned his provisional government and set up their own puppet régime.

Thus, a split developed in the nationalist movements of French Syria and British Palestine, in response to the different policies being pursued by the colonial powers. Those in central Syria focused their attention on the French occupation, whilst those in Southern Syria concentrated on the British and the Zionists. 60 years later these events still have an effect on the interplay of nationalist interests in the Middle East, and particularly on the conflict between the Palestine movement and Jordan about the future status of the Palestinians.

The kingdom of Jordan, like Feisal, is Hashemite. When Feisal instructed his people in Damascus to stay out of the struggle that was developing in Palestine with the Zionists, he demonstrated his inability to lead the Pan-Arab movement, and played into the hands of the Franco-British policy of creating small manageable national states.

The French occupation encouraged the Christian minority of Northern Syria to congregate on the Mediterranean coast where the French influence was most strongly felt. The Christians, though proud of their Arabic language and traditions, wanted to shake off Muslim domination. In 1926 France, acceding to Christian pressure, set up Lebanon as a separate republic.

After ceding Northern Syria to the French, the British set about the division of the South. In compensation to Sharif Hussein for not honouring the agreement to support his Pan-Arab state after the war, the British installed one of his sons, Feisal, as king of Iraq, and another, Abd'ullah, as the ruler of Transjordan. In addition they approved Hussein's proclamation of himself as king of Hejaz (North West Arabia). The creation of the separate states of Palestine and Transjordan gave Britain control over the routes from their oil fields in Iraq to the Mediterranean. In effect, Britain now had political and economic control over the region linking the Tigres-Euphrates, the Persian Gulf, the Nile Valley and the Mediterranean, through the hands of the ancient and respected Hashemite family.

But no sooner had Britain established itself as a dominant power in the Middle East than other factors, the seeds of which had already been sown, began to make themselves felt. The first of these was the expansion of the United States' oil interests. Other factors were the re-emergence of the Saud family dominance in Arabia, the reaction of the Arabs to the Zionist ambitions in Palestine, and the increasing strength of the nationalist movements in the region. It was not nationalist aspirations, and certainly not Muslim rivalries, which created the geopolitical map of the modern Middle East. Yet once the boundaries had been created, they took on a significance of their own, and most have survived to the present day. Once political structures had been created within these boundaries, regardless of whether the unit was economically viable or religiously compatible, another dimension was added to the ideas of Muslim brotherhood and Pan-Arab unity: patriotic nationalism.

The ascendancy of the Saud family in Arabia began in 1902 when the youthful Abdul Aziz ibn Saud emerged from exile in what is now Kuwait and recaptured the family's traditional capital, the mud-brick oasis town of Ridayh. Abdul Aziz had remained loyal to the fundamentalist Wahhabi doctrine, and had stayed aloof from the dealings of the British and the Hashemites in the North, concentrating instead on consolidating his power in central Arabia. By 1925 he was strong enough to challenge and win control of the Hashemite Hejaz, the traditional cradle of Islam. Two years later he was in control of two-thirds of the Arabian peninsula, and was in a position to demand, and get, British recognition. After overcoming a series of revolts and tribal wars he had, by 1932, brought most of the territories of the Arabian peninsula into the kingdom of Saudi Arabia. This done, he declared himself king.

## The Challenge of Zionism

If the sub-division of Greater Syria into national states helped to pave the way for the creation of Israel, it also helped ultimately to create the nucleus of the strongest opposition: the national identity of the Palestinians. It was a long time, however, before this became an effective force. The immediate effect of the sub-division was to dissipate the strength of the growing nationalist movement as it was forced to concentrate on an increasing number of local issues. As a result the Palestinians felt isolated and betrayed, and left to face the mounting pressure of Zionism alone.

Zionism, a political movement founded in Europe, seeks to provide a homeland (preferably, though not necessarily, in the land of the Jews' spiritual ancestors) for the oppressed and persecuted Jewish people of the world. Originally it did not seek to establish a sovereign Jewish state.

It is a common misconception in the West that Arab unity or Arabism has been brought about largely by the threat of Zionism. This is no more true than saying that Zionism has been largely brought about by the threat of Nazism. At the end of the First World War, when the Balfour Declaration first made Zionism a real threat to Palestine, Arab consciousness was working in its own quite different way. As the Arabs saw it, there was no such place as Palestine. What had been Palestine in biblical times had long since been absorbed as part of the Ottoman province of Syria, and the people who had lived there for centuries, whether Muslims or Christians, regarded themselves as Arabs, not as Palestinians.

Muslims regard Jews as a religious group, not as a nation. Certainly for them there is no generic connection between the Jews who emigrated in waves to Palestine at the end of the First World War, and the Jews who had lived in the Middle East for 2000 years. The immigrants had come almost exclusively from Eastern Europe and Southern Russia and their ancestors had been converted to Judaism in the eighth century: none had originated in the Middle East. Muslims in general, and Arabs in particular, make a distinction between the possibility of a Jewish homeland as part of an Arab state, which might in principle be acceptable, and a politically Western oriented Zionist sovereign state, which is not.

Living in Palestine in 1919 there were about 60,000 Jews and 10 times that number of Arabs. Under the British administration, Jewish immigration increased, and the Jews began to make it clear that their eventual aim was the establishment of an independent state. This triggered off a series of riots, in which the Arabs struck back at the nearest available target: the Jews. In the years leading up to the Second World War much blood was shed on both sides, but Jewish immigration proceeded apace, and their achievements in building up their nation were impressive. With the help of massive injections of foreign (mostly Jewish) capital and the immigration of skilled European and American Jews the homeland became a prosperous miniature state on the European model. By the mid 1930s the Arab population were becoming increasingly concerned by the prospect of total Jewish control. The creation of a Jewish state by partition was being openly canvassed, and this threat, reinforced by the national frontiers surrounding it, strengthened the notion of Palestinian nationalism.

The Second World War, and the events leading up to it, concentrated the minds of Arabs, Jews and British alike. At the start of the war the open hostility between Arabs and Jews in Palestine had reached dangerous proportions. Arab resentment of Zionism was no longer centred exclusively in Palestine but had spread throughout the Arab world. In the meantime, the persecuted Jews of Europe were desperately looking for sanctuary, and for many a natural refuge was Zionist Palestine. When the danger of war with Germany became real, Britain dramatically reversed its policy which had for so long favoured the Jews. A White Paper was published, drastically limiting Jewish immigration, and stating flatly that it was not British policy that Palestine should become a Jewish state. Britain's intention was obvious. Although she could not foresee that the war would leave the Middle East virtually intact (apart from North Africa), Britain clearly did not want to enter the war with the Arab nations becoming increasingly hostile to her foreign policy.

But if the Arabs in general greeted the new policy with relief, it made the Zionists into bitter enemies. It provoked the formation of a dangerous underground movement, which staged an open armed revolt against the British in 1939 when Britain refused to revise the ban on immigration to accommodate the Jewish refugees from Nazi Europe.

Even so, by 1947 there were over 600,000 Jews living in Palestine, and more than twice as many Arabs who owned 95% of the land. But the Zionist pressure eventually bore fruit as the result of the terrorist campaign in Palestine, and a propaganda campaign in the West. The break came when President Truman, abandoning Roosevelt's promise to King Abdul Aziz that the US would make no commitments regarding Palestine without first consulting the Arabs, publicly advocated the immediate admittance of 100,000 Jews into Palestine. This statement marked the beginning of the United States's political involvement in the Middle East, and signalled its ascendancy at the expense of Britain. The Arabs viewed this turn of events with despair, especially when the British Foreign Office began to make it clear that it was ready to wash its hands of the Palestinian affair. It was easy to see that the vacuum would be filled by the United States with its powerful Jewish political lobby. The Arabs argued that the events in Europe were none of their making, but their aspirations and interests were being once more swept aside in order to pacify the wave of Christian guilt which swept the world when the results of Nazi persecution became generally known.

The Arabs found themselves in the position of having to plead their case to a Western audience in terms that they would understand, and they failed. Their case was rooted in the Islamic standards of justice and the complexities of Arab history, and was constructed on a sense of the shame that the colonial powers should feel for the way they had dealt with the Arabs in the past. It was no match for the Zionist propaganda, Western in its origin and language, and based on a mixture of humanitarian ideas and pragmatic solutions carefully tuned in to a real sense of Western guilt.

Britain finally referred the whole Palestine question to the United Nations in 1947 and a special committee recommended partition of the land into separate Arab and Jewish states. The Jews accepted the idea, because by now the establishment of any kind of Jewish state was an overriding priority. It was flatly rejected by the Arabs for exactly the same reasons that they had advanced all along: the land belonged to the Arabs and had done so for centuries; the Jews were not a nation, and never had been; neither the United Nations nor anybody else had the right to dispose of Muslim territory; and no Muslim could agree to relinquishing Islamic land to the infidel without a fight.

Following intense Zionist and American pressure the UN General Assembly endorsed the idea of partition and the following year a provisional Israeli government established itself in Tel Aviv. At the same time armies from Egypt, Lebanon, Syria, Transjordan and Iraq were advancing on the frontiers of the new state. The first Middle East war was about to start, and Islam began to move back into the centre of world events.

The Arab armies were unable to overcome the poorly equipped but highly motivated Israeli forces. At the end of the war all Palestinian territory was occupied by either Israel or Transjordan, with the Gaza strip under Egyptian administration. The Palestinians were left with nothing.

## National Liberation Movements

The Second World War, like the First, accelerated social change, but the changes which took place in the Muslim countries were motivated more by anti-colonial objectives than by pro-Islamic sentiment.

Yet it is noticeable that although each country has found its own way to independence, every national leader to emerge has been a devout Muslim. Furthermore, there are only two significant political movements whose constitutions aim at setting up a democratic secular state, rather than a state where, at the very least, Islam is the official religion. There are the Ba'th Socialist Party, and, paradoxically in view of the support received from Muslim states, the Palestine Liberation Organization.

Although, until the Iranian Revolution, the concept of Islam had not been used directly in national self-determination, its inherent qualities of opposition to foreign domination, anti-corruption, and justice, have always been at hand to trigger off a national response. Moreover, while various Muslim countries have shown a willingness to import selected Western ideas on social equality, collective ownership and other socialist concepts, including equality for women, all have stopped short of embracing either Communist or Marxist methods. However politically leftist have been the policies of Iraq, Syria, Egypt and Libya, their leaders, as devout Muslims, have rejected quite specifically all atheistic philosophies.

## Modern Political Structures

The variety of forms of government seen in Muslim countries relates to the economic and political realities from which each emerged rather than to Koranic doctrine. These have given rise to the full spectrum of political forms: single-party states, parliamentary states, socialist states, states ruled by military junta, constitutional monarchies, parliamentary states based on Islamic and other religious groupings, and two types of fully fledged Islamic states, one pro- and the other anti-monarchy.

None of these has been remarkable for its stability. Even the oldest of them has been established for barely 50 years, and most of them for very much less. Many are subject to frequent changes, which suggests that they are moulded less in the tradition of Islam than by the political upheavals that historically accompany national independence. Even

Society and Politics 91

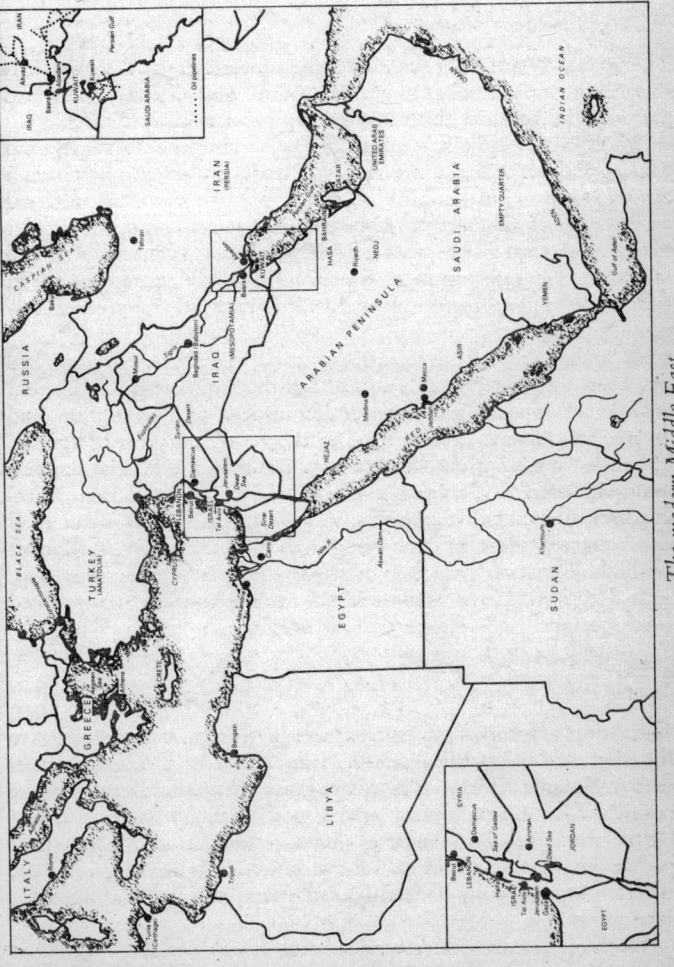

The modern Middle East

Turkey, which has not suffered from a colonial past, and is the only country to have adopted a modern Western parliamentary system, has been taken over by a military junta three times in the last 20 years. The rest, with two exceptions, appear to have more in common with newly independent non-Muslim states than they have with each other on the question of representative government. The two exceptions are the fully-committed Islamic states of Saudi Arabia[1] and Iran.

## Unity and Division

There are occasions and issues on which solidarity is readily achieved among Muslims, and others which trigger off the deepest conflicts.

A distinction worth drawing is that between the Islamic concept of Muslim brotherhood, and the political concept of Arab unity. The first holds the pedigree of the Koran, the Prophet, and the *Sunna*. The second is a modern political weapon, conceived and launched by Gamal Abdul Nasser when President of Egypt. Until that time the inhabitants of the Arabian peninsula, and in particular the Bedu, considered themselves the only true Arabs, and many of them still hold this view. Until Nasser's time, many Middle Eastern peoples, particularly the Egyptians, regarded themselves as quite distinct from the Arabs. Nasser's definition, which has now become generally accepted, is that an Arab is someone whose language, and therefore culture, is Arabic. This includes not only Muslims, but the adherents of all other religions, including Christians and Jews. But by definition it excludes Muslim states such as Turkey, Iran and the Indian sub-continent.

By contrast, the concept of Muslim brotherhood automatically includes all Muslims in the Islamic community, and excludes all others. The idea is deeply rooted in the very origins of Islam. Once the Prophet had won over the communities of Medina and Mecca, he set about converting and forming alliances with the surrounding tribes. The seal of an alliance was that the tribe submitted to Islam and as a result it became an inflexible rule that those who had become believers must not be attacked. It is this principle which virtually put an end to the traditional aggressive attitude of the Arab tribes towards each other, and, with their aggressiveness turned outwards, resulted in the spectacular spread of Islam.

The great achievement of the *ulama* is that for nearly 1000 years these religious scholars maintained the structure of Sunni society vir-

1. There are a number of small states along the Arabian Gulf which have systems of government very similar to that in Saudi Arabia. These include Kuwait, Bahrain, Qatar and the United Arab Emirates. They are ruled by an Amir (ruler) rather than a king and orthodox Wahhabi law is generally less strictly enforced, although this varies from state to state.

tually intact, by insisting that there were certain matters it was not in their power to alter. This suited their rulers well enough, especially as they controlled the appointment and promotion of the *ulama*. But its significance for today is the place that this unbroken tradition of social stability has in the hearts of the masses. This resistance to change has been reinforced by intractable minority problems in many states as a result of the break-up of the Ottoman empire. The Copts in Egypt, the Sunni Kurds and the Shi'ite Arabs in Iraq, and the Christians in Lebanon have presented insoluble problems for political unity, and reinforced the underlying resistance of the Sunni communities to change. The political changes in the Middle East since the Second World War have been largely brought about by the emergence of an increasingly powerful middle class, which has been educated either in the West or, at least, within the framework of a modern educational system. This has had a far reaching effect on commercial, technical, intellectual and political life in virtually every country. Significantly, though, it has had little or no religious impact.

## Race and Class

The European political idea of equality has been accepted by the orthodox Muslim mind only in limited areas. Islam is indifferent to race and colour, and although sharp distinctions are sometimes made between groups of people, they are based on class and social prejudice rather than on racial discrimination. Prejudice takes a different form from that frequently found in the West. Thesiger, travelling in the Empty Quarter of Arabia in the early 1950s, noted of his travelling companions that

> at first glance they seemed to be little better than savages...but I was soon disconcerted to discover that, while they were prepared to tolerate me as a source of very welcome revenue, they never doubted my inferiority. They were Muslims and Bedu and I was neither. They had never heard of the English, for all Europeans were known to them simply as Christians, and more probably infidels, and nationality had no meaning for them...Arabs have little if any sense of colour bar; socially they treat a slave, however black, as one of themselves... I remember asking some Rashid who had visited Riyadh how they had addressed the king, and they answered in surprise, 'we called him Abd'al Aziz, how else would we call him except by his name?' and when I said 'I thought you might call him Your Majesty', they answered 'we are Bedu. We have no king but God'.

The attitude of the Koran to slavery is similar to that of the New Testament. Both accept the social institution of slavery, and then give directions to make it more tolerable. Islam inherited slavery from ancient Arabia, and reformed its worst excesses, as it did in the case of inheritance, marriage, divorce and retribution. The basic social purpose of Islam was not to transform its essential class structure, but to carry out reforms in order to create a more stable and unified society. Thus, on the whole, slaves seemed to have been well treated. It was considered a pious act to free slaves, and in the case of unintentional killing, the freeing of a slave was the price to be paid to the community. Islam made it impossible to take a fellow Muslim in slavery, this being inconsistent with the idea of Muslim brotherhood. This was the limit of enlightenment in seventh century Islam.

## Modern Islamic States: Saudi Arabia and Iran

Although there are many countries in which Islam is the official religion, in which the leaders are pious Muslims, and in which Islamic law and tradition play a prominent part, there are very few which can claim to have retained Islam in its entirety. Saudi Arabia and several of the small Gulf states are examples. But these countries retain their Islamic character by virtue of resistance to change and in particular to change inspired by Western values which might undermine the values of Islam. Other countries, on achieving national independence, have made positive efforts to retain, and in some cases to expand, various aspects of traditional life, but there is only one state which has consciously and wholeheartedly abandoned all Western influence as being corrupt, evil, and anti-Islamic and has instituted a programme to reconstitute a fully-fledged Islamic state. That is Iran.

It is interesting to examine the two constitutional and political paths down which Saudi Arabia and Iran are travelling, not so much for the purposes of comparison but to see the variety and complexity of ideas that can be accommodated within the scope of Islam.

Saudi Arabia is an orthodox Sunni state, occupying territory whose people have more or less followed the teaching of the Prophet and the *Sunna* in an unbroken tradition dating from the time of Mohammed. Abdul Aziz ibn Saud reunited the territories of Arabia with the traditional weapons of the Sword and the Message, and he won the allegiance of the tribes by the traditional diplomacy of intermarriage.[1]

Iran became an Islamic Republic in 1979. This event was preceded by waves of public protest, civil unrest, and riots against the régime of the Shah (king). At first the civil revolt had no clear aim or leadership, and involved a number of political factions, as well as the Muslim clergy.

---

1. He is said to have had some 100 wives and over 100 children.

The widespread and popular feeling was focused on such general issues as freedom from foreign exploitation and interference, civil rights, civil justice, and an end to corruption in public life. It quickly became apparent that the only force that was influential enough to unite the forces of revolt was the Muslim clergy who had been preaching in their mosques for years the Islamic virtues of social justice, honest dealing, and the superiority of Islam over the infidel. Once the clergy delcared themselves, they transformed the revolt into an Islamic Revolution, provided its slogan *'Allah'hu akbar'* (God is greatest), and provided the leader for the occasion: Imam Khomeini. By contrast with Abdul Aziz, Khomeini played down the role of physical force (although it was there for him to order it) and relied on the morality and justice of his message. The forces which the Shah relied upon to maintain power — the military, Savak (secret police) and in the last resort his foreign allies[1] — proved inadequate. The armed forces, even the Royal Guard, would not fight to defend the régime, Savak was decimated by popular action, and the Shah's allies did nothing.

Perhaps the most significant aspect of these events is that a cornerstone of the Shah's policy was to 'modernize' his country with the maximum speed. This involved importing Western values, as well as Western technology, at the expense of traditional values, and this policy was at the root of his struggle with the clergy. Iran was run like a private company, and every state and commercial transaction involved a 'commission' to the royal family. Political power was maintained by faith in military and para-military force alone. The expectations of the people, the dissatisfaction of the business community and the residual strength of Islam were not given enough weight in the Shah's analysis. The miscalculation was to bring about his downfall.

Saudi Arabia is an absolute monarchy and has no written constitution. Political power rests exclusively in the hands of the king, and he makes appointments to all government posts, and those of all government agencies. The king rules through a Council of Ministers by issuing royal decrees which become statute law. Each minister takes on ministerial and departmental responsibilities, similar to those in a parliamentary system. Political power and religious orthodoxy are part of each other, based upon the Koran, *Sunna* and the *hadith* as interpreted by the Wahhabi sect. There is thus no distinction between the legislature and the executive, and religious/political power is enforced by the *ulema* (religious scholars) and the *mutawwa* (secret police).

The Council of Ministers debates the policy of the state, and makes

---

1. The American CIA overthrew the nationalist government in 1954 and reinstituted the monarchy with the Shah at its head.

decisions which require the royal assent. A committee system based on the idea of council is common in many aspects of Saudi life. Although the decision of a committee cannot be appealed against in a higher court, every individual has the right of access to the king, and may appeal to him directly.

The country is divided into four administrative regions with appointed officials, and each region is sub-divided into districts presided over by a local leader or *sheikh*. The *ulema* have a strong influence on all national or local affairs, and it is their duty to preserve the rule of law on all issues.

There are no elections of any kind in Saudi Arabia. Political parties, trade unions, trade and professional associations and institutions are illegal. The Hanbali school of law is officially recognized. Its interpretation of the *sharia* is possibly the most orthodox and conservative, and accounts for the *sharia's* surviving virtually intact.

The economy is a capitalist free enterprise system, but because the ovewhelming wealth of the country is created through its oil deposits, the government has the power not only to direct the economy, but to control it. The king, through the Council of Ministers, controls and directs the State revenue as he sees fit, and this combined with the intermarriage of the Saud family with the tribes secures his power base. Although government agencies control development and the economy, with the notable exception of defence, they do not normally engage in direct trading. This is left to private enterprise. It is illegal for foreign interests to own land, or to hold a majority interest in Saudi companies or corporations. Official monetary policy is administered by the Saudi Arabian monetary agencies (SAMA) which have the power and functions of a bank.

Foreign investment is encouraged, and it is common for the government to employ foreigners and foreign contractors. There is no constitutional objection to a foreign military presence or base although strict conditions could be imposed in such cases on religious grounds.

As an orthodox Islamic state, Saudi Arabia is bound to support the just cause of Muslims in foreign policy. The Saudis contribute a greater proportion of their gross national product in foreign aid than any Western nation, the United States included.

By contrast, Iran has established a fundamentalist Islamic state by revolutionary change and has formalized it with a written constitution.

The official introduction to the constitution of the Islamic republic of Iran, published in 1980, states: 'the fundamental characteristic of this revolution in relation other movements in Iran in the last century is its Islamic content'.

The constitution which was approved in a referendum by 98 per cent of the electorate represents the only attempt in modern times to define an Islamic state in writing. It is considered here as an expression of the abiding faith in the eternal nature of Islam.

The introduction acknowledges the contribution made by women in the solidarity which overthrew the old régime, and defines the Islamic method of government as 'the political objective of a nation that organizes itself in order to be able to move forward to its common ideal and objective, the movement towards God'. This is to be done by:

— Participation by all members of the community in all the stages of political decision making.
— Continuous and equitable leadership of the clergy.
— Allowing women greater liberties and an assumption of higher responsibilities.
— Setting up defence forces not to protect the country's frontiers, but to carry on a crusade in the name of God until the law of God is established throughout the world.
— Establishing a judicial system, consisting of judges fully acquainted with Islamic principles... remote from any unhealthy connection with other branches of government.
— The mass media being in the service of an Islamic culture.
— Working so that the present century will witness the victory of the deprived peoples of the world and the defeat of their oppressors.

All laws and regulations are to be on the basis of Islamic principles as laid down by the Guardian Council. The Leader of the community is to be a religious lawyer, and is accepted by the majority of the people. Among his duties are: selection of religious lawyers for the Guardian Council; appointment of the highest judicial authority; acting as supreme commander of the armed forces; the appointment of all bodies responsible for the security and defence of the State; and dismissing the President if considerations of the national interest make this necessary. The Assembly of Experts has the right to dismiss the Leader.

The President is next in authority to the Leader of the nation, elected by the direct vote of the nation for four years. The three powers of legislature, executive and judiciary are independent of each other and the President is the link between them all. All are under the authority of the Leader. The legislature is the National Assembly whose representatives are elected by universal suffrage and secret ballot. Its duration is six years. Zoroastrians, Jews, and Christians will have one representative each in the National Assembly. The National Assembly cannot make laws in contravention of the official religion of the country.

The official religion is Islam. Sunni sects are guaranteed freedom of religious expression, as are Jewish and Christian Iranians (within the framework of the law). The policy of the government towards non-Muslims is based on justice and goodwill. All citizens are to enjoy equal rights with no distinction of race, colour, language or creed; men and women have equality before the law. Provided the Islamic principles of the Republic are not flouted, political parties, groups, societies, guilds, and Islamic societies are legal.

The economy of the Islamic Republic is based on the public, private, and co-operative sectors. Private ownership is fully respected. The government will appropriate all money derived from usury, bribery, theft, gambling, and illicit trade practices, and either return it to its owner or divert it into State funds.

The army of the Republic is described as an Islamic army which is an army of the people. The establishment of military bases in Iran by foreign countries is prohibited. Foreign policy is based on independence, defence of the rights of all Muslims, non-alignment with dominating and aggressive powers, peaceful relations with non-destructive powers and the rejection of every type of aggression and domination of one nation by another. The Islamic Republic shall not withhold its support from deprived peoples of the world against their oppressors. Political asylum can be granted, but not to traitors.

It is clearly the intention of the new constitution that ultimate political power should lie with the religious authorities. The popular will is given familiar expression by election of the President and the National Assembly. The judge in this matter is the Guardian Council, half of which is appointed by the Leader and half by the judiciary. The judiciary is appointed by the Leader. Effectively, therefore, the Leader controls the National Assembly. He has power also to dismiss the President. Yet it cannot be said that the religious authorities, through the Leader, control policy by formulating it: this is the function of the civil government. The Islamic element is written into the constitution to run parallel with the elected parliament, and to check that no legislation is enacted which is un-Islamic. This will seem a contradiction to those weaned on the sovreignty of parliament, but it is quite consistent with the general principle that man is in need of divine guidance, and the particular Shi'ite belief that the *imams* are divinely inspired to provide it.

Although modern Iran, Saudi Arabia and the Gulf states have relied upon the ideology of Islam for their main political features, other Muslim states have not. Moreover, there is nothing in the constitution of Islam or in its development which has prevented the formation of a privileged class of power and wealth; nor has it played any role in

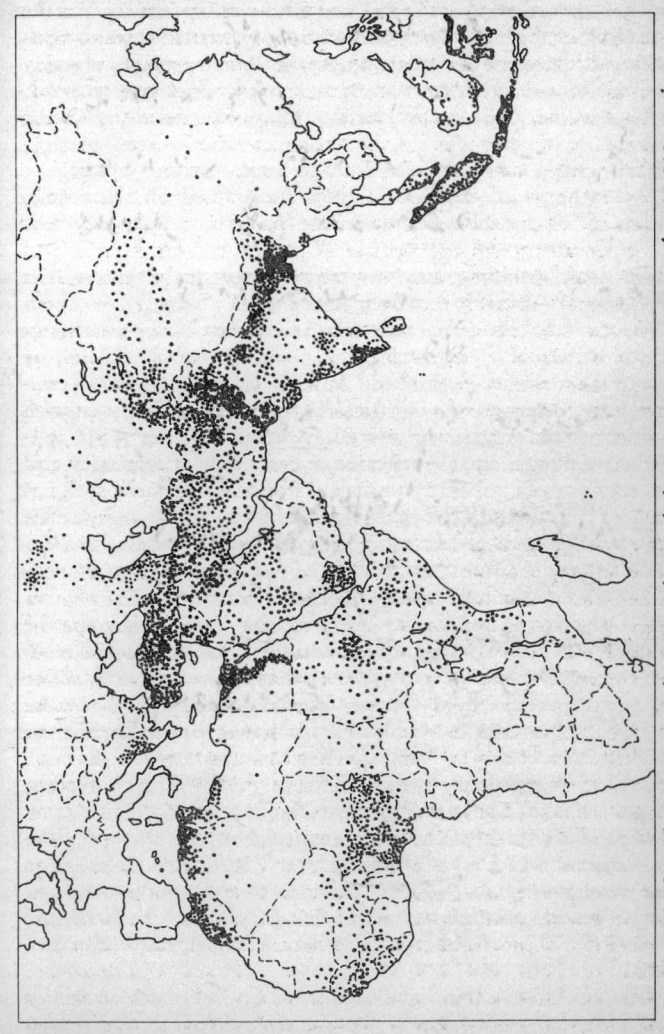

*Areas of Muslim presence at the present day, each dot representing approximately 100,000 people*

checking or modifying the penetration by capitalist economy in most modern states. Generally the development of the capitalist sector is low, and as a result individualistic traditions are not as deeply rooted as in the West, but this may be due more to Islam's colonial history than to its ideological stance. Similarly, the orientation of some Muslim states towards socialism has nothing to do with Islam, except in so far as the principle of Muslim brotherhood may serve to endorse a society without social privilege. But Islam had to look to Europe for its socialist ideas: to the French revolution for the idea that a democratic state is viable, and to the Russian revolution for the idea that a state without privileged classes is possible.

The alignment of political forces is changing very fast in Islam, particularly in the Middle East, and the pace of change has accelerated dramatically this century. Muslim states unite politically on certain religious and cultural issues, notably the integrity of Islamic territory and the sanctity of its holy places. Less solid and reliable is the unity of Muslim brotherhood, which can be fairly fragile in the face of territorial disputes or sectarian differences, and can result in Arab against Iranian and Sunni against Shi'ite. But both will normally sink their differences if the essential interests of Islam are threatened. A second factor supporting the solidarity of Islamic countries is the idea of Pan-Arab unity, a cultural identity based on language and a common historical heritage, and defined by Hafez Al-Assad of Syria as the struggle of the Arab peoples to achieve equality with the other peoples of the world. Its ultimate aim is the political unity of all Arabs.

But there are also issues which provoke conflict. Territorial disputes are as common in Muslim countries as anywhere else, especially if economic advantage is at stake. On social and economic issues alignment is likely to be decided by whether capitalist or socialist ideology holds power, and this factor, together with strength of nationalist feeling, will determine whether a country identifies with the Eastern or Western bloc, or with neither.

## Chapter 5
# Social Behaviour and Customs

The Islamic world of today is derived from seventh century Arabian society transformed by Mohammed's Message, adapted to the needs of one of history's great empires, and steeped in a thousand years of unchanging tradition. Although many of the customs and traditions can be traced back to ancient Arabia, the aim of Islam to determine the day to day course of every believer's life makes all accepted social customs in a sense Islamic. It is important to distinguish between social custom and social life. Social customs can be readily identified, but, because of the supremacy of the family in Islam, family and social life tend to be the same thing. Social life in a Western sense, embracing organizations, pastimes, clubs and other activities outside the home, exists only in a very limited form.

## Traditional Hospitality and Courtesy

Perhaps the custom for which Muslims, and certainly Arabs, are most renowned is their traditional hospitality. This special kind of hospitality has its origins in the desert. Thesiger writes:

> I pondered on this desert hospitality and compared it with our own. I remembered other encampments where I had slept, tents on which I had happened in the Syrian desert and where I had spent the night. Gaunt men in rags, hungry looking children had greeted me, and bade me welcome with the sonorous phrases of the desert. Later they had set a great dish before me, rice heaped around the sheep which they had slaughtered, over which my host poured liquid golden butter until it had flowed down onto the sand; and when I had protested, saying 'Enough, enough', had answered that I was a hundred times welcome. Their lavish hospitality always made me uncomfortable, for I had known that as a result of it they would go hungry for days. Yet when I left them they had almost convinced me that I had done them a kindness staying with them.

Perhaps the most famous story of all is the story of a Bedu *sheikh*, who was known as 'the host of the wolves', because whenever he heard a wolf howl around his tent he ordered his son to send a goat out in the desert, saying that he would have no-one call on him for dinner in vain.

The Bedu take traditional hospitality to even greater extremes and it is to them that most Arabs look with admiration. As inviolable as the bond between host and guest is the bond between travelling companions in the desert. This is perhaps the strongest bond of all, transcending even tribal and family loyalties. Tradition demands that the travelling companion, be he a Christian, Jew or slave, be defended against any attack, even from Muslims, and a travelling guest will be expected to do the same.

Traditional generosity takes many forms, and sometimes the giving of presents seems to an outsider out of proportion to the occasion. To admire effusively something belonging to one's host is not good manners. This can be taken as asking for it as a gift, and a host is quite likely to insist that his guest keeps it.

An essential function in social intercourse is the exchange of views, and there is an accepted way of doing this. In answer to the usual question 'What's your news?' the reply will never be that the news is bad. Regardless of what has actually happened, until the formalities have been observed, the coffee drunk and other refreshments taken, the real news will not be discussed. Bad luck, misfortune, or even disaster may have occurred, but the telling will come in allotted time. Coffee is made with great ceremony in the desert, and many people in the towns take a great interest in serving the wide variety of blends available. An attendant serves coffee from a metal pot into a small handleless cup. The cup should always be taken in the right hand. The attendant will wait and replenish the cup when it is empty. To take one or two cups full is polite, more than three is greedy. The only way to stop the cup being continually replenished is to shake it two or three times when offering it back to the attendant.

## Ritual Ablution, Bathing, Shaving

Ablution is described by Mohammed as 'the heart of faith and the key of prayer', and it is founded on the authority of the Koran:

> O believers, when you stand up to pray
> wash your faces, and your hands up to the
> elbows, and wipe your heads, and your feet
> up to the ankles.

(Koran 5:5)

Ablutions are absolutely necessary as a preparation for the ritual prayer, and detailed descriptions are laid down for washing all the prescribed parts of the anatomy. A specific prayer is recited at each stage of the proceedings. The ablution need not be performed before each of the five periods of prayer if the person is sure of having avoided every kind of impurity since the last ablution. Also laid down is the necessity to wash the whole of the body after certain periods of impurity. Brushing the teeth is a religious duty.

In all large mosques and most houses there are bathrooms both for ordinary purposes and for religious purification. According to Mohammed decency should be observed in bathing in public, and the body should not be exposed from the waist downwards.

The shaving of the beard is forbidden by tradition. The Prophet is recorded as saying: 'Do the opposite of the polytheists: let your beards grow long and clip your moustachios.' The shaving of the head is allowed providing the whole and not a part is shaven, for the Prophet said: 'Shave off all the hair of the head or let it alone'. It is the custom to shave the head in Afghanistan but not in other Islamic countries.

## Food and Taboos

All religions emanating from the Middle East contained food taboos. There are several messages in the Koran directed against the pagan eating habits, criticizing the pagans for not enjoying the good things provided by God. Subsequent tradition and later generations have interpreted and sometimes expanded the original prohibitions. Some members of the pious Wahhabi sect have interpreted the ban on intoxicants to include all drugs and stimulants, including tobacco, coffee and tea.

A Muslim always eats with his right hand and avoids, if possible, touching food with his left. This is because Satan is believed to eat and drink with the left hand. Further, the left is the unclean hand which he washes after relieving himself. It is bad manners to pass anyone anything or to accept anything with the left hand. There is normally water available for washing before a meal.

There are other rules connected with eating. A Muslim pronounces the name of God over the food, and he eats what is nearest to him. Muslims will be taught not to hurry to table in advance of others, not to eat quickly or in excess, and to eat one mouthful at a time. They will be told not to study the food, but to pay attention to the other people present. The underlying virtue is self-discipline based on the idea that hunger is preferable to gluttony, and that physical appetites must be controlled.

A man must sit properly to eat, and not recline. Traditionally, all eat with the right hand from a common plate (the Bedu still do), and from this derives the exhortation to eat what is nearest. But it is permissible to pick and choose the fruit. A meal should begin and end with salt. The sexes eat separately, although it is now not uncommon for non-Muslim European women to be included as guests.

It is not considered polite for Muslims to linger at table after meals. Many have the (to a Westerner) disconcerting habit of departing without ceremony when they have eaten their fill.

All unclean things, except intoxicants, may be used as medicine, or, in extreme necessity, as food. Food must not only be lawfully slaughtered and lawfully prepared, it must also be bought with money honestly gained.

Eating is a part of religion, so food is controlled by law and the rules connected with it are codified by the moralists. The Koran says that all good things on earth may be eaten, and that bad things are forbidden (7:157). Consequently, a Muslim distinguishes not between what is edible and what is not, but between food which is lawful and food which is forbidden. A Muslim must not eat pork, nor the flesh of an animal which has not had its throat cut whilst still alive. Most of them will not eat meat slaughtered by anyone other than a Muslim, or by a boy who is uncircumcised, although some Muslims will eat meat killed by a Christian. The consumption of blood is also forbidden. An exception to the general rule is found in the case of fish and locusts, in that they are permitted without ritual slaughter because they have no blood. The Shafi'i view is that all marine creatures are permitted, but other schools of law distinguish between species. There is considerable confusion in this and other areas between the various interpretations of the law, however, and custom varies considerably from place to place.

Lawyers have tried to classify those things which were not expressly forbidden, and have formulated the general rule that anything may be eaten of which the Arabs approve. If the Arabs give a strange animal the name of a clean animal, then it may be eaten; if there is no name for it in Arabic it may be eaten if it resembles a clean animal. Classes of unclean animals are birds and beasts of prey, crawling things, those animals which men are commanded to kill and those which they are forbidden to kill.

Hunting gives very wide scope for theological hair-splitting. If the hunter evokes the name of God when he releases his arrow or sets his hound on the game, the prey is lawful food. But if the dog was not trained the prey is lawful only if the hunter cuts its throat before it dies, which is invariably done.

# Drink and Alcohol

Prohibition was not part of Mohammed's original message. At first, in the Koran, we find wine praised as one of God's bounties to humanity:

> We give you to drink...
>     pure milk, sweet to drinkers.
> And of the fruits of the palms and the vines, you take
>     therefrom an intoxicant
>     and a provision fair.
>
> (Koran 16:67)

But excesses among the believers became too disruptive and interfered with prayer, and a later revelation took a different stance:

> They will question thee concerning
> wine, and arrow-shuffling.[1] Say 'In both
> is heinous sin, and uses for men,
> but the sin in them is more heinous
>     than the usefulness.
>
> (Koran 2:216)

This was seen as disapproval rather than prohibition, and wine was not forbidden until:

> O believers, wine and arrow-shuffling,
> idols and divining-arrows are an abomination,
> some of Satan's work; so avoid it; haply
>     so you will prosper.
>
> (Koran 5:92)

It is not surprising that alcohol was finally forbidden as once the ritual of praying five times a day became the hallmark of the faith, it is difficult to see a time when the effects of drinking would not be present during one of the prayers.

After the conquest of Mecca Mohammed is said to have refused a present of wine, and to have had the wine poured away. W Montgomery Watt[1] suggests that if the prohibition was on wine in the strict sense (as distinct from other intoxicants) it could be interpreted as a prohibition on trading with enemies, as wine was normally imported from Syria and Iraq. A more likely reason for the prohibition, however, is the connection of wine with *maysir* (arrow-shuffling) in the verses quoted above from the Koran. *Maysir* was a pagan practice by which 10 men bought a camel, slaughtered it and drew lots for the portions. It has been suggested that the Koranic objection to *maysir* was not that it was a form of gambling, but that it

1. Gambling.

was closely connected with the pagan religion. It seems possible, therefore, that the main reason for the prohibition of wine may have been some as yet unestablished connection with pagan religion.

There are laws to be observed when drinking. In tradition blessings should be uttered before and after drinking. The cup should be held in the right hand, but opinions differ on whether drinking is permitted standing up. It is forbidden to drink out of the mouth of a water skin, nor should one drink like a dog or in other unseemly ways, nor should one drink the whole in one draught. If drinking in company, the cup should be passed to the right. It is thought that knowledge in these matters distinguishes the believer from the infidel.

## Greetings

*Salam alekum* (peace be on you) is the traditional greeting, and the reply is *we alekum salam* (and on you be peace). This is still used universally in Arabic speaking countries, although other forms of greetings are used as Western influence grows.

*Salam alekum* is, according to the Koran, the greeting which is given to the blessed in Paradise or on entering Paradise. It is commanded to the Prophet:

> And when those who believe in Our signs come
> to thee, say, "Peace be upon you"

(Koran 6:154)

Shaking hands is encouraged by tradition, and is founded upon the express example of Mohammed himself. He is said to have remarked: 'There are no two Muslims who meet and shake hands but their sins will be forgiven before they separate'.

Salutation is a religious duty:

> And you are greeted with a greeting,
> greet with a fairer than it, or return it;
> surely God keeps a watchful count
>   over everything.

(Koran 4:88)

Mohammed is said to have instructed people on precisely who greets whom in what circumstances: 'The person riding must salute someone on foot, and the small must salute the larger, a person of higher degree the lower', and so on. He is also said to have remarked that 'the nearest people to God are those who salute you first'. By tradition a man does not salute a woman unless she is old, although the Prophet is said to have done so.

1. *What is Islam?*, Longman, 1979.

# Mosques

In the Message revealed by Mohammed, sanctuary for prayer was not a fundamental necessity; humility in the presence of God can be shown anywhere. In the beginning the *salat* (ritual worship) was performed in houses, or in any quiet place. The first mosque, literally a place for prostration, was built by the Prophet in Medina, but there was nothing sacred about its character. Its courtyard contained huts for his various wives, and believers and unbelievers went about freely inside. It was a general meeting place for Mohammed's followers; various tents and structures were put up at random, and in it all manner of affairs and business were conducted. Originally, therefore, the mosque was a place in which the believers assembled for prayer with the Prophet, and where he gave out regulations affecting the social life of the community. It had no specific form or content and what distinguished the earliest mosque from the Christian church, or the Meccan temple, was the absence of any specially dedicated ritual object. From this developed the general type of Muslim mosque, which, depending on circumstances, emphasized the place as a social centre or a place of prayer.

In the early centuries of Islam mosques were built in vast numbers and gradually their sanctity increased. The expression *Bait Allah* (House of God), which was first used only for the *Kaaba* came now to be applied to any mosque. As a result one could no longer enter a mosque at random as had been permitted in the time of the Prophet. The custom of taking off one's sandals before entering a mosque goes back to the early days of Islam. The believer, on entering, should place his right foot first and utter certain prayers, and when inside should perform two *rak'as* (a section of the *salat*). He should put on fine clothes for the Friday service, and rub himself with oil and perfume. It is evident from some *hadiths* that many did not want women in mosques, though it seems that no-one has any real authority to stop them entering. Other *hadiths* say that they should leave the mosque before the men, and sometimes a special part of the mosque was railed off for them. According to some, women must not enter the mosque during menstruation, and they should not be perfumed.

Although the mosque became a sacred place, it did not totally cast off its old character as a place of public assembly. Over the years it has been used as a place of business, and of shelter for strangers. As a result of spending the night in a mosque it naturally came about that people ate there, and in the end elaborate and formal banquets were held.

Although the *salat* can be performed anywhere, it is particularly meritorious to perform it in the mosque because this expresses adherence to the community. This is especially true of the Friday *salat*, which can only be performed in the mosque and is obligatory for every free male Muslim who has reached years of discretion.

An oath is particularly binding when taken in a mosque, and the contract of matrimony (but not the ceremony) is also often concluded there. The form of divorce effected by the *li'an* (disclaimer of paternity because of the wife's alleged adultery) takes place in the mosque.

The *qibla* is the direction of prayer, which in a mosque is marked by a niche in the wall facing the direction of Mecca. This niche is called the *mihrab*, and is often elaborately decorated. Every Friday mosque has a *minbar* — a kind of elevated pulpit located near the *mihrab*. In addition, mosques usually have a *kursi* — a wooden stand, a seat and a desk. The desk is for the Koran, and the seat for the reader. Carpets are often used to improve the appearance of mosques, and the custom of performing the *salat* on a carpet is ascribed by *hadith* to the Prophet himself. Later the chief mosques had the floor covered with a great number of sumptuous carpets, but some puritans rejected this fashion, preferring the bare ground. The Wahhabis still do.

Lighting is of particular importance, especially on ceremonial occasions, and has divine significance. In the month of Ramadan the level of illumination is increased, both inside and outside the building.

It was inherent in the character of Islam that religion and politics could not be separated. The same individual was ruler and chief administrator in the two fields, and the same building, the mosque, was the centre of gravity for both politics and religion. The Caliph was the appointed leader of the *salat*, and the appointed spokesman of the Muslim community, and as such he was the *imam*. The significance of the mosque for the State is therefore embodied in the *minbar*. When homage was first paid to Abu Bakr by those who had decided the choice of the Prophet's successor, he sat on the *minbar*. He delivered an address, and as the people paid homage to him he assumed the leadership. It was the same with the following Caliph, and this tradition was never abandoned. The Friday sermon (*khutba*) was delivered in the name of the Caliph or government and this is still so today. Gradually this system changed and the *imam* no longer represented a political office.

In modern times it is not always clear whether visitors are welcome to mosques and shrines, particularly those containing relics of the Prophet and of martyrs. It is necessary to approach a holy place with caution, and it will invariably be made clear whether unbelievers are permitted or not. According to strict religious dogma only the holy cities of Mecca and Medina are reserved exclusively for Muslims, and whether unbelievers are allowed in other holy places seems to be more a matter of local custom than religious ruling. Before crossing the threshold it is always necessary to remove one's shoes or to wear the overshoes supplied in some places.

## The Prophet's Tomb

The Prophet's tomb should not be visited in the *ihram* or pilgrim dress: men should not kiss it, touch it with the hand, or press the bosom against it as at the *Kaaba*, or rub the face with dust collected near the sepulchre. Those who prostrate themselves before it are held to be guilty of a deadly sin. To spit upon any part of the mosque, or to treat it with contempt, is held to be the act of an infidel.

## Dress

The Koran encourages Muslims to wear their good clothes when they go to the mosque.

According to *hadith* silk is not lawful for men to wear, but it is for women.[1] Men are prohibited from wearing gold or silver ornaments, but they are allowed a silver signet ring. Handkerchiefs must not be carried in the hand.

The Prophet said: 'Wear white clothes, because they are the cleanest and the most agreeable; and bury your dead in white clothes'. His own dress is said to have been extremely simple, and he never wore long robes to the ankle. It is said that a gold ring distracted his attention whilst praying, so he changed it for silver.

The 20th century has seen drastic changes in dress in most parts of the Middle East, largely as a result of Western influence. In most towns and cities men usually go in Western dress of some kind. An exception is in the Arabian peninsula, but even here, except for Oman and Yemen, the traditional turban has been abandoned in favour of a stylized form of traditional Bedu dress. These garments were normally worn only by the better off *sheikhs*, the ordinary Bedu for the most part being able to afford little more than simple shirts and loincloths. Nowadays stylized dress takes the form of a long shirt stretching to the ankles called a *thobe*, usually white in colour. A black *abba*, an overgarment stretching to the ground, is often worn over this by wealthy or important people. On the head is worn a kerchief called a *keffie* which is held in place by a cord round the head (*akal*), traditionally of camel hair. The headdress can by drawn across the face to shield it from sun and dust storms.

## Charms

The use of amulets or charms is very widespread in Islamic countries.

---

1. Further details of women's dress are to be found on page 140ff.

They are often carried in small bags, lockets or purses, worn around the neck or fastened to the arm or turban. As soon as they are 40 days old, children are given amulets which may take the crude form of a shell, a piece of bone, or be made of gold or silver. Inscribed on them can be found a bewildering variety of devices, from the names of angels and verses from the Koran to magic squares and figures of animals and men. Figurative inscriptions are rarely found among Arabs, although they are common in Persia and India. The hand, usually called the hand of Fatima, is a very popular symbol among Muslims. It is carried around the neck, often cut from gold or silver, and is said to revoke the evil eye. The Shi'ites interpret the fingers as the five saints: Mohammed, Ali, Fatima, Hasan and Husain. The talisman, still known as Solomon's Seal and worn by Muslims and Jews alike, represents a six pointed star. Strictly, only the name of God or verses from the Koran should be used for amulets.

Muslim theology, which forbids sorcery, tolerates the use of amulets. They are usually made by Dervishes, who belong to the various brotherhoods, and are only of value when they are received from their hands.

## Names

The teachings of Mohammed greatly influenced the names given to his followers. 'The best names given in the sight of God are Abd'allah (servant of God), Abdu'r-Rahman (the servant of the Merciful One)' ... 'You must not name your slaves Yasar (Abundance), Rabah (Gain), Najih (Prosperous), because if you ask for one of your servants and he is not present, it will mean that abundance, gain, prosperity are not in your home ... The vilest name you can give a human being is Maliku'l-amlak or King of Kings, because no-one can be such but God himself.'

Custom continued to use the names of ancient Arabia, but modified in accordance with the teachings of Mohammed. Single names are common, as Mohammed, Musa (Moses), Da'ud (David), Ibrahim (Abraham), Hasan, Ahmad. The prefix Abu means father of and Umm or Ummu means mother of. Thus Abu Issa is father of Jesus. Ibn means son of, as ibn Umar, son of Umar. Bizarre names are often found in desert regions, such as Abu Hurairah, the kitten's father. Sometimes trade names are used, for example, Hasan al-Hallaj, Hasan the dresser of cotton. Finally, people are sometimes called after their birthplace, as al-Bukhari, native of Bukharah.

Arabic names often undergo drastic modifications when the English tongue fails to get round them. For example, Saladin, the celebrated defender of Islam against the Crusades should properly be

Salahu'din, 'the peace of religion'.

## Entertainments

### Music, Singing and Dancing

There is an inconsistent and shifting balance between what strict religious authority lays down from time to time, and what popular custom evolves. The distinction comes out very clearly in the general area of public and private entertainment. Strict authorities believe that Islam forbids frivolous pleasures such as singing, dancing, playing and playing music of any kind. Yet it is evident that music is deeply rooted in the popular culture of North Africa, Lebanon and Egypt in particular, as well as Muslim South Africa and South East Asia. Furthermore, as if to compound the contradiction, many of the most talented and skilful performers are women.[1]

The general condemnation of music probably derives from the pious Wahhabi doctrine, and its influence on the Saud family. Certainly, the nearer one gets to the heartland of Islam, the weaker is the musical tradition, and in Saudi Arabia, where musical instruments were banned until a generation ago, it hardly exists at all.

Tradition has it that the Prophet was opposed to music, though the evidence for this is rather sketchy. This applies also to singing. It is generally held to be unlawful by Muslim theologians, and is based on a quotation from Mohammed: 'singing and hearing songs causes hypocrisy to grow in the heart, even as rain causes the corn to grow in the field'. The Sufis, who use music and song as an act of worship, say Mohammed only forbade songs of an objectionable character, but the general body of opinion is against them.

Dancing is also held to be unlawful by some authorities, although it is not forbidden either in the Koran or by tradition. According to Bukhari, the Prophet expressly permitted it on the day of the great festival. Those who hold dancing to be unlawful quote 'walk not in the earth exultantly' (Koran 17:39), although it is difficult to see how this can be used as a basis for prohibition. The Sufis dance as a religious exercise.

Whistling is mentioned in the Koran and the text is generally taken to mean that it is an idolatrous custom and is therefore forbidden.

---

1. The Egyptian singer, Umm Kulthum, was probably the most popular Arab in modern times, and her work was known and loved throughout the Middle East. Her death brought Cairo to a standstill, and mourners at her funeral outnumbered those for ex-President Nasser.

## Theatre

Similar attitudes prevail towards theatrical performances, although the reasons here are more complex. There is in Islamic law a specific prohibition on payment for performance. In addition the segregation of women creates a major problem for the theatre.

## Cinema, Broadcasting and Photography

The general prohibition on any kind of social change caused considerable problems with the introduction of photography, films, and wireless and television broadcasting. Islamic hostility to the making of images relates originally to the Koranic condemnation of the making and worshipping of idols. Subsequent religious authority in many places has expanded this prohibition to include all figurative illustration and art. The justification for this view is that God alone can create living things, and it is a sin and a blasphemy to attempt to imitate God. It is widely believed that on the Day of Judgement all those who have made images will be confronted by them and commanded to bring them to life. If they are not able to do so, they will be condemned to the fire of Hell. Consequently, in conservative Islamic countries it is quite rare to find any figurative art, what there is being confined to private houses. It is almost unknown in a public setting.

Outside Arabia the situation is different. Painting flourished under the Moghuls in India and in Persia the art of miniature painting and manuscript illustration is unsurpassed. Even so, it is quite common to see paintings with the faces despoiled by a subsequent religious purge. It is rare for a painting to show the face of the Prophet; the few artists who have painted scenes from Mohammed's life show him veiled.

All this has had consequences for photography and its development. Although photographs of heads of state are now common in all Muslim countries, this is a quite recent development. In Saudi Arabia and the Gulf States the photographing of women can provoke a hostile reaction. They were not allowed to be photographed, even for passports, until very recently, and many Muslim countries will still not ask for a woman's photograph for any official purpose. The situation is changing rapidly, but strangers taking photographs of people are sometimes unwelcome.

Wireless and television were eventually accepted because of their potential to spread the Message. Most of the air-time for Saudi television is devoted to the Koran and religious subjects, and any programme will be interrupted, without any transitional announcement, by the call to prayer.

Acceptance of public cinemas depends upon the strength of religious authority. There are none in Saudi Arabia, for example, but Cairo has many cinemas showing films from Europe and the USA, as well as local productions.

## Sport

Sport appears to be the only important activity for which Islam does not lay down any special requirements, and every Muslim country seems to have adopted without qualification the sports suited to its climate and temperament. Sport is generally encouraged at all levels for both sexes, from participation in schools and colleges to international competition. The only restriction in some countries is that placed on women performing in public, and on those very few sports or games for mixed sexes.

No Muslim countries seem to have objections (except perhaps political ones) to joining all kinds of international sporting bodies, including the Olympic movement.

## Animals

In Islam a dog is an unclean beast, and 'dog' is used as a term of abuse, especially when referring to unbelivers. According to the *hadith*, food which has come into contact with dogs becomes impure, and water may no longer be used for ritual purification. Vessels which have been licked by a dog must be cleaned several times and dogs make the *salat* worthless when they come into the vicinity. It is believed that angels will not enter a house where there is a dog, and that Satan occasionally appears in the form of a black dog. It is permissible to keep dogs only for hunting, herding and watching, but it is said that 'whoever possesses a dangerous dog keeps good fortune away from his house'.

Most people believe that when a dog howls without apparent cause in the neighbourhood of a house, it forbodes death to one of the residents; for the dog, they say, can distinguish the form of Azrael, the angel of death, hovering over the doomed abode, whereas man's spiritual sight is dim because of his sins.

For thousands of years the Arabs have domesticated the camel, and without it human survival would not have been possible in most of Arabia and the surrounding desert regions. In the Koran the animal given to man to ride upon is mentioned as an example of God's wisdom and kindness. Camels are a lawful sacrifice at great festivals and on other occasions, and *zakat* is payable on them. In law a driver is responsible for any damage done by the animals in his charge.

According to a *hadith*, Mohammed said: 'Cats are not impure, they keep watch around us'.

The Koran describes cattle (the title of the sixth *sura*) as being the gift of God:

> It is God who appointed for you the cattle,
> some of them to ride
> and some for you to eat.

(Koran 40:79)

Mohammed's affection for horses is said to have been very great. The qualities of horses are much discussed in the *hadith*, even to the point of describing ideal colouring. It is laid down that in taking a share of plunder a horseman is entitled to a double share.

Bestiality is said by Muslim jurists to be the result of a most vitiated appetite and of the utmost depravity. It is unlawful but there is no *hadd*, only a discretionary punishment. According to law the beast should be killed and, if it is a lawful species, burnt.

## Deportment

The traditions take some pain to explain the precise manner in which the Prophet walked, sat, slept and got up, but the accounts are not always consistent with each other. As a result, what appeared to be ordinary bodily functions turn out to have religious, if not legal, connotations. Tradition is very particular about sitting. Muslims must sit on the ground in places of public worship. In social gatherings superiors always sit higher in the order. It is bad manners to present the soles of one's feet towards a person in the company. There is even an order in which the shoes must be taken off (the right one first). Muslims are urged to sleep with their heads in the direction of Mecca. Some authors give ethical advice on how to walk and when to kneel, how to spit, and even how to blow your nose. But the overriding message is that the individual should conduct himself in public so as not to cause inconvenience or disgust to others, and in private so as to acquire good habits.

It is considered a duty to repond to a sneeze and say something like 'God be praised', which is similar to the Jewish custom. Mohammed said: 'God loves sneezing and hates yawning'.

The Prophet adopted certain ancient practices called *fitrah* (nature) which were common practice before his time. There are ten qualities of the Prophet: clipping the moustache so that it is clear of the mouth, not cutting the beard, cleansing the teeth, cleansing the nostrils with water at the ablutions, cutting the nails, cleansing the finger joints, pulling out hairs under armpits, shaving the pubic hair, washing with water after passing urine, and cleansing the mouth at ablution.

## Vices and Virtues

In summary, then, a pious Muslim has a formidable list of social vices to avoid, and a daunting list of social virtues to cultivate.

According to strict custom Islam forbids frivolous pleasures (such as singing or music making), slander, lying, meanness, coarseness, intrigue, treachery, disloyalty in friendship, disavowal of kinship, ill nature, arrogance, boasting, sly scheming, insult and obscenity, spite and envy, inconstancy, aggressiveness and tyranny. According to Mohammed God has included in Islam the finest qualities and noblest virtues which are: kindliness and generosity in dealings between man and man, accessibility, free giving of what is lawful, feeding the poor, the dissemination of peace, visiting a sick Muslim, escorting the bier of a dead Muslim, being a good neighbour, honouring the aged, giving food and accepting invitations to eat with others, granting forgiveness, making peace between men, open handedness, generosity and liberality, being the first to give greeting and restraining one's anger.

A believer's word is his bond, and a Muslim must keep his promise. The Prophet is said to have hated untruths and although he was ready to accept cowards and misers as believers he refused to regard a liar as a true Muslim. Liars were classed in the same category as promise-breakers, men of bad faith and hypocrites. These are constantly denounced in the Koran, but lying as such is nowhere specifically mentioned. There may be circumstances under which it is justified, or even preferred to the truth, as, for example, where an innocent man might come to grief or danger if the truth were told.

*Chapter 6*
# Family and Domestic Life

### Family Structure

The family is the only group based on kinship or affinity which traditional Islam recognizes in law, and it is the bedrock of Islamic society. It is not surprising, therefore, that it should remain the focus and pivot of a Muslim's life. About a third of the Koran is devoted to family matters and relationships, and the importance of the family in Islam can hardly be exaggerated. The only other group recognized by tradition is the brotherhood of believers; all others, whether social or political, have been discouraged or forbidden, and this is still the case in conservative Islamic countries. Islam is the only religion which forbids the formation of groups and organizations, the justification being that it is a complete way of life, and by definition needs no man-made accessories.

The Muslim marriage is a contract in which both parties have rights and duties. It is a husband's duty to provide for his family, to treat his wives equally, and to keep them in the style to which they are accustomed. It is a woman's duty to look after her family and her husband, though not his house guests. She has control of the household, and although the religious education of the children is a joint responsibility, she often adopts a leading role here too. Grandmothers are often important in this respect. There is no community of property. A wife by law retains her own property, including her marriage dower, and has complete freedom of dealing. In rural communities she is expected to help with the cultivation of land and the care of animals. Conflicts arising from a disparity of wealth, or from expectation in terms of marital duties, are largely avoided by arranged marriages which aim at compatibility in social class.

The Koran in fact created a revolution in the status of women. Before this the women of Arabia had had no legal rights before the law. For the first time in the history of Oriental legislation the principle of women's rights was recognized.

> Women have such
> honourable rights as obligations, but
> their men have a degree above them.
>
> (Koran 2:228)

And Mohammed said: 'Ye men, ye have rights over your wives, and your wives have rights over you'.

Traditionally, the qualities a Muslim looks for in his wife are chastity, contentment, respectfulness, submissiveness, and a humouring nature.

According to the *sharia*, a husband is not guardian over his wife except in terms of the contractual obligations of marriage. But if he does not carry out the basic duties, he is liable to imprisonment for neglect of maintenance. The evidence of a husband concerning his wife is not accepted by the Sunnis, but is allowed in Shi'ite law. Islamic law demands that a husband shall treat his wives equally and reside equally with each of them, unless one forgoes her right in favour of another wife.

A husband is legally bound to maintain his wife and her domestic servants, whether she and her servant belong to the Muslim faith or not. This is a contractual obligation of the husband, and lasts as long as the wife is subjected to the marital controls. The maintenance of a wife includes everything connected with her support and comfort, including her right to claim a home for her own exclusive use, the scale of which is consistent with her husband's means. In practice, however, these duties vary considerably from place to place.

According to tradition Mohammed said: 'That is the most perfect Muslim whose disposition is best, and best of you is he who behaves best to his wives' and 'Admonish your wives with kindness, because women were created from a crooked bone of the side; therefore, if you wish to straighten it, you will break it, and if you let it alone it will always be crooked.'

## Fathers

In the Sunni law of inheritance a father receives one sixth of his son's or grandson's property. If the son dies unmarried without children the father takes the whole. According to the law of retaliation a father cannot be punished for taking the life of his son, because, as Hanifa has said, 'as the parent is the official cause of his child's existence it is not proper that the child should require or be the occasion of his father's death'. It is forbidden for a son to harm his father, even if in the army of an enemy, or to throw a stone at him if he is convicted of unlawful intercourse. In the law of evidence the testimony of a father brought against his child is not admitted in a court of law.

## Mothers

Kindness towards a mother is required by the Koran. 'Be kind to parents, and the near kinsman' (Koran 4:40). Mothers cannot be compelled to nurse their children, but they are not allowed to move them to a strange place without their husband's permission.

## Children

While the Koran does not prescribe rituals relating to birth, or training and instruction of the young, the subject is frequently referred to in tradition.

After the birth of a child, when he has been properly washed and dressed, he is carried by the midwife to the assembly of male relatives and friends. Someone present then recites the *azan* (call to prayer) in the infant's right ear and the *iqamah* (the second call to prayer) in the left ear. The Maulawi[1] then chews a little date fruit and inserts it into the infant's mouth, a custom said to have been founded on the example of Mohammed. After this alms are distributed and prayers recited for the health and prosperity of the child. According to tradition the amount of silver given as alms should be the same weight as the hair on the infant's head: the child's head being shaved for this purpose. After this the house is open to friends and neighbours to bring presents and congratulations.

The child should be named on the seventh day, the name being taken from either some member of the family, or saint, or some name suggested by the astrological situation. Also on the seventh day Mohammed established a ceremony of sacrifice to God. In the name of the child two goats are sacrificed for a boy, and one for a girl. The goats must be under one year old and without any blemish. The animal is dressed and cooked and, while it is being eaten, the assembled offer a prayer, although modern custom varies.

The mother is ritually purified on the 40th day, after which she is free to go about as usual. As soon as the child is able to talk, or when he has attained the age of four years four months and four days he is taught the *Bism'illah*, the first words of the Koran: *Bism'illah ir-Rahman ir Rahim* (in the name of God the Merciful, the Compassionate).

Children, and particularly, sons, are considered a blessing. There is no hierarchy of birth; the eldest son enjoys no privilege of either treatment or inheritance. Older children are expected to set an example,

---

1. From *maulà*, a term generally used for a learned man.

and to teach the younger ones such things as the ritual prayer.

Children are taught what is expected from them, and what they can expect in return. They learn to respect older people, to be helpful to neighbours and generous to guests. As a result of the strong family bond, crime rates generally are very low in most places, and non-existent in others. If necessary families will act together to defend their rights; and their commitments, such as marriage and funeral expenses, are treated as a joint responsibility.

In pre-Islamic times the principle ruled that 'the child follows the bed' — that is, its paternity was reckoned to be the husband of its mother at that time. Bearing in mind that marriage and divorce were both frequent and swift, paternity was frequently not given to the natural father. Islam modified the principle by laying down that a pregnant woman, when widowed or divorced, could not re-marry until the child was born. As a general rule a child born in wedlock is considered legitimate, and is recognized by the husband, providing it is born more than six months after cohabitation begins. A husband may, but is not obliged to, acknowledge a child born in less than six months. The legitimacy of a child born after cohabitation ends varies with various sects. For the Shi'ites the time limit is 10 months, Hanafi law makes the limit two years, and the Shafi'ite and Malikite codes provide for a period of four years.

The law that the child follows the bed is linked with the *hadith* stating that 'the adulterer gets nothing'. A child therefore belongs to its mother's husband even if he is not the natural father. In these circumstances, Shi'ite law gives paternity to the husband unless he disallows it formally by pronouncing the *li'an* (see page 108) against his wife. This may be withdrawn later if the husband wishes to acknowledge paternity. In any case, an adulterer cannot claim paternity of a child.

In general, therefore, Islam places few obstacles in the way of recognizing the legitimacy of children. Only if a Muslim man knows he has no right to a woman as his wife or as his concubine, or if a Muslim woman marries a non-Muslim are the children of such unions declared illegitimate. Consequently, at the present day, except in Iran, 'bastard' will very rarely be heard as a term of abuse, but 'son of a whore' is not uncommon.

By a curious anomaly in Islamic law, kidnapping a freeborn child does not incur the *hadd* punishment of amputation, because a free person is not property. However, the scholar Abu Yusuf adds that if the child has jewellery or other valuables attached to him worth more than 10 *dirhams*, then property is violated, and amputation is the punishment. Amputation is also inflicted for stealing an infant slave, because a slave is property.

Although in Islamic law of inheritance all sons share equally, in cases of chieftainship or monarchy, the eldest son normally has perference; but his is not automatic and he must demonstrate that he is equal to and fit for the position. Very often when the eldest son is passed by, because he has not satisfied the community of his suitability, a younger brother is selected as ruler. If none of the children is considered suitable to inherit the leadership or the crown, a brother might be selected for the position.

In the case of orphans, under the *sharia* law the burden falls upon the widow to manage as best she can. The tribe will not have more than a general obligation to provide for the destitute, and a new husband is under no compulsion to feed extra mouths if he does not want to. Charitable and pious foundations exist to take charge of children without parents or kinsmen, and they then become a charge on the community.

A male child is not required to observe all the customs of the Muslim law until he has reached puberty, but it is the duty of the parents and guardians to teach him the prayers as soon as he has been circumcised. When a child has finished reciting all of the Koran once through the occasion is marked by the scholar presenting his tutor with presents.

The Koran lays down few regulations on bringing up children. Where parents are married and cohabiting they are jointly responsible for rearing their children, the father providing the material necessities, and the mother taking charge of their physical well-being and religious training. In the case of a dispute the mother has custody of children during their infancy. The exact period of custody is not specified in the Koran and the various schools of law have different ideas on the subject. The Shi'ites, for example, specify two years in the case of a boy, and seven years for a girl. The Shafi'ite school, on the other hand, specified seven years as a general rule, at which age the child is considered to be able to discriminate and can choose with which parent it wishes to live. However, the mother in such cases must be respectable, stable, and unmarried.

The extended family is as important as the family unit. It is an important day when a son is married, because the family is increased by the addition of a daughter-in-law, who is received by, and under the protection of, the bridegroom's family. Similarly, when a daughter is married, she passes into the care of another family, although she does not change her family name. This is retained as a symbol of her status in the new situation, and as a link with her blood relations, to whom in the last resort she can turn for protection.

Unlike the Christian and Jewish religions, there are in Islam no religious ceremonies connected with birth, marriage, death, circumcision, attainment of adulthood, or even commitment to and acceptance of the faith. Such ceremonies as exist are prescribed by custom, rather than religion, although prayers may be said, and an *imam* might take part in the various ceremonies.

## Birth

Although there is no ceremony connected with birth there are legal definitions relating to childbirth. According to Hanafi law a married woman's claim to motherhood of a child must be supported by the testimony of one woman. In the case of a father, his testimony alone is accepted.

The testimony of a midwife alone is valid in respect of birth, but legal parentage is established by the fact of the mother of the child being the wife of the husband. According to *hadith*, if the woman is in her *idda* (suspended divorce), the testimony of the midwife with respect to birth is not enough. The evidence of two men, or one man and two women, is required.

Contraception is a relatively modern social concern, and there is no guidance in either the Koran or the *Sunna* for modern Muslims. However, in recent times various religious authorities[1] have considered the question and have concluded that contraception is permissible under Islamic law. Although one of the functions of marriage is procreation, this is conditional upon the availability of the means to bear the cost of a child's education and training, so that he can be properly brought up, and not develop anti-social ways. There are genuine traditions which allow methods for restricting procreation, and these are seen as no different from the use of pharmaceutical contraceptive methods. Equally, it is not considered right that pregnancies should injure the health of a woman or weaken her unduly.

Mohammed is often quoted as saying that 'the greatest catastrophes are many children and meagre sustenance', and this is often used as a slogan in Islamic family planning organizations. The fact that the Prophet allowed coitus interruptus has encouraged the legal schools to sanction it, but the Maliki school insists that the wife must agree to this procedure, whatever her age. Similarly in Iraq, Pakistan, Afghanistan and Syria, the Shi'ite Ga'afareyz condone this method if it is agreed with the wife at the time of marriage. According to the Prophet withdrawal should not be practised with a free woman unless she agrees.

Muslims distinguish abortion from contraception, because it is an assault on life and therefore could be a criminal act; they believe that it

---

1. The Grand Mufti of Jordan, December 1964, and the Fatwa Committee, Al Azhar University, March 1953.

is a crime after 'quickening of life' has taken place — that is when the movement of the foetus can be felt. This is consistent with tradition which has special rules concerning an assault on a pregnant woman and subsequent damage to a foetus. After the quickening as taken place, a foetus has human rights in law including the rights of inheritance and blood money. However, if the mother's life is endangered by the pregnancy, the lesser evil is to be allowed and the mother must be saved. The only other ground for abortion appears to be if there is a strong possibility that the baby will be born deformed. The underlying assumption, therefore, is that the foetus has a right to live, but that it is not an absolute right.

Throughout the Middle Ages it was common for Muslim physicians to advise their patients on contraception. One of them, Avicenna (ibn Seena) (died 1037 AD), in his *Laws of Medicine* described 20 methods of contraception, most of which had apparently been used for hundreds of years.

The attitude of modern Islam towards birth control varies according to population size, birth rates and economic and material resources. In Kuwait and Saudi Arabia contraception is advised only for medical reasons. In Tunisia and Egypt[1] the governments officially approve and encourage birth control. This is true also of Pakistan and Turkey, and the reasons for adopting the policy are economic rather than religious.

A clear distinction is made between contraception and permanent sterilization, which all authorities agree is not permitted.

## Circumcision

Circumcision of both males and females seems to have been common in early Arabia, and the custom was absorbed by Islam. It is not mentioned in the Koran, but a *hadith* describes it as *sunna* (traditional, customary) for men and honourable for females.

For males the operation is described as cutting off the whole of the skin which covers the glans, and for females as cutting off a small part of the skin in the highest part of the genitals to expose the clitoris[2]. The age at which circumcision takes place varies according to local custom. In *hadith* it is said that Ibrahim (Abraham) was circumcised at the age of 80. In Mecca children are circumcised between the age of three and seven years, girls without festivities, and boys with great ceremony. In Egypt boys are, or were, circumcised at the age of five or six years. Sometimes the operation is performed in groups of children, the

1. Egypt currently has one of the world's biggest growth rates, projected to double within 30 years.
2. This operation is not unknown in the West.

richest family paying the whole cost. The formal procession is led by a boy who is, obscurely, dressed with ceremony and pomp as a girl. It is common for the local barber to perform the operation. In North Africa a child born with a short foreskin is considered a great blessing.

In the circumcision of females it is particularly important to distinguish between what Islam prescribes and what is accorded to local custom. The *Shorter Encyclopaedia of Islam* gives the following translation of al-Nawawi (1283AD):

> Circumcision is obligatory according to al-Shafi, *Sunna* according to Malik and the majority .... As regards females, it is obligatory to cut off a small part of the skin in the highest part of the genitals .... The second view within the limits of our school is that circumcision is allowed, but not obligatory.

This description is a far cry from the mutilation practised in some countries up to modern times. In Egypt, according to Nawal El Saadawi, an Egyptian woman doctor, circumcision meant the amputation of the whole or part of the clitoris of young girls in a primitive operation. In the Sudan it was even more drastic, with the removal of all the external genital organs: the clitoris and the inner and outer lips (*labia majora* and *minora*). The wounds were then stitched up. No-one seems able to give a reason for these rituals, and certainly no justification can be found in any of the legal manuals of Islam. In recent years these practices have declined.

The treatment of circumcision in general does not have a prominent place in the books of Islamic law, but importance and value is still attached to it in popular opinion. Its merits and demerits are still contested by physicians: some consider it a barbaric ritual and others a hygienic operation, some believe it heightens sexual gratification, and others that it diminishes it.

## Collective Responsibilities

An individual is responsible to the family for social behaviour, and the family is responsible to society for the behaviour of the individual. If an individual does harm, the family will be held responsible for the consequences, and if wrong is done to an individual, his family will automatically support him. This has important consequences, particularly in respect of upholding the law. The violence and lawlessness of Western cities is a source of continuing amazement to Muslim communities. They are surprised the police cannot find lawbreakers, when they know that in their own community they would be found and punished within a few days. Their young men are more afraid of what the family will do or say than they are of the police. An individual is therefore very cautious in his dealings and behaviour because it will be subject to the scrutiny of his relatives and his community, all of whom will be involved in any wrongdoing. The reputation of an individual man or woman reflects upon the family.

If trouble occurs between families, there are in some countries customary procedures to be followed as well as legal ones. For example, in the case of a road accident in which a boy is knocked down, even if the police vindicate the driver this will be irrelevant so far as the driver's family is concerned. The first thing for them to do is to visit the boy's family and arrange a truce, so that the boy's family will not retaliate to restore family honour. If the boy dies, the driver's family has to pay a fixed sum in compensation for accidental death. If he recovers, the truce ends and there is a ceremonial feast which representatives of both families attend. The driver's family will give thanks to God for the boy's wellbeing, and the boy's family will express forgiveness, acknowledging that it was an accident. Documents are signed to say that peace is restored.

The ultimate responsibility of the family, then, is to defend its honour. This includes the way all members behave in society and particularly includes the chaste behaviour of its women. A family is responsible for the esteem with which it is regarded, and it is the unavoidable duty of its men to defend and preserve the honour of the family.

If family honour is violated the shame attached to it can be a harder punishment to bear than any prescribed by the law. Even in cases of *hadd* offences, the pressure of social opinion can not only modify the punishment, but also inflict an alternative which is meant to be as severe. For example, the legal penalty for unlawful intercourse in Oman is stoning to death, or one year's imprisonment and the accompanying shame. In North Yemen, if stoning is ordered, the stones are always pebbles, cast from a distance where they will inflict only shame.

## Respect for Elders

In Islam there is a profound respect for knowledge and experience. As these qualities are normally associated with age, respect for one's elders is deeply ingrained. This veneration derives in part from the fact that Islam is a legalistic system which necessitates knowing the rule for each occasion. Equally, the stability of the family depends on, among other things, stable judgement and guidance, and both of these considerations establish the elderly in a privileged position.

A sense of hierarchy is particularly strong in the family. A younger person will automatically rise to his feet when an older relative comes into the room. If he wears a traditionally cut *thobe* (see page 109) with loose sleeves he will hide his hands as a sign of deference.

The respect for knowledge is demonstrated by the power and authority of the *ulema* (religious scholars), who derive their position from their knowledge of the Koran and *Sunna*, or, in the case of the Shi'ites, from the *imams*, on whom the community relies for guidance in all aspects of human behaviour.

## Neighbours

The Sunni define neighbours as those who worship in the same mosque. The Shi'ites generally refer to a neighbour as one living in close proximity (40 cubits)[1], whilst others maintain that the term covers the occupants of 40 houses on either side. This can be important in matters of real estate. A neighbour has the next right after a partner in the sale and purchase of houses and land. The Prophet laid down that a neighbour has a superior right to purchase a house (next to an immediate relative), and this applies also to land. If the neighbour is absent the owner must wait until his return before selling.

The Koran urges kindness to neighbours, and tradition has it that 'he is not a perfect Muslim who eats his fill and leaves his neighbour hungry'.

According to tradition there was a man who once said to the Prophet 'There is a woman who worships God a great deal but she is very abusive to neighbours'; the Prophet replied 'She will be in the fire'. The man then told him 'But there is another woman who worships little and gives but little in alms, but she does not annoy her neighbours with her tongue'; the Prophet said 'She will be in Paradise'.

## Houses and Homes

Muslim family relationships, whether through observance of the religious laws or through custom or both, have a direct bearing on the layout and design of houses.

In the first place, a typical Muslim will be keen to live in very close proximity to the homes of his brothers and other close male relatives. The private and secluded nature of family life makes it an advantage for members of an extended family to be readily accessible. If a man is away from home, or some misfortune befalls him, he is secure in the knowledge that there is a trusted man on hand to protect and look after his family.

Secondly, houses and apartments were, and are, designed to suit the way of life of the family. There are separate entrances for the men and

---

1. A cubit is the length of a forearm, ie about 18-22 inches.

for the women and children. In rural districts, and in some suburban settings, there are often separate huts, or buildings for the two parts of the family. If the family is rich, there might well be separate palaces within a common enclosure or estate. The nature of the establishment and the degree of luxury does not alter the principle. The men's apartment will always have a *majlis* (literally 'a meeting of the parties'). In prosperous households, each adult male will have his own *majlis*. The *majlis* is used for entertaining relatives, guests, and business acquaintances. The favourite time for gathering is after sunset, and normally there are regular times at which the heads of families, or leaders of the community can be found in their *majlis*. This means that families and friends can congregate regularly, to discuss the events of the day, and the nearer the group is to its Bedu origins, the more the gossip will hinge on the minutest detail of events. In accordance with Islamic tradition and tribal custom, there is little or no formal ceremony in the *majlis*, although politeness and courtesy are indispensable. The courtesies are exactly the same whether a king is entertaining a head of state, or a *sheikh* is listening to a grievance from his poorest follower. Provided there is physical room, access is readily available to all. Even a total stranger will be entertained, and he will not be asked his business: he must broach the subject first in his own time.

The traditional style of furnishing was described by Sir Richard Burton[1] in the 1880s:

> The *diwan* — it must not be confused with the leathern perversion which obtains that name in our club smoking room — is a line of flat cushions ranged around the room...varying in height unto the fashion of the day...It should be about three feet in breadth and slope very gently from the outer edge towards the wall for the greater convenience of reclining. Cotton stuffed pillows with chintz for summer and silk for winter are placed against the wall and can be moved to make a luxurious heap. A seat of honour is denoted by a small square cotton stuffed silk coverlet placed in one of the corners which the position of the windows determines, the place of distinction being on the left of the host.

The reference to the windows relates to their positioning to give efficient cross ventilation of air. Before the invention of air-conditioning, window sills were normally built to the floor for the benefit of the *majlis'* reclining occupants. Nowadays modern chairs are normally used.

A dining room is usually located next to a *majlis* offering direct access. Adjacent will be found facilities for guests to perform ablutions before and after a meal. In a prosperous household, living accommodation for guests is attached to the *majlis*.

---

1. *Personal Narrative of a Pilgrimage to Al Madinah and Meccah,* Dover Publications, NY, 1887.

The women's entrance gives access to the family rooms, the kitchen and the bedrooms. Access is forbidden to this part of the house to all men who are not close relatives. *Haram* is Arabic for forbidden, and *harem* is a derivation. Gardens and outdoor spaces are normally surrounded by high walls.

In a traditional house there are no rooms set aside specifically for sleeping. Male visitors and friends will sleep in the verandas, or in the *diwan* on the first floor. It is also common to sleep on the roof in hot weather, and wide staircases are often built up to this level so that beds can be carried out. Masonry parapets at roof level are often built to screen the roof from public view, but are normally perforated to allow the cross circulation of air. Apart from being used for sleeping the flat roofs are often used for a variety of household purposes such as drying corn, linen and fruit.

Houses with wind towers are a Persian invention, but can often be found on the Arabian side of the Gulf. The wind towers project above roof level and are so designed to catch a breeze from any direction and direct it down into the dwelling. This system of natural ventilation is quite sophisticated, and is controlled by a series of opening shutters set in the external walls, which may be adjusted to give the best conditions at different times of the day.

It is distinctly uncivil behaviour to enter a Muslim's house without his permission, as both the Koran and tradition stress. It is, strictly speaking, necessary for a man to ask permission of his mother to see her, even if they live in the same household.

Mohammed had very firm views about money and real estate. He is reported to have said 'verily the most unprofitable thing that eateth up the wealth of a believer is building'.

## Death and Burial

Death occurs at a time appointed by God. Precise preparations are made to prepare the body for the wait for the Resurrection and the Day of Judgement.

When a Muslim is dying, after having made his will, a learned reader of the Koran is sent for to recite *sura 36*, in order that, by hearing it, the spirit of the man might experience an easy release.

The Koran says nothing about funerals, but the manuals of law describe the ritual in minute detail. As soon as a Muslim is dead, he is laid on a stretcher with his head in the direction of the *qibla* (direction of prayer), after which begins the ritual washing. The body is then wrapped in shrouds, the number and nature of which depends upon custom, but the colour is generally white. After this the *salat* for the dead is performed which includes an additional prayer for the deceased and must be meticulously followed. This ceremony takes place in the house of mourning, not in the mosque or in the graveyard (which is considered too polluted for the sacred book). The nearest relative is an appropriate person to recite the service, but it is usually said by the family *imam*. It is forbidden to perform the *salat* to an unbeliever, nor may he be washed, but he must be buried. A martyr is not washed, in order not to remove traces of blood which are the hallmark of his martyrdom; nor is it necessary to pray for his soul. Keeping watch over a dead body is not prescribed in the manuals of law, although it is common in Egypt. Tradition disapproves of the old Semitic custom of burning a light by the side of the deceased. The dead are seldom interred in coffins, but this is not forbidden.

The burial service was established by Mohammed and varies little from place to place, although the ceremonies connected with the funeral procession vary according to local custom. In Egypt and other places, for instance, the male relations and friends of the deceased precede the corpse, whilst the female mourners follow behind. In India and Afghanistan women do not usually attend the funeral, and relatives and friends walk behind. There is a tradition among some Muslims that no-one should precede the corpse, as the angels of death go before it.

The stretcher is carried to the burial place by men, even when the deceased is a woman. The corpse of a woman must be hidden from the eyes of the public. Whether bystanders stand up at a funeral procession depends upn the school of law. Some do in the presence of the angels of death, and others do not because it is a Jewish custom. It is recommended to follow a funeral procession, but it is forbidden to do so on horseback, since the angels of death go on foot.

It is considered meritorious to carry the bier, but unlike Christians who customarily walk slowly to the grave, Muslims carry out the procession quickly. Mohammed is reported to have said that it is good to carry the dead quickly to their graves so that the righteous person arrives sooner to happiness; if the deceased was unrighteous, it is well to put wickedness away from one's shoulders. There is merit in attending a funeral whether it be for a Muslim, Jew or Christian.

The burial itself is performed by an odd number of men; the body is laid down in the grave with the head in the direction of the *qibla*, after which the bystanders each cast three handfuls of earth on the grave. Either on the deathbed or in the grave, the confession of faith is recited into the deceased's ear. This is to remind him to give the right answer when the angels interrogate him in his grave.

The manuals of law specifically disapprove of any ornamenting of graves, even by an inscription, although the location of the head may be marked by a stone or piece of wood. In spite of this prohibition, elaborate tombs have often been constructed out of popular esteem especially over the graves of saints. The grave of a woman is covered with a garment.

On the third day after the burial it is usual for relatives to visit the grave and to recite selections from the Koran. If they can afford it, they pay learned men to recite the whole of the Holy Book. During mourning the relatives do not wear any bright clothing nor do they change any soiled garments.

Before and after the burial, visits of condolence are paid, and the manuals of law give detailed prescriptions on exactly what one should say. It is recommended to hold a banquet after the burial, but not on the same day. On this occasion passages from the Koran are recited, and the good works of the deceased are remembered.

Suicide is not mentioned in the Koran but it is forbidden in tradition. Mohammed said 'whosoever shall kill himself shall suffer in the fire of Hell'. It is also related that Mohammed refused rites to a suicide, but it is nonetheless usual in Islam for them to be performed. He is said also to have refused the *salat* unless debts of the deceased had already been paid. In law therefore the mourners are recommended to settle debts quickly. The *hadith* is contradictory as to whether Mohammed held the *salat* on behalf of those who had been legally executed.

The burning of the dead (or the living) is strictly forbidden, although there is nothing to confirm the impression that the burning of the corpse in any way prevents his soul from entering Paradise. Tradition has it that a dead body is as fully conscious of pain as a living one.

Weeping and excessive lamentation at the graves of the dead is clearly forbidden by the Prophet, who is reported to have said 'whatever is from the eyes (tears) and whatever is from the heart (sorrow) are from God; but what is from the hands and tongue is from the Devil. Keep yourselves, O women, from wailing, which is the noise of the Devil'. However, the custom of wailing at tombs of the dead is common in all Muslim countries.

## Chapter 7
# The Status of Women

### The Status Defined

> Men are the managers of the affairs of women
> for that God has preferred in bounty
> one of them over another, and for that
> they have expended of their property.
> Righteous women are therefore obedient,
> guarding the secret for God's guarding.
> And those you fear may be rebellious
> admonish; banish them to their couches,
> and beat them. If they then obey you,
> look not for any way against them.
>
> (Koran 4:38).

In these few words, God has made known the status of women in relation to men. In relation to other matters the status, rights and duties of women are defined with various degrees of rigidity, but in this the message is clear, finite and complete; it is not a matter for discussion or compromise. The Koran also states:

> Your women are a tillage for you; so come
> unto your tillage as you wish.
>
> (Koran 2:223).

Women in this context means wives, and clearly they are to be seen as subject to a husband's control. To what extent this attitude was a legacy of pre-Islamic times is unclear. Some authorities have suggested that among many tribes in ancient Arabia a form of polyandry had existed in which government was by matriarchy. This may have been true either if property was not inherited, or if such as there was was inherited through the female line. It is also possible that the harsh realities of the desert encouraged the restriction of the numbers of females; certainly the burial of unwanted girls at birth seems to have been common. One of the significant changes brought about by the Koran was the unconditional forbidding of this practice. Islam also recognized poverty as a cause of this and other abuses, and sought to relieve this situation by compulsory giving of alms. At the same time the doctrine that no believers were to be taken captive prevented the taking of Muslim prisoners and led to the gradual disappearance of marriage by capture. That custom was still widespread in the Prophet's time and, although women taken into captivity might be treated with great consideration and even regard, the possibility of marriage by capture reduced the general status of women to chattels. Personal freedom and independence, however, were hardly burning issues in ancient Arabia. Apart from the ability to possess and dispose of property,[1] and the choice of a marriage partner (the two matters are not unconnected), men were in a similar position to women in this respect. Even so it seems to have been rare, though not unknown, for women to exert their will on questions of marriage, and it has been suggested that the cases which are often quoted to prove that the status of women was high are those of exceptional people, and have been preserved for that reason.

In the early Muslim era there seems to be little doubt that the woman was subordinate either to her husband, or to her nearest male kinsman. His rights over her were the same as over any other property, but an interesting corollary was that, like his other property, he had to watch over it. His wife's honour was entirely in his hands, and it was his responsibility to see that it was not violated. If he failed in his duty to mount suitable protection over her, no stigma attached to the woman for alliance with another man. Proprietry marriage carried with it no moral or legal sanctions, although within the tribe his rights to his wife or other property would be respected. But if a man from another tribe seduced a married woman, he committed no unlawful or dishonourable act, and poets constantly boasted of their conquests. Seducers, however, were fair game for the vengeance of both the husband's and the wife's kinsmen.

In addition to marriage by capture there existed, before Mohammed's day, marriage by contract. This made no difference to the status of women, as the suitor paid a sum of money to the woman he wished to marry, and sometimes to the father also. This payment gave the husband exclusive rights to the services of his wife.

---

1. Inheritance only became a problem when there was a significant amount of property to inherit. In the harsh nomadic life of the desert, inheritance was largely irrelevant. Apart from a few personal possessions, the only significant property was the camel herds on which the survival of the group depended. Settlement based on agriculture was very limited in scope, but the establishment of the caravan trade made settlement in towns both possible and necessary, and led to the accumulation of wealth in the hands of individuals. This shift of emphasis reflects the attitude of a society moving from a communal basis to an individualistic one.

## Property Rights

Payments such as those made in a marriage by contract have a bearing on whether women in pre-Islamic times could own property. Although there is contradictory evidence, direct payments to women suggest that they could. This view is also supported by the position of Mohammed's first wife, Khadija, who all sources agree was a wealthy widow in her own right. Indeed, according to tradition, Mohammed encountered considerable financial hardship when she died, which suggests that, instead of her husband and daughters inheriting on her death, her assets reverted to her nearest male kin as custom demanded.

In the matter of inheritance the Koran made important social reforms. No doubt some of the principles involved in the revised laws were brought about by the circumstances of the times. Tradition relates that after the battle of Uhud a widow of one of the fallen complained to Mohammed that she and her three children were left destitute because her husband's inheritance had reverted to his kinsmen, perhaps because the husband's family was hostile to Mohammed's cause. The Prophet received the revelation:

> To the men a share of what parents and kinsmen
> leave, and to the women a share of what
> parents and kinsmen leave, whether it be
> little or much, a share apportioned.
>
> (Koran 4:7)

Later in the same *sura* more detailed instructions were given concerning what proportions of a man's inheritance were to be given to his family and relations. Equality was not the purpose, because sons inherited twice as much as daughters, but strict provision was made for wives, mothers and daughters depending upon the numbers involved and the numbers of male relatives entitled to a share. There was also a clear statement that husband and wife should retain control over their own property; there was no provision for common ownership, and a woman retained her complete freedom of dealing. A woman also had exclusive rights over her wedding dower, which probably confirmed existing practice. The Koran forbids any coercion of women in respect of their property and it is illegal for a husband to withhold divorce from a woman who is entitled to it if his motive is to retain her possessions within the family. It is also illegal to divorce a wife on a false charge so that a husband may retain some of the property lawfully belonging to her.

In matters of property, therefore, women have been guaranteed by law a share in inheritance since the seventh century. In this respect they were ahead of some of their sisters in the West. This long tradition of the right to property has encouraged women who are so minded to conduct business in their own right.

In certain of the more conservative countries it is necessary for them to do this through the services of a *wakil*, or commissionaire, who deals with all the necessary face to face business. This cumbersome arrangement naturally does not encourage women to participate in commerce, but in countries where constitutional changes have been made, Muslim women participate openly in business affairs. Although it is the common Muslim view that women are unsuited to working in public and holding public office, there is no edict to this effect in the Koran.

## Marriage

In Islam marriage is a contract and not a religious ceremony. The taking of more than one wife, which to many outsiders appears to be a licence, was in fact, at the time, a limitation. Before Mohammed there was no limit to the number of wives a man might have, except that dictated by his means. The Koran limits the number to four and at the same time recognizes that there might be difficulty in treating wives with impartiality. In modern times, it is comparatively rare in most Muslim countries for a man to have more than one wife at a time. Apart from Western influences on relationships there are few men who can afford the separate establishments required by law, custom and expediency. The Koran provides that polygamy for women is forbidden, and they are always restricted to one husband.

There are many *hadiths* on the subject of marriage and one in particular deserves notice here. That is, that no woman can be married without her consent. It is a popular misconception that arranged marriages are part of the Islamic faith; it is, more accurately, an Eastern custom which is not confined to Muslims. It is true that the practice is firmly established in almost all Islamic countries, but it is not a religious requirement, and the Koran says nothing about it.

Moreover, an arranged marriage is not the same as a forced marriage, and, while custom encourages the first, it does not sanction the second. Marriage in the East is seen as uniting two families rather than two individuals. (Mohammed himself used marriage with several of his wives to strengthen alliances with neighbouring tribes.) As such the choice of a suitable partner is the concern and business of the whole family. Nor is an arranged marriage a marriage of convenience. It is usual, rather than exceptional, for family relationships to be very close, and it is against a background of love and trust that parents will select what they judge to be suitable matches for their children. This is not to say that there is no family pressure, but, as in the West, this is usually reserved for what parents consider an unsuitable match. Pressure usually concerns a father's relationship with his son. If a father wishes to be united with a certain family, he will make it known to his son that he would particularly like him to marry a particular girl and more often than not the son will comply with his father's wish. Marriage is thus seen not as a way of achieving individual satisfaction or happiness but as a way of caring for needs, ensuring the survival of the family unit, and providing an environment in which religious precepts and obligations may be fulfilled.

Koranic law and custom both lay down specifications as to whom a man may marry. In general the Koran makes it lawful to marry any woman except an idolatress. Chaste women who have received revealed scriptures (that is, Jews and Christians) are approved. The Shafi'ites make it almost impossible to wed non-Muslim women, although the Prophet did not confine his marriages to believing women. On the other hand, by Koranic law, a Muslim woman may marry no-one but a believer, although this custom has been modified in certain countries.

Islamic law made sweeping changes to pagan custom as regards marriages which were prohibited as incestuous. It is not lawful for a man to marry either the widow or the divorced wife of his father, nor is he allowed to marry the sister of a woman to whom he has been married. Such marriages were allowed in pre-Islamic times. It is also prohibited for a man to marry his daughters, his sisters, his aunts on either side of the family, his brother's and his sister's daughters, his son's wives, a woman and her daughter, or a woman who is already lawfully married. A law peculiar to Islam is that forbidding marriage between two people suckled by the same foster mother, or between the foster mother and the person who has been suckled. The law also prohibits a man from marrying his grandmother or granddaughter, or a woman and her niece at one time.

Islam has no fixed age limits for marriage, and quite young children may be married legally; one of Mohammed's wives was betrothed to him at the age of six. A bride is not handed over to her husband, however, until she is fit for marital congress. Betrothal may take place at any age. In practice, either the age limit for marriage is laid down by the State, as in the USSR,[1] or judicial obstacles are put in the way of child marriage without actually making it illegal, as in Egypt where marriages cannot be registered unless the parties have reached a specified minimum age. Nevertheless, in Egypt not many girls remain unmarried after 16, but here, as elsewhere, there is a tendency for the marriageable age to increase.

The preliminaries to a first marriage are, with some exceptions,

[1]. USSR here refers to the Muslim Republics in the South which are subject to Soviet law.

similar in most Muslim communities. Traditionally, whether the family or the bridegroom selects a prospective wife, it is the bridegroom's mother or near female relative who calls on the mother of the girl and asks her to put the matter to her husband. If the suitor's mother receives an evasive reply, the matter normally ends there. If the girl being married is a virgin she may be ignorant of negotiations that are proceeding, and in theory she may be promised to a man she has never seen.

On an appointed day the *imam* (prayer leader) goes with the prospective bridegroom and his friends to ask the girl's father formally for his daughter's hand. The amount of the *mahr* (marriage dower) is then settled. Next, the *imam* recites prayers and sends to a *qadi* to ask him to grant the necessary permission to marry, after which the two people are considered betrothed.

There are variations on this arrangement, notably among the Bedu of the North African desert, where direct courtship takes place, and in Chinese Turkestan where children are not segregated. Among the Tuareg of the Sahara women choose their own husbands.

Although the wedding ceremony itself is simple, great importance is attached to it. The wedding normally takes place in the house of the bride's father where the guests assemble. An *imam* invites a representative from both families to act as the two witnesses, whose presence are essential to the wedding. It is the witnesses, not the bride and groom or the *imam*, who sign the wedding contract. They must be adult males of sound mind and Muslims. If two suitable men are not available, two Muslim women may take the place of one of them. At least two witnesses are required and they must possess the legal qualifications for a witness. Their presence is required not simply for evidence, but as essential to the validity of the marriage.

When the contract is signed, the *imam* formally asks the two families' representatives if they consent to the terms of the marriage; he then puts the hands of the bride and bridegroom together, so that their thumbs touch. He holds them in this position and recites a prayer after which all present recite the opening chapter of the Koran. The formal wedding is then over. A feast invariably follows and the host provides the best entertainment he can. It is, of course, his business to see that all the food, drink and vessels are ritually lawful.

The *wali* can only give a bride in marriage with her consent, but in the case of a virgin silent consent is sufficient. Only the father or grandfather has the right to marry his daughter or granddaughter against her will so long as she is a virgin. As minors are not in a position to make a declaration of their wishes which is valid in law, they can only be married at all by a *wali*.

The man can demand from his wife readiness for sexual intercourse and general obedience; if she is continually disobedient she loses her claim to support and may be chastised by the man. The latter in his turn is expressly forbidden to take upon himself the vows of continence. The prescriptions of the law regarding the rights and duties of husband and wife cannot be modified by the parties in the contract.

An important feature of the marriage contract is the *mahr*, the value of which must be specified although there are no prescribed limits. The *mahr* is paid to the bride, probably in two instalments, and until the first agreed instalment is paid the bride is within her rights to refuse to comply with any of her husband's wishes. The second instalment might be held in reserve in case her husband should die, or she is divorced. The actual position of the married woman is in all Muslim countries dependent on local conditions and on many special circumstances. Yet it is not a contradiction of this to say that the legal prescriptions regarding marriage are as a rule most carefully observed.

Apart from the modern tendency of Muslims to limit themselves to one wife by choice, legislation in various countries has added to the decline of polygamy. It is illegal in the USSR and China, and it was abolished in Turkey in 1926 with the introduction of the Swiss Civil Code. It has become more difficult in Egypt and other countries in recent years.

Modern Egyptian legislation illustrates the tendency towards bringing marriage under closer control by the State and towards adopting, with orthodox Muslim arguments, some of the leading Western ideas on this subject. Nevertheless, marriage, at least between Muslims, remains governed here, as elsewhere, by *sharia* law. Turkey and Albania are so far the only Muslim countries which have regulated this institution, together with the whole of family law, by the wholesale adoption of modern codes.

In pre-Islamic Arabia a form of temporary marriage (*mut'a*) was known and it persisted until after the Prophet's death. The Caliph Umar attempted to abolish the practice which is regarded as illegal by the Sunnis. It is permitted in Shi'ite countries where justification is found for it in the Koran (4:24). The object of a *mut'a* marriage is not to establish a home or beget children. It is a personal arrangement between two parties as a means of providing a man with a wife for a specified period, at the end of which both parties are free to part, providing the woman has received the fee due to her. Families are not involved, and no ceremony is necessary. One tradition declares that Mohammed made it unlawful because it differed little from prostitution, but other traditions appear to sanction the practice. Consequently, in Shi'ite countries, the Muslim may take a Christian, Jewish or Muslim woman for a fixed period of time varying between hours and years. There has to be a contract drawn up by the officiating *mulla*[1] in which the payment and the term must be specified. The contract binds the parties to each other for a specified period unless they agree to divorce by mutual consent. The children of such a marriage are legitimate and have the right to share inheritance, but the two parties to the contract do not inherit from each other.

It is almost certain from tradition that the Prophet permitted *mut'a* amongst his followers, especially on the longer campaigns. Even the Sunnis have practically the same arrangement; those who wish to live as husband and wife for a certain period simply agree to do so, without stipulating it in the marriage contract. Irregular unions regarded by the *sharia* as unlawful have been permitted by local custom in various parts of Islam at different times. Although the *mut'a* marriage is generally regarded as forbidden to Sunnis, in recent times it has been unofficially acknowledged as valid by certain people in the sacred city of Mecca. Even the prohibition against the marriage of sisters to the same husband has not always been obeyed. Up to the time of the Wahhabis in the mid 18th century a husband of the Asir tribe might lend his wife to a guest[2], and there was a time when a man might enter into a partnership of conjugal rights with another man in return for his services as a shepherd. In some parts of Baluchistan a host might provide an unmarried, but nubile girl, for the better entertainment of the guest. All modern authorities agree, however, that such practices, outside the contract of *mut'a*, are tribal rather than Islamic.

The position regarding concubinage is now academic as only slaves may be held as concubines. Slavery has now been abolished in all Muslim countries.

## Prostitution

There is no doubt that prostitution existed before the days of the Prophet and it seems that there was no stigma attached to those who patronized prostitutes. Islam brought about a change, but in spite of official disapproval most Muslim countries have not succeeded in suppressing prostitution completely.

## Unlawful Intercourse

There is no concept of adultery in Islamic law. Sexual intercourse is either lawful or unlawful, and unlawful intercourse is not a transgression against a marriage partner, but a crime against God.

---

1 Persian form of Arabic *ulama*, learned man, scholar in the widest sense.
2. According to some recent accounts this custom is still to be found among the Bedu.

Unlawful intercourse is a serious crime, but the evidence required by the Koran makes it practically impossible to prove. A confession must be repeated three times, and the evidence of four witnesses is required who must actually have seen the act take place. Tradition has passed down a story of A'isha, one of Mohammed's wives being suspected of unlawful intercourse. The case was resolved only by a Koranic revelation which not only exonerated A'isha, but also laid down that in future four witnesses must be produced to prove such accusations. If, however, the case is proved, the Koran demands a harsh punishment, but there are two versions of what this should be.

> The fornicatress and the fornicator –
> scourge each one of them a hundred stripes,
> and in the matter of God's religion
> let no tenderness for them seize you.
>
> (Koran 24:2)

Alternatively:

> Such of your women as commit indecency,
> call four of you to witness against them;
> and if they witness, then detain them
> in their houses until death takes them
> or God appoints for them a way.
>
> (Koran 4:19)

It is generally assumed that the first of these is an earlier passage, and there is a provision that if the accuser cannot substantiate his case he will receive 80 lashes for casting imputations on chaste women.

The second punishment is more ambiguous, and it is believed that in the early days of Islam guilty women were simply locked up. At some stage, however, the punishment seems to have been changed to stoning to death, although it is difficult to see how the text of the Koran can be used to justify this.

To rationalize different punishments for the same offence, subsequent jurists have divided offenders into two classes – those who are *muhsan* and those who are not. The former are free men or women, sane and mature, who are in a position to enjoy lawful marriage. The penalty for these is death by stoning. The penalty for people who are not *muhsan* is 100 lashes if they are free men or women (and half that number if they are slaves).

A husband who accuses his wife of illegal intercourse but is not able to bring the necessary evidence, must testify four times by God that he speaks the truth, and a fifth time that the curse of God shall be on him if he lies. A wife can defend herself and escape punishment, by testifying to similar oaths, but in any event the marriage is annulled, and under no circumstances may the husband resume cohabitation.

## Divorce

The Koran has much to say about the circumstances and provisions of divorce, but it has nothing to say about the grounds for divorce. It has been assumed that a husband needs no grounds to divorce his wife, and the *sharia* law is structured accordingly. A wife does not have a similar right. In some respects the right of the husband is derived from pre-Islamic practice where a man only needed to repeat the dismissal notice three times to be clear of all obligations to his wife. The difference in Islamic practice is that after the first and second repudiations (*talak*) a man may take back his wife without her permission, providing he does so before the end of the period of waiting required by law before she might marry another man. But if he pronounces the formula for the third and final time, he loses all further right to her and cannot resume a relationship until she has first been married and divorced by another man. A *talak* pronounced in jest is considered legal and binding.

The circumstances under which a woman may claim divorce are restricted. If two non-Muslims are married and the woman then adopts the faith but her husband does not, she may claim divorce. If it is the husband who is converted but not the wife, the *qadi* decides between them.

In general the other grounds on which a woman can seek divorce are few and often difficult to prove. They are:
- Grave chronic diseases and physical defects (including impotence) which prevent marital intercourse.
- Non-payment of the *mahr* before completion of the marriage.
- Inability of the man to provide support (this separation is not final as long as the woman's *idda* runs).
- Non-fulfilment of special conditions and obligations of the marriage contract.
- Ill-treatment of the wife by the husband, but only if repeatedly and seriously done – this separation may be either revocable or final.

Another ground on which divorce can be sought is rebelliousness in the woman or incompatibility in the man, and general discord between husband and wife; this case has special rules based on *sura* 4:35. The *qadi* appoints two referees, one from the family of each consort, who first attempt a reconciliation. If their efforts fail they decide the question of guilt; if the fault is on the woman's side the husband is empowered to use the Koranic means of compulsion (admonishment, confinement, beating). If it is on the side of the man it is annulled by the referees. If the fault is on both sides the marriage is annulled and the referees decide about the payment or return of the *mahr*. The verdict of the referees is confirmed by the *qadi*.

In many places custom is stronger than the strict provisions of the *sharia* law. For example, in some communities where virginity is considered to be of paramount importance, a bride claiming to be a virgin can be divorced if she turns out not to be, notwithstanding the fact that neither the Koran nor the Prophet attached any importance to it. Similarly, although divorce is specifically condoned by the Koran, in the United Provinces of India it is considered shameful because it brings shame on the family.

The *khul* is a special form of divorce by which the wife purchases her freedom. Under the arrangement separation is legal after the partners have made a bona fide agreement in return for compensation. Some sects allow the possibility of a divorce by agreement without compensation. Modern practice varies in different countries according to the strength of secular constitutions. In the USSR, China, Turkey and Albania women are on a par with men for marriage and divorce. In other areas, notably Saudi Arabia and the Gulf States, the original word of Islam stands virtually intact.

Before a woman may remarry, she must wait a period of three menstrual cycles. She continues to be regarded as a wife during this time until it is established that she is not pregnant. If she is, the husband is encouraged by custom to take her back until the child is born, for it belongs to him if conceived legitimately. The woman is forbidden to marry anybody else until the child is delivered. During the period of suspended divorce (*idda*) a husband may take back his wife and resume cohabitation. In unscrupulous hands this divorce procedure can be used to keep a woman in a perpetual state of being neither divorced nor married and can be used to extort property or payment from unwilling wives. The Prophet expressly forbade this practice, and the Koran seeks to restrict the practice of a woman ransoming herself from marriage. This was apparently a common procedure before Mohammed's time and Islam has modified the worst excesses.

## Seclusion of Women

The seclusion and veiling of women is a subject peppered with ambiguities and contradictions. It has been suggested that in ancient Arabia the Bedu women of the desert went unveiled and associated freely with men, whilst women in the towns were veiled. One source says that in the Prophet's own tribe, the Quraysh, veiling was generally observed. Another authority has it that in ancient Mecca unmarried daughters and female slaves were dressed in their finery and paraded to attract possible suitors and buyers. If this was successful the women were said to have resumed their veils once and for all.

> Wives of the Prophet, you are not as other
> women ... speak
>    honourable words.
> Remain in your houses; and display not
> your finery, as did the pagans of old.
>
> (Koran 33:32)

And:

> O Prophet, say to thy wives and daughters
> and the believing women, that they draw
> their veils close to them; so it is likelier
> they will be known, and not hurt.
>
> (Koran 33:59)

The suggestion here is that this command came in the early days when the believers and their wives were likely to be molested and harassed by a hostile public. But it also indicates that veils were then common, otherwise they would simply have drawn attention to themselves.

There were special rules for Mohammed's own wives in terms of veiling and seclusion. The Koran specifically asks the followers not to enter his house without permission, and to address his wives 'from behind a veil'. The intention of these commands is open to different interpretations. The first is that the wives of the Prophet were entitled to special consideration and that they should act as an example of how women should be treated and behave, implying that all women should be secluded and veiled. But it may also relate to the physical conditions under which Mohammed and his wives were living. Mohammed's establishment in Medina consisted of a walled courtyard, inside which each of his wives had a hut reserved for her use. Mohammed had no apartment of his own, and he would spend one day with each wife in turn. But the courtyard was also used as a common meeting place for his followers, as a place of prayer, and as the general focus for many activities of the new movement. As the Message spread and the ranks of the faithful grew, the pressure of numbers on the Prophet's household must have been suffocating, so it is possible that neither he nor his wives would have had any privacy without such special protection. Subsequent generations of Muslim jurists have interpreted the Koran very much in line with the first option, although there is no clear command that all women should be veiled and secluded. The general tenor of the text in terms of modesty and chastity, combined with the revelations placing men in charge of the affairs of women, has resulted in seclusion sometimes taking an extreme form.

The evidence suggests that, so far as the Prophet's own family was concerned, he wished to follow the ordinary conservative custom of his tribe. But it is hard to see how the events of the time taken as a whole can be interpreted to exclude women completely from public life. The Prophet himself had no objection to praying in the presence of women. Until at least 300 years after the *Hijra*, women enjoyed the right to pray in the mosque, and the Caliph Omar is said to have appointed a Koran reader especially for them at public worship.

It seems that the rigid seclusion of women grew up over generations, although it is not possible to say when the *harem* system began to be general. It has been suggested that the early interpreters of the Koran were men of Persian origin amongst whom such seclusion was traditional. At all events the system was firmly established by the Middle Ages, particularly among the town dwellers, where settled prosperity resulted in special buildings staffed by eunuchs. The practice was not nearly so widespread among the peasants of the field and the Bedu of the desert, and there are records of travellers among these people who were shocked by the lack of modesty shown by women in the presence of men, and by the open friendship between unrelated men and women in public. It is impossible for a man to shut his wife up if he is living in a tent and requires her to work, fetch water and firewood and herd the goats.

It seems likely, then, that in the early days of Islam, when the new religion was coming to terms with established tribal custom, there was a much more flexible and open attitude towards the status of women. By the Middle Ages religious authority had passed to the centres of learning in Turkey and Persia, who imposed their own more rigid codes of behaviour.

Interpretations differ as to the meaning of 'letting down the veil'. Some say it means that women must cover their faces and heads, some say that the eyes need not be covered, and yet others insist that the face may be uncovered but the forehead and hair must not be shown. Thus various traditions and customs have been established and the present day situation varies from place to place.

In Saudi Arabia, all women still go fully veiled in public. Both the veil and the *abba*, an over-garment stretching to the ground, are black. But there are some subtle distinctions to be seen. Generally, the older women wear veils so thick that even in the brightest sunlight it is impossible to see an outline of the face, while young girls often wear thin veils through which their features can be seen quite clearly, and which are little more than a token. Fashions clearly change, as in 1853 Sir Richard Burton described the women of Yanbu, in Arabia, as having veils covering only the lower part of their faces.

In the Gulf States, the women also wear the *abba* which is used to cover their heads, but the lower part of the face is covered by a *petula*, leaving the eyes visible. A *petula* is a leather or fabric mask covering the nose and mouth, tied at the back of the head. In all these countries the over-garments are worn only in public. What is worn underneath seems to be a matter for personal choice, providing it is modestly tailored to the wrists and neck and reaches the ankles.

In Iran the over-garment is the *chador* which is similar in style to the *abba*. The custom in respect of veiling varies from place to place depending upon the strength of religious community or Western influence. In some religious centres, the women are veiled, and in the cities many women go in Western dress.

Wherever it is the custom, women must cover their faces in the presence of all men, except close relatives. They will certainly do so in the presence of a strange man, but will not bother in the presence of a boy.

In modern times, especially among the younger families of the Arabian peninsula, it is possible to see how custom rather than religious dogma decides on the degree to which women are secluded in various circumstances. In Saudi Arabia, for example, although it is unheard of for a Saudi woman to attend any mixed gathering or company unaccompanied, Saudi couples do attend mixed parties both in their own country and abroad. The more usual arrangement, however, is for the woman to adhere strictly to Saudi custom whilst at home, and to adopt a different style of dress and behaviour whilst abroad. It is not therefore unusual to find a young Saudi wife not permitted even to go shopping by herself in Riyadh (in which case the husband does the shopping), but whilst in London and Paris to be out in the city from dawn till dusk alone, dressed in the latest Western fashion. This seems to be an increasingly common arrangement which is tailored to suit the situation, particularly when the woman has been educated abroad.[1]

## Sex

The Arabic word for marriage and sexual intercourse is the same: *nikah*.

Islam has never placed any restriction on the gratification of sexual pleasure and enjoyment, providing it is within the limits prescribed by the law. This is an unbroken tradition which stretches back to the Prophet himself, and at no time has there been any of the guilt or inhibitions which Christians have placed on sensual pleasures over the ages. Mohammed is known for certain to have had 10 wives and at least three concubines, and from that time the idea that sex is enjoyable has been taken for granted by Muslims. Sexual intercourse is regarded as no different from any other natural function of the body. It is discussed

1. There is justification in the *sharia* for differing behaviour in Islamic territory and elsewhere.

freely even when children are present, and sexual satisfaction is positively encouraged. One *hadith* goes so far as to suggest that the best in a Muslim community is he who contracts most marriages. Celibacy is against the *Sunna*, is positively discouraged and appears to be unknown except among Sufis. The Bedu of the desert, when on journeys, can be celibate for months on end, yet not one of them, even the most austere, would regard celibacy as a virtue. They want sons, and consider that women are provided by God for the satisfaction of men. Deliberately to refrain from using them would be not only unnatural, but also ridiculous, and the Bedu, like most Arabs, are very susceptible to ridicule. Sexual satisfaction is allowed to be mentioned as a blessing in prayer or thanksgiving.

Homosexuality is condemned in the Koran:

> What, do you come to male beings,
> leaving your wives that your Lord created
> for you? Nay, but you are a people
> of transgressors.
>
> (Koran 26:165)

However, it does not appear to be uncommon, or condemned by popular opinion.

The Muslim attitude towards virginity is inconsistent. To the Prophet it seemed quite unimportant, as only one of his wives was a virgin when he married her. Although many of his marriages can be considered as political alliances, this was not true of all of them, and his overriding consideration seemed to be that widows and divorced women should be included in the community through remarriage. Yet in some Muslim countries, particularly in North Africa, the importance attached to virginity in a bride can be obsessive. However, such attitudes could be more properly described as tribal rather than Islamic.

Attitudes towards chastity are also not entirely straightforward. Apart from the legal aspect, unchaste or immodest conduct is seen as bringing dishonour not only upon the girl herself, but on the whole family, and to a lesser extent, on her tribe. It is the inescapable responsibility of the near male relatives to protect not only the honour of their women, but to demonstrate publicly that the honour of the family is encapsulated in the chastity of their women. It is therefore the clear duty of men to redeem the family honour if it has been violated. What constitutes violation and the action taken in redemption can both take an extreme form. A woman does not actually have to do anything to bring disgrace. It can be enough that she is talked about, and that people believe she has been unchaste, or is capable of unchaste conduct. There are many examples of a brother killing his sister in such circumstances, and everyone concerned thinking he is completely justified in his action. Compared with the honour of a family, one life is of little importance. Yet an Arab will use his sister's name as a battle cry, and go to any lengths to help and protect her. Dishonour has to do with losing face, and this is not necessarily related to anything that has happened; it is more a matter of what people believe has happened. It is therefore the collective responsibility of a family to see to it that they are respected. It is possible for a man who knows that his wife has been unfaithful to him to do nothing if discretion has been shown and no public attention is aroused.

Not all Muslims react in the same way, however. Some of the Bedu tribes regard it as barbarous to kill a girl even if she has been immoral. But as usual the Bedu are a case apart; Thesiger was once advised by one of them that if he wanted to try his luck: 'next time you see a girl who pleases you, sit down next to her in the dark, push your camel stick through the sand until it is underneath her, then turn it over until the crook presses against her. If she gets up, gives you an indignant look, and marches off, you will know that you are wasting your time. If she stays where she is, you can meet her next day when she is herding the goats.'

## Employment and Public Life

Among the states of the Arabian peninsula there are significant differences in attitude towards the public status of women, notwithstanding that each sees itself cast strictly in the mould of Islam. In Saudi Arabia women are not allowed to take any employment, except in institutions and organizations run exclusively for their own sex, where it is obligatory that all staff should be female. This applies not only to schools, colleges and hospital departments, but also to shops selling exclusively women's clothes. This general rule applies also to foreign Muslims and to Western women, who are generally allowed into the country only if accompanying a near male relative. There are very few exceptions to the rule. Television broadcasts, films from other countries with women taking part, and airlines employ foreign stewardesses as a matter of course, presumably to look after the women passengers. Apart from jobs, women are expected to play no part in public life, including not being allowed to drive motor cars. All women, including Westerners, are expected to dress modestly in public, although foreigners, including Muslims, are not expected to adhere to the strict Saudi standards of seclusion. It is still to be expected that both Saudi and foreign women not properly dressed, especially during Ramadan, could receive from the Morals Police (controlled by the *ulema* – the religious authority in Islam) a few sharp cracks with a stick or a dab of green paint on exposed ankles and arms. In the Gulf states by contrast, foreign women are allowed to take jobs, conduct business openly and drive cars, and are allowed considerable latitude in the way they conduct their private lives and dress in public.

The seclusion of women, and the denial of any kind of public role, has emphasized the special problems of developing countries. It is apparent from all the development programmes published by Saudi Arabia and the Gulf States in recent years, that the one commodity they are notably short of is human resources. They must import not only unskilled labour, but also managerial and technical resources. A great self-imposed handicap is being felt by excluding half of the population from the process. In addition, many of the facilities necessary for development must be duplicated: lecture rooms, laboratories, medical facilities, recreation projects, restaurants and even mosques are provided for each sex. Yet women are encouraged to take up the educational opportunities open to them. They may study abroad, and are given generous state assistance to obtain degrees and qualifications in foreign colleges and universities. At present the numbers involved are small: those who have attained the necessary standards are few, and to study abroad women normally have to be accompanied by their husbands.

In Egypt, by contrast, since the Revolution of 1952, there are no laws that discriminate between the sexes in relation to education and employment. There are women members of Parliament (though only six) and for some years there has been a woman in the Cabinet. But some contradictions remain. So far no woman has been appointed a judge, and women are not allowed to hold public office of an executive nature, such as Governor of a province, or Mayor. Women employed in the public sector receive wages equal to those of men, although many complain that opportunities for training and promotion are not equal. Even so, when women take the equal place in work that the law provides, the right that Islam has given women to control their own possessions and money could put them in a more advantageous position than their sisters in the West.

Yet in many Muslim countries one area of the law seems at odds with another. The labour laws in places like Egypt, Syria and Iraq allow women to be employed outside the home. Yet marriage regulations and family law give a husband an uncontested right to refuse his wife permission to leave the house, go to work, or travel.

It is a curious paradox in Islamic law that a woman may execute the office of *qadi*, except in cases of *hadd* and *kisas* in conformity with the rule that she may not give evidence in these cases. There is no prohibition against a woman assuming the government or head of state. Rulers of the Muslim state of Bhobal in central India were women for several generations in the 19th century.

## Women Saints

Strict Islamic authorities do not approve of canonization. Nevertheless, Islamic sects and movements, notably the Sufis, through their mystical interpretations of the Message, have not only saints, but women saints; this comes about because the Sufis are preoccupied with the importance of the spiritual Message to be received through the mystical experience, so that outward form and sex simply is not important. (It is remarkable that in the oldest Turkish mystical order (Yesviya) women took part in the ceremony (*dhikr*) unveiled.) This is consistent in that Mohammed taught that the attainment of the divine lies not in appearance, but in purpose. On this basis scholars have admitted women into the ceremonies of Islam.

However, when it comes to considering women taking a lead in religious matters, the compliments become somewhat backhanded. 'If it is possible to have learnt two thirds of the faith from A'isha (one of Mohammed's wives), then it is possible to learn some of the truth of religion from one of her handmaidens . . . A woman on the path of God becomes a man, she cannot be called a woman' said Al-Din Attar writing of Rabi'a, a female Sufic saint. Perhaps the depth of Muslim feeling on the subject of women could not be better summarized.

## Swiss Civil Code in Turkey

The most important change to the status of women in Islam came with Turkey's adoption of the Swiss Civil Code in 1926 which replaced the religious law – the *seriat* (Arabic: *sharia*) – governing marriage. Among other features, the new code retained the Muslim practice of separating the property of the spouses. It permitted abandonment by the husband as grounds for divorce, and for the first time allowed marriage between Muslim women and non-Muslim men. Perhaps the most important feature of the 1926 Civil Code is the complete revision of the procedures for contracting marriage. Instead of the traditional contract between families, the new code recognized only a contract between individuals established at a civil ceremony. Thenceforth unregistered unions were considered illegal, their offspring illegitimate, and both parents and children ineligible for certain government assistance.

However the new Civil Code had only a limited effect in the countryside, and illegal traditional marriage continued to produce illegitimate children. This became so common that the government enacted several bills to legitimize millions of children. In the half century since the Republican reforms, civil marriage is now much more widely accepted, but whether there has been any basic change in the relationship between the sexes is less clear.

To a considerable extent the outward signs of sexual segregation are disappearing. Women no longer occupy special sections of buses and trains, and do not have special areas in cinemas. Although, especially in the cities, women move about with apparent freedom, it is still a mistake to think in terms of the social relationships that exist in Northern Europe or the United States. Women enjoy the right to vote and have legal equality. They commonly take all kinds of jobs at all levels, and form an increasing proportion of students. But many old ways remain. Men generally do not take their wives to public entertainments nor introduce them to friends. The basic social institutions of the coffee house and the guest room are still exclusively male preserves.

\* \* \*

Although it is outside the scope of this book to relate the Women's Movement to Islam, it is nonetheless worth noting that criticism of Islam is much more likely to be levelled from the Western, rather than the Muslim, wing of the movement. The general role played by women in the Iranian Revolution is remarkable, and it is noticeable that even the most strident Muslim feminist and political revolutionary is unlikely to attack Islam as such. Nawal El Saadawi[1], for example, whilst making the most virulent attack on the structure and nature of Arab society in general and the position of women in particular, describes Islam as 'one of the most tolerant and least rigid of religions, rational in many of its aspects, adaptable and leaving scope for change'. At another point she remarks on 'the broadmindedness and tolerance of Mohammed the Prophet of Allah, when compared with other prophets and religious leaders'. She considers that the Christian Church has exercised an even more ferocious oppression of women than the Islamic, Arab or Eastern cultures. Furthermore, the first blow for women's liberation can be said to have been struck at the very beginning of Islam. 14 centuries ago Muslim women succeeded in changing the exclusive use of the male gender in the Koran itself. They said: 'We have proclaimed our belief in Islam, and have done as you have done. How is it then that you men should be mentioned in the Koran and we ignored?' Until then the only reference in the holy book was to Muslims, but from then on the Koran speaks of 'the Muslims, men and women, and the believers, men and women'.

1. *The Hidden Face of Eve*, Zed Press, 1980.

*Chapter 8*
# Commerce and Trade

This chapter does not offer any advice on how to do business in Islamic countries. It seeks to outline the attitudes and qualities of the Muslim mind which affect, consciously or otherwise, modern practices and methods.

## The Traditional Role of Commerce

The language and ideas of the Koran reflect the fact that it was first addressed to people engaged in commerce. The Prophet was a successful merchant. The Meccan caravan trade was central to the life of the community, and the commercial terms used in the Koran are seen by scholars as expressing fundamental points of doctrine, and not simply as illustrating ideas. The Koran states that the deeds of a man are reckoned in the book; the Last Judgement is a reckoning; each person receives his account; the balance is set up and a man's deeds are weighed; each soul is held in pledge for the deeds committed; if a man's actions are approved he receives his reward; and to support the Prophet's cause is to lend a loan to God. It is not surprising therefore, bearing in mind the literal nature of the Koran, that commerce has always had a significant place in the minds of Muslims.

In the 14th century Ibn Khaldun said:

> It should be known that commerce means the attempt to make a profit by increasing capital, through buying goods at a low price then selling them at a high price, whether these goods consist of slaves, grain, animals, weapons, or clothing material. The accrued amount is called profit. The attempt to make such a profit may be undertaken by storing goods and holding them until the market has fluctuated from low prices to high prices. Or the merchant may transport his goods to another country where they are more in demand than in his own. Therefore, an old merchant said to a person who wanted to find out the truth about commerce: 'I shall give it to you in two words: buy cheap and sell dear.'[1]

1. Maxime Rodinson, *Islam and Capitalism*, Allen Lane, 1974

It is true that the Koran emphasizes the uselessness of wealth in the face of God's judgement and warns against the temptation to neglect religion that wealth brings, but it has nothing to say against the accumulation of private property, or inequality in terms of wealth and possessions. It looks with favour upon commercial activity, and confines its criticism to condemning fraudulent practices, and requiring abstention from trade during certain religious festivals. The Prophet is believed to have said that 'the trustworthy merchant will sit in the shade of God's throne at the day of Judgement'. According to holy tradition, trade is a superior way of earning one's livelihood, and 'a *dirham* lawfully gained from trade is worth more than 10 *dirhams* gained in any other way'.

Nevertheless strict Islamic law and custom restrict an individual's right to hold property in certain basic respects. It is not permissible, for example, to make a charge for such primary products as water and grass. The right of ownership is also subsidiary to the right of everyone to life. A man dying of hunger is justified in taking the minimum of food he needs to keep alive at the expense of the legitimate owner, and is permitted to use force if he can do it in no other way. Indeed, according to the Shi'ites, refusal to give food to a starving man amounts, in effect, to complicity in killing him.

There are no more restrictions placed upon a Muslim business man or trader than are placed upon his counterpart in the West, but restrictions can occasionally have important consequences. For example, the Koran emphasizes the prohibition of a certain game of chance (*maysir*). As a result, any gain accruing from chance or undetermined causes is prohibited. It would not be allowed, for example, to promise a workman a fleece for skinning six sheep, because it is not possible to know for certain whether the skin may not be damaged during the course of the work.

Certain commercial practices are forbidden by the *Sunna*: those which are either fraudulent, involve trade in impure goods (wine, pigs, animals that have died by means other than by ritual slaughter) or in goods that are common to everyone (water, grass and fire). Speculation in food, especially with a view to cornering the market, is forbidden. Above all, the selling of any commodity where there is an element of uncertainty is prohibited. This includes, for example, sale by auction, since the seller does not know what price he will get for his object; or any sale in which the merchandise is not precisely numerically defined.

Although Islam has never raised any objection in principle to the capitalist mode of production, at times religious opinion has condemned the making of certain goods, or certain forms of exploitation which conflicted, not so much with the scriptures, as with a tradition which had acquired religious validity after centuries of stagnation. This applies, for example, to the making of alcoholic drinks, or the employment of women as productive workers. Attitudes in Islam have changed over the centuries; in particular, the habit of condemning any practice that did not go back to the time of the Prophet has been abandoned. At one stage, innovation (*bid'ah*) of any kind was condemned out of hand, and this applied, for example, to the use of coffee and tobacco when they were first introduced. More recently, a distinction has been drawn between innovations which are praiseworthy, and those which are not. Thus many innovations that were condemned in their time were subsequently endorsed by religious leaders, whose predecessors had taken an opposite point of view. Opponents and supporters of the new ways were never short of texts or arguments to back up their mutually contradictory opinions.

The situation in Saudi Arabia, the most orthodox Islamic state, illustrates the point. The strictly orthodox Wahhabi sect controls all religious matters, and its religious scholars were initially opposed to many modern innovations. But its political leaders, notably King Abdul Aziz ibn Saud, himself a sincere Wahhabite, were able to overcome opposition to, for example, the telegraph, the telephone and broadcasting.

Islam modified only marginally the attitude of ancient Arabia towards accumulated material wealth. As we have seen, it introduced *zakat* (alms) to provide for the needy, and also revised the laws of inheritance to give a fairer distribution within the family. But it has no objection at all to individuals or groups acquiring vast wealth, providing the guidelines laid down by the Koran are observed. The Christian idea that it is easier for a camel to pass through the eye of a needle [1] than for a rich man to enter the Kingdom of Heaven is quite alien to Muslims.

## The Example of the Prophet

Because of the Prophet's responsibilities to the community, there was no distinction between the public exchequer and his personal possessions. Shortly before his death, he compelled newly conquered groups by formal treaty to hand over a fixed proportion of their income or property each year. A special tax was imposed upon Christian Arabs, but this was no higher than the contributions required from Muslims. The Prophet was also not averse to accepting private gifts and legacies. Besides these, Mohammed received a fifth of all spoils taken from the enemy, as compared with the quarter required by tradition by Arab

---

1. This image is reserved for sinners: 'nor shall they enter Paradise until the camel passes through the eye of the needle' (Koran 7:39).

chiefs. In addition, the Prophet had the right to share equally the thing or person he liked best before the general distribution. If the plunder were won by negotiation, rather than battle, Mohammed took it all.

After the capture of Khaybar, the owners were left in possession, but Mohammed sequestered half the produce on behalf of the Muslims. His position imposed a number of heavy financial obligations. As he was engaged full-time in public and religious affairs, he could not earn his living as others around him did. As the *Sayyid*[1], he was necessarily engaged in extensive hospitality, and gave generous gifts to those around him. The Koran commanded him, like other men, to give generously to his relatives, to orphans, beggars and travellers. He had also to contribute towards ransoming captives.

From the very beginning, therefore, business and financial affairs have occupied an important place in the administration and functioning of the religious community, and there is certainly no contradiction between the rich and the pious in Islam. Nevertheless, the rich are urged to do good works, and the love of wealth for its own sake is condemned. Damnation and hell-fire are promised the sinner who thinks he can ransom himself on the Day of Judgement:

> Nay, verily it is a furnace
> snatching away the scalp,
> calling him who drew back
>   and turned away,
> who amassed and hoarded.

(Koran 70:15)

## Associations and Combinations

Religious authority condemns practices that interfere with the free play of supply and demand. A tradition is said to have come from the Prophet himself condemning obligatory price fixing or the laying down and fixing of price levels. This general edict, together with the Koranic prohibition on conclaves in general, has had far reaching effects on the organization of people in work situations in strict Islamic countries. It effectively prohibits, in theory, the organization of any trade union, trade association, chamber of commerce, guild, professional association or institute, learned society, academic association, charitable organization or political party. In addition it could be taken to mean that no prices, wages, salaries, or fee scales can be laid down. But in practice these principles are applied selectively. The most obvious example is the strenuous effort of some OPEC countries to control oil prices, but other more parochial examples can be found. In most countries the government controls hotel prices, air fares and

---

[1]. A term now used as a mark of respect.

some food prices, and has a set salary structure for government employees. In those same countries combinations of workers to fix wage rates, or associations of professionals to fix fee scales, are illegal.

One important result of this is that professionalism is almost unknown in most Muslim countries and poorly understood in the rest. Professional firms and consultants are treated like traders or contractors when it comes to price, but are expected to behave differently from contractors when it comes to performance.

## Customs in Business

There are general rules for conducting business affairs, and naturally these are best understood by Muslims. There is a very strong tradition for conducting business and concluding agreements on a verbal basis. Such agreements are as binding as any other kind. It is essential to a man's honour that, having reached an agreement, it should be fulfilled. Probably for this reason, there is rarely any pressure for an agreement to be concluded. Discussions might range over a long period, whilst all aspects of a deal are considered. One can be quite sure that however long and detailed the discussion, an Arab will remember precisely what was said and the terms of any agreement reached.

It is an extraordinary characteristic that, however long or involved or complicated negotiations might be, it is very rare for an Arab to take notes of a meeting, a result, perhaps, of the immensely strong oral tradition which stretches back centuries. It began with committing to memory the epic poems of the desert, and continued with learning the whole of the Koran by heart. Modern education in many places consists of committing all school books to memory, and it is not surprising therefore that the average Arab has a prodigious capacity for remembering detail. The Bedu seem to be positively suspicious of the European habit of committing everything to paper, and in a traditional *sharia* court only oral evidence is accepted; written evidence is not generally allowed.

A Muslim, both by his religion and ancient tradition, is honour bound to stand by the terms of an agreement. Westerners sometimes get into difficulties when they expect not only the terms, but also what they consider to be the spirit of an agreement, to be implemented. An Arab may insist on the letter of an agreement which could seem to contradict the spirit. This is not a devious conspiracy; rather is it a mistake to consider that any agreement or contract has a spirit. This tradition goes back a very long way and is illustrated in an incident involving the Prophet Mohammed. While Mohammed was living in Medina, he concluded a treaty with his enemies in Mecca, which provided, among other things, that tribes and individuals were free to enter into alliance with the Muslims or the Meccans as they desired. However, minors under the protection of either side were not allowed to defect, and had to be handed back to their parents. One youth from a Meccan clan was a Muslim sympathizer, and attempted to join Mohammed in Medina. Mohammed sent the young man back under guard. The youth killed one of his guards and returned undaunted to Medina, but Mohammed again attempted to return him, thus fulfilling his treaty obligations and at the same time demonstrating that the youth was not under the protection of the Muslim community. The youth, however, left Medina and set up camp on a coast road nearby. Here he gathered around himself 70 or so sympathetic Meccan Muslims and set about raiding the Meccan caravans that passed their way. Now another provision of the treaty was that Mohammed's supporters would stop attacking Meccan caravans, but as the youth and his followers were operating outside Mohammed's technical control, Mohammed could not be considered in breach of the treaty. On the other hand, the Meccans, if they wished to do so, were free to use violence on the raiders without provoking Mohammed and his community. In the end, the raiders became such a thorn in the side of the Meccans that they asked Mohammed to take them into his community, thereby waiving their rights under the treaty. By Arab standards Mohammed's conduct was formally correct, and was never challenged by the Meccans.

According to *hadith* the intent of the believer is more important than his action, and this has to be considered in relation to the object to be attained. In other words, the end does not justify the means; it would be an evil act to build a mosque with extorted money, whether the builder was conscious of the source of the money or not. Business must therefore be transacted according to certain rules. A Muslim has to be careful that an act valid in law does not leave opportunity for injustice to be done which will provoke the anger of God; morality must take precedence over a legal contract. If a man purchases food in a time of famine in order to hoard it and sell it at high prices, it is wrong according to the *sharia* because it is against the interests of the community, regardless of whether the contract is commercially valid.

All actions must be based upon sound knowledge and it is the duty of a trader to acquire the necessary knowledge. If, for example, counterfeit money or faulty goods are put into circulation, the man first dealing in them must take the burden of ascertaining their true value. Having done so, he must dispose of them or put them out of circulation. If he does not they might be passed on to another who does not know, and who might become a transgressor through no fault of the first merchant. The danger here is one of general distribution to the public harm. Likewise, transactions that harm individuals are forbidden. It is a general principle that a Muslim should desire for fellow Muslims that which he desires for himself and reject for them what he rejects for himself. This means that he shall not praise a commodity for qualities it does not possess, nor conceal its faults or any fact concerning weight or quality which would prevent the sale.

However, a foreigner should be aware that, as in most aspects of moral and social behaviour, there is a sliding scale; all men are not dealt with equally. A brother has many special claims, a more distant member of the family fewer and a non-related fellow Muslim fewer still. Lastly come *jar* (protected foreigners). A non-Arab Muslim is to be treated with favour rather than cold justice. Christians and Jews, and others by and large, should reckon to have the strict letter of the contract enforced.

The three worst vices are folly, meanness and falsehood. Lies which avert harm and bring benefit may be justified, but they are still vile. A man who boasts of his possessions, although he is telling the truth, is nevertheless vile. The vilest of all men is he who boasts of what he has not.

Yet a great gap exists between theory and practice in business. The *sharia* entirely forbids the sale of certain things because they are ritually unclean, such as dogs, pigs, wine, dung, or unclean olives, yet it is lawful, though disapproved, to buy grape juice from one who has extracted wine, weapons from one who has used them against God, or any goods from a man whose property is illicitly acquired. It is illegal to sell anything for which no use can be found: vermin, wild animals not used for hunting, or things not actually in existence – for example, fruit not yet on the tree, or goods not manufactured. It is illegal to sell that which cannot be delivered or that which would cause harm in delivery. A sale is illegal in which the exact quantity or quality of the goods is unknown. A sale must take place and delivery must be completed within three days of the contract being settled, and a purchaser cannot claim possession of goods until they are actually delivered. Until then the seller is responsible for them: if the buyer dies before delivery the sale is void.

There are two views about the sale of commodities which the purchaser has not seen. The first is that it is illegal. The second is that it is legal if a description of the thing is given and the buyer has the option of purchasing, if the goods, when seen, comply with the descriptions.

Conditions in general, except where they are of essence to the contract, nullify sale. Thus a contract cannot be made where one side sells a barrel of oil for $10, if the other side reciprocates by selling a rifle for $5. However, it is lawful to sell goods for a profit if the costs and the amount of the profit are disclosed. In this way one commodity can be bartered for another.

## Making Contracts

The requirements of the *sharia* that a contract has to be completed within three days is clearly impracticable in many cases. One way round this is to make an advanced payment (*salam*) in order to secure an option on the goods which may be rejected if they do not conform to the specification. Alternatively, it is possible to arrange a contract with a skilled workman (under *istisna*) to make an article, so that an advanced payment does not have to be made, nor a period stipulated.

Some commercial dealings between Muslims go back further than Islam itself. The conditions and arrangements are dictated by custom, and it is seldom that details are specified in commercial contracts. Much is left to the pedigrees of the parties concerned, and everything customary is deemed to be included.

It is in the nature of a Muslim's belief and way of life to take all things literally, and consequently to offer nothing superfluous to a situation. In recent times more than one Western contractor, when handing over a completed building, has been startled to be asked by his Arab client for the motor car shown on the artist's sketches in the early days when the design was being discussed.

The concluding of an agreement is not to be confused with the bargaining process that precedes it. For the average Westerner, if he takes part in it at all, this is normally considered a tedious, if not embarrassing, process, a simple game of numbers played to arrive at an eventual price. For an Arab, it is the stuff of life, in which personality and imagination is given full play. In essence it is the art of compromise without backing down or losing face, and at each stage, a reason must be given for changing one's position, however implausible the reason might logically appear. Whether the bargain is being struck in the verbal violence of the camel market, or in the dusty quiet of a government office, the underlying procedure is essentially the same, and if the bargain is well made, the pleasure expressed by both parties at the end will be genuinely enjoyed.

Another pitfall for the unwary Westerner is the way in which details of negotiations are or are not connected. If, for example, a development project was being discussed in London or New York, it might be agreed at an early stage that one party would provide the land, another the finance, and a third the contracting services. As the discussions progressed, however, the general strategy could be modified if a better one emerged. Not so in Riyadh or Cairo; once a verbal agreement has been made, even though it does not cover the whole situation, and even if a better strategy can be found, it is inviolate. Any attempt by one of the parties to modify an aspect of the agreement, especially if in doing so he appears to be delivering less than originally promised, will be seen as dishonourable and unbusinesslike.

## Usury

The Koran specifically forbids usury (*riba*) on no less than four occasions. In a commercial centre like Mecca in Mohammed's day, the taking of interest was probably commonplace. The Koranic disapproval of interest dates from the period after the *Hijra*, and it has been suggested that it appears to be directed against the Jews rather than against the Meccans. In the Koran the Jews are accused of practising usury though forbidden so to do. It is possible that when Mohammed and his followers first settled in Medina and appealed for material support, the Jews refused a contribution but offered to lend money at interest. By adopting this position they were in a way refusing to accept Mohammed's claim to Prophethood, and this may explain the Koranic insistence that usury is wrong. It has also been suggested, however, that the idea underlying the prohibition of usury was that all believers are brothers and therefore ought to help one another financially as well as in other ways.

In present day Muslim countries the situation regarding usury varies from place to place. From the beginning of the 19th century pressure has been brought to bear on traditional Islamic values by the colonial expansion of the European powers, and the financial institutions exported from the West. When the Ottoman Civil Code was promulgated in the 1870s there was no mention of loans at interest. This made it possible in 1888 to establish the Agricultural Bank, whose written constitution allowed it openly to lend and borrow money at interest. The present day situation varies, therefore, from a country like Turkey, which places no religious restrictions on its financial and economic institutions, to a country like Saudi Arabia, whose law quite specifically forbids the charging of interest. Even in Saudi Arabia, however, not all business transactions are free from interest charges; for example, the Saudi Industrial Development Fund (owned by the government) grants loans to licenced projects at an annual interest rate of two per cent. On the other hand, the loan granted by Saudi Arabia to Syria in 1950 was expressly defined as being free of interest. In between these two examples is a country like Pakistan, which has made great efforts to introduce Koranic legislation into its law. Its draft constitution provided for the elimination of interest as one of the most important principles underpinning the new state. However, the final text in 1956 referred simply to the rapid elimination of *riba* as one of the aims to be strenuously pursued, along with, for example, the welfare of the people. In the meantime, its banks raise and lower their interest rates like any others.

This situation is possible because there are those who believe that all forms of usury are forbidden, and those who distinguish between usurious interest, which is to be condemned, and participation in the profits of the business, which is legitimate. Some believe that a second category is that of interest paid by banks.

The prohibition on usury presents considerable problems for modern Muslim banks. In a fundamental sense a Muslim bank is a contradiction in terms, since in essence the business of the bank is characterized by the creation of profit through charging interest. Recently, one Arab bank based in the Lebanon has been formed to conduct its business strictly in accordance with Koranic practice. Essentially its business is to lend money and thereby derive profit, but instead of charging interest it takes a share in the equity of the project or enterprise. This makes it similar in character to a European merchant bank, and presumably restricts the nature of its business. It represents an interesting attitude towards economics, as only enterprises that are productive and potentially profitable would attract loans. Loans for the purposes of consumption are virtually ruled out. As a result of religious ideology a new way of recirculating money has come into existence, and one of the cornerstones of society, the banking system, has been transformed. Instead of banks being institutions for the manipulation of money as a commodity, they are forced into a constructive and creative role, and take a share in the social success or failure of private or public enterprise.

However, these restrictions on normal commerce have been either ignored or, in many cases, observed to the letter of the law so as to make nonsense of them. Interest might be allowed to accumulate in a bank account without the beneficiary withdrawing any of it. A money lender might take interest indirectly through payment in kind. A common way of evading the law is for a loan to be made and the recipient to hand over some property. The property is then bought back at an inflated value.

However usury is interpreted, it seems to be generally agreed that the total amount of interest charged must never exceed the principal of the debt:

> O believers, devour not usury, doubled
> and redoubled, and fear you God; haply so
>   you will prosper.
>
> (Koran 3:125)

By the same token the charging of compound interest is expressly forbidden.

There are those pious Muslims who believe that the sin of *riba* is not only endangering the structure of Islam, but has already undermined and corrupted the institutions of the West. What is more, they point out, usury is specifically forbidden to both Christians and Jews as well as Muslims. But these other religions have failed, and, in the clash between Islam and the Christian world, the latter is in the wrong, and must be the one to yield. Examples have been given of cooperative loan societies being set up in Muslim India since the end of the last century. These were influenced to some extent by the cooperative movement in Europe, but they represent a successful, if modest attempt to fulfil the financial needs of the community within the Muslim ideology.

## Debt

The teachings of the Koran are in the mainstream of the oral tradition of the Arabs. The rules and directions it gives to the faithful for living their lives, even in such contracts as marriage, divorce and inheritance, are to be observed orally through ceremonies and rituals. It is only debt that should be recorded in writing and witnessed:

> O believers, when you contract a debt
> one upon another for a stated term,
> write it down, and let a writer
> write it down between you justly.

(Koran 2:281)

The result of forbidding usury is that a debtor cannot make his situation worse by postponing repayment: the debt cannot increase by the accumulation of interest. Yet clearly a debt is to be viewed as a serious matter.

## Insurance

Insurance represents another example of changing attitudes. Until recent years orthodox opinion frowned upon insurance so that it was almost unknown in Muslim countries. This was a result partly of resistance to innovation, and partly of the fact that conservative opinion held insurance to be an attempt by man to frustrate the will of God. If it is God's will that a man should suffer loss, misfortune, or disaster, it is a Muslim's duty to submit, not to seek compensation. It has taken the huge capital investments made possible by oil revenues in Saudi Arabia and other Middle Eastern states to change this attitude. The risks involved in leaving such large investments uninsured have proved too much for any responsible government. Although in many Muslim countries certain restrictions and rules are laid down for insuring property, it is now a common practice.

## Decision Making

It is part of the faith that there are no intermediaries between God and man. One result of this is that in Muslim countries the head of any organization, ministry, or department, will not generally delegate decisions. This nearly always makes the concluding of any business, however trivial, a time-consuming matter. It is usually easy enough, even for an outsider, to find the right man to see, and, in principle, direct access to very important and busy people is usually easy enough to arrange. But at this point practical difficulties often arise. First, it is difficult to find people in their offices; one consequence of decisions being taken personally is the mobility required of all businessmen and officials. The alacrity with which the modern Arab leaps on and off aeroplanes is remarkable and he is inclined to treat continents like adjoining parishes[1]. Having run your man to ground, the second problem is conducting a private interview. The *majlis* tradition has spilled over into all but the most modern business practice and government administrations. Most offices are physically fairly large with comfortable chairs arranged continuously around the walls. The chairs are occupied by people who have some business to conduct, or some enquiry to make, or are visiting a business acquaintance to pass the time of day, or by friends and relatives paying a social call, or, in the case of public offices, by people off the street wanting somewhere to sit down out of the sun. The host sits behind his desk which has on his left and right one or two additional chairs. In a busy office there might well be three or four different meetings or discussions going on with the occupant at the same time. The other people in the room might join in with one or more of the discussions, or be having conversations between themselves, or simply adopt the role of onlookers. This is not nearly so chaotic as it at first appears, and, as in most things Islamic, there is an underlying structure. The seat of honour is to the left of the host. In most cases this will be given as a matter of courtesy to a foreigner, but its occupant is expected to know when a more important visitor arrives, and be prepared to relinquish it. When this happens all discussions stop until the formalities have been completed with the new visitor and the nature of his business ascertained; at a suitable moment the host might revive the previous discussion and continue to conduct two or three meetings at once. When this happens it can be assumed that no serious business can be concluded. At no time will anybody be made to feel that he ought to leave, or that he has outstayed his welcome. The arrival of a senior member of the host's family or tribe will immediately take precedence over any business discussion. Another facet of the principle of instant availability is that the host

1. In 1977 Saudi Arabia ran out of passports!

himself, unless he is the king, ruler or president, is a subject of the system. If his superior requests his attendance, he departs immediately, leaving a roomful of unfinished business to be dealt with at a later date.

For Arabs business is never carried on at the expense of social ritual. The most refreshing experience for the outsider is the willingness with which people make themselves available, and with a little patience almost anyone can be seen without secretaries or assistants acting as intermediaries. Naturally, an introduction helps a good deal, and much importance is attached to being 'known', that is, being passed on as a suitable person by friends, relatives, or business acquaintances. In any event, a visitor can be almost certain of a courteous, even friendly reception, and of receiving a hearing which varies from polite interest to real enthusiasm. This should not be taken as encouragement, let alone agreement to any proposal. Everyone gets a similar hearing, and this gives time an unstructured appearance, which partly explains the apparent chaos of many establishments.[1]

It is a Muslim characteristic that business is not separate from the rest of life, and there is therefore no reason why it should operate under different rules and conditions. As with other aspects of life the day to day objective is not to get things done, or even to acquire riches, it is the ancient desire to win prestige in other men's eyes, and to win a respected and important place in society. In Islam it is people who regulate and dominate business, not business that dominates them.

But, finally, it must be remembered that, in business as well as in all other matters, it is not man that ultimately orders events, but God. Awareness of the divine will runs parallel with all human decisions, and can override them at any turn. God's will is everywhere, and nothing is too trivial for his attention. A visa will be granted or a contract made *inshallah* (God willing), a building will be completed if *maktoob* (it is written), and some extraordinary human achievement like a moon landing will be greeted with *La illah il-Allah* (There is no God but God).

---

1. It is noticeable that some of the younger executives in rapidly developing countries like Saudi Arabia have chosen to occupy very small offices with room for only the minimum of furniture and only two or three visitors' chairs. This does nothing to relieve bottlenecks, but it does create a certain order, and enables work to be processed.

# Conclusion: The Oil Factor

For Muslims in general and Arabs in particular it is no coincidence that the richest oil deposits in the world are to be found under the cradle of Islam. For them it is surely part of the divine will that Islam should take its rightful place at the centre of world events, having suffered the injustice and indignity of domination and exploitation by foreigners for generations.

At a critical point in history, when the Arabs were ready to receive the Message, God sent his Prophet. Shortly afterwards the rest of the world felt the effects in spectacular fashion. Similarly now, just at the moment when the whole industrial world becomes critically dependent on oil for survival the Islamic world finds itself not only awash with it, but needing comparatively little for its own use. Things could hardly have been better arranged. Furthermore, it could well happen that, within a few years, the positions of Islam and the rich nations could be dramatically reversed. Oil could provide enough wealth for the Middle East not only to dominate the economy of the western world, but to gain a major, if not controlling, interest in it. The thing most likely to stop this happening is not the ability of the West toprevent it, but Islam's inability to resolve its own internal political conflicts. As if this possibility was not dramatic enough, oil is also high on the list of strategic subjects important enough to trigger off a war involving the major powers. In either event the rise of Islam in the 20th century based on oil is hardly less important than its rise in the seventh, based on the Message.

The story began at the turn of the century, when the British Admiralty decided to convert its fleet, by far the largest in the world, from coal to oil fuel. This led to Britain financing the first successful oil exploration in the Middle East, and in 1908 large deposits of oil were proved to exist in Persia.

Serious competition between the Western powers began in the Middle East after the First World War, stimulated by the dramatic increase in industrial production and the manufacture of motor vehicles. On the face of it Britain was well placed at the end of the war.

Besides her Persian concession she controlled Iraq and the eastern shore of the Persian Gulf, where the richest deposits were found. However, when the Pan-Arab state which Britain had promised failed to materialize, the various Arab Amirs (rulers) let it be known that they were open to offers for oil concessions. The next 10 years saw the most intense competition between oil companies, at the end of which the United States came out best with the concessions of Saudi Arabia and Bahrain; Britain was second best with Persia, Qatar and half of Kuwait. The oil fields of Iraq were controlled by a British-Dutch and American consortium.

After the Second World War the major international oil companies expanded their operation in the nations of the Middle East until by the early 1950s they were virtually states within states, dictating not only oil prices but domestic and foreign policies. They maintained peace by paying the ruling families and governments enough to keep their personal exchequers filled, under royalty contracts initiated and executed between the wars.

Perhaps significantly, the first reaction to these arrangements came from Iran in 1951 against the British controlled Anglo-Iranian oil company. Buoyed up on a wave of anti-imperialism, the nationalist movement set out to reject British influence by nationalizing Anglo-Iranian, undaunted by the knowledge that Iran had little of the technical or management expertise to run the company assets.

The only other oil producer in the region was motivated not by political but by financial ends. There was no interest in revolutionary nationalism in the entrenched and deeply conservative monarchy of the Saud family, but when King Saud and the generation of Saudis learnt that Aramco, the American consortium, was paying more to the United States treasury in income tax than it was to Saudi Arabia in royalties, pressure mounted for revisions to treaties negotiated before the war. The problem for Aramco was how to meet the Saudi point that a foreign government was receiving more from the exploitation of their own mineral wealth than they were. To ignore the demands and rely upon the terms of properly negotiated treaties would risk spreading unrest, and undermine their extremely profitable position. But to increase royalties out of company earnings would, of course, decrease the profits. With the approval of the United States government Aramco proposed that the concession treaties should be left as they were, but that Saudi Arabia itself should impose an income tax on oil. As a royalty as well as a tax was paid on each barrel, this would effectively double the Saudi revenue. The consortium profit would not be affected because it could write off taxes levied in Saudi Arabia against the taxes due in the United States. Both Aramco shareholders and the Saudi government were suitably pleased with the solution; so much so that Aramco's lawyers were invited to draft the Saudi income tax legislation. The US government was not so pleased when it realized later the huge tax revenues it had lost through this arrangement.

The tension in the Gulf was largely eased in 1954 when the Iranian nationalist government was overthrown by the American CIA, and a consortium of British, French, Dutch and American companies was given access to Iran's oil.

Stability had been restored to the region, at least on the surface, but it was not to last very long. In 1956 Britain, France and Israel invaded Egypt in a last desperate attempt to stem the tide of Arab nationalism, and re-establish their imperial interests by military means. This triggered a violently anti-Western reaction throughout the Middle East, including riots in Kuwait among the large immigrant worker population of Egyptians and Palestinians. Although the Suez invasion was a military defeat for Egypt, it paradoxically rallied the forces of Pan-Arab nationalism solidly behind President Nasser, and accelerated the pace of declining Western influence.

But the decade of the 1950s was not merely important for development of nationalism, it was also the decade in which the owner countries became aware of the economic power residing in their oil sources. Once more the first significant move came in Iran. The overthrow of the Iranian nationalist government in 1954, orchestrated by the United States, had restored to power the Shah Pahlevi. This apparently dependent and easily led young man learned quickly from his American tutors, and in 1957 enacted a law which was to revolutionize the oil industry. This was to be called the Joint Venture law, and it provided that in future international oil companies would not only pay for concessions and pay royalties and taxes but in addition they would pay half the residual profit to Iran. This included profits not only from the production of oil, but from all its various by-products. In effect the future profits of all foreign oil companies would be halved.

The Arabs on the other side of the Gulf were not slow to follow suit. The tiny sheikhdoms along the coast, which with the help of the British had remained independent from Saudi Arabia, embraced the idea with considerable enthusiasm. From then on joint venture was a standard procedure in the exploitation of the rich oil fields on the Arabian coast. The oil companies were quick to appreciate the significance of this turn of events and began to sound warning signals to the political forces at home of possible future crises in oil supplies. Both sides began to focus on the issue of oil as the crucial factor in their future relationship with each other: the West because of its vital importance to its industrial base, and the East because of the potential economic development it offered. Once the basic message had sunk in,

Conclusion: The Oil Factor 165

nationalism took a decisive turn. It was no longer good enough to reject foreign troops and the colonial administration that went with them, it was now necessary to overcome the economic imperialism, headed by oil companies, which, to an increasing number of Arabs and Iranians alike, was even more insidious. This mood came to a head in Iraq in 1958 when an anti-Western government was established by revolution and openly threatened Britain's control of its considerable oil reserves.

Shortly afterwards matters reached a crisis point in Saudi Arabia. Crown Prince Faisal had been appointed by the Saudi royal family to replace his brother, King Saud, in order to bring the country's finances under control. In spite of the Kingdom's considerable income through taxes and royalties, it was on the verge of bankruptcy with debts close to $500 million. Just at the time when Faisal had contained the situation by fiscal controls based on future oil revenues, the oil companies slashed the price of oil and reduced Saudi Arabia's income by $30 million for the following year.

The Saudi response was swift and devastating. First they negotiated a new kind of contract with a Japanese company for offshore exploration. It gave Saudi Arabia 56 per cent of all profits made, no matter where and in what form. For the first time a condition was imposed that the oil must not be sold to 'enemies of the Arabs'. From the point of view of the Saudis the contract was better than a joint venture agreement because it released them from any capital participation or risk.

Secondly, in 1960 the Saudis organized the Organization of Petroleum Exporting Countries (OPEC), an alliance that was ultimately to alter the balance of economic power in the world. The basic purpose of OPEC was to present a united front to the oil companies, and to negotiate standard terms and prices. The first real test for the organization came from an unexpected source: the Arab-Israeli six-day war in 1967. Although its member countries had agreed not to allow their different politics to interfere with united action, the war divided them along predictable political lines. The Arab countries of the Gulf embargoed the oil supplies to Israel's supporters in Europe and the United States, whereas Iran, Venezuela and Libya did practically the opposite and stepped up production to make good this shortfall. Although the Arab embargo remained in force for only one week, the cash-flow situation in Saudi Arabia was so critical that at the end of the week the treasury was empty. The first time that the oil weapon was openly used as a political instrument by an almost exclusively Muslim body it ended in failure.

But even this failure was not without its positive side. The Arabs, although dismayed by their inability to hold OPEC together in a crisis, were furious at the treachery displayed by Libya under the leadership of

King Idris. Nor was this disapproval restricted to the Arab countries which felt betrayed, it found expression also in Libya itself, notably among a group of disgusted and pious army officers, led by Lieutenant Qadhafi. This internal unrest and disapproval of the Libyan régime was compounded by the spiralling corruption which took place after the 1967 war. The war had closed the Suez Canal and the rich and accessible oil fields of Libya were suddenly in a highly favoured position, and their products in greater demand than ever. At the end of 1969 Qadhafi made his move and staged a totally unexpected *coup d'état*. The new régime not only quickly purged Libya of its most pernicious foreign influences, it also instituted a vitally new element in dealing with foreign oil companies. Qadhafi's first instinct was to nationalize the entire Libyan oil industry at a stroke, but he was dissuaded from this by the voices in the revolutionary Council who argued that there would be enough trained Libyans to run the facilities. Instead Qadhafi selected one operator, Occidental, which had no other source of supply, and put pressure on it to renegotiate existing contracts, giving substantial increases in taxes, royalties and prices. Rather than close down its business, Occidental agreed, and from then on contracts on existing concessions which had to date been fixed and sacrosanct were renegotiable.

The significance of the exercise was not lost on the other oil producers. The following year they called an OPEC meeting in Tehran, and confronted the major oil companies with demands for huge increases in revenues. Rather than face the threat of nationalization, the companies acceded to the demands, and agreements concluded effectively doubled the income of the producers. The companies passed on these costs to their consumers.

The real significance of Qadhafi's breakthrough was not so much the increase in wealth derived by the producers, as the realization that the political initiative was passing into their hands. Oil minister Sheikh Yamani of Saudi Arabia took up the initiative. He demanded participation in all phases of the companies' existing operations, with an ever increasing share in the ownership, culminating in 100 per cent ownership and control of all foreign oil companies. Aramco, the first target, resisted selling any of its equity as long as possible, but in the end was forced to agree under the threat of legislation which would compel it to do so. Oil companies in other countries were forced to follow suit, and the Western domination of the Middle Eastern oil resources ended.

By the time of the 1973 Arab-Israeli war, the Muslims were able to impose a second but effective oil boycott, which not only provoked an energy crisis in the West but also caused a quadrupling of price, taking the Western economy to the edge of an economic crisis, and a dazzling increase in the oil revenues of the producing states.

Although the producing countries have had control of their oil industries for less than a decade, there has already been a massive transfer of wealth from the Western industrialized world into the coffers of Islam. Nor is the process complete, as each year the acquisition of capital grows. This represents an historically unique situation, for up until now wealth has flowed inexorably from the less developed to the more developed regions of the world. The events in the last few years have dramatically reversed this process, and for the first time the world has seen a region which is both under-developed and rich. Yet even the basic economic and political implications of the oil factor have not yet penetrated the Western consciousness to any depth.[1]

Nor has the massive scale of the dramatic transfer of revenues, and ultimately wealth, been appreciated. The monetary figures are so astronomical that, for all except bankers and treasury officials, they border on abstractions. As figures and estimates vary according to source, and statistics fluctuate from year to year, we shall use a comparative rather than a statistical method to gauge the scale of this shift in wealth, at the risk of oversimplifying the matter.

The United States is by far the richest nation in the world, with a gross national product of $1000 billion dollars. It has a total money supply of just over one quarter of that amount. Most economic experts agree that this is the sum that will pour into the Treasury of Saudi Arabia alone, in the form of oil revenues, in a period of five consecutive years.

If these figures are going to vary relative to each other in the foreseeable future they are likely to favour the Saudis. All sources agree that at the present rate of production Saudi Arabia has oil reserves for at least another 150 years, and possibly twice that long. Clearly, Saudi Arabia, with a population of only some eight million, cannot absorb such vast sums into its economy, even if it wanted to. Most, but not all, is recycled in the form of investments in the Western economy in general, but the only financial medium large enough to absorb the surplus is the dollar market, and the vast majority of Saudi Arabian assets are held in the United States.

In 1976 the Saudi oil industry earned about $37.8 billion, or just over $100 million a day. At that rate of oil production Saudi Arabia would be able to buy all shares listed on the New York Stock Exchange in 26 years, all the gold bullion in US central banks (including the IMF) in four years at $145 per ounce, all real estate in Manhattan in five months, and the whole US communications industry (all TV stations,

---

1. A CBS News-New York Times public opinion poll taken in 1978 indicated that 48 per cent of Americans did not believe that the United States imports oil.

radio stations, newspapers and magazines) in approximately four weeks.

But Saudi Arabia is not the only Muslim country with huge surplus revenues derived from oil. If the demand for Middle East oil continues at the present rate, in 10 years the total Arab accumulation of monetary reserves could amount to $600 billion, enough, in theory, for the Arab world to buy the majority interest in the publicly owned American business and industrial complex: in other words into majority ownership of the United States. It is not only the scale of this change which is difficult to grasp, but also the pace. It was only a generation ago that the power station at Jeddah was powered by coal imported from Britain, and hardly longer when the wheel was introduced to Saudi Arabia fixed on the axle of a motor car.

The oil factor has shifted Islam back dramatically into the centre of world politics. Of all the OPEC members, it is only the Muslims in general, and the Arabs in particular, that have budget surpluses; the remainder have overall deficits. Furthermore, there is an increasingly deeply held conviction among Arabs that oil will solve their political problems, and that the Arab nation, and with it Islam, will be restored to its former dominant position in the world. This is a view held not just by a few immature students, but by the majority of Arab leaders, politicians, economists, bankers and academics, as well as by political zealots throughout the Arab world. The oil under the sea and sand of the Middle East is not seen as Saudi, Kuwaiti, or Qatari oil, even by its owners. Throughout the entire Arab world it is universally regarded as Arab oil, to be used to further the interests of the Arab people, and to finance the rise of the Arab nation. It is to be used as an instrument of ideology and political will, and was placed there by God for this reason.

*Appendix 1*
# The Islamic Calendar

The Islamic calendar starts from the Christian year AD 622 when the Prophet and his small band of followers emigrated from Mecca to the sanctuary of Medina. Known as the *Hijra*, the emigration was the first united act of the Muslim community and demonstrated its determination to survive at all costs; this was subsequently designated the Muslim year AH1. But the difference between the Islamic and the Christian Gregorian calendar is not simply the date of its inception; Islam officially uses a lunar calendar of 12 lunar months, giving the year 354 days. This means that all the months, including those of the pilgrimage and fast, come about 11 days earlier each year by solar reckoning. The Arabs in pre-Islamic times also used a lunar calendar but they kept it in sequence with the solar year by inserting an extra month where necessary. This practice was forbidden by the Koran, although no-one has provided a logical explanation for the change.

It has been pointed out that the Muslim adoption of the lunar year shows the non-agrarian character of Islam; Islam is often said to mould or influence every aspect of life, but it has not penetrated the agricultural life of the million Muslim peasants. Their farming methods, and some of the religious ideas connected with them, continue to observe the solar seasons.

*Appendix 2*
# Modern Islamic States

Apart from Saudi Arabia and Iran, whose constitutions have been outlined in Chapter 4, modern Islamic States have adopted a wide variety of political structures and state legislatures. There follow brief descriptions of some of these. There are, of course, many other states with Islamic populations, but the following examples are chosen to highlight the variety of structures that can be accommodated within Islam.

## Algeria
*State religion:* Islam (with provision for other beliefs).
*Form of government:* 1976 Constitution provides for single party socialist state.
*Power of head of state:* Executive powers for 6 year renewable term. President of Council of Ministers, High Security Council and Supreme Court, and head of Armed Forces. Appoints ministers, initiates legislations, and can dissolve legislature.
*Type of legislature:* National People's Assembly elected by universal suffrage for 5 years. Meets for 6 months a year and can legislate on all issues except national defence. Referanda widely used.
*Distribution of seats:* 261 members elected to NPA from list drawn up by FLN (Front de Libération Nationale).
*Legal system:* Criminal justice system as in France.
*Date of independence:* 1962.

## Arab Republic of Egypt
*State religion:* Islam.
*Form of government:* Republic:Democratic Socialist State.
*Power of head of state:* President nominated by Assembly and confirmed by plebiscite for 6 year term.
*Type of legislature:* Governed by People's Assembly, single chamber legislature with 5 year term. Has 372 elected members and 20

nominated by President. Universal suffrage: compulsory voting by men.
*Distribution of seats:* 1979 election returned: National Democratic Party (Sadat) 330; Socialist Labour Party 29; Liberal Socialist Party 3; Independents 10.
*Legal system:* National Courts system established 1883 and amended 1931 and 1946. No religious courts, but *sharia* law still governs some family affairs.

*Date of independence:* 1946.

## Jordan

*State religion:* Islam (the King can trace an unbroken descent from Mohammed).
*Form of government:* Constitutional monarchy.
*Power of head of state:* King has executive power, appoints PM and cabinet, orders general elections and approves and promulgates laws through Assembly in joint session. Has power to override veto and must approve treaties.
*Type of legislature:* National Assembly comprising: 1. Council of Notables – members appointed. 2. Council of Deputies – by general election.
*Distribution of seats:* Council of Notables – 30 members, 15 from East and 15 from West Bank. Council of Deputies – 60 members, 30 from East and 30 from West Bank. Traditional composition: 48 Arab Muslims, 10 Christians, 2 Circassians.
(Political parties outlawed in 1963. Last election held in 1967. In 1976 Assembly met and agreed to indefinite postponement of elections and dissolution, as it was no longer possible to hold elections on West Bank. National Consultative Council appointed by King's decree in 1978 to advise King and cabinet on legislation. 60 appointed members.)
*Legal system:* Law based on Islamic law for both civil and criminal matters, except for personal matters concerning non-Muslims. System of High Courts and Magistrates Courts, and religious courts for both Muslims and Christians.
*Date of independence:* 1946.

## Lebanon

*State religion:* Population almost equally divided between Muslims and Christians.
*Form of government:* State offices divided according to religion in

accordance with National Pact 1943. 1926 Constitution with frequent amendments.
*Power of head of state:* President must be a Maronite Christian elected by two thirds majority of Chamber of Deputies. Has power to initiate laws. In exceptional circumstances can dissolve the Chamber and force an election.
*Type of legislature:* Chamber of Deputies seats allocated by a system of proportional representation based on religious groupings. Election by universal suffrage for 4 year term.[1] President of Chamber is a Shi'ite Muslim. The Prime Minister must be a Sunni Muslim.
*Distribution of seats:* Maronites 30; Sunnis 20; Shi'ites 19; Greek Orthodox 11; Greek Catholic 6; Druse 6; Armenian Orthodox 4; Armenian Catholic 1; Protestant 1; Other 1 – (ie 53 Christian, 45 Muslim): Total 99.
*Legal system:* Law and justice based on codes derived from modern theories of civil and criminal legislation. Higher, lower and appeal courts. Islamic, Christian and Jewish religious courts deal with affairs of personal status.
*Date of independence:* 1946.

## Socialist People's Libyan Arab Jamahiriyah

*State religion:* Islam (the Holy Koran is the country's social code).
*Form of government:* Since 1977 the Jamahiriyah (State of the Masses) was promulgated and the official name of the country changed.
*Power of head of state:* The Secretary of the General People's Committee has functions similar to those of Prime Minister.[12]
*Type of legislature:* The constitution provides for 'Direct people's authority as the basis for political order. The people shall practice its authority through people's congresses, popular committees, trade unions, vocational syndicates and the General People's Congress, in the presence of the law'.
*Distribution of seats:* The General People's Congress has 1000 delegates from the above organizations. It appoints its own General Secretariat and the General People's Committee whose members head the 20 government departments which execute national policy.

---

1. Elections suspended since 1976 as a result of civil war.
2. Since reorganization in 1979 Colonel Qadhafi has retained his position of leader of the Revolution. But neither he nor former RCC colleagues have any official posts.

*Legal system:* Civil, Commercial and Criminal Codes based mainly on Egyptian models. *Sharia* courts have jurisdiction over family matters. A commission was set up in 1971 to revise Libyan Law.
*Date of independence:* 1951.

## Morocco

*State religion:* Islam.
*Form of government:* Constitutional Monarchy.
*Power of head of state:* King is supreme civil and religious authority. Appoints all ministers, has right to dissolve Parliament and to approve legislation. He is Commander in Chief of armed forces, can declare a state of emergency and initiate constitutional amendment.
*Type of legislature:* Single chamber with 226 deputies. 88 seats elected by indirect electoral college representing town councils, regions, commerce, industry, agriculture and trade unions. 176 seats elected in general election.
*Distribution of seats:* There are 8 parties represented in chamber of representatives. Government party is King's Party. Also a system of local elections.
*Legal system:* All judges appointed by the King, on advice of Supreme Council of Judiciary.
*Date of independence:* 1956.

## Islamic Republic of Pakistan

*State religion:* Islam.
*Form of government:* Martial law (since 1977). (The 1973 Constitution provides for a constitutional democracy based on the principles of Islam. Equal rights, freedom of expression and the press, and the rule of law.)
*Power of head of state:* The Chief Martial Law Administrator has powers capable of being imposed by the military. (The constitution provides for a President who acts on the advice of the Prime Minister. He is elected for 5 years and must be a Muslim.)
*Type of legislature:* In July 1977, following martial law, all fundamental rights provided for in the constitution were suspended. In 1978 a provision was made for separate electoral registers for Muslims and others. The constitution provides for a Lower House consisting of 200 members elected directly for 5 years by universal suffrage. Senate has 63 members for 4 years. Senators elected by provinces and tribal areas.
*Distribution of seats:* The martial law administration provides for a

20 member cabinet, and a 4 member Military Council.
*Legal system:* In 1979 martial law established the supremacy of military courts in trying all offences. The constitution provides for an independent judiciary, and a system of higher and lower courts. There is a *sharia* bench at High Court level which ensures that Islamic law is enforced as the law of the state.
*Date of independence:* 1947.

## Democratic Republic of Sudan

*State religion:* Islam (with freedom of religion guaranteed to large Christian minority and others).
*Form of government:* One party socialist state.
*Power of head of state:* President nominated by Sudanese Socialist Union. Responsible for upholding constitution. Appoints Vice-President, Prime Minister and Ministers, Commander in Chief of armed forces, and security forces, and Head of Public Service. Has power to declare state of emergency which may suspend all civil rights other than that of resort to courts.
*Type of legislature:* People's Assembly, 304 members: 274 elected by universal suffrage for 4 years, 30 nominated by President.
*Distribution of seats:* All members must either belong to or be approved by Sudanese Socialist Union.
*Legal system:* Judiciary independent from state, but appointed by President. Civil Division of Judiciary headed by Chief Justice; *Sharia* Division headed by Grand *Qadi*. System of civil courts, criminal courts and local courts, with courts of appeal. *Sharia* courts deal with personal and family matters.
*Date of independence:* 1956.

## Syria

*State religion:* Islam.
*Form of government:* Constitution describes system as 'Socialist Popular Democracy'.
*Power of head of state:* President (who must be a Muslim) has wide powers. Nominated by People's Council and elected by referendum for 7 year term. Appoints cabinet, military personnel and civil servants. Commander in Chief of armed forces. Can amend constitution.
*Type of legislature:* People's Council elected by direct universal suffrage.
*Distribution of seats:* 195 members controlled by Ba'ath Socialist Party via the Progressive Front of National Union.

*Legal system:* Civil judicial system introduced in 1974 with higher and lower courts and Courts of Appeal. Personal Status Courts based on *sharia* for Muslims.
*Date of independence:* 1946.

## Tunisia

*State Religion:* Islam.
*Form of government:* One party state.
*Power of head of state:* President with wide powers; can legislate when Assembly not in session. Constitution provides that President is elected for a maximum of 3 consecutive terms of 5 years.[1]
*Type of legislature:* National Assembly. Single chamber system with limited authority.
*Distribution of seats:* In practice only members of Destourian Socialist Party elected.
*Legal system:* Integrated civil and religious courts.
*Date of independence:* 1956.

## The People's Democratic Republic of Yemen

*State religion:* Islam.
*Form of government:* One party (Marxist-Leninist) state.
*Power of head of state:* President appointed by Presidium.
*Distribution of seats:* All seats in SPC held by Yemen Socialist Party.
*Legal system:* Justice administered by the Supreme Court and Magistrates' Courts. The judicial system is a mixture of civil, Islamic and local law.
*Date of independence:* 1967 (as People's Republic of Southern Yemen).

---

1. Bourgiba elected President for life in 1974.

*Appendix 3*
# Mohammed's Wives

Christianity has for its teacher, inspiration, and example a chaste and celibate bachelor who preached monogamy and set an example of sexual abstinence, which to this day is preached by the Christian church. As a consequence, the idea that a religion should actively promote sexual fulfilment and specifically discourage celibacy is difficult for many Westerners to accept. But not only does Islam preach this message, it also has it sanctified by its founder and Prophet[1]. Yet, as in all other matters in Islam, sexual relationships must be conducted within certain rules laid down by law.

There have been various interpretations placed on Mohammed's attitude towards women, and the motivations behind his marriages. His first wife apart, some Western scholars and many Muslims regard all his marriages as political in character, suggesting the need for him to secure the allegiance of a particular family or tribe in order to strengthen the position of the new faith. It is undoubtedly true that this is an important element in most of his choices, but some scholars believe that ordinary human instincts sometimes prevailed.

Whatever the precise truth of the nature and range of Mohammed's attraction to women, it is a fact that not only was he given divine authority to marry many women, but the relationships he had with them are referred to in the Koran itself, and have resulted in formulations in Islamic law which have affected permanently the status of Muslim women, and defined other important legal issues.

Probably because he was poor Mohammed remained a bachelor until he was 25. His first wife was Khadija bint Khuwaylid. She was a prosperous widow of Mecca who at 40 had already been married twice and had several children. Mohammed's marriage to Khadija was to have a security, warmth and affection that never wavered, and so long as she lived Mohammed did not take another wife. Mohammed used to say that she was the best of all the women of her time, and that he

---

1. Mohammed said: 'When a Muslim marries he perfects his religion'.

would live with her in Paradise in a house built of reeds, in peace and tranquillity.

Khadija gave Mohammed several children. Four daughters survived: Zaynad, Ruqayya, Fatima and Umm Kalthun, but all their sons died in infancy. During Khadija's lifetime Mohammed adopted his young cousin, Ali, and Khadija made him a present of a slave, called Zayd. Mohammed gave him his freedom and adopted him as a son.

It must have been an important matter to Mohammed that he had no male heir, bearing in mind that to Arabs and Semitic people in general this was a source of shame, (men who suffered it were called *abtar*, which means, roughly, mutilated), particularly in the circumstances of pre-Islamic Mecca, where polygamy was quite widespread and divorce was simple and frequent. It is possible that Mohammed did not take a second wife because his marriage contract with Khadija made that condition, but it is also possible that he chose to keep faith with Khadija.

Besides being Mohammed's first wife Khadija was also the first believer. She died in 619AD when Mohammed was nearly 50. She was the one who had believed and chosen him before anybody else, even before God. Initially she offered him social position and protection, and subsequently she had given him support and faith. Her position as Mohammed's employer, wife and follower is unique. After her death Mohammed was inconsolable, and Khawla, wife of Uthman, suggested he should marry A'isha bint Abn Bakr, or a widow, Sawda bint Zama. He married both.

Sawda was one of the first to embrace Islam. She was a charitable and good natured woman and as she was not young when the Prophet married her it is likely that his reasons were purely domestic, as there were children to look after. Certainly it is hard to find any kind of political motive.

As Sawda grew older Mohammed preferred to spend more of his time with A'isha, and in 8AH he divorced her. But Sawda asked to be taken back, offering to yield her day (the Prophet spent a day with each wife in turn) to A'isha, as her only desire was 'to rise on the Day of Judgement as his wife'. Mohammed agreed, and *sura* 4:128 was revealed allowing husband and wife to seek mutual agreements. Sawda died in Medina in 54AH.

A'isha was only six at the time of her betrothal but the marriage was not consummated until she was about ten. By all accounts A'isha was Mohammed's favourite wife and won a special place in his heart. She turned out to be a bright and vivacious young woman who not only inadvertently left an indelible mark on Islamic law, but had considerable political influence in her own right after the Prophet's death.

In the year 6/628 she was accompanying Mohammed back from an expedition when she was accidently left behind, the party believing she was inside the enclosed litter they were carrying. Finding herself alone at the overnight camp she happened to be found by a young man called Safwan. He set her on his camel and leading the animal by the rein caught up the main party. The sight of these two arriving alone gave rise to grave accusations and many influential Muslims were scandalized. The Prophet consulted Ali, who advised him to repudiate A'isha (hence her lifelong hostility towards Ali). The matter was resolved finally by a revelation (Koran 24:10) which lays down that no charge of illegal intercourse is valid unless it is supported by four witnesses, and that those who accuse but cannot bring witnesses shall be flogged.

The incident had other far reaching consequences. It was to result in the Prophet's wives being given more protection, and therefore seclusion from the mass of the followers. Revelations came to say that it was forbidden to enter any of their huts unannounced or to talk to the women except through a curtain. In addition they were to keep their faces covered.

A'isha was 18 when Mohammed, sick and dying, took to his sickbed in her hut, and she nursed him till the end. Subsequently she opposed the caliphate of Uthman, and when Ali, her mortal enemy, was elected Caliph she did her utmost to raise the Muslims against him. She fought on the side of Talha and al-Zubair in the battle against Ali in 36/656, being in the thick of the fighting. She opposed the plan to bury al-Hasan ibn Ali[1] at the side of the Prophet, arguing that the tomb was her property. In spite of extremely influential opposition, she had her way.

She died in 58/678 and was buried in Medina. A'isha occupies a prominent place among the most distinguished traditionalists: she reported no less than 1210[2] traditions directly from the mouth of the Prophet.

In about 2/624 Mohammed took a third wife. He wanted to secure the cooperation of Umar, so he married his daughter Hafsa, who at 20 was already a widow. For some reason still obscure she was repudiated almost at once, but restored to favour by divine command in consideration of her Muslim virtues. In Mohammed's *harem* she took the side of A'isha in endeavouring to secure the succession of Mohammed for Abn Bakr and Umar. Yet on the whole, in contrast to A'isha she played a modest political role, even during her father's caliphate.

Hafsa could read and write, and some authorities have it that the

---

1. Eldest son of Ali and Fatima, daughter of the Prophet.
2. Bukhari and Moslem, the two master-compilers of Islamic tradition, accepted 228 and 242 respectively.

*suhuf* (the separate leaves of the Koran, not yet set in order) came into her possession on the Prophet's death as a gift of honour. Hafsa had no children and died aged about 60.

Just over a year after his marriage to Hafsa the Prophet married Zaynab bint Khuzaima, who like Hafsa was widowed at the battle of Badr. She was known as the Mother of the Poor, but her presence was not to complicate life in the *harem* for long, as she died shortly afterwards.

Mohammed's fifth wife was the proud and beautiful Umm Salama, whose husband had died of wounds shortly after the battle of Uhud. She had several children by him, and her deep and abiding love for him explains her reluctance to remarry. She had offers from both Abu Bakr and Umar which she refused. Even the Prophet was not accepted without pressing his suit with some fervour and persistence. Finally she yielded and the marriage took place in 4/626. The introduction of the aristocratic Makhuzumite Umm Salama into the *harem* involved more than personal jealousies; she provided the nucleus of the political faction favouring Fatima and Ali as the heirs to power, rather than the fathers of A'isha and Hafsa.

But it is the story of Zaynab bint Jahsh, the Prophet's sixth wife, as normally told by Western scholars, that gives most offence to Muslims. These scholars, insisting that they are using the original collected texts, generally conclude that this is one case where Mohammed was ruled by nothing but physical desire. The Muslims reply that this treatment merely shows the extent to which Western racial and religious prejudice distorts the truth, and that the marriage was made to win the support of her powerful kinsman Abu Sufyan.

The essential facts seem to be that Zaynab, Mohammed's cousin, although a great beauty, was at 30 still unmarried until the Prophet (it is said with Zaynab's reluctance) arranged a marriage between her and Zayd, his freedman and adopted son. Some years later Mohammed, while calling to see Zayd at his home, chanced to see Zaynab in light disarray, and left in some confusion saying 'Praise be to Allah, who transforms men's hearts'. On hearing about this from his wife, Zayd went immediately to the Prophet and offered to divorce Zaynab if he wished to marry her. Although Mohammed sent him away urging him to keep his wife for himself, Zayd divorced her anyway.

After the usual period of waiting was over the Prophet married Zaynab, after specific permission from God, recorded in the Koran (33:36). Nevertheless he incurred the displeasure and criticism of the community, not because of any physical desire on Mohammed's part, but because custom regarded the marriage as incestuous, the position of an adopted son being the same as that of a natural son. A new revelation silenced the criticism by making the distinction, and by specifically permitting marriage with the divorced wife of an adopted son (36:38).

In the two years following his marriage to Zaynab, five new women joined the six wives. The first was the comely young Jewess Raihana bint Zaid of the Nadir tribe. She had married into the Qurayza tribe and had lost her husband and other male relatives in the massacre[1]. Tradition is undecided about her actual status in the *harem*. Some say she was a proper wife, others that she preferred to remain a slave concubine, which would enable her to retain her faith and escape from the limitations of seclusion.

Mohammed's next two marriages were certainly political in motivation. The first was to Ramla, daughter of Abu Sufyan, the leader of the Meccan opposition. She had embraced Islam in defiance of her father and had emigrated to Abyssinia with her husband, who died there. She was about 35 when she married the Prophet, who perhaps was signalling Islam's inevitable victory by uniting with his most able opponent's daughter, and the powerful Umayyads.

The next and last wife to join the household was Mayanna bint al-Harith whose wedding is thought to have taken place in 7/629. She was a young and attractive widow of 26. Her brother-in-law was the uncle of Mohammed, and the marriage, which took place in Mecca during his first visit for 7 years, can be seen as a wish on the Prophet's part for reconciliation with his own tribe.

Although the political nature of the Prophet's marriages is clear enough it is evident that feelings played their part both in the relationships Mohammed had with his wives, and between the wives themselves. In all material and mundane matters it was quite possible for Mohammed to treat them all with equality, but by common consent A'isha was his most beloved wife, although she never threatened the special place of Khadija, as Mohammed himself once told her.

For their part his wives during his lifetime were fertile ground for both political rivalries and personal jealousies, but they did not hesitate to speak their minds in answer to or in argument with Mohammed. Indeed in a domestic situation they were quite able to take on both Abu Bakr and Umar, when his friends seemed to be interfering in asking them to moderate their demands on the Prophet[2]. Yet it says a good deal for Mohammed's singular talents that in the thick of establishing a new religion, and transforming Arabian society, he could accommodate the affection and conflicts of the extraordinary women in his

---

1. See page 24.
2. Ibn Sa'd, Vol VIII, 129.

household. Yet one thing was missing. Apart from Khadija, none of his wives bore him any children. It was as if, once his mission was revealed, he was to have access to all except this.

After his death Mohammed's widows became known as the Mothers of the Believers. In 20/641 when he initiated state pensions from the tremendous revenues resulting from the conquests, the Caliph Umar placed them at the head of the list. At the same time he seems to have prohibited them from attending the mosque or going on the pilgrimage to Mecca.

It is difficult to be sure of the relationships between the widows at this period. No more stormy scenes are recorded, nor any challenge to A'isha's favoured position financially or otherwise. In public policy and conduct the Prophet's widows generally behaved and were treated as a unit and given a place of honour in the community. It seems that they continued to live most of the time in the mosque apartments and must have seen a good deal of each other. A few incidents connected with Zaynab's death indicate that they lived amicably, Mohammed's memory drawing them together as his presence sometimes pulled them apart.

A'isha was to live a widow for another 50 years, and although interesting anecdotes are recorded about some of the other widows the traditions give much attention to this remarkable and able woman. She played a full part in the politics and conflicts, ideological and physical, that marked the tumultuous and unprecedented changes brought about by the rise of Islam. Indeed, her involvement in the public affairs of the new Muslim state have provoked responses which have lasted to this day. To the Shi'ites she is a curse, while the orthodox Sunnis continue to sing her praises and honour her memory.

# NON-FICTION

## GENERAL
| | | |
|---|---|---|
| ☐ Truly Murderous | John Dunning | 95p |
| ☐ Shocktrauma | Jon Franklin & Alan Doelp | £1.25 |
| ☐ The War Machine | James Avery Joyce | £1.50 |
| ☐ The Fugu Plan | Tokayer & Swartz | £1.75 |

## BIOGRAPHY/AUTOBIOGRAPHY
| | | |
|---|---|---|
| ☐ Go-Boy | Roger Caron | £1.25 |
| ☐ The Queen Mother Herself | Helen Cathcart | £1.25 |
| ☐ Clues to the Unknown | Robert Cracknell | £1.50 |
| ☐ George Stephenson | Hunter Davies | £1.50 |
| ☐ The Borgias | Harry Edgington | £1.50 |
| ☐ The Admiral's Daughter | Victoria Fyodorova | £1.50 |
| ☐ Rachman | Shirley Green | £1.50 |
| ☐ 50 Years with Mountbatten | Charles Smith | £1.25 |
| ☐ Kiss | John Swenson | 95p |

## HEALTH/SELF-HELP
| | | |
|---|---|---|
| ☐ The Hamlyn Family First Aid Book | Dr Robert Andrew | £1.50 |
| ☐ Girl! | Brandenburger & Curry | £1.25 |
| ☐ The Good Health Guide for Women | Cooke & Dworkin | £2.95 |
| ☐ The Babysitter Book | Curry & Cunningham | £1.25 |
| ☐ Pulling Your Own Strings | Dr Wayne W. Dyer | 95p |
| ☐ The Pick of Woman's Own Diets | Jo Foley | 95p |
| ☐ Woman X Two | Mary Kenny | £1.10 |
| ☐ Cystitis: A Complete Self-help Guide | Angela Kilmartin | £1.00 |
| ☐ Fit for Life | Donald Norfolk | £1.35 |
| ☐ The Stress Factor | Donald Norfolk | £1.25 |
| ☐ Fat is a Feminist Issue | Susie Orbach | 95p |
| ☐ Living With Your New Baby | Rakowitz & Rubin | £1.50 |
| ☐ Related to Sex | Claire Rayner | £1.25 |
| ☐ The Working Woman's Body Book | Rowen with Winkler | 95p |
| ☐ Natural Sex | Mary Shivanandan | £1.25 |
| ☐ Woman's Own Birth Control | Dr Michael Smith | £1.25 |
| ☐ Overcoming Depression | Dr Andrew Stanway | £1.50 |

## POCKET HEALTH GUIDES
| | | |
|---|---|---|
| ☐ Migraine | Dr Finlay Campbell | 65p |
| ☐ Pre-menstrual Tension | June Clark | 65p |
| ☐ Back Pain | Dr Paul Dudley | 65p |
| ☐ Allergies | Robert Eagle | 65p |
| ☐ Arthritis & Rheumatism | Dr Luke Fernandes | 65p |
| ☐ Skin Troubles | Deanna Wilson | 65p |

NAME ..........................................................

ADDRESS ......................................................

............................................................

Write to Hamlyn Paperbacks Cash Sales, PO Box 11, Falmouth, Cornwall TR10 9EN.

Please indicate order and enclose remittance to the value of the cover price plus:

U.K.: Please allow 40p for the first book 18p for the second book and 13p for each additional book ordered, to a maximum charge of £1.49.

B.F.P.O. & EIRE: Please allow 40p for the first book, 18p for the second book plus 13p per copy for the next 7 books, thereafter 7p per book.

OVERSEAS: Please allow 60p for the first book plus 18p per copy for each additional book.

Whilst every effort is made to keep prices low it is sometimes necessary to increase cover prices and also postage and packing rates at short notice. Hamlyn Paperbacks reserve the right to show new retail prices on covers which may differ from those previously advertised in the text or elsewhere.

# Bibliography

Abbott, Nabia *Aishah the Beloved of Mohammed* Univ of Chicago Press, 1942
Arberry, A J *The Koran Interpreted* Oxford Univ Press, 1964
Burton, Sir Richard *Personal Narrative of a Pilgrimage to Al Madinah and Meccah* Dover Publications, New York, 1887
Coulson, N J *A History of Islamic Law* Edinburgh Univ Press, 1964
Gibb, H A R *Islam* Oxford Univ Press, 1953
Gibb, H A R and Kramers, J H *Shorter Encyclopaedia of Islam* E J Brill, Leiden, 1974
Guillaume, Alfred *Islam* Pelican Books, 1967
Jaber, Kamel Abu *The Arab Ba'ath Socialist Party: History, Organization, Ideology* Syracuse Univ Press, 1966
Kiernan, Thomas *The Arabs* Abacus Books, 1978
Levy, R *Social Structure of Islam* Cambridge Univ Press, 1957
Quilici, Folco *Children of Allah* Chartwell Books Inc, 1978
Rodinson, Maxime *Islam and Capitalism* Allen Lane, 1974
Rodinson, Maxime *Mohammed* Allen Lane, 1974
Said, Abdel Moghny *Arab Socialism* Blandford Press, 1972
Schacht, J *An Introduction to Islamic Law* Oxford Univ Press, 1962
US Govt Printing Office *Area Handbook for the Republic of Turkey* 1973
Waddy, Charis *The Muslim Mind* Longman, 1976
Watt, W Montgomery *Bell's Introduction to the Qur'an* Edinburgh Univ Press, 1978
Watt, W Montgomery *Companion to the Qur'an* Geo Allen and Unwin, 1967
Watt, W Montgomery *Muhammed in Madina* Oxford Univ Press, 1956
Watt, W Montgomery *Muhammed, Prophet and Statesman* Oxford Univ Press, 1974
Watt, W Montgomery *What is Islam?* Longman, 1979

## Background Reading

Arberry (transl) *Ring of the Dove* Luzac, London, 1953
Byron, Robert *The Road to Oxiana* Macmillan, 1937
Fernea and Bezirgan *Middle Eastern Women Speak* Univ of Texas Press, 1977
Saadawi, Nawal El *The Hidden Face of Eve* Zed Press, 1980
Thesiger, W *Arabian Sands* Allen Lane, 1977